THE EXTINCTS

QUEST FOR THE UNICORN HORN

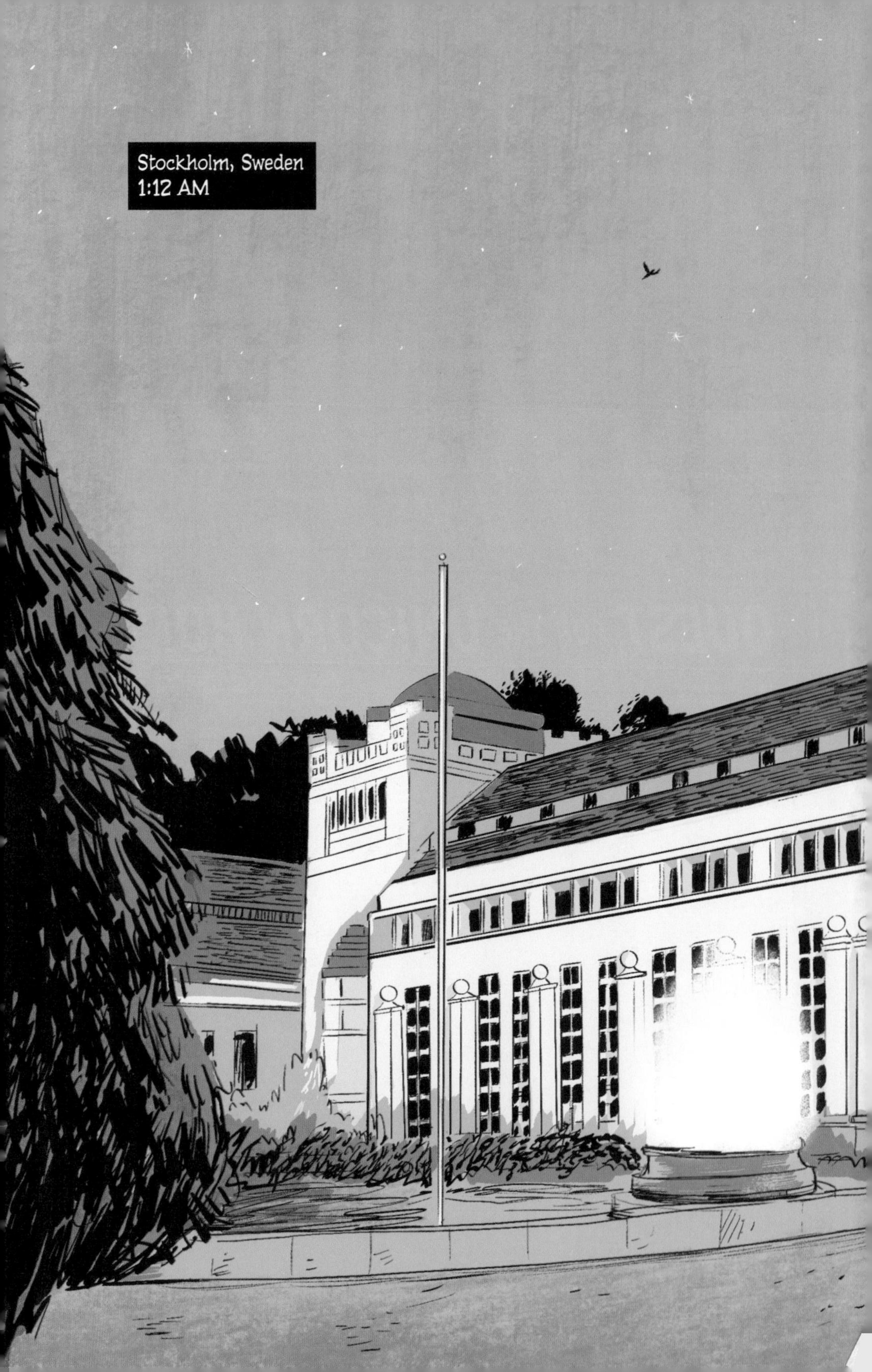

Stockholm, Sweden
1:12 AM

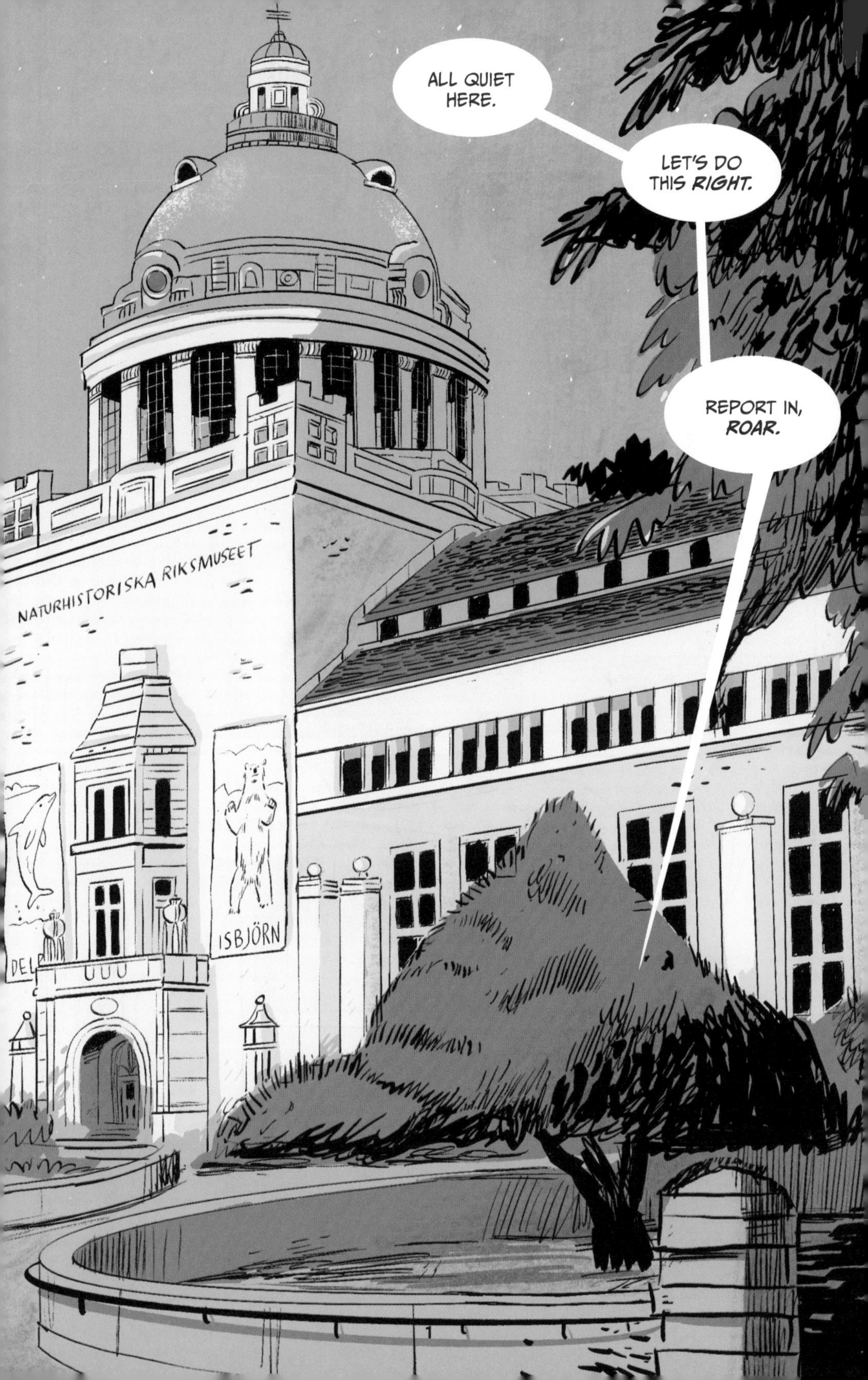
ALL QUIET HERE.
LET'S DO THIS *RIGHT.*
REPORT IN, *ROAR.*
NATURHISTORISKA RIKSMUSEET
DEL
ISBJÖRN

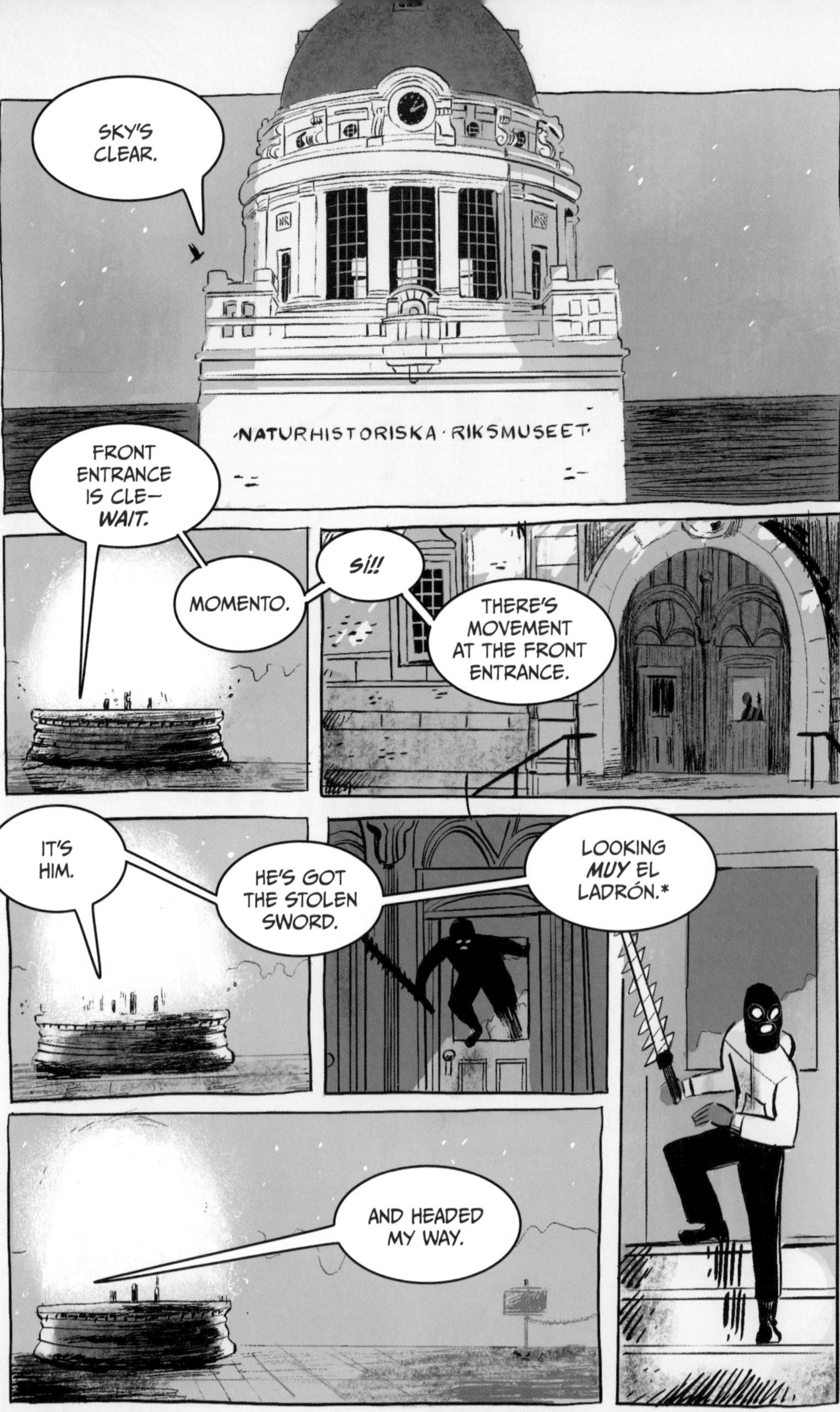
SKY'S CLEAR.
NATURHISTORISKA · RIKSMUSEET
FRONT ENTRANCE IS CLE— *WAIT.*
MOMENTO.
SÍ!!
THERE'S MOVEMENT AT THE FRONT ENTRANCE.
IT'S HIM.
HE'S GOT THE STOLEN SWORD.
LOOKING *MUY* EL LADRÓN.*
AND HEADED MY WAY.

*Translated: Thief.

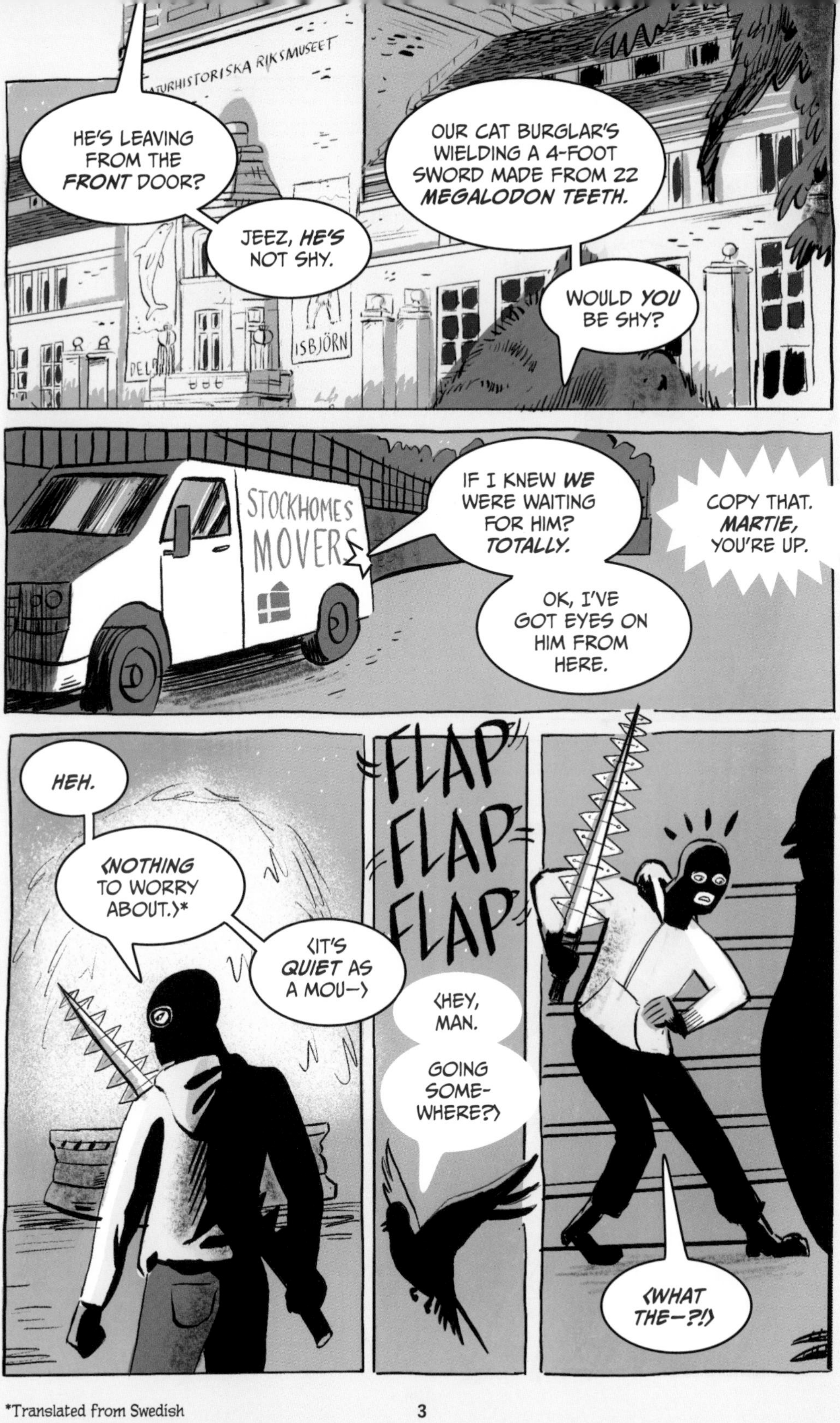
NATURHISTORISKA RIKSMUSEET
HE'S LEAVING FROM THE *FRONT* DOOR?
JEEZ, ***HE'S*** NOT SHY.
OUR CAT BURGLAR'S WIELDING A 4-FOOT SWORD MADE FROM 22 *MEGALODON TEETH.*
WOULD ***YOU*** BE SHY?
ISBJÖRN
STOCKHOMES MOVERS
IF I KNEW ***WE*** WERE WAITING FOR HIM? ***TOTALLY.***
COPY THAT. ***MARTIE,*** YOU'RE UP.
OK, I'VE GOT EYES ON HIM FROM HERE.
HEH.
‹*NOTHING* TO WORRY ABOUT.›*
‹IT'S ***QUIET*** AS A MOU—›
FLAP FLAP FLAP
‹HEY, MAN.
GOING SOME-WHERE?›
‹*WHAT THE—?!*›

*Translated from Swedish

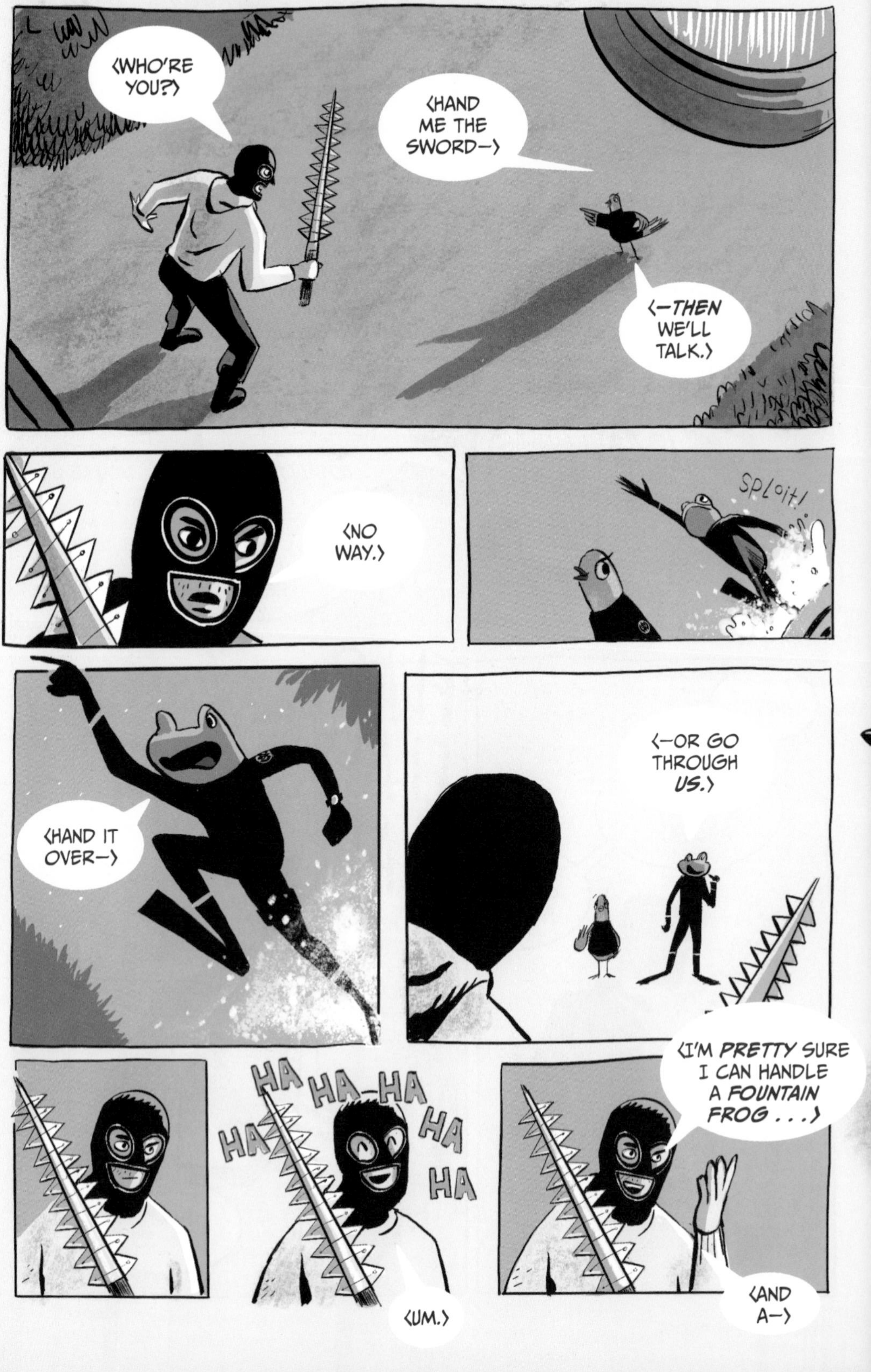
⟨WHO'RE YOU?⟩
⟨HAND ME THE SWORD—⟩
⟨—*THEN* WE'LL TALK.⟩
⟨NO WAY.⟩
SPLOIT!
⟨HAND IT OVER—⟩
⟨—OR GO THROUGH *US.*⟩
HA HA-HA HA HA HA HA
⟨UM.⟩
⟨I'M *PRETTY* SURE I CAN HANDLE A *FOUNTAIN FROG . . .*⟩
⟨AND A—⟩

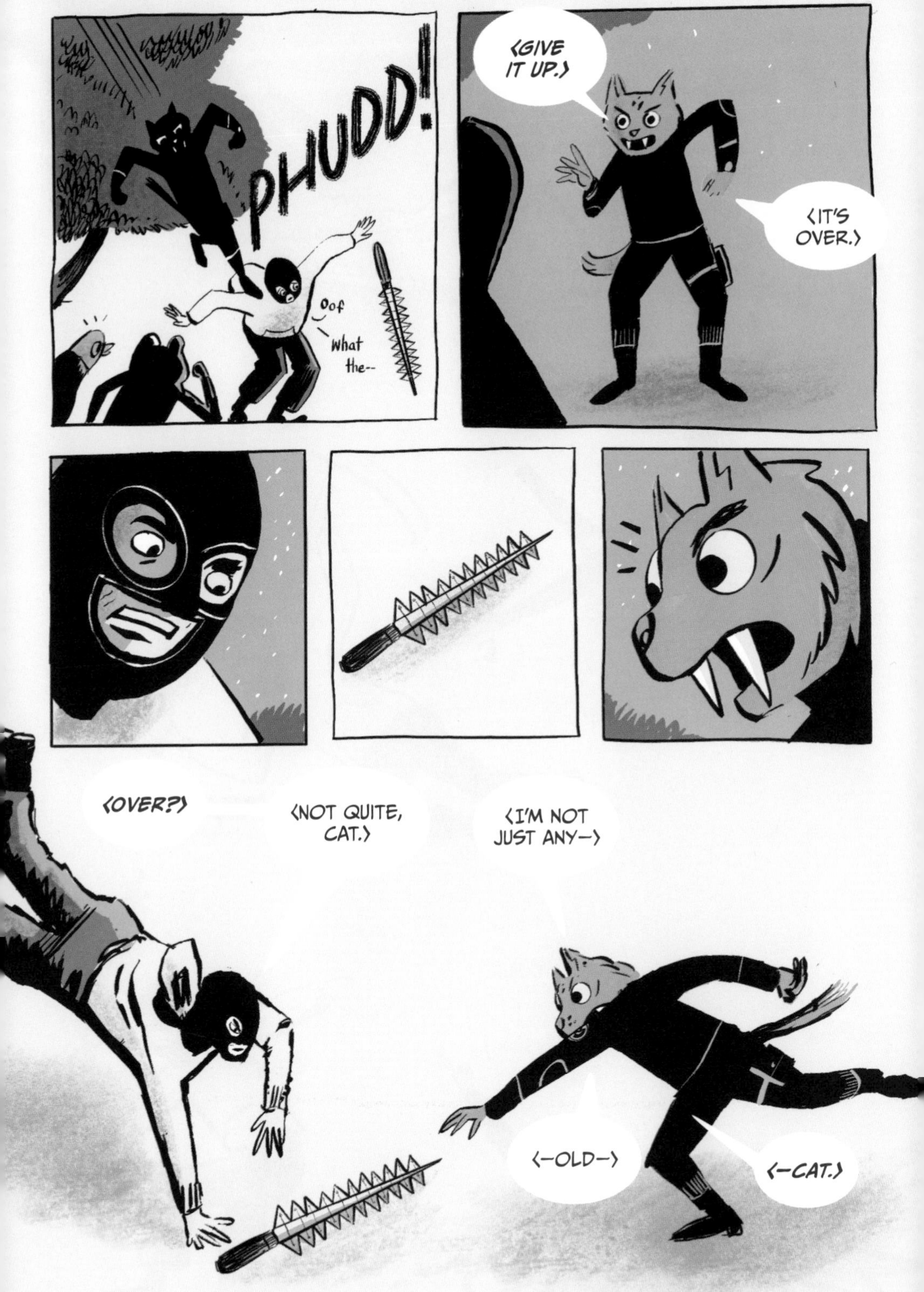
PHUDD!
Oof
What the--
‹GIVE IT UP.›
‹IT'S OVER.›
‹OVER?›
‹NOT QUITE, CAT.›
‹I'M NOT JUST ANY—›
‹—OLD—›
‹—CAT.›

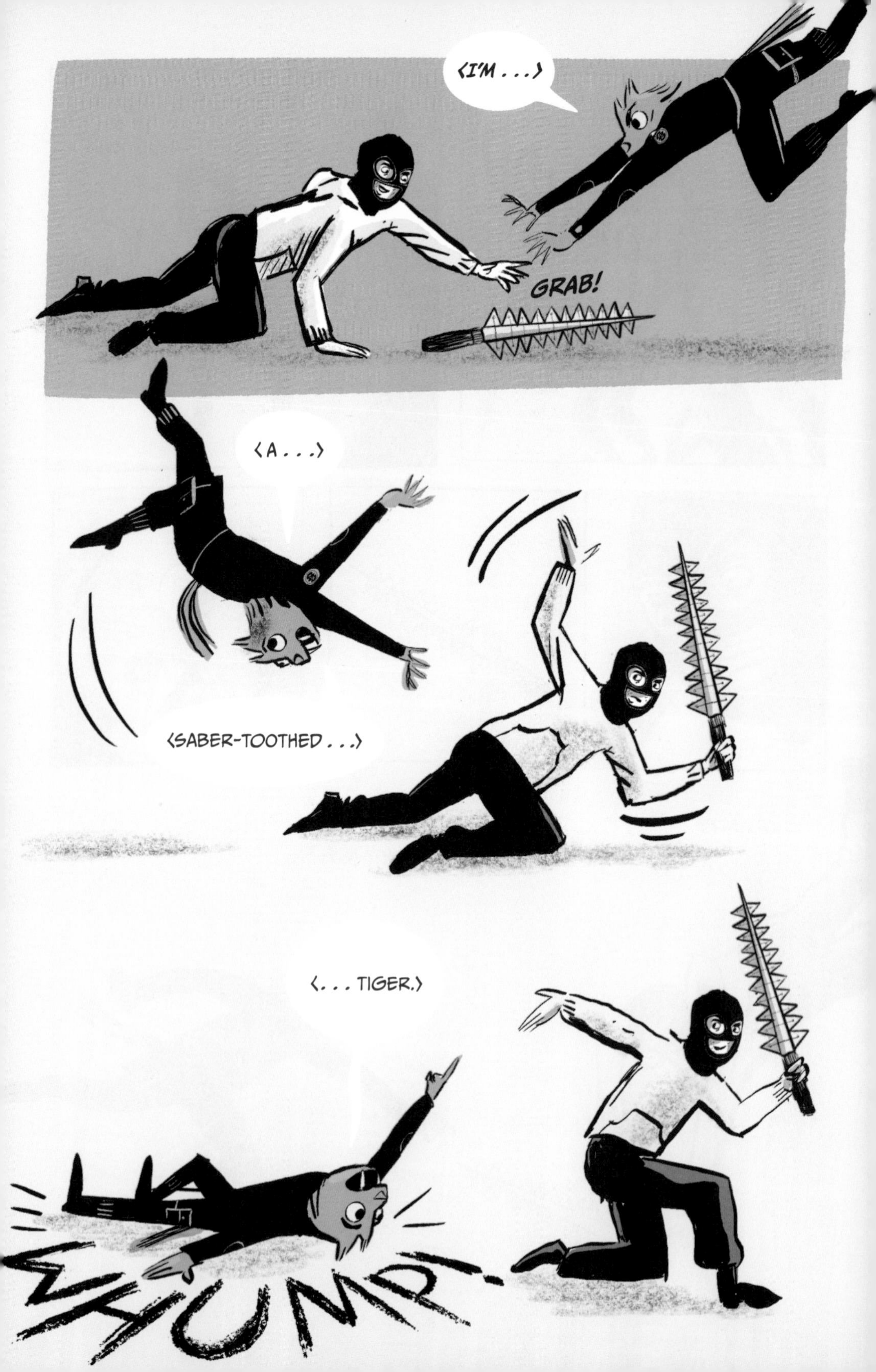
⟨I'M . . .⟩
GRAB!
⟨A . . .⟩
⟨SABER-TOOTHED . . .⟩
⟨. . . TIGER.⟩
WHUMP!

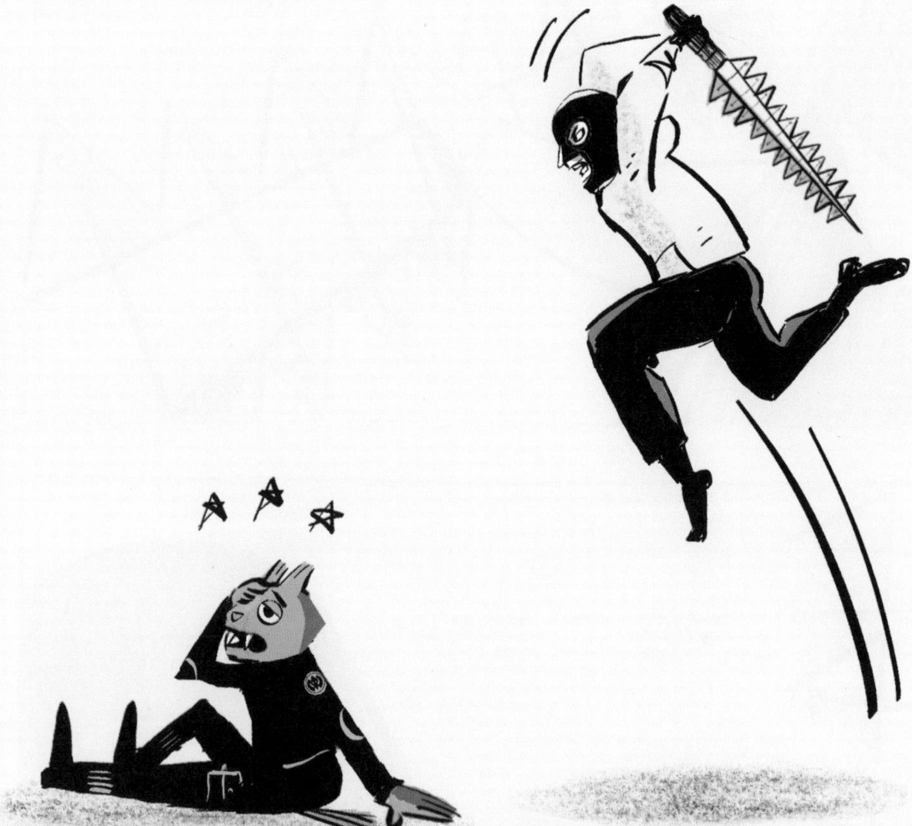

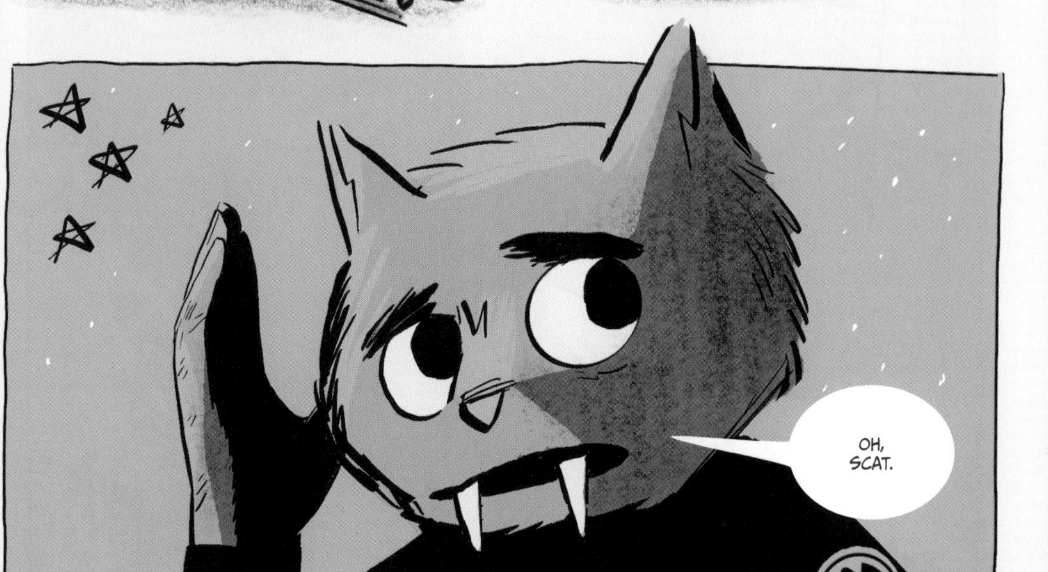
OH,
SCAT.

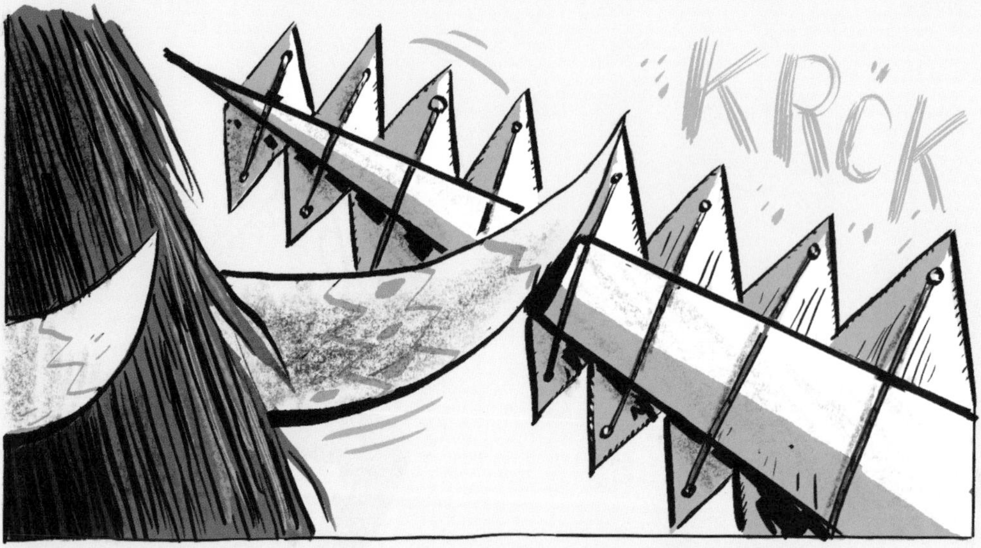
KRČK

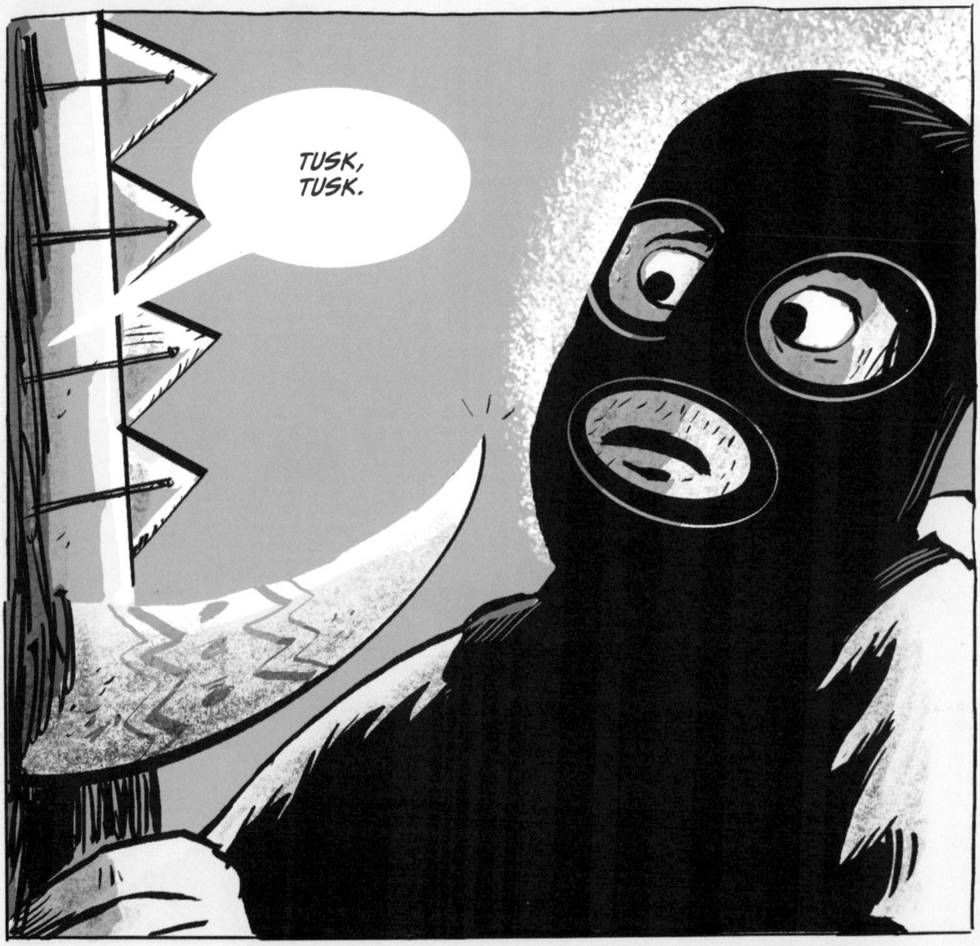
TUSK,
TUSK.

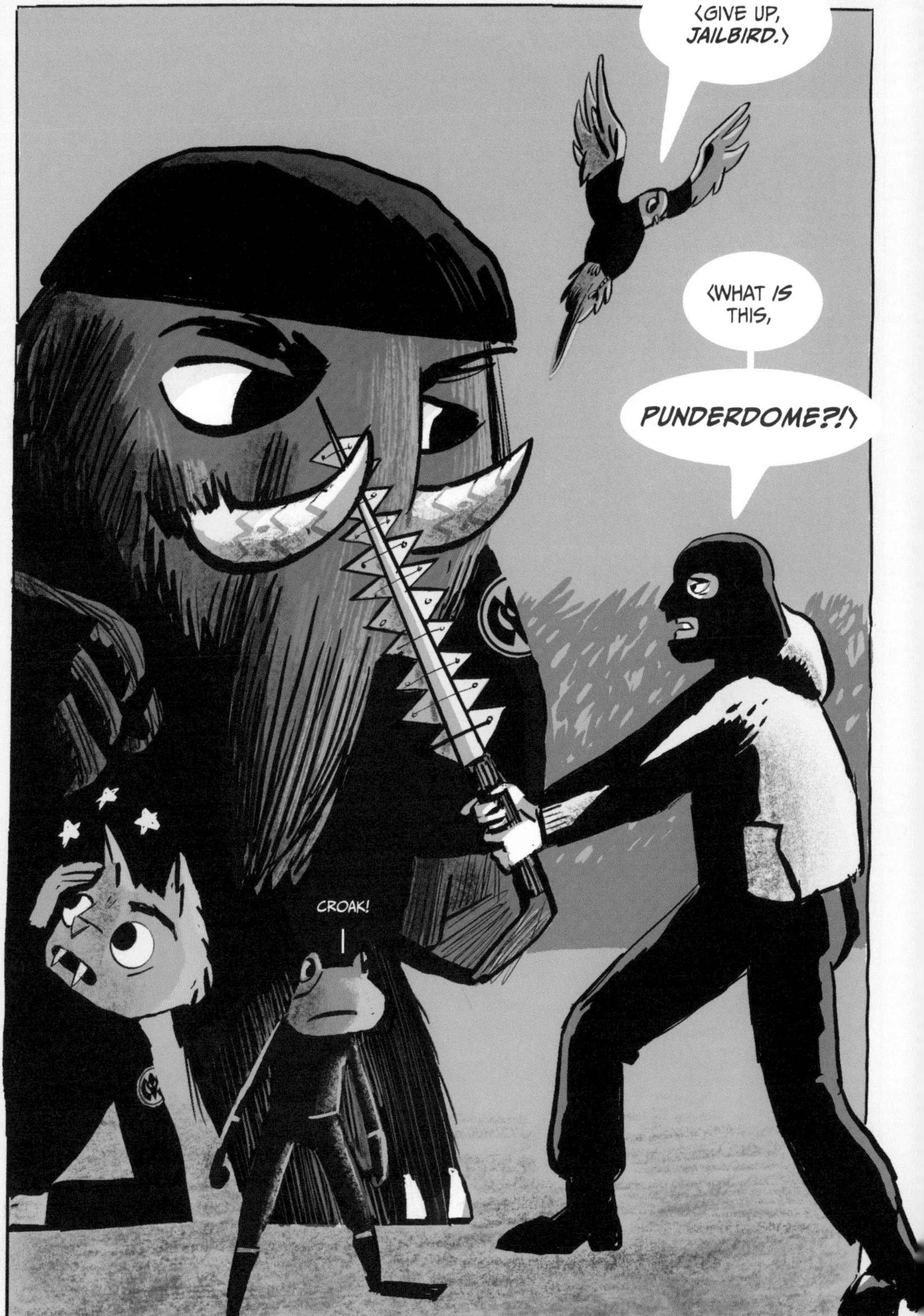

⟨GIVE UP, JAILBIRD.⟩
⟨WHAT IS THIS,
PUNDERDOME?!⟩
CROAK!

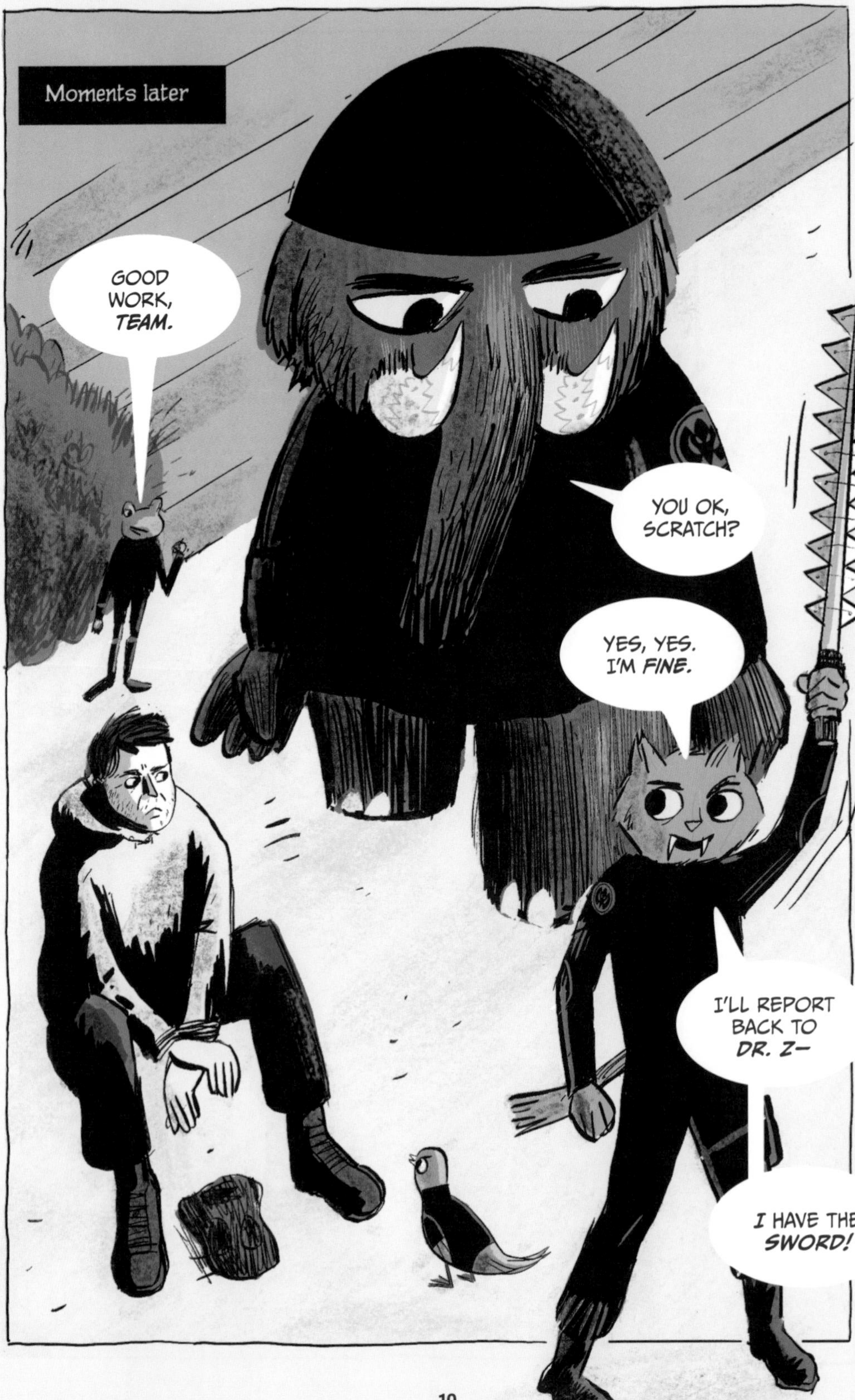
Moments later
GOOD WORK, TEAM.
YOU OK, SCRATCH?
YES, YES. I'M FINE.
I'LL REPORT BACK TO DR. Z—
I HAVE THE SWORD!

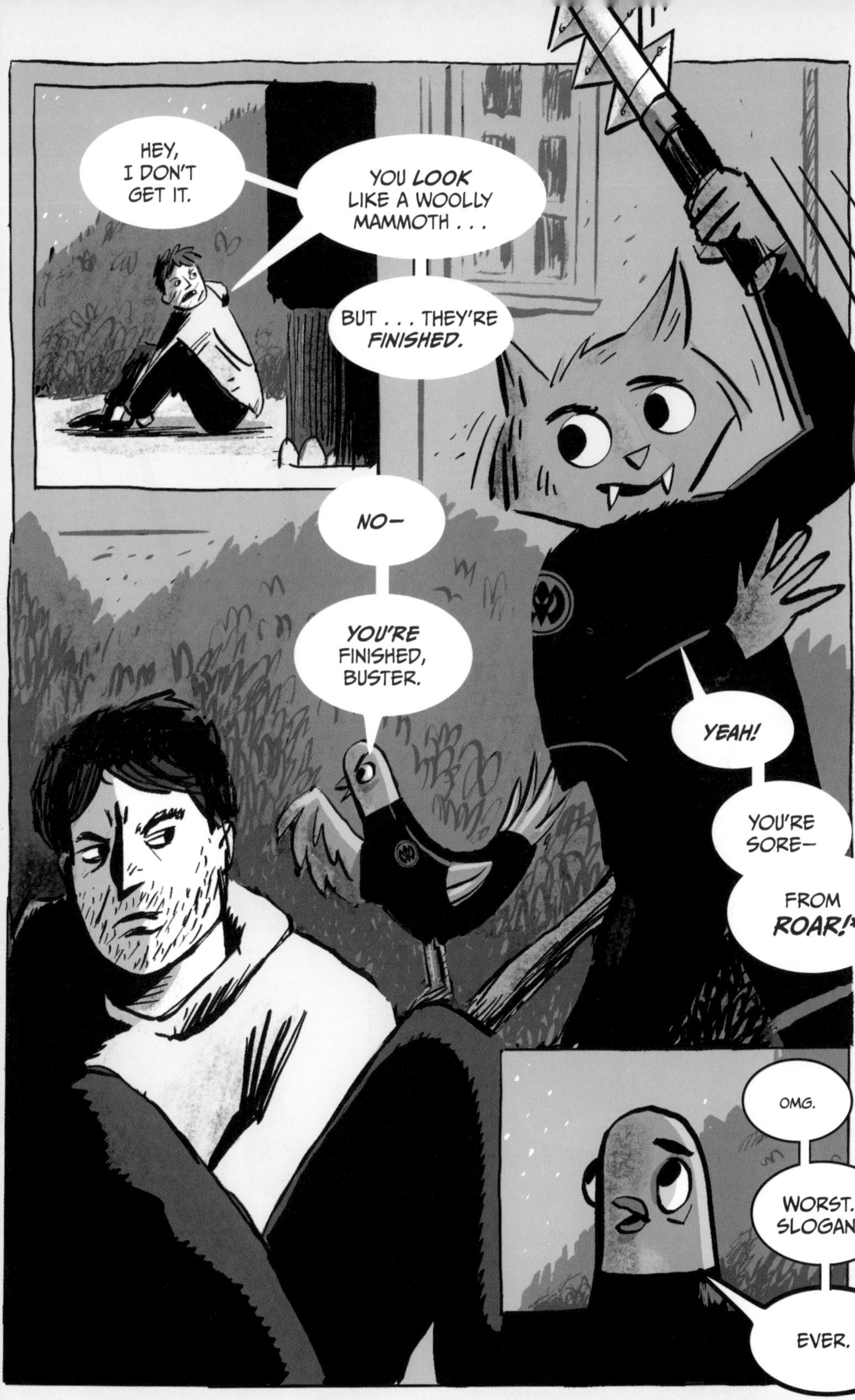
HEY, I DON'T GET IT.
YOU LOOK LIKE A WOOLLY MAMMOTH . . .
BUT . . . THEY'RE FINISHED.
NO—
YOU'RE FINISHED, BUSTER.
YEAH!
YOU'RE SORE—
FROM ROAR!*
OMG.
WORST. SLOGAN.
EVER.

*Rescue Ops Acquisition Rangers

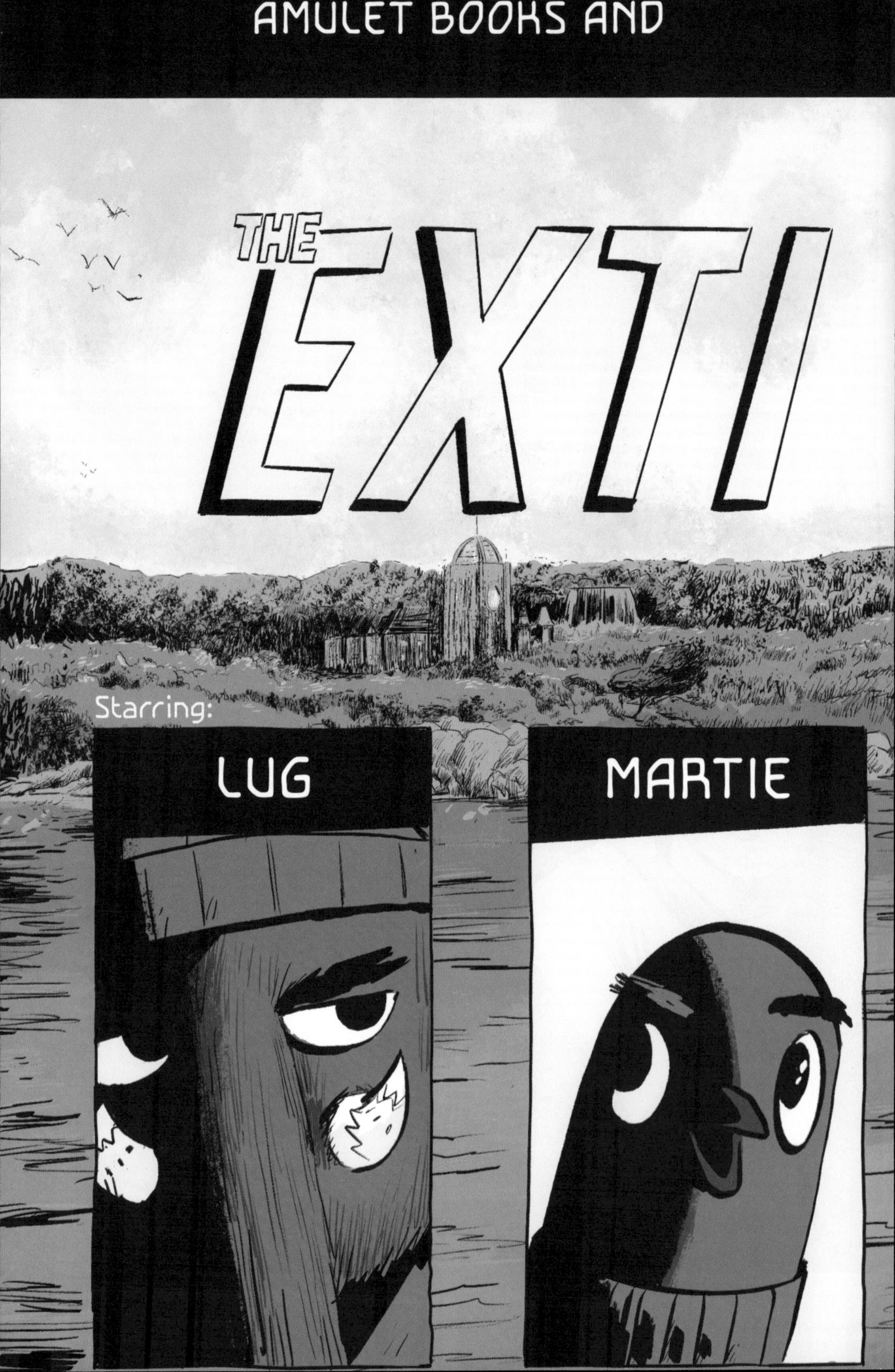
AMULET BOOKS AND
THE EXTI
Starring:
LUG
MARTIE

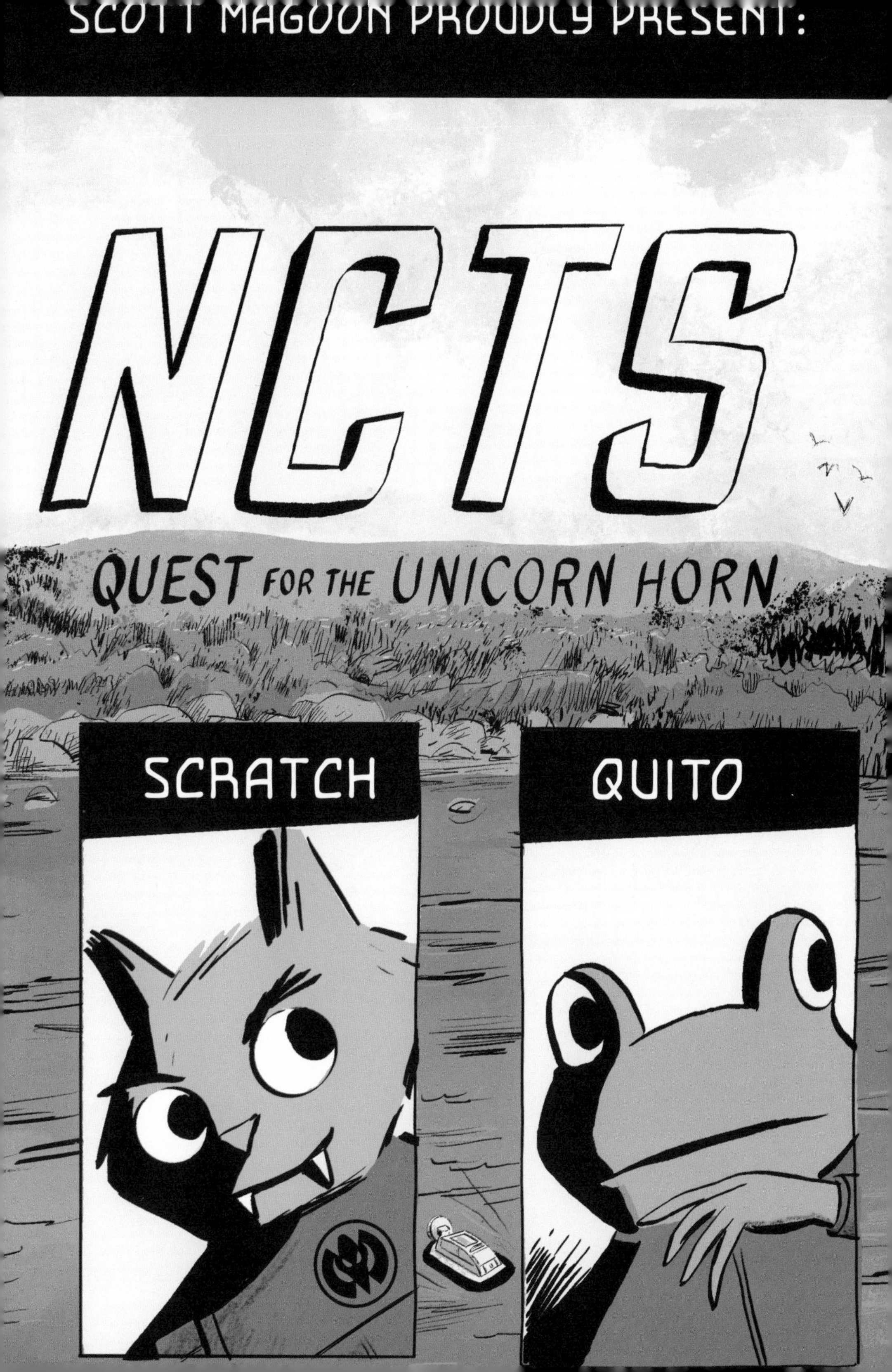
SCOTT MAGOON PROUDLY PRESENT:
NCTS
QUEST FOR THE UNICORN HORN
SCRATCH
QUITO

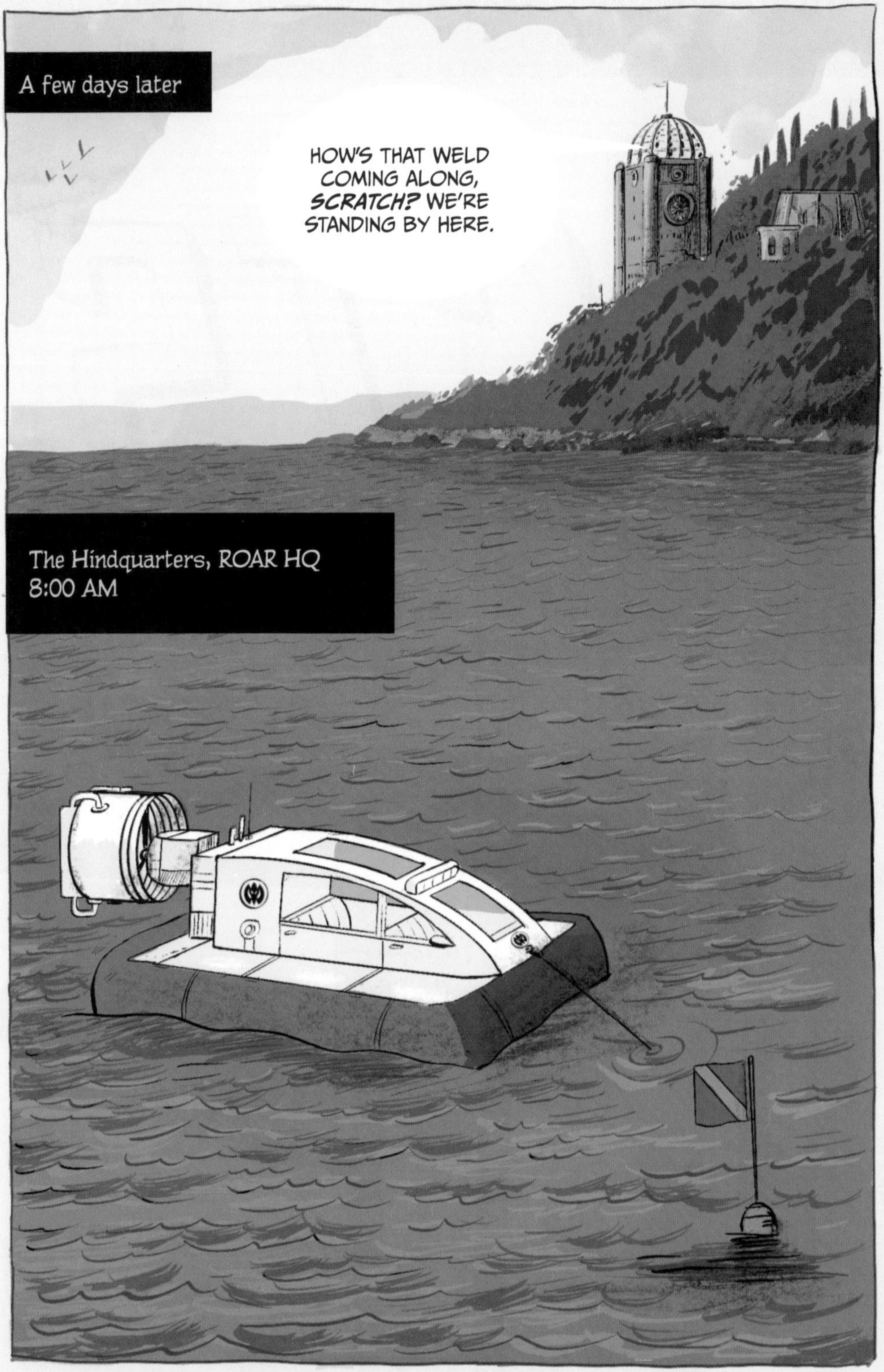
A few days later
HOW'S THAT WELD COMING ALONG, SCRATCH? WE'RE STANDING BY HERE.
The Hindquarters, ROAR HQ
8:00 AM

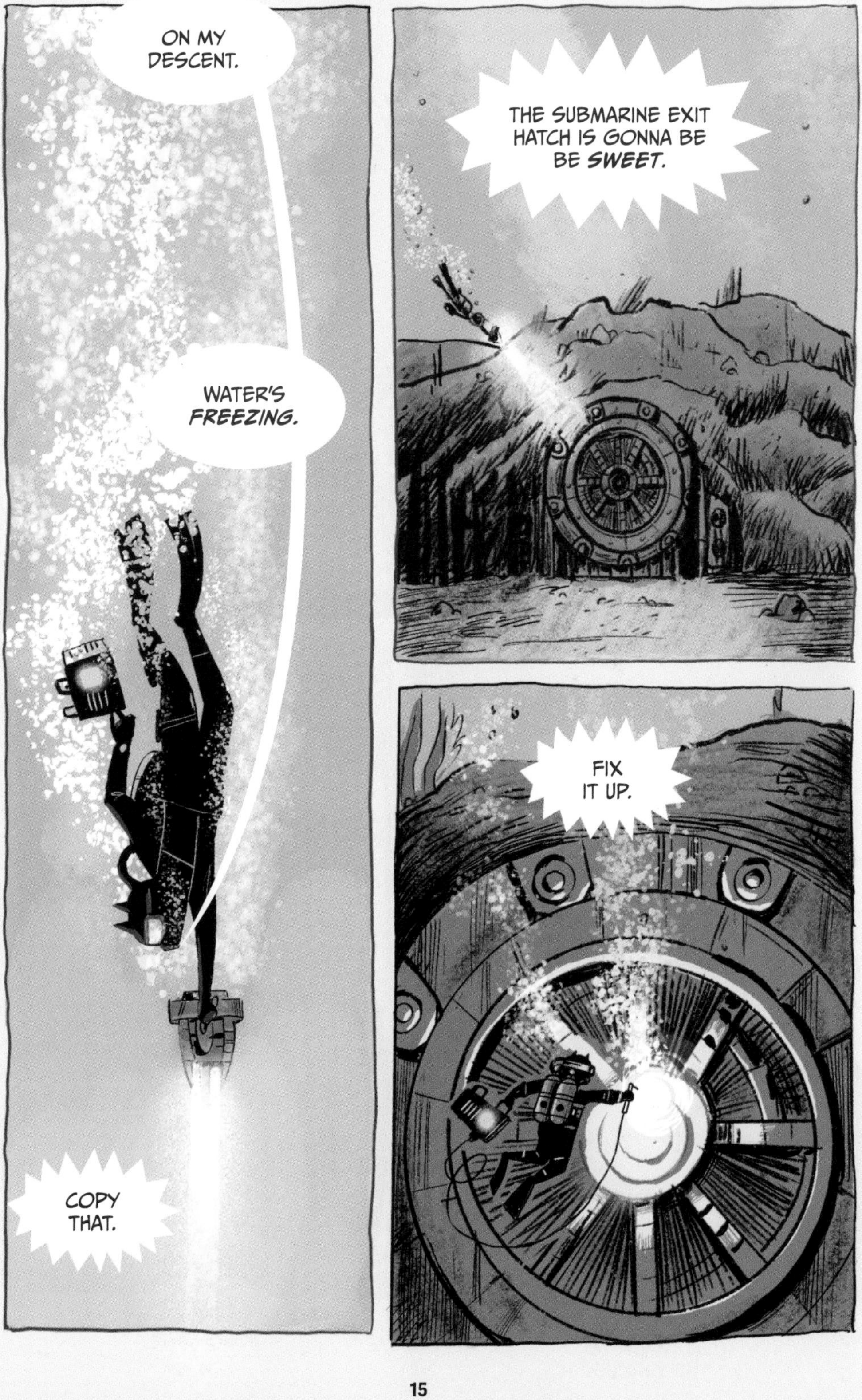
ON MY DESCENT.
WATER'S *FREEZING.*
COPY THAT.
THE SUBMARINE EXIT HATCH IS GONNA BE BE ***SWEET.***
FIX IT UP.

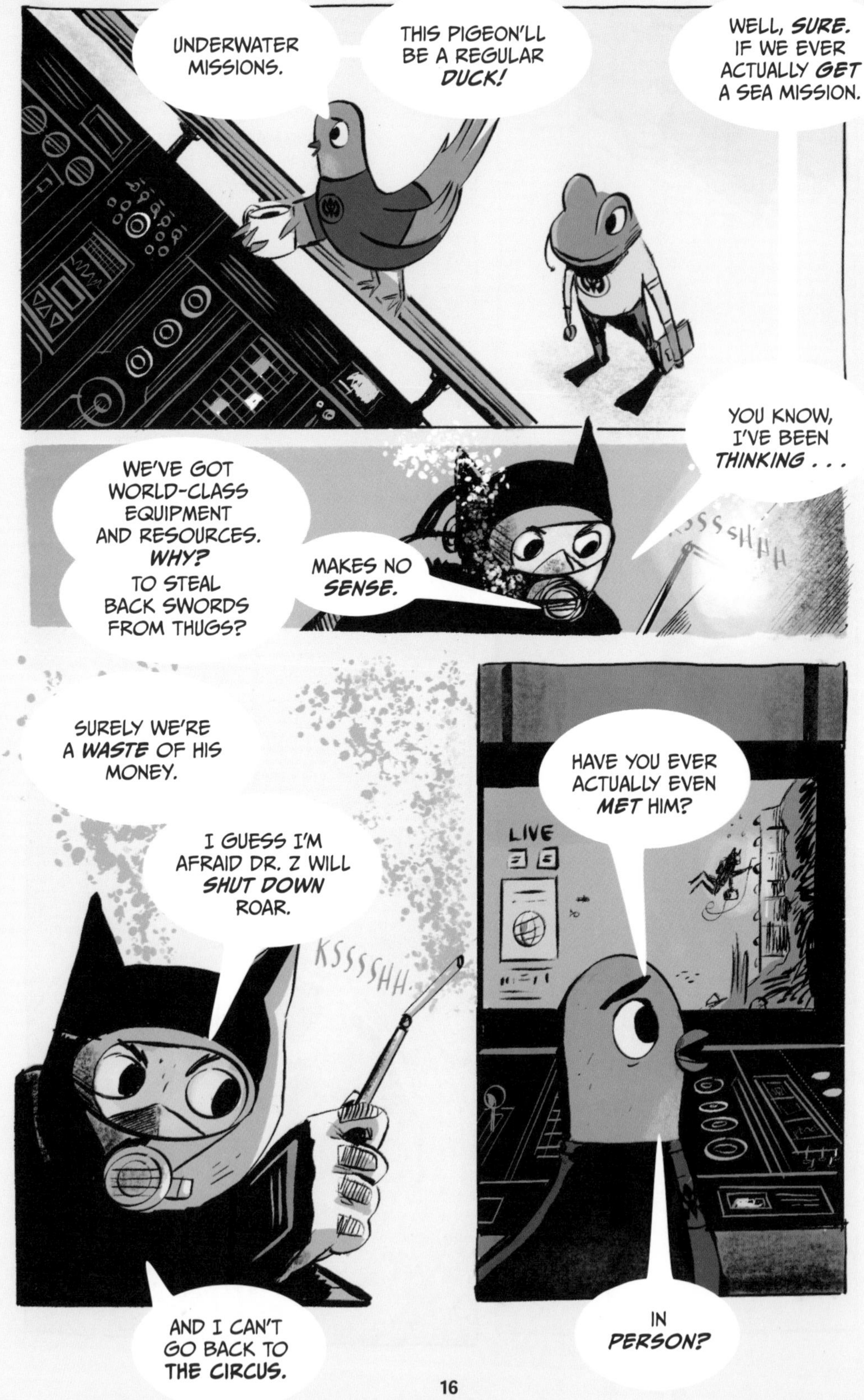
UNDERWATER MISSIONS.
THIS PIGEON'LL BE A REGULAR DUCK!
WELL, SURE. IF WE EVER ACTUALLY GET A SEA MISSION.
YOU KNOW, I'VE BEEN THINKING . . .
WE'VE GOT WORLD-CLASS EQUIPMENT AND RESOURCES. WHY?
TO STEAL BACK SWORDS FROM THUGS?
MAKES NO SENSE.
KSSSSHHH
SURELY WE'RE A WASTE OF HIS MONEY.
I GUESS I'M AFRAID DR. Z WILL SHUT DOWN ROAR.
KSSSSHH
AND I CAN'T GO BACK TO THE CIRCUS.
LIVE
HAVE YOU EVER ACTUALLY EVEN MET HIM?
IN PERSON?

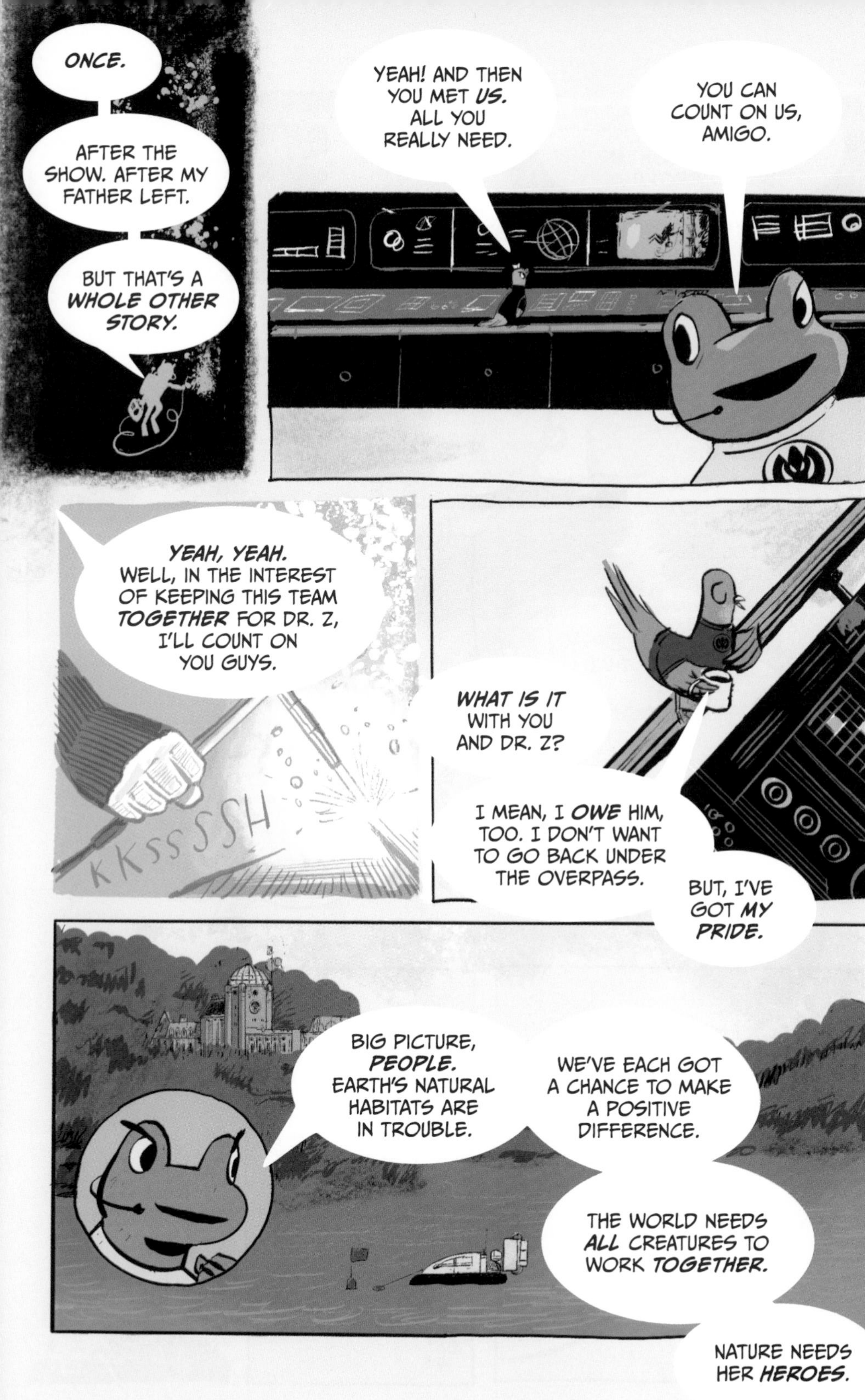
ONCE.
AFTER THE SHOW. AFTER MY FATHER LEFT.
BUT THAT'S A WHOLE OTHER STORY.
YEAH! AND THEN YOU MET US. ALL YOU REALLY NEED.
YOU CAN COUNT ON US, AMIGO.
YEAH, YEAH. WELL, IN THE INTEREST OF KEEPING THIS TEAM TOGETHER FOR DR. Z, I'LL COUNT ON YOU GUYS.
KKSSSSH
WHAT IS IT WITH YOU AND DR. Z?
I MEAN, I OWE HIM, TOO. I DON'T WANT TO GO BACK UNDER THE OVERPASS.
BUT, I'VE GOT MY PRIDE.
BIG PICTURE, PEOPLE. EARTH'S NATURAL HABITATS ARE IN TROUBLE.
WE'VE EACH GOT A CHANCE TO MAKE A POSITIVE DIFFERENCE.
THE WORLD NEEDS ALL CREATURES TO WORK TOGETHER.
NATURE NEEDS HER HEROES.

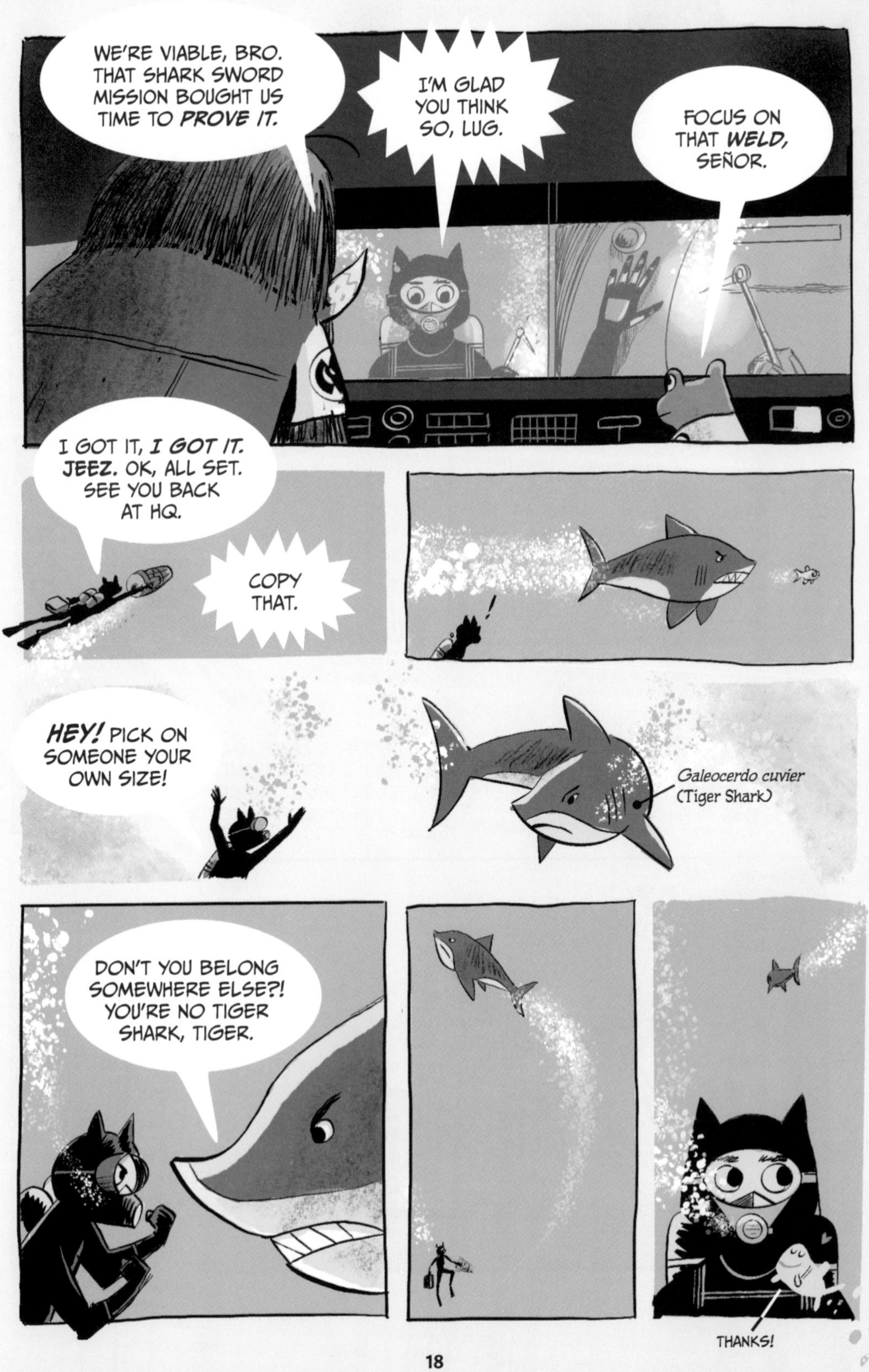
WE'RE VIABLE, BRO. THAT SHARK SWORD MISSION BOUGHT US TIME TO *PROVE IT.*
I'M GLAD YOU THINK SO, LUG.
FOCUS ON THAT **WELD,** SEÑOR.
I GOT IT, ***I GOT IT.*** **JEEZ.** OK, ALL SET. SEE YOU BACK AT HQ.
COPY THAT.
!
HEY! PICK ON SOMEONE YOUR OWN SIZE!
Galeocerdo cuvier
(Tiger Shark)
DON'T YOU BELONG SOMEWHERE ELSE?! YOU'RE NO TIGER SHARK, TIGER.
THANKS!

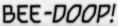
Moments later

SCRATCH, BETTER *HIGH TAIL IT OUTTA THERE* AND HEAD BACK.

DR. Z'S CALLING.

BEE-*DOOP!*

Incoming transmission from Dr. Z.

ROGER THAT! I'M EN ROUTE. SCRATCH OUT.

Later still

HM. IT'S A GARBLED TRANSMISSION—

GAIA,* SEE WHAT YOU CAN DO TO STRENGTHEN THE SIGNAL.

Boosting signal.

AH, BETTER.

HERE HE IS . . .

ZZZZAK!

GREETINGS, DR. Z! WHAT CAN WE DO FOR YOU?

*GAIA: Global Animal Information Access

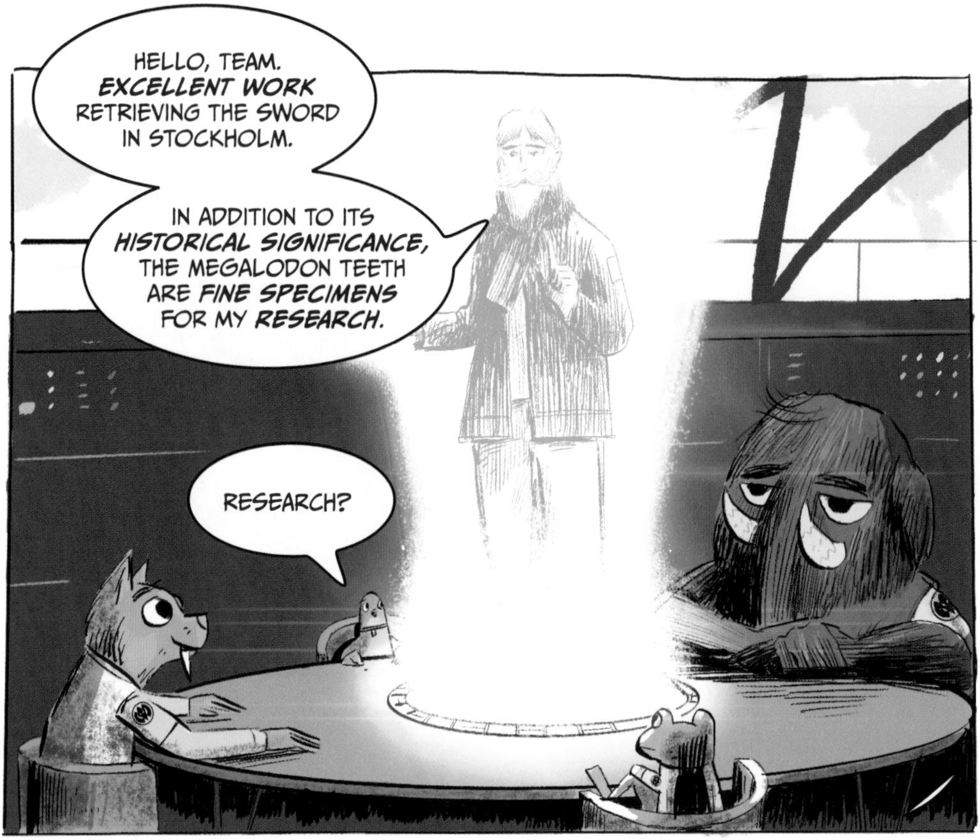
HELLO, TEAM. **EXCELLENT WORK** RETRIEVING THE SWORD IN STOCKHOLM.
IN ADDITION TO ITS **HISTORICAL SIGNIFICANCE,** THE MEGALODON TEETH ARE **FINE SPECIMENS** FOR MY **RESEARCH.**
RESEARCH?

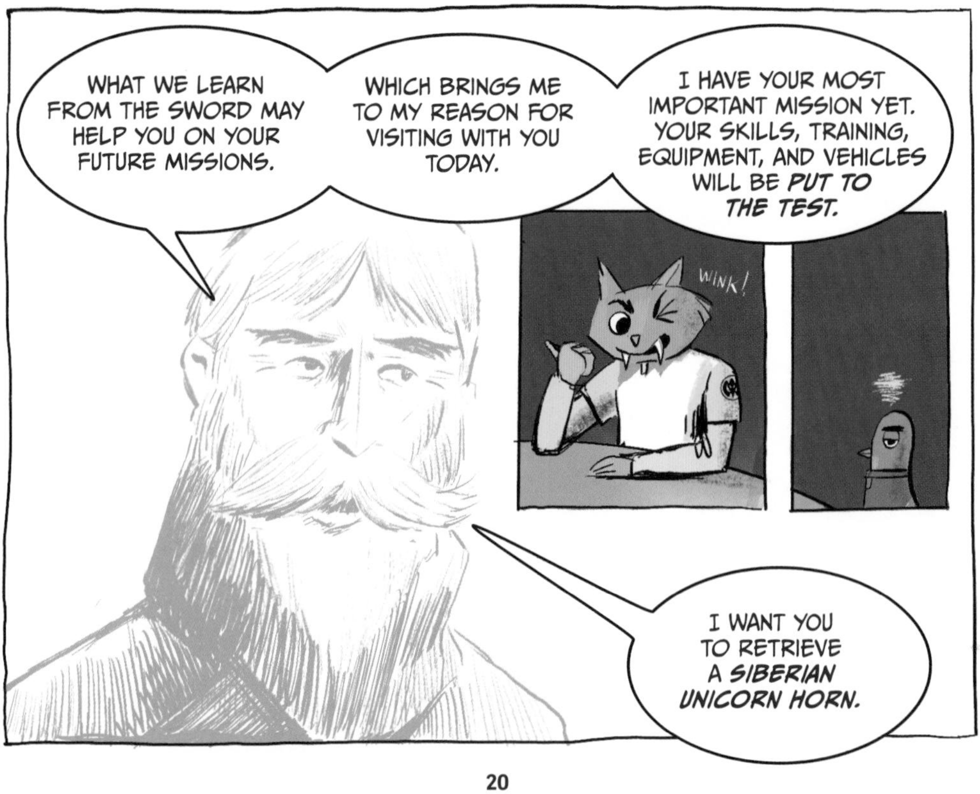
WHAT WE LEARN FROM THE SWORD MAY HELP YOU ON YOUR FUTURE MISSIONS.
WHICH BRINGS ME TO MY REASON FOR VISITING WITH YOU TODAY.
I HAVE YOUR MOST IMPORTANT MISSION YET. YOUR SKILLS, TRAINING, EQUIPMENT, AND VEHICLES WILL BE **PUT TO THE TEST.**
WINK!
I WANT YOU TO RETRIEVE A **SIBERIAN UNICORN HORN.**

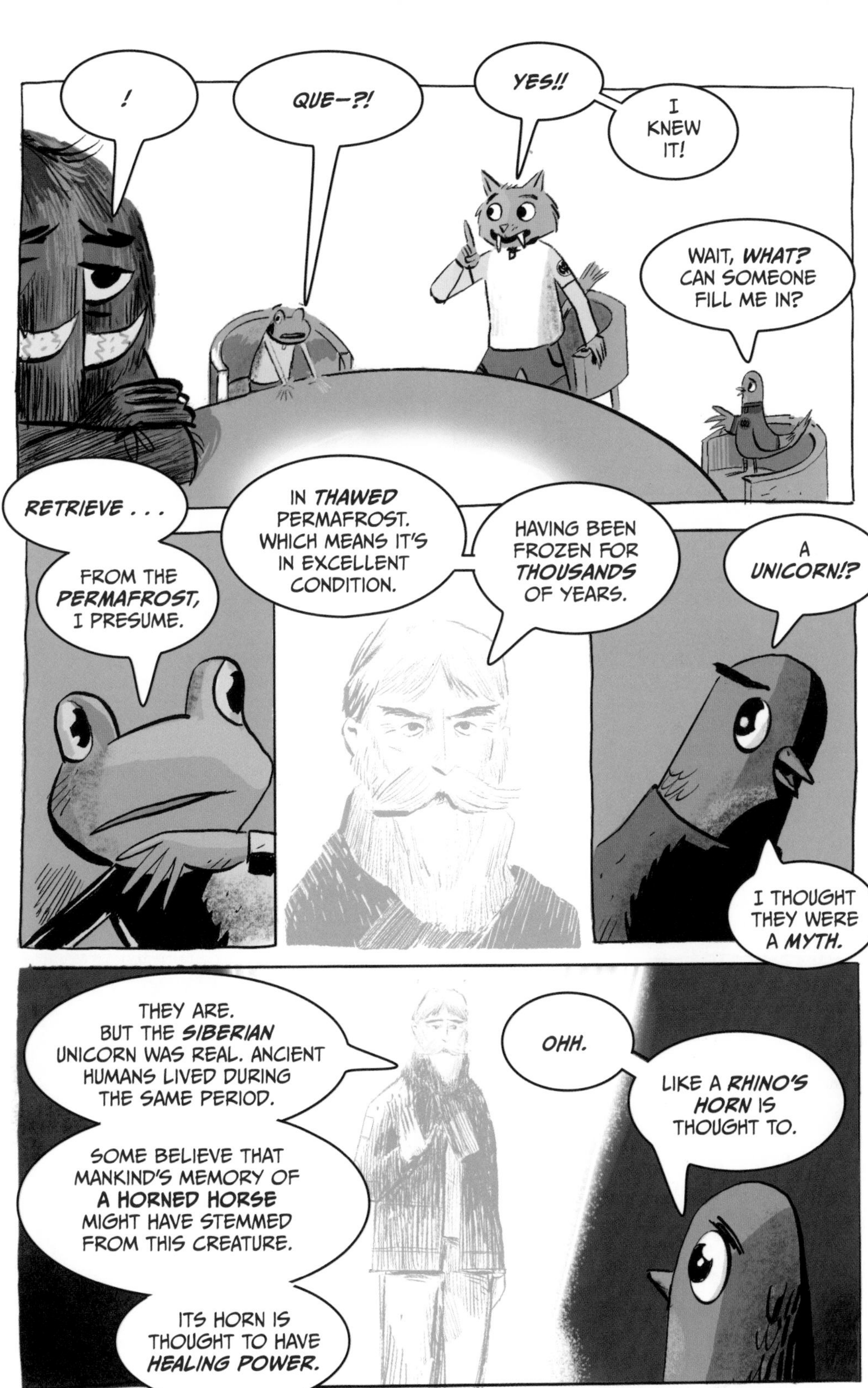
!
QUE–?!
YES!!
I KNEW IT!
WAIT, WHAT? CAN SOMEONE FILL ME IN?
RETRIEVE . . .
FROM THE PERMAFROST, I PRESUME.
IN THAWED PERMAFROST. WHICH MEANS IT'S IN EXCELLENT CONDITION.
HAVING BEEN FROZEN FOR THOUSANDS OF YEARS.
A UNICORN!?
I THOUGHT THEY WERE A MYTH.
THEY ARE. BUT THE SIBERIAN UNICORN WAS REAL. ANCIENT HUMANS LIVED DURING THE SAME PERIOD.
SOME BELIEVE THAT MANKIND'S MEMORY OF A HORNED HORSE MIGHT HAVE STEMMED FROM THIS CREATURE.
ITS HORN IS THOUGHT TO HAVE HEALING POWER.
OHH.
LIKE A RHINO'S HORN IS THOUGHT TO.

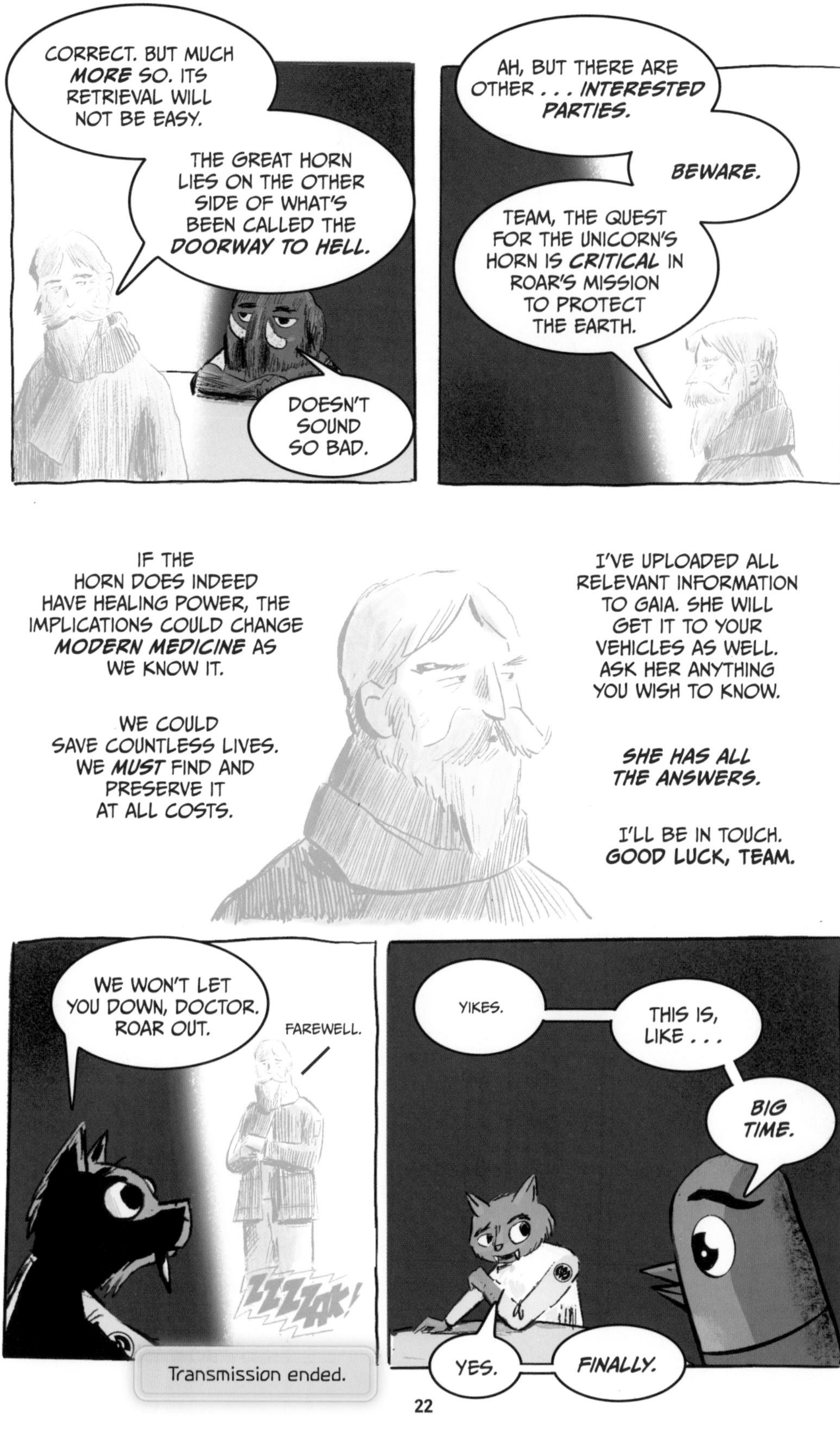

CORRECT. BUT MUCH MORE SO. ITS RETRIEVAL WILL NOT BE EASY.
THE GREAT HORN LIES ON THE OTHER SIDE OF WHAT'S BEEN CALLED THE DOORWAY TO HELL.
DOESN'T SOUND SO BAD.
AH, BUT THERE ARE OTHER . . . INTERESTED PARTIES.
BEWARE.
TEAM, THE QUEST FOR THE UNICORN'S HORN IS CRITICAL IN ROAR'S MISSION TO PROTECT THE EARTH.
IF THE HORN DOES INDEED HAVE HEALING POWER, THE IMPLICATIONS COULD CHANGE MODERN MEDICINE AS WE KNOW IT.
WE COULD SAVE COUNTLESS LIVES. WE MUST FIND AND PRESERVE IT AT ALL COSTS.
I'VE UPLOADED ALL RELEVANT INFORMATION TO GAIA. SHE WILL GET IT TO YOUR VEHICLES AS WELL. ASK HER ANYTHING YOU WISH TO KNOW.
SHE HAS ALL THE ANSWERS.
I'LL BE IN TOUCH. GOOD LUCK, TEAM.
WE WON'T LET YOU DOWN, DOCTOR. ROAR OUT.
FAREWELL.
ZZZZAK!
Transmission ended.
YIKES.
THIS IS, LIKE . . .
BIG TIME.
YES.
FINALLY.

SIBERIAN UNICORN
Elasmotherium sibiricum
Extinct: 35,000 years ago
Cause: Loss of food & hunted by humans
Weight: 4 tons
Length: Up to 15 feet
Height: Up to 7 feet at shoulder
Diet: Tough, dry grasses
Temporal Range: Late Pliocene to Late Pleistocene

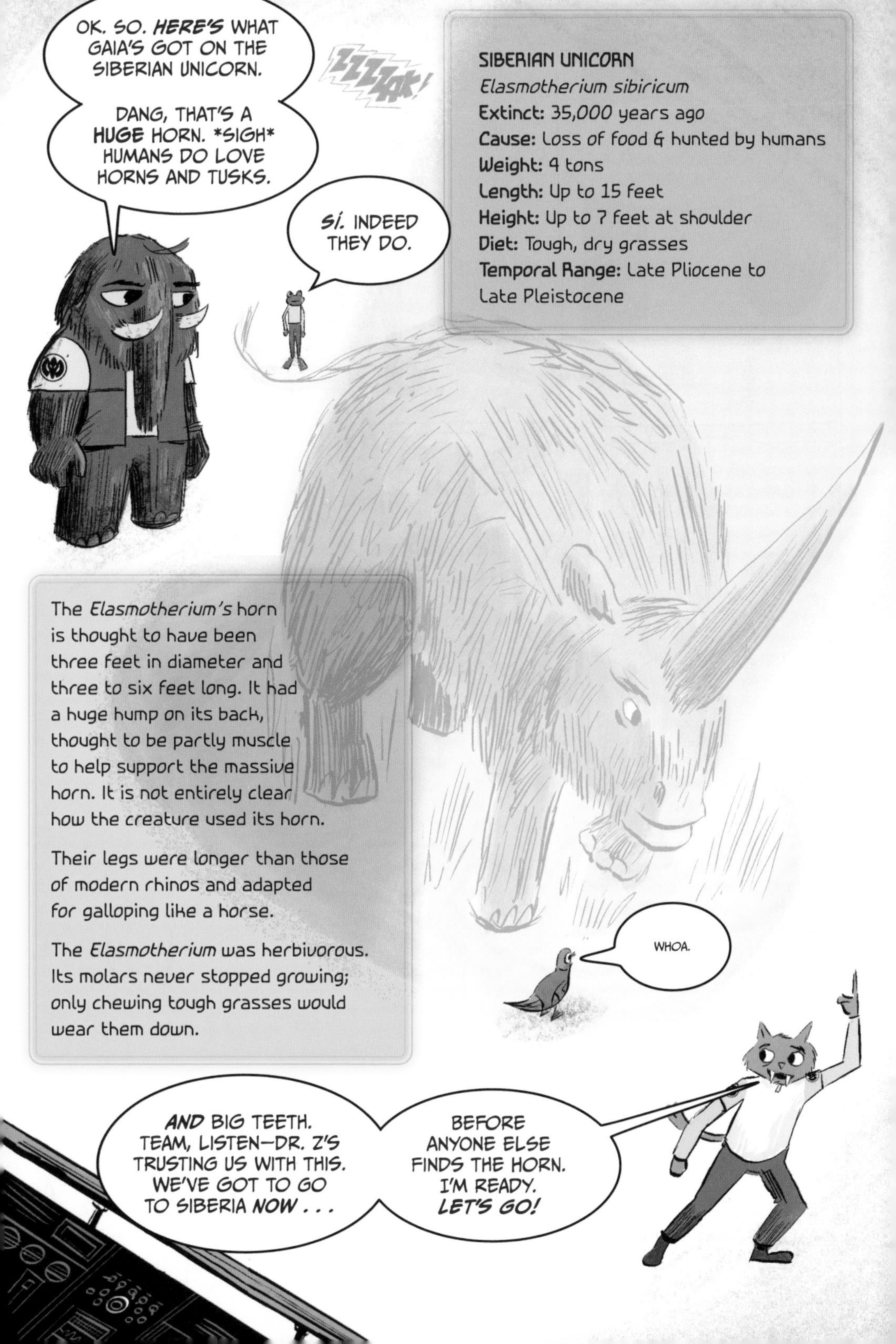
OK. SO. HERE'S WHAT GAIA'S GOT ON THE SIBERIAN UNICORN.
DANG, THAT'S A HUGE HORN. *SIGH* HUMANS DO LOVE HORNS AND TUSKS.
ZZZZAK!
SÍ. INDEED THEY DO.
WHOA.
AND BIG TEETH. TEAM, LISTEN—DR. Z'S TRUSTING US WITH THIS. WE'VE GOT TO GO TO SIBERIA NOW . . .
BEFORE ANYONE ELSE FINDS THE HORN. I'M READY. LET'S GO!

The *Elasmotherium's* horn is thought to have been three feet in diameter and three to six feet long. It had a huge hump on its back, thought to be partly muscle to help support the massive horn. It is not entirely clear how the creature used its horn.

Their legs were longer than those of modern rhinos and adapted for galloping like a horse.

The *Elasmotherium* was herbivorous. Its molars never stopped growing; only chewing tough grasses would wear them down.

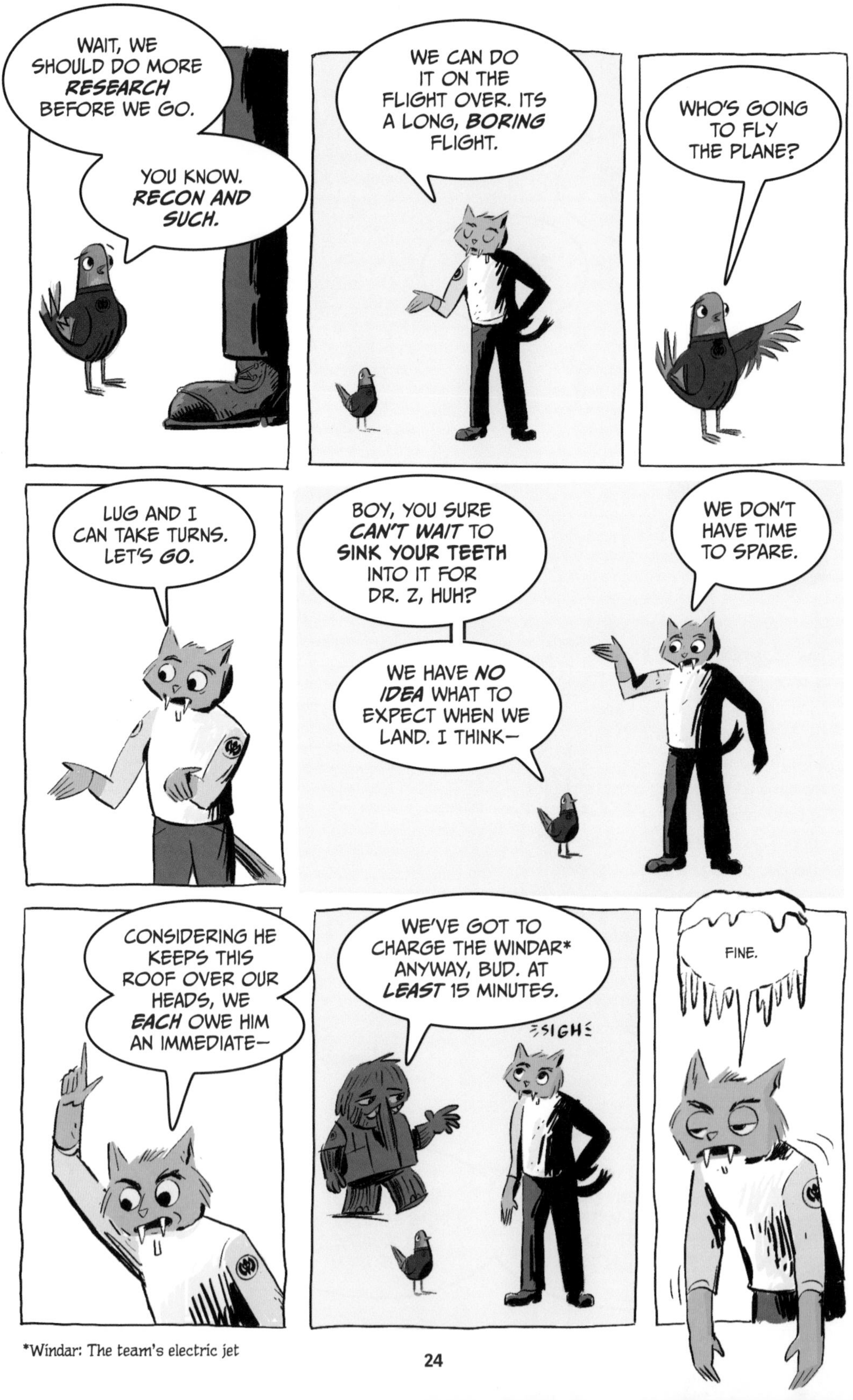
WAIT, WE SHOULD DO MORE RESEARCH BEFORE WE GO.
YOU KNOW. RECON AND SUCH.
WE CAN DO IT ON THE FLIGHT OVER. ITS A LONG, BORING FLIGHT.
WHO'S GOING TO FLY THE PLANE?
LUG AND I CAN TAKE TURNS. LET'S GO.
BOY, YOU SURE CAN'T WAIT TO SINK YOUR TEETH INTO IT FOR DR. Z, HUH?
WE HAVE NO IDEA WHAT TO EXPECT WHEN WE LAND. I THINK—
WE DON'T HAVE TIME TO SPARE.
CONSIDERING HE KEEPS THIS ROOF OVER OUR HEADS, WE EACH OWE HIM AN IMMEDIATE—
WE'VE GOT TO CHARGE THE WINDAR* ANYWAY, BUD. AT LEAST 15 MINUTES.
SIGH
FINE.

*Windar: The team's electric jet

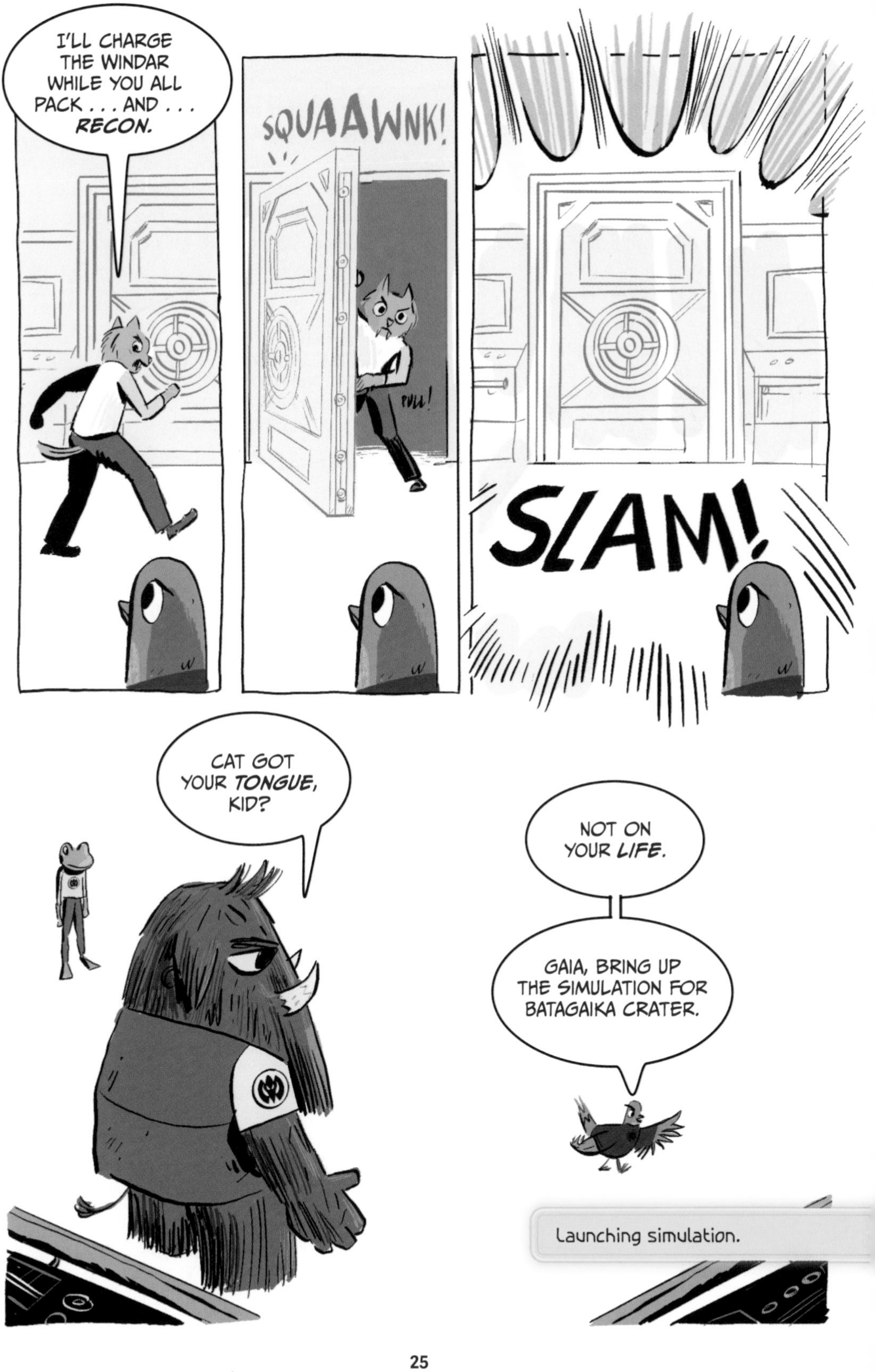
I'LL CHARGE THE WINDAR WHILE YOU ALL PACK . . . AND . . . *RECON.*
SQUAAWNK!
PULL!
SLAM!
CAT GOT YOUR *TONGUE,* KID?
NOT ON YOUR *LIFE.*
GAIA, BRING UP THE SIMULATION FOR BATAGAIKA CRATER.
Launching simulation.

This is the great Batagaika crater, located in the East Siberian taiga, in the Sakha Republic of the Russian Federation. The pit began to form In the 1960s after the area was deforested and thawing permafrost sank the area. Flooding erosion also expands the crater's size. It is a depression half a mile long, up to 330 feet deep, and is still growing at a rate of about 40 feet per year. The permafrost walls of the pit are constantly thawing, making the walls dangerously unstable.

Paleontologists found ice age fossils buried in the mud around the crater, including reports of the Siberian unicorn horn.

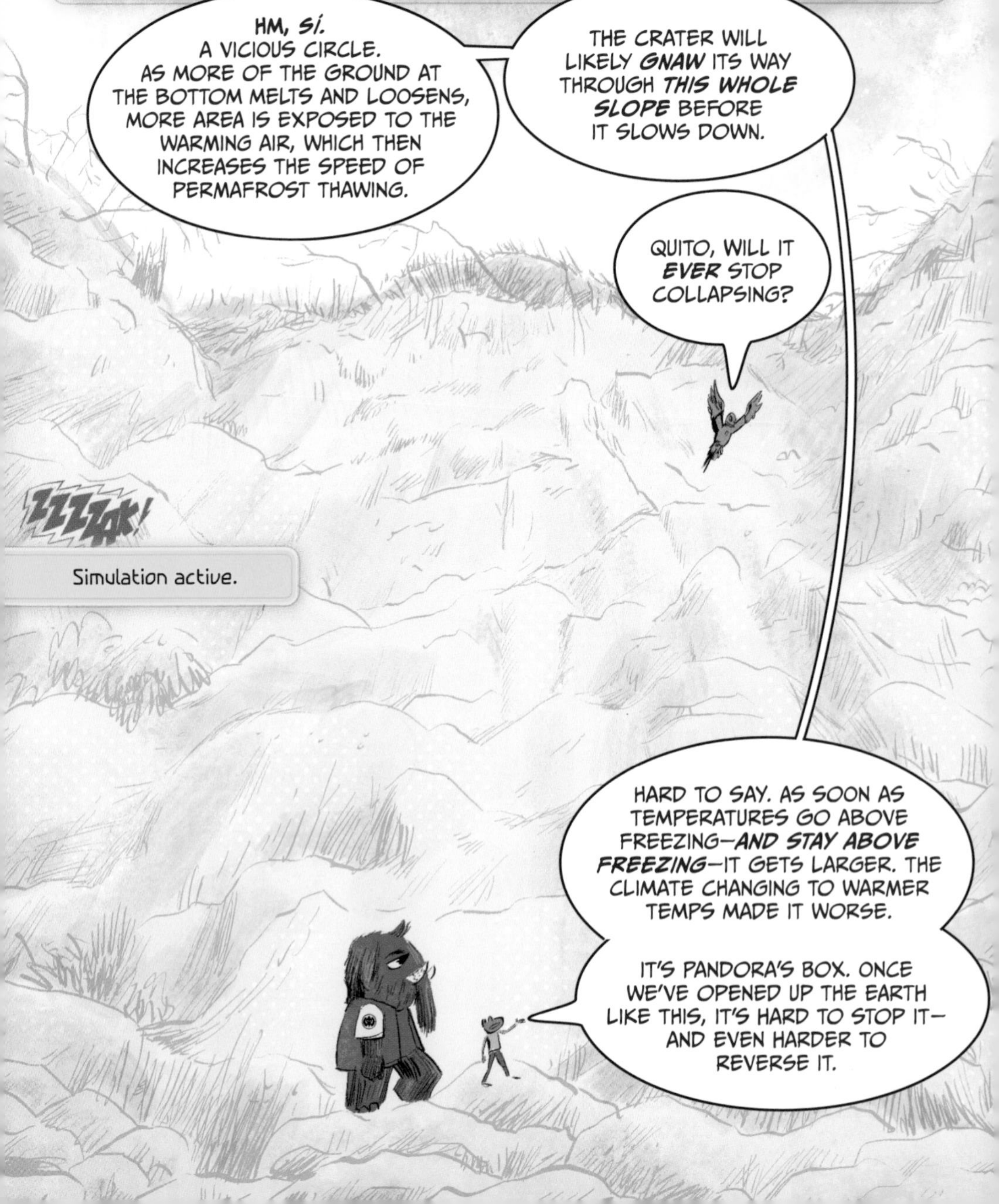
HM, *SÍ.* A VICIOUS CIRCLE. AS MORE OF THE GROUND AT THE BOTTOM MELTS AND LOOSENS, MORE AREA IS EXPOSED TO THE WARMING AIR, WHICH THEN INCREASES THE SPEED OF PERMAFROST THAWING.
THE CRATER WILL LIKELY ***GNAW*** ITS WAY THROUGH ***THIS WHOLE SLOPE*** BEFORE IT SLOWS DOWN.
QUITO, WILL IT ***EVER*** STOP COLLAPSING?
ZZZZAK!
Simulation active.
HARD TO SAY. AS SOON AS TEMPERATURES GO ABOVE FREEZING—***AND STAY ABOVE FREEZING***—IT GETS LARGER. THE CLIMATE CHANGING TO WARMER TEMPS MADE IT WORSE.
IT'S PANDORA'S BOX. ONCE WE'VE OPENED UP THE EARTH LIKE THIS, IT'S HARD TO STOP IT—AND EVEN HARDER TO REVERSE IT.

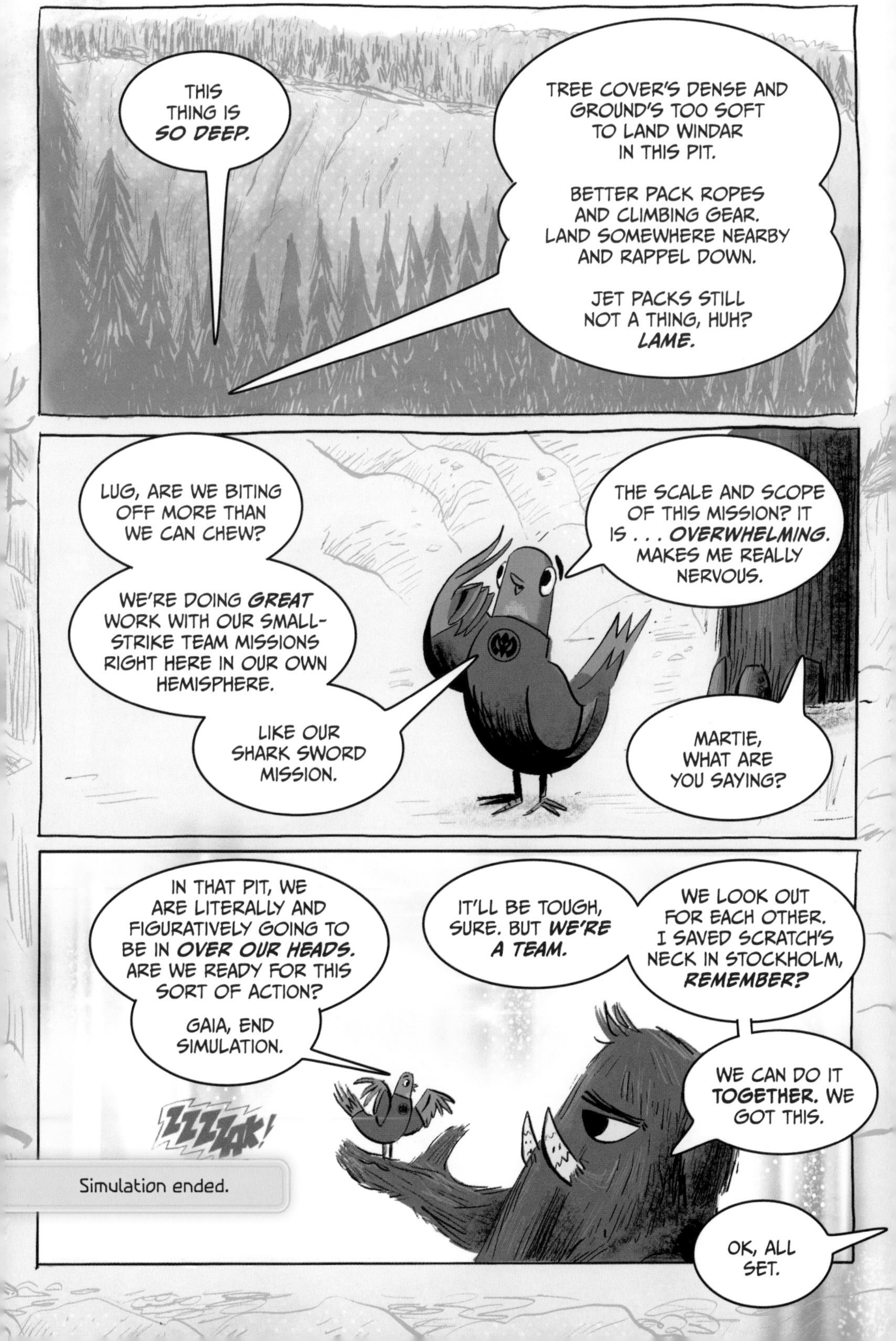
THIS THING IS *SO DEEP.*
TREE COVER'S DENSE AND GROUND'S TOO SOFT TO LAND WINDAR IN THIS PIT.
BETTER PACK ROPES AND CLIMBING GEAR. LAND SOMEWHERE NEARBY AND RAPPEL DOWN.
JET PACKS STILL NOT A THING, HUH? *LAME.*
LUG, ARE WE BITING OFF MORE THAN WE CAN CHEW?
WE'RE DOING *GREAT* WORK WITH OUR SMALL-STRIKE TEAM MISSIONS RIGHT HERE IN OUR OWN HEMISPHERE.
LIKE OUR SHARK SWORD MISSION.
THE SCALE AND SCOPE OF THIS MISSION? IT IS . . . *OVERWHELMING.* MAKES ME REALLY NERVOUS.
MARTIE, WHAT ARE YOU SAYING?
IN THAT PIT, WE ARE LITERALLY AND FIGURATIVELY GOING TO BE IN *OVER OUR HEADS.* ARE WE READY FOR THIS SORT OF ACTION?
IT'LL BE TOUGH, SURE. BUT *WE'RE A TEAM.*
WE LOOK OUT FOR EACH OTHER. I SAVED SCRATCH'S NECK IN STOCKHOLM, *REMEMBER?*
GAIA, END SIMULATION.
WE CAN DO IT **TOGETHER.** WE GOT THIS.
ZZZZAK!
Simulation ended.
OK, ALL SET.

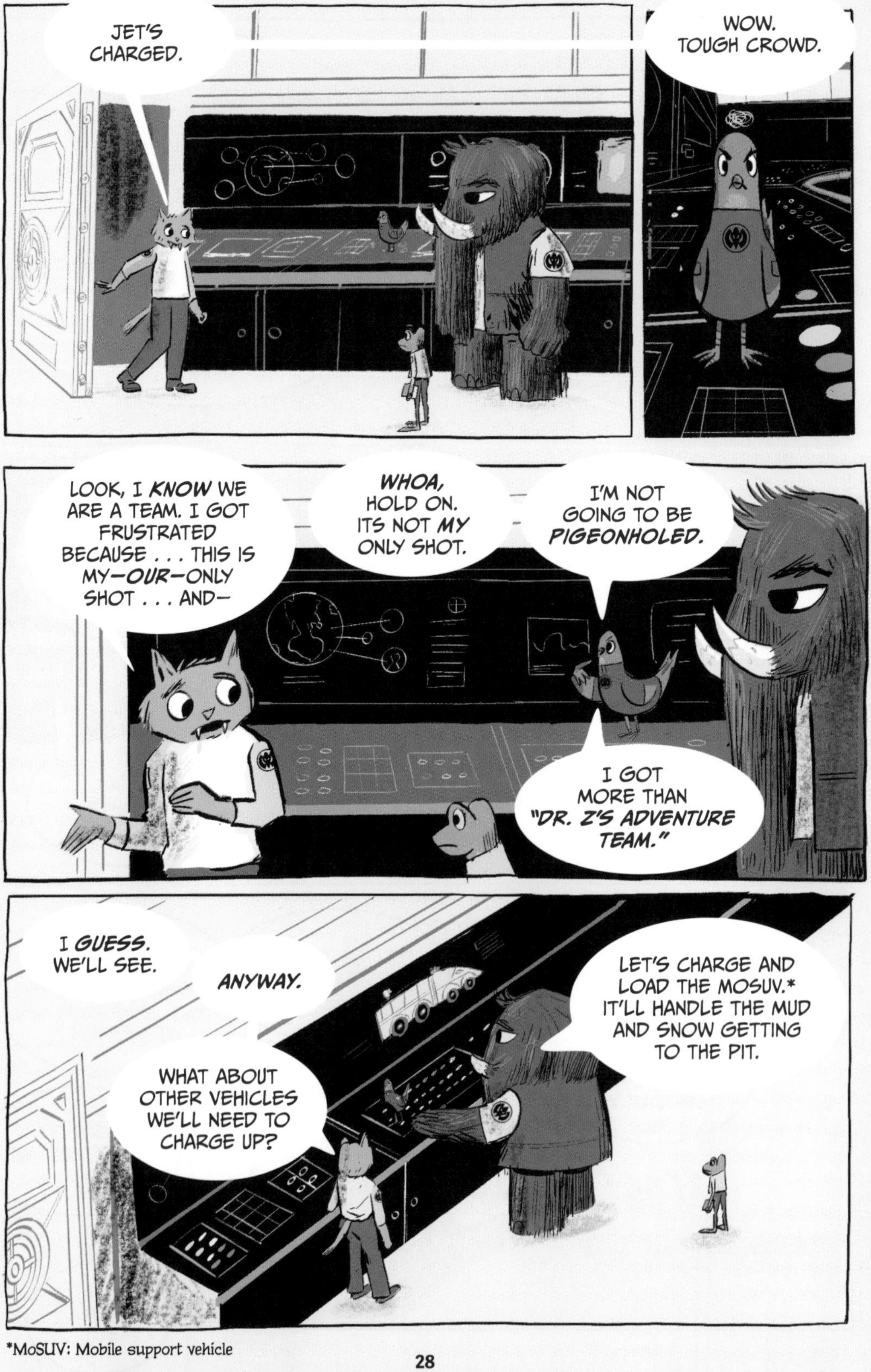
JET'S CHARGED.
WOW. TOUGH CROWD.
LOOK, I *KNOW* WE ARE A TEAM. I GOT FRUSTRATED BECAUSE . . . THIS IS MY—*OUR*—ONLY SHOT . . . AND—
WHOA, HOLD ON. ITS NOT *MY* ONLY SHOT.
I'M NOT GOING TO BE *PIGEONHOLED.*
I GOT MORE THAN *"DR. Z'S ADVENTURE TEAM."*
I *GUESS.* WE'LL SEE.
ANYWAY.
LET'S CHARGE AND LOAD THE MOSUV.* IT'LL HANDLE THE MUD AND SNOW GETTING TO THE PIT.
WHAT ABOUT OTHER VEHICLES WE'LL NEED TO CHARGE UP?

*MoSUV: Mobile support vehicle

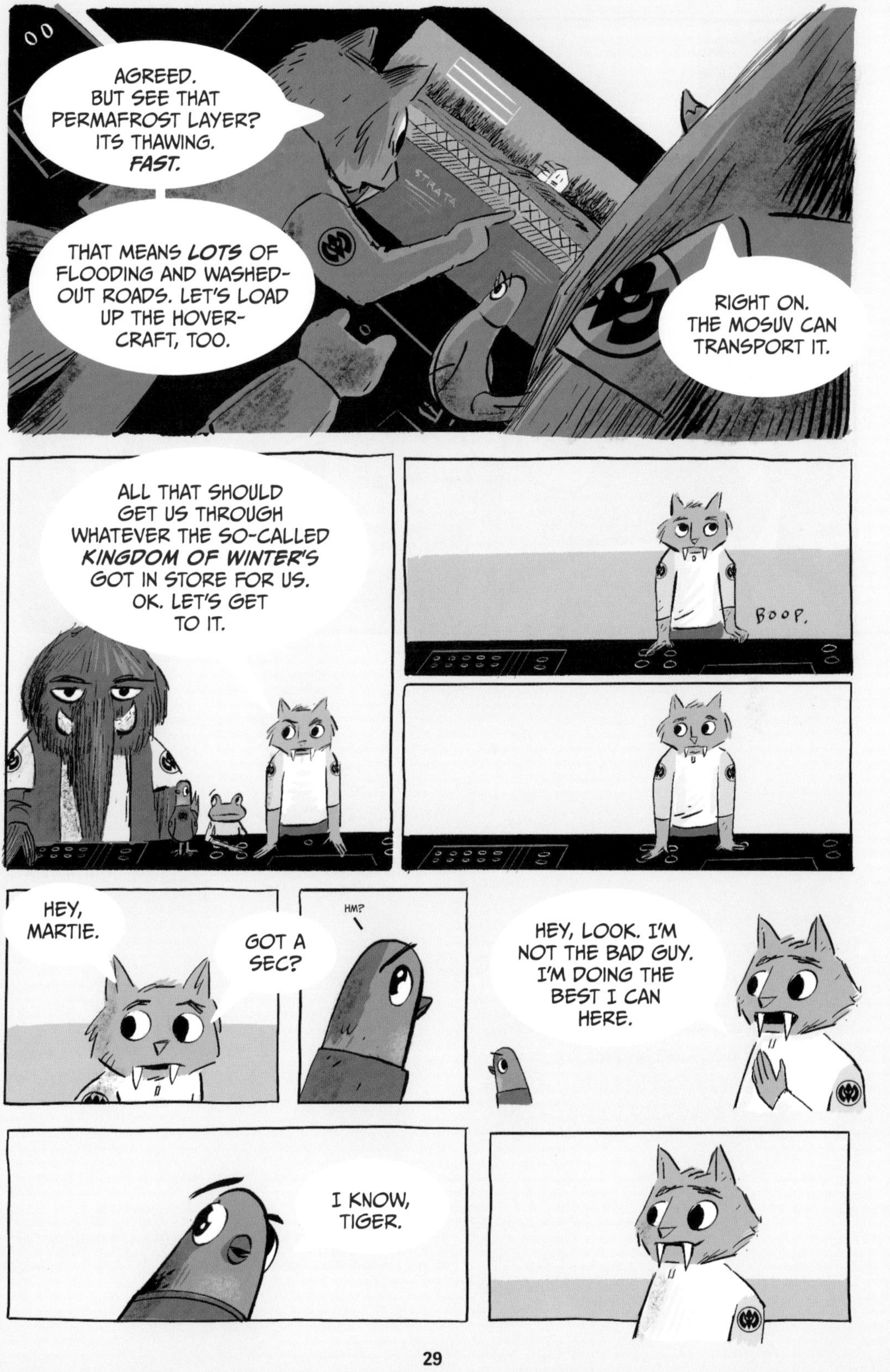
AGREED. BUT SEE THAT PERMAFROST LAYER? ITS THAWING. *FAST.*
STRATA
THAT MEANS *LOTS* OF FLOODING AND WASHED-OUT ROADS. LET'S LOAD UP THE HOVER-CRAFT, TOO.
RIGHT ON. THE MOSUV CAN TRANSPORT IT.
ALL THAT SHOULD GET US THROUGH WHATEVER THE SO-CALLED *KINGDOM OF WINTER'S* GOT IN STORE FOR US. OK. LET'S GET TO IT.
BOOP.
HEY, MARTIE.
GOT A SEC?
HM?
HEY, LOOK. I'M NOT THE BAD GUY. I'M DOING THE BEST I CAN HERE.
I KNOW, TIGER.

Minutes later

MY WINGS WOULDN'T MAKE THIS TRIP! SIBERIA IS *SO* FAR AWAY.

SÍ. THE REGION'S COME TO MEAN REMOTE AND DESOLATE. HAS BEEN FOR HUNDREDS OF YEARS. GAIA, INFO ON SIBERIA?

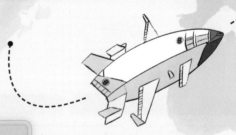

Empress Elizabeth exiled prominent political prisoners to Siberia beginning in 1744. It took a year's journey to reach Siberia from St. Petersburg in those days. Today, it's still remote. There are only two highways in Yakutia. The one built using Gulag prisoners' labor under Communism is mostly unpaved dirt.

Flight time: 16 hours, 47 minutes, 10 seconds

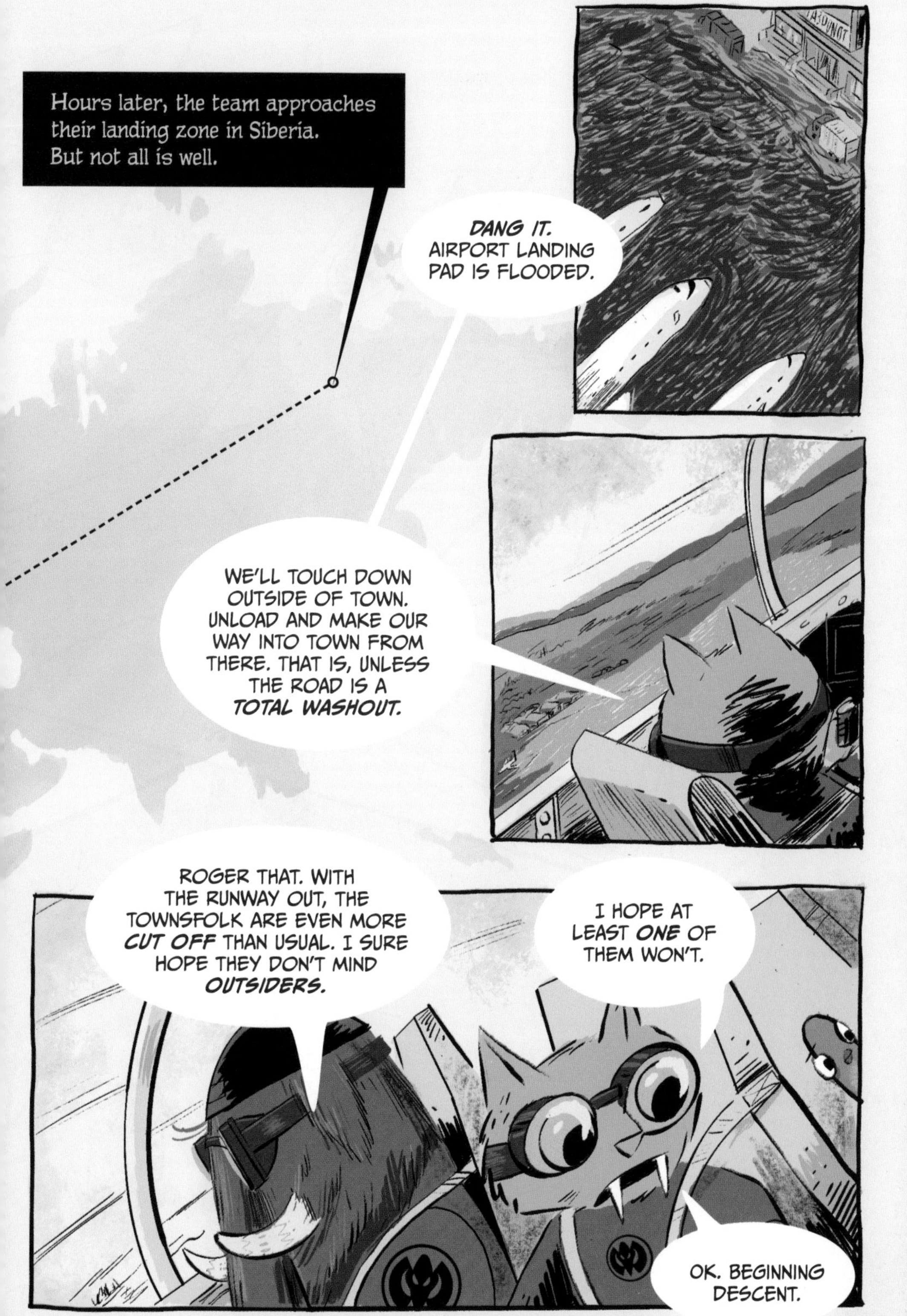

Hours later, the team approaches their landing zone in Siberia. But not all is well.
DANG IT. AIRPORT LANDING PAD IS FLOODED.
WE'LL TOUCH DOWN OUTSIDE OF TOWN. UNLOAD AND MAKE OUR WAY INTO TOWN FROM THERE. THAT IS, UNLESS THE ROAD IS A TOTAL WASHOUT.
ROGER THAT. WITH THE RUNWAY OUT, THE TOWNSFOLK ARE EVEN MORE CUT OFF THAN USUAL. I SURE HOPE THEY DON'T MIND OUTSIDERS.
I HOPE AT LEAST ONE OF THEM WON'T.
OK. BEGINNING DESCENT.

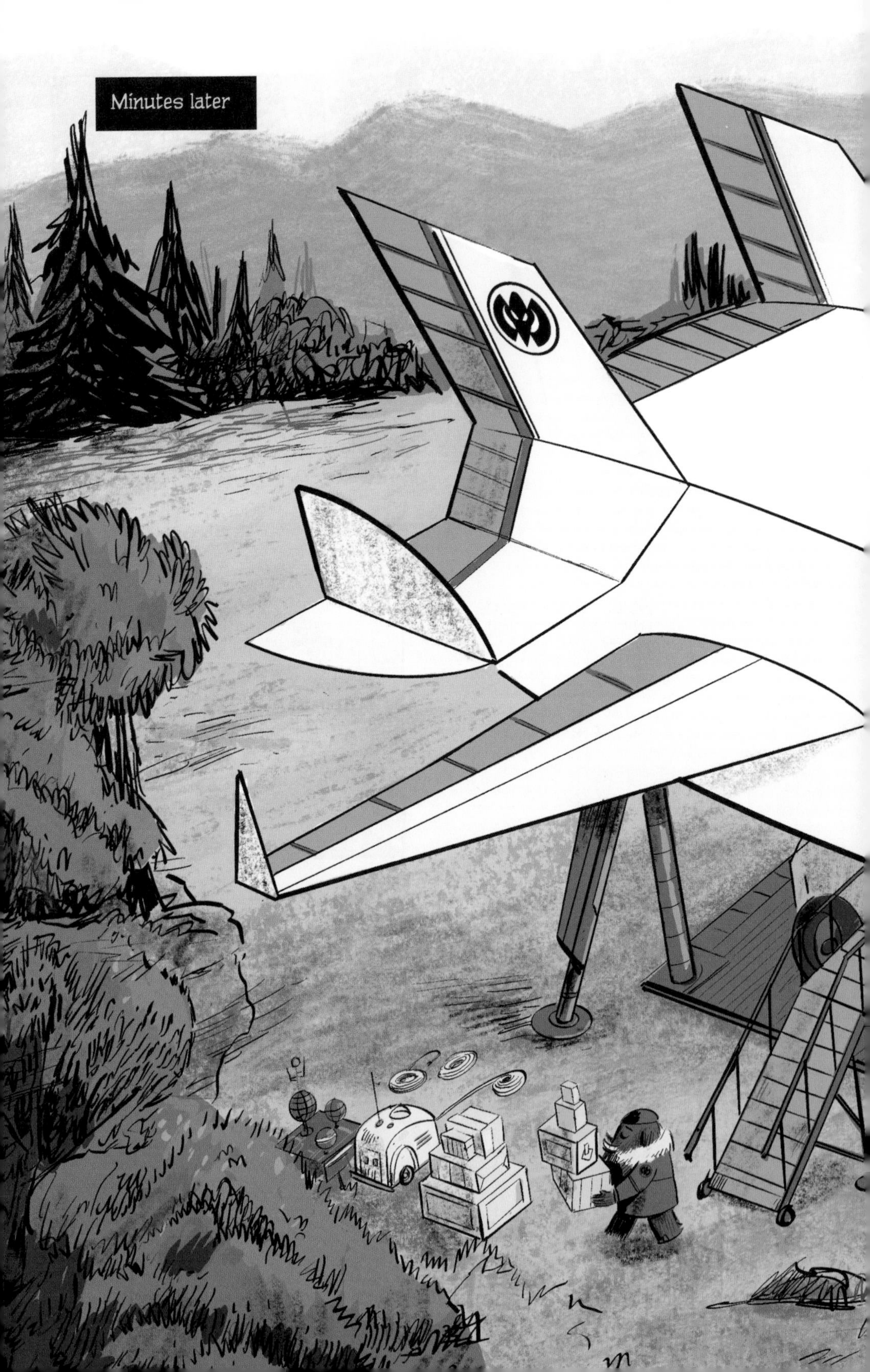
Minutes later

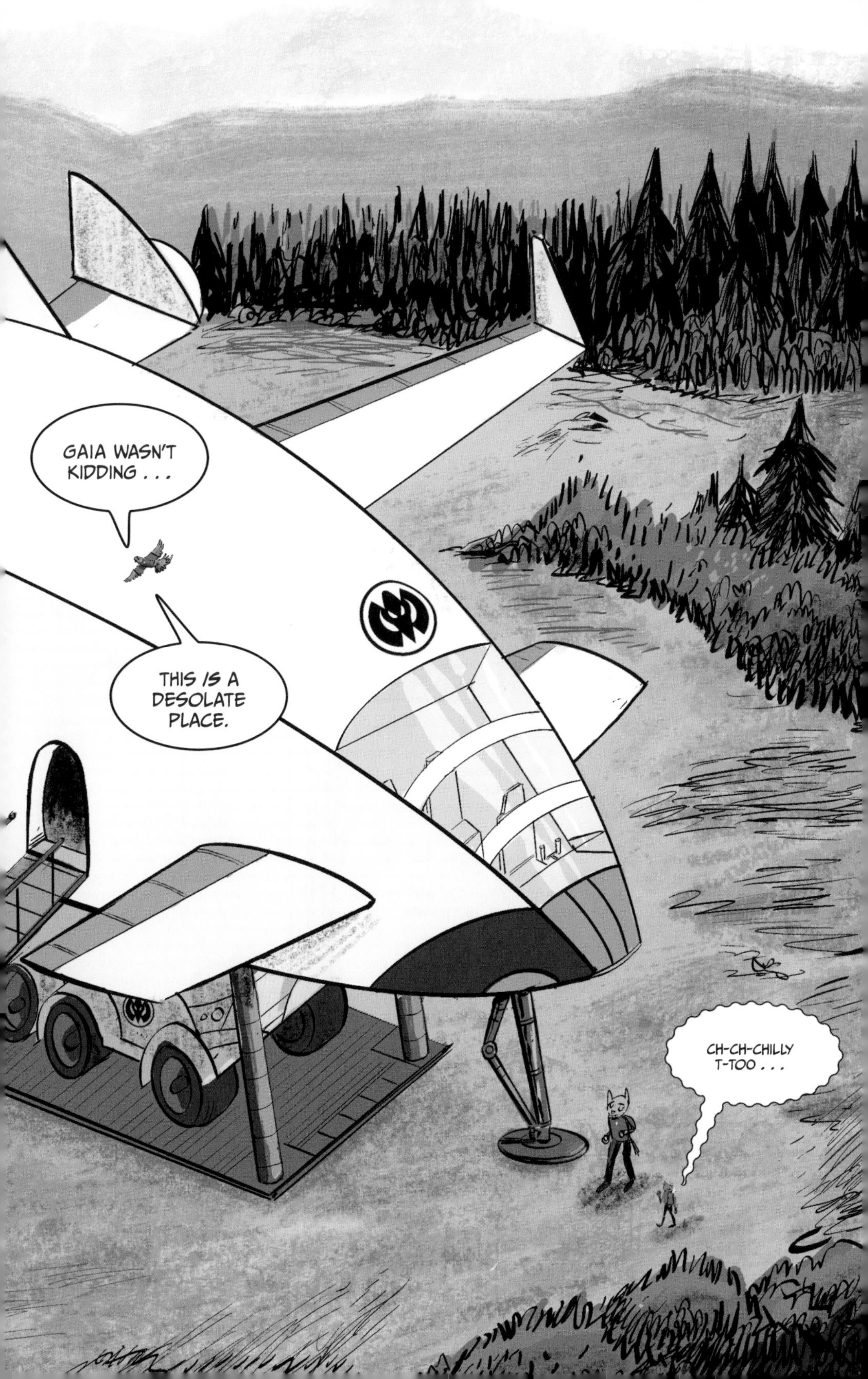
GAIA WASN'T KIDDING . . .
THIS IS A DESOLATE PLACE.
CH-CH-CHILLY T-TOO . . .

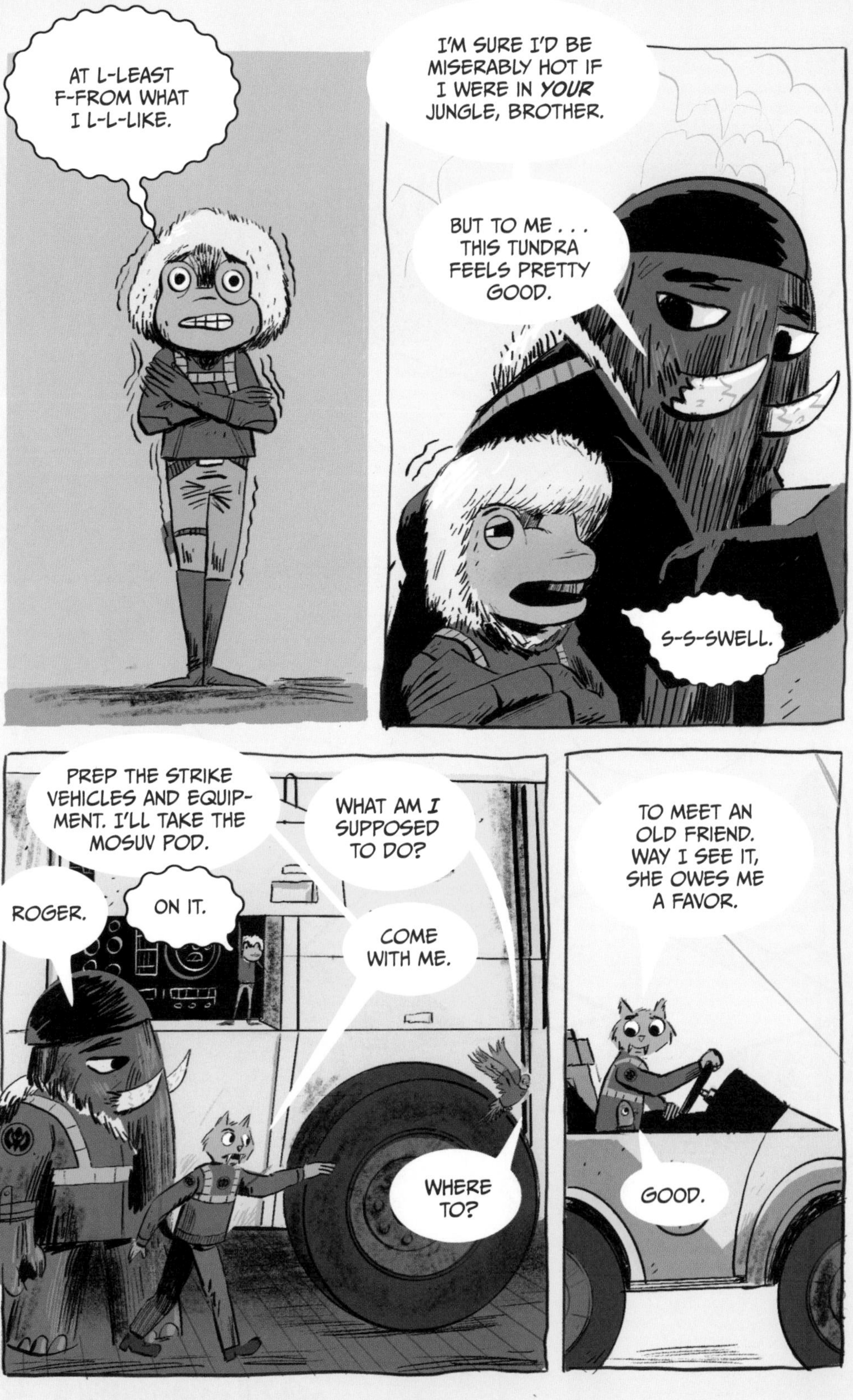
AT L-LEAST F-FROM WHAT I L-L-LIKE.
I'M SURE I'D BE MISERABLY HOT IF I WERE IN *YOUR* JUNGLE, BROTHER.
BUT TO ME . . . THIS TUNDRA FEELS PRETTY GOOD.
S-S-SWELL.
PREP THE STRIKE VEHICLES AND EQUIPMENT. I'LL TAKE THE MOSUV POD.
ROGER.
ON IT.
WHAT AM *I* SUPPOSED TO DO?
COME WITH ME.
WHERE TO?
TO MEET AN OLD FRIEND. WAY I SEE IT, SHE OWES ME A FAVOR.
GOOD.

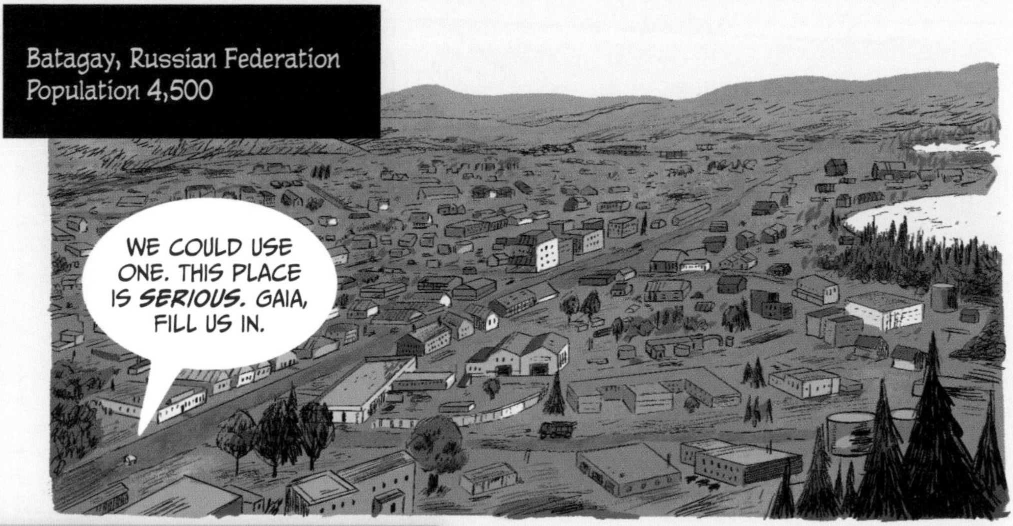
Batagay, Russian Federation
Population 4,500
WE COULD USE ONE. THIS PLACE IS *SERIOUS.* GAIA, FILL US IN.

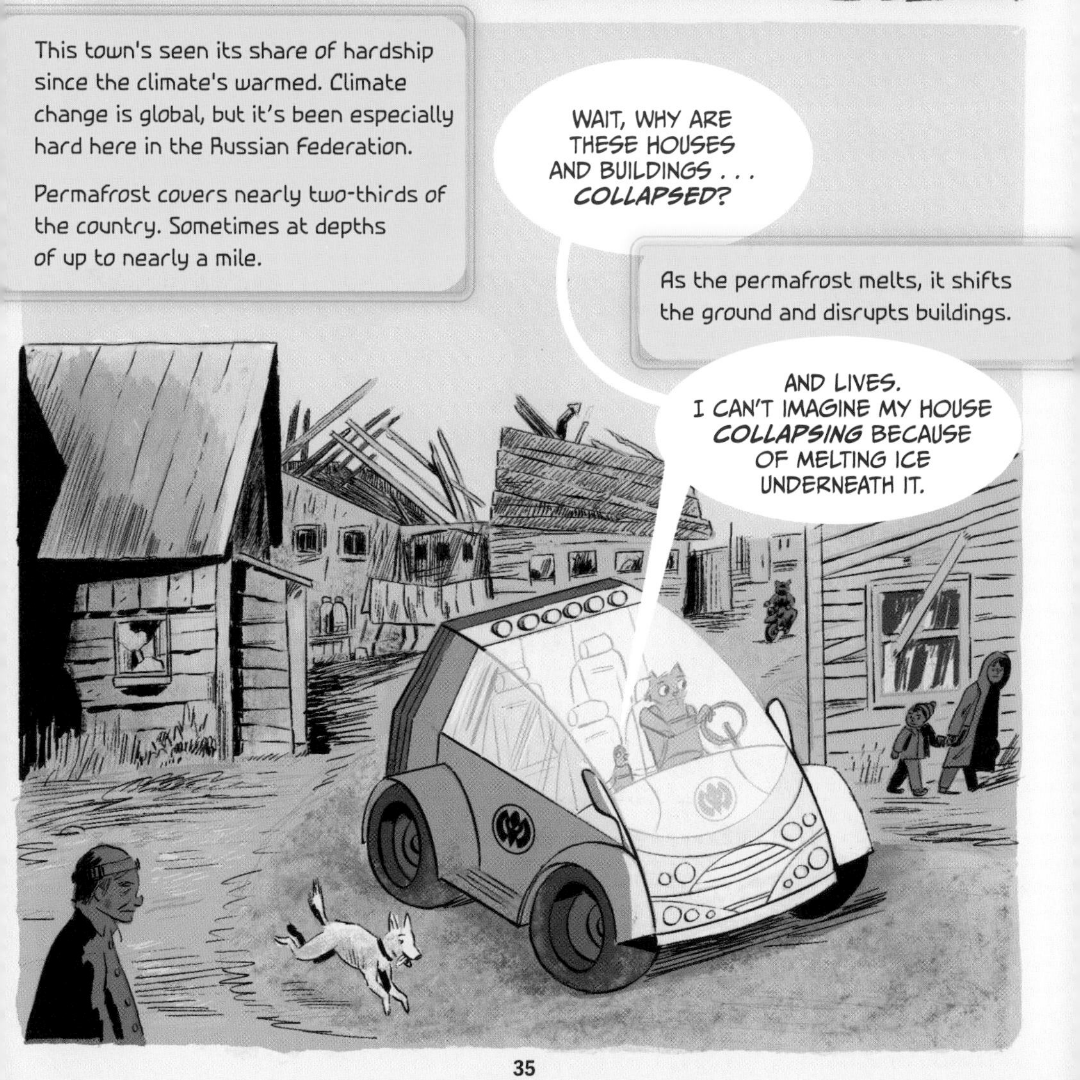
This town's seen its share of hardship since the climate's warmed. Climate change is global, but it's been especially hard here in the Russian Federation.
Permafrost covers nearly two-thirds of the country. Sometimes at depths of up to nearly a mile.
WAIT, WHY ARE THESE HOUSES AND BUILDINGS . . . *COLLAPSED?*
As the permafrost melts, it shifts the ground and disrupts buildings.
AND LIVES. I CAN'T IMAGINE MY HOUSE *COLLAPSING* BECAUSE OF MELTING ICE UNDERNEATH IT.

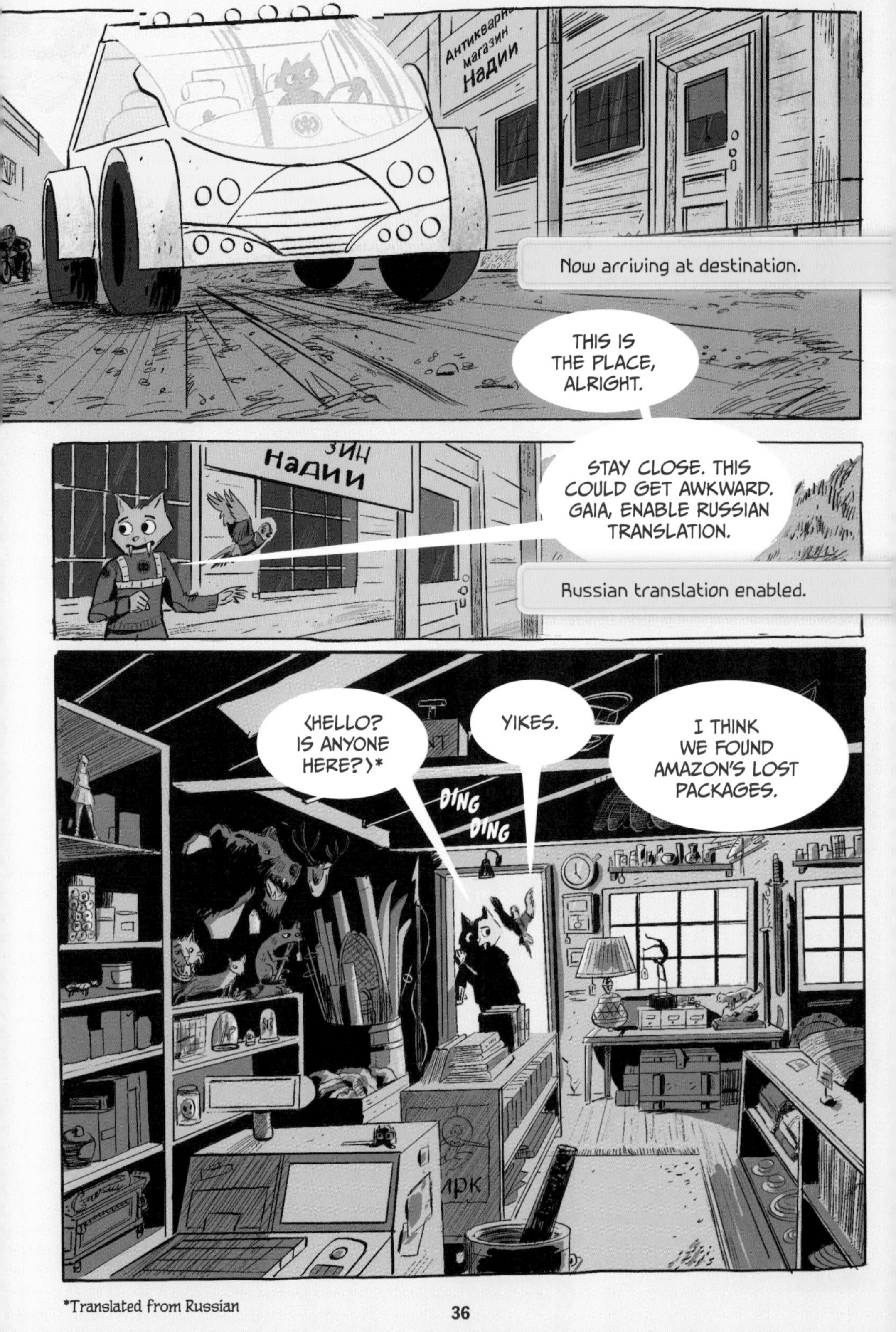
Антикварны
магазин
Надии
Now arriving at destination.
THIS IS THE PLACE, ALRIGHT.
зин
Надии
STAY CLOSE. THIS COULD GET AWKWARD. GAIA, ENABLE RUSSIAN TRANSLATION.
Russian translation enabled.
DING DING
<HELLO? IS ANYONE HERE?>*
YIKES.
I THINK WE FOUND AMAZON'S LOST PACKAGES.

*Translated from Russian

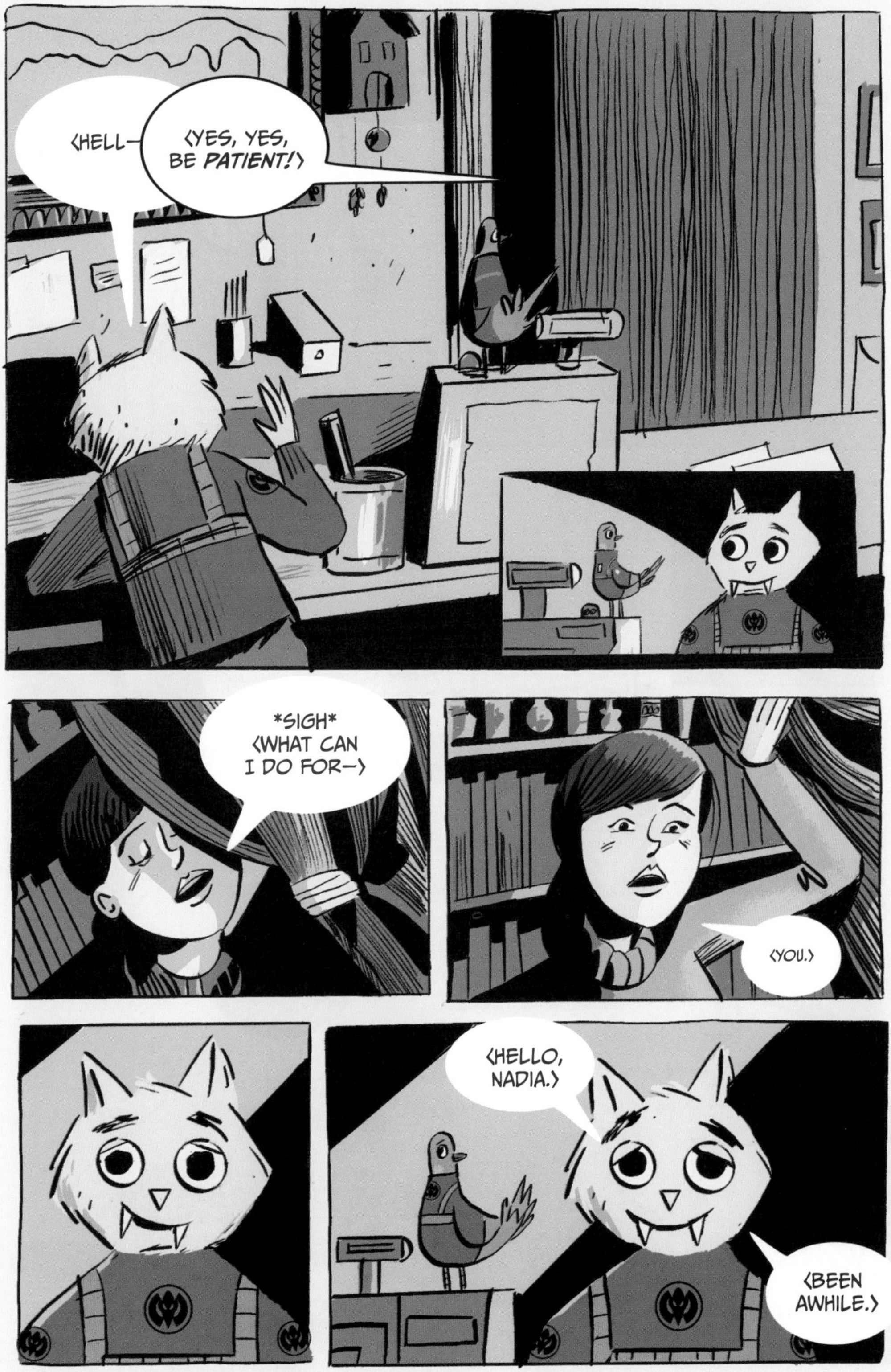

‹HELL—
‹YES, YES, BE *PATIENT!*›
SIGH ‹WHAT CAN I DO FOR—›
‹YOU.›
‹HELLO, NADIA.›
‹BEEN AWHILE.›

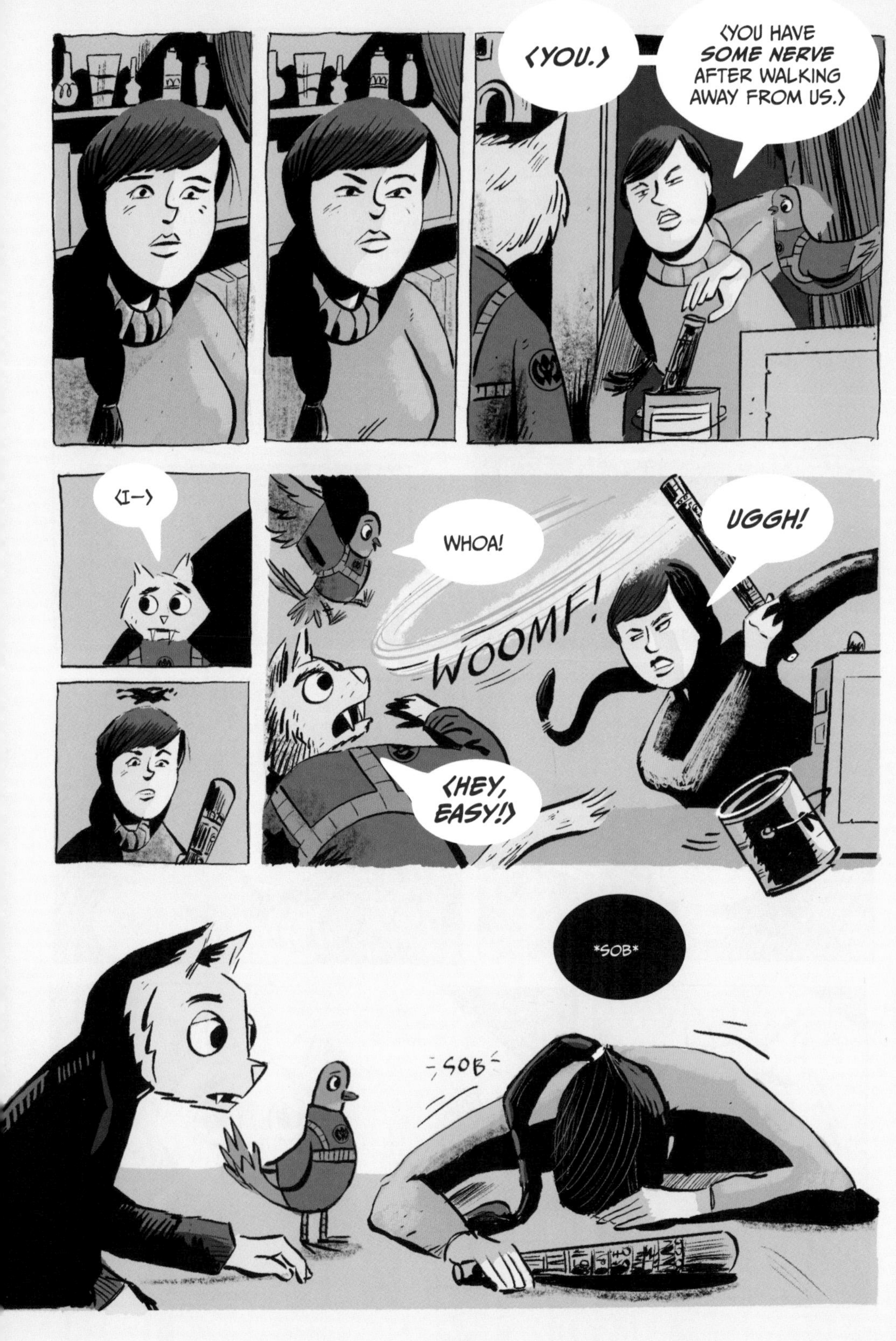
⟨YOU.⟩
⟨YOU HAVE SOME NERVE AFTER WALKING AWAY FROM US.⟩
⟨I—⟩
WHOA!
UGGH!
WOOMF!
⟨HEY, EASY!⟩
SOB
SOB

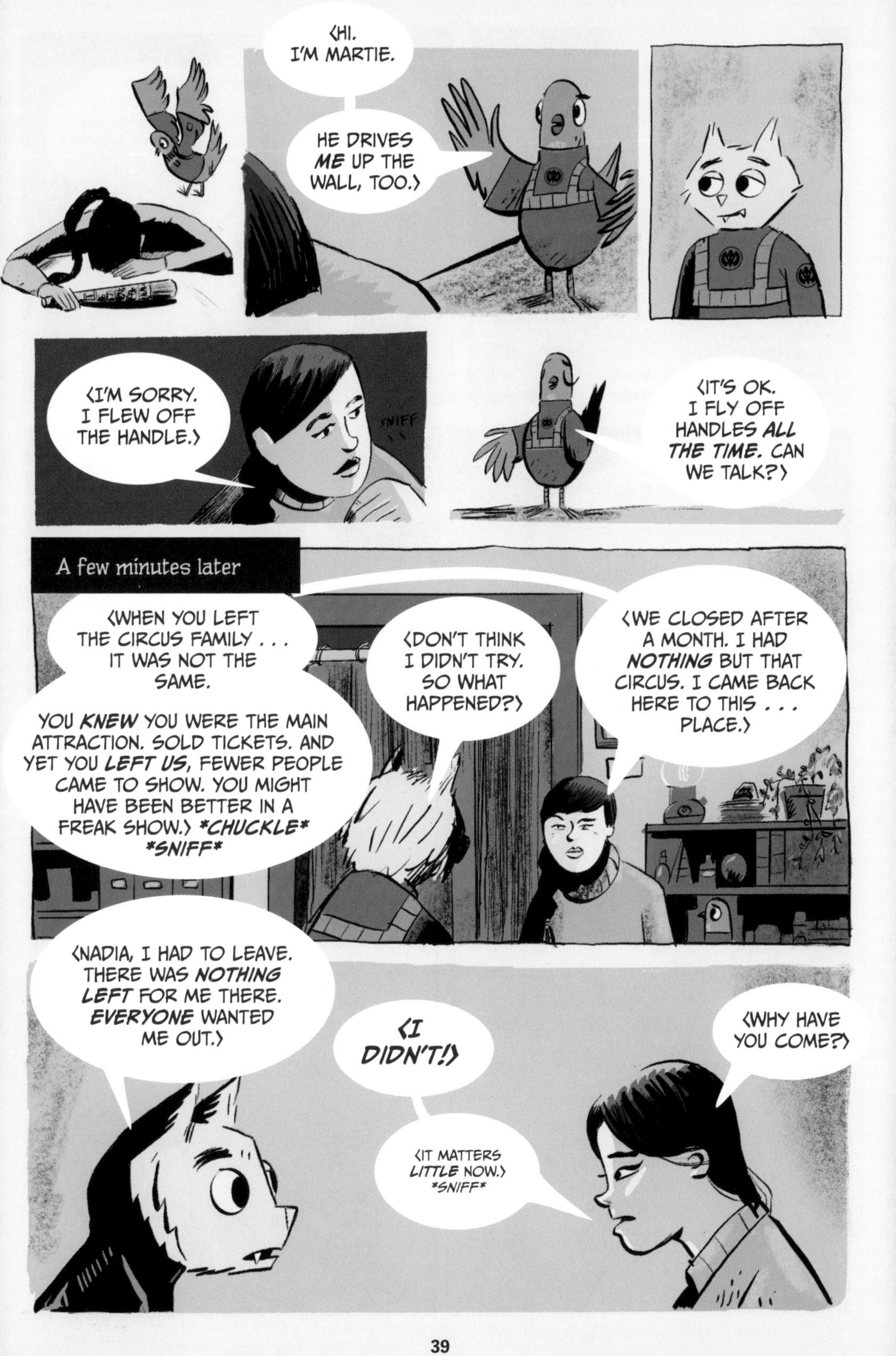

‹HI. I'M MARTIE.
HE DRIVES ME UP THE WALL, TOO.›
‹I'M SORRY. I FLEW OFF THE HANDLE.›
SNIFF
‹IT'S OK. I FLY OFF HANDLES ALL THE TIME. CAN WE TALK?›
A few minutes later
‹WHEN YOU LEFT THE CIRCUS FAMILY . . . IT WAS NOT THE SAME.
YOU KNEW YOU WERE THE MAIN ATTRACTION. SOLD TICKETS. AND YET YOU LEFT US, FEWER PEOPLE CAME TO SHOW. YOU MIGHT HAVE BEEN BETTER IN A FREAK SHOW.› *CHUCKLE* *SNIFF*
‹DON'T THINK I DIDN'T TRY. SO WHAT HAPPENED?›
‹WE CLOSED AFTER A MONTH. I HAD NOTHING BUT THAT CIRCUS. I CAME BACK HERE TO THIS . . . PLACE.›
‹NADIA, I HAD TO LEAVE. THERE WAS NOTHING LEFT FOR ME THERE. EVERYONE WANTED ME OUT.›
‹I DIDN'T!›
‹IT MATTERS LITTLE NOW.› *SNIFF*
‹WHY HAVE YOU COME?›

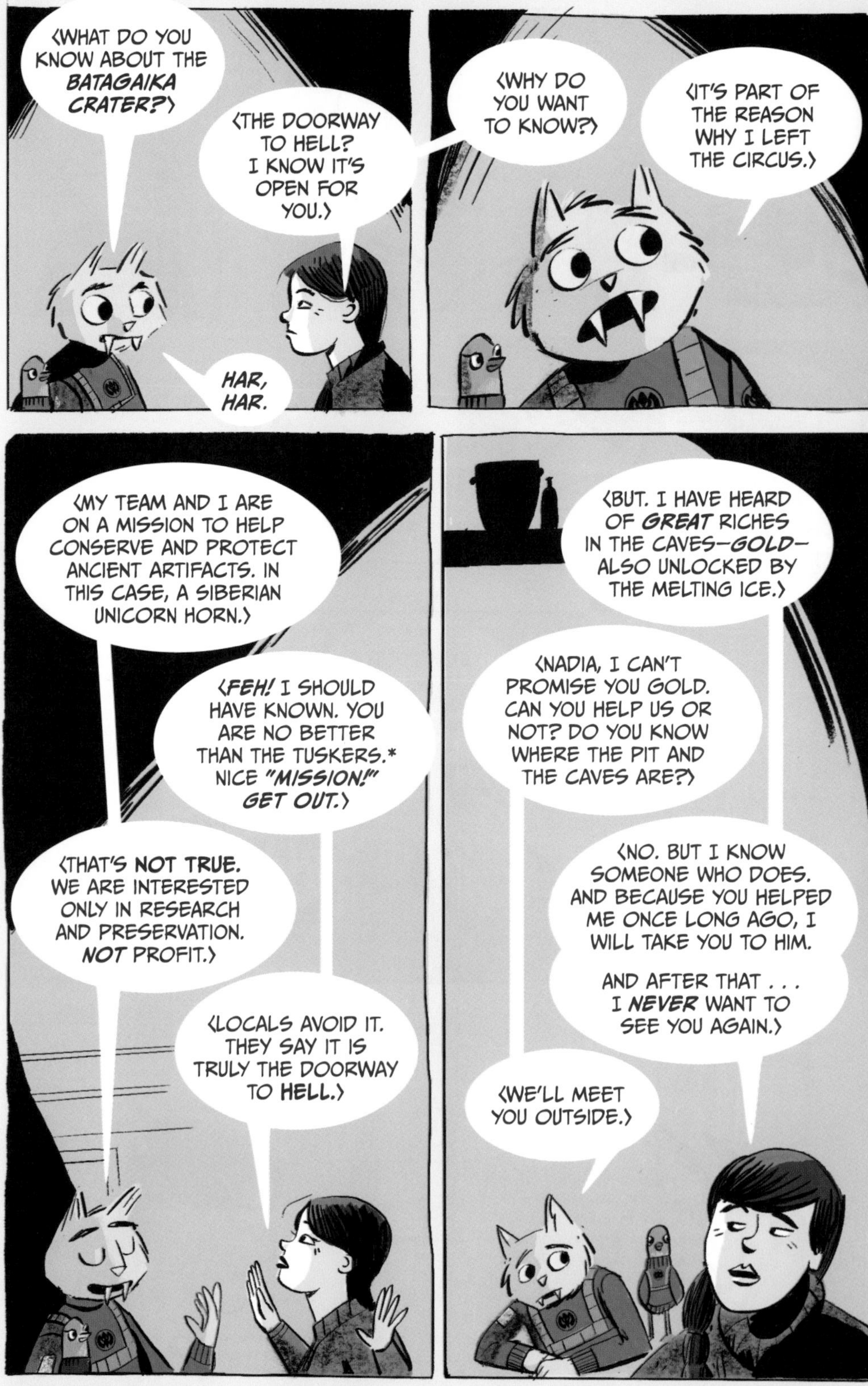
⟨WHAT DO YOU KNOW ABOUT THE BATAGAIKA CRATER?⟩
⟨THE DOORWAY TO HELL? I KNOW IT'S OPEN FOR YOU.⟩
HAR, HAR.
⟨WHY DO YOU WANT TO KNOW?⟩
⟨IT'S PART OF THE REASON WHY I LEFT THE CIRCUS.⟩
⟨MY TEAM AND I ARE ON A MISSION TO HELP CONSERVE AND PROTECT ANCIENT ARTIFACTS. IN THIS CASE, A SIBERIAN UNICORN HORN.⟩
⟨FEH! I SHOULD HAVE KNOWN. YOU ARE NO BETTER THAN THE TUSKERS.* NICE "MISSION!" GET OUT.⟩
⟨THAT'S NOT TRUE. WE ARE INTERESTED ONLY IN RESEARCH AND PRESERVATION. NOT PROFIT.⟩
⟨LOCALS AVOID IT. THEY SAY IT IS TRULY THE DOORWAY TO HELL.⟩
⟨BUT. I HAVE HEARD OF GREAT RICHES IN THE CAVES—GOLD—ALSO UNLOCKED BY THE MELTING ICE.⟩
⟨NADIA, I CAN'T PROMISE YOU GOLD. CAN YOU HELP US OR NOT? DO YOU KNOW WHERE THE PIT AND THE CAVES ARE?⟩
⟨NO. BUT I KNOW SOMEONE WHO DOES. AND BECAUSE YOU HELPED ME ONCE LONG AGO, I WILL TAKE YOU TO HIM.
AND AFTER THAT . . . I NEVER WANT TO SEE YOU AGAIN.⟩
⟨WE'LL MEET YOU OUTSIDE.⟩

*Tusk hunters who sell mammoth tusks for profit

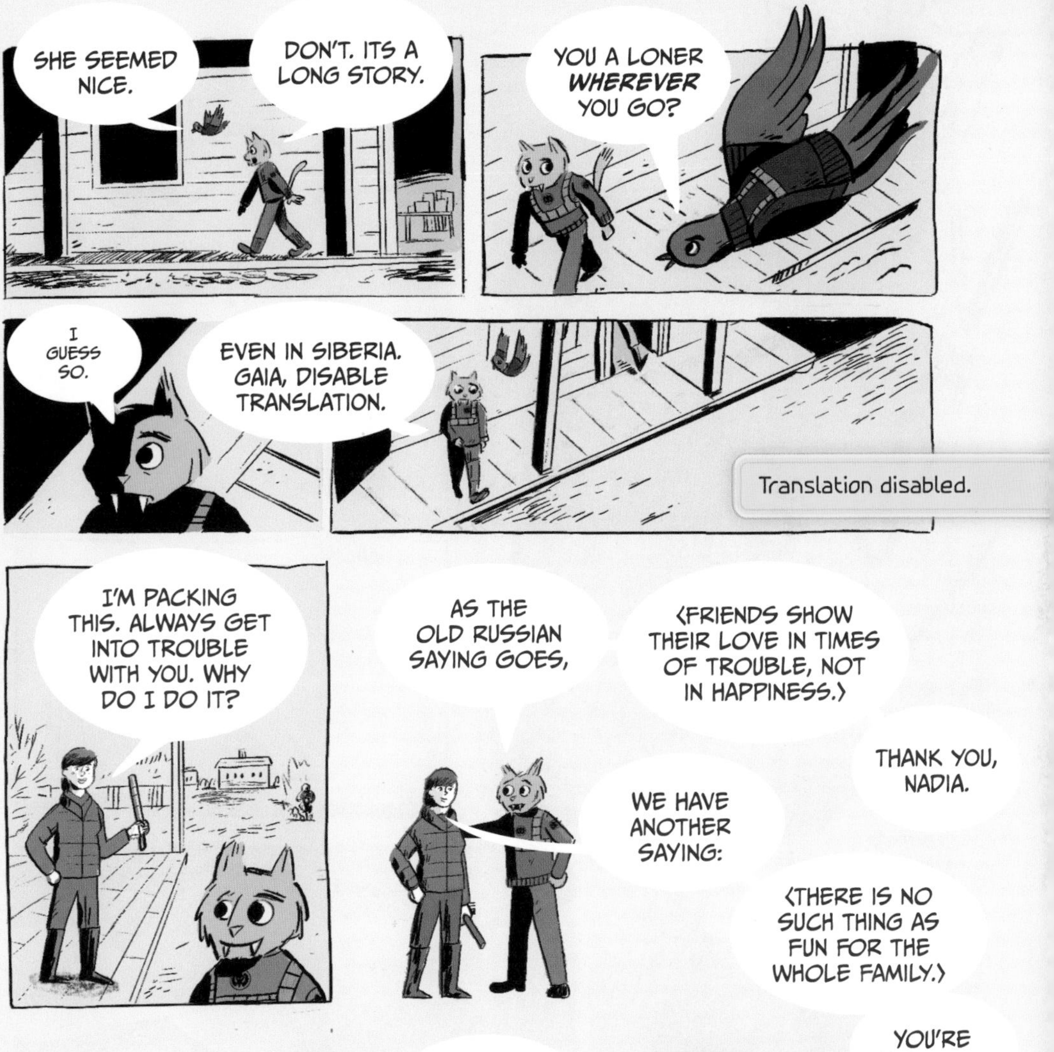

SHE SEEMED NICE.
DON'T. ITS A LONG STORY.
YOU A LONER *WHEREVER* YOU GO?
I GUESS SO.
EVEN IN SIBERIA. GAIA, DISABLE TRANSLATION.
Translation disabled.
I'M PACKING THIS. ALWAYS GET INTO TROUBLE WITH YOU. WHY DO I DO IT?
AS THE OLD RUSSIAN SAYING GOES,
‹FRIENDS SHOW THEIR LOVE IN TIMES OF TROUBLE, NOT IN HAPPINESS.›
THANK YOU, NADIA.
WE HAVE ANOTHER SAYING:
‹THERE IS NO SUCH THING AS FUN FOR THE WHOLE FAMILY.›
YOU'RE WELCOME.
I DON'T KNOW *WHAT* YOU GUYS ARE SAYING, BUT—
WHAT THE—?!
THP!
THP!
THP!

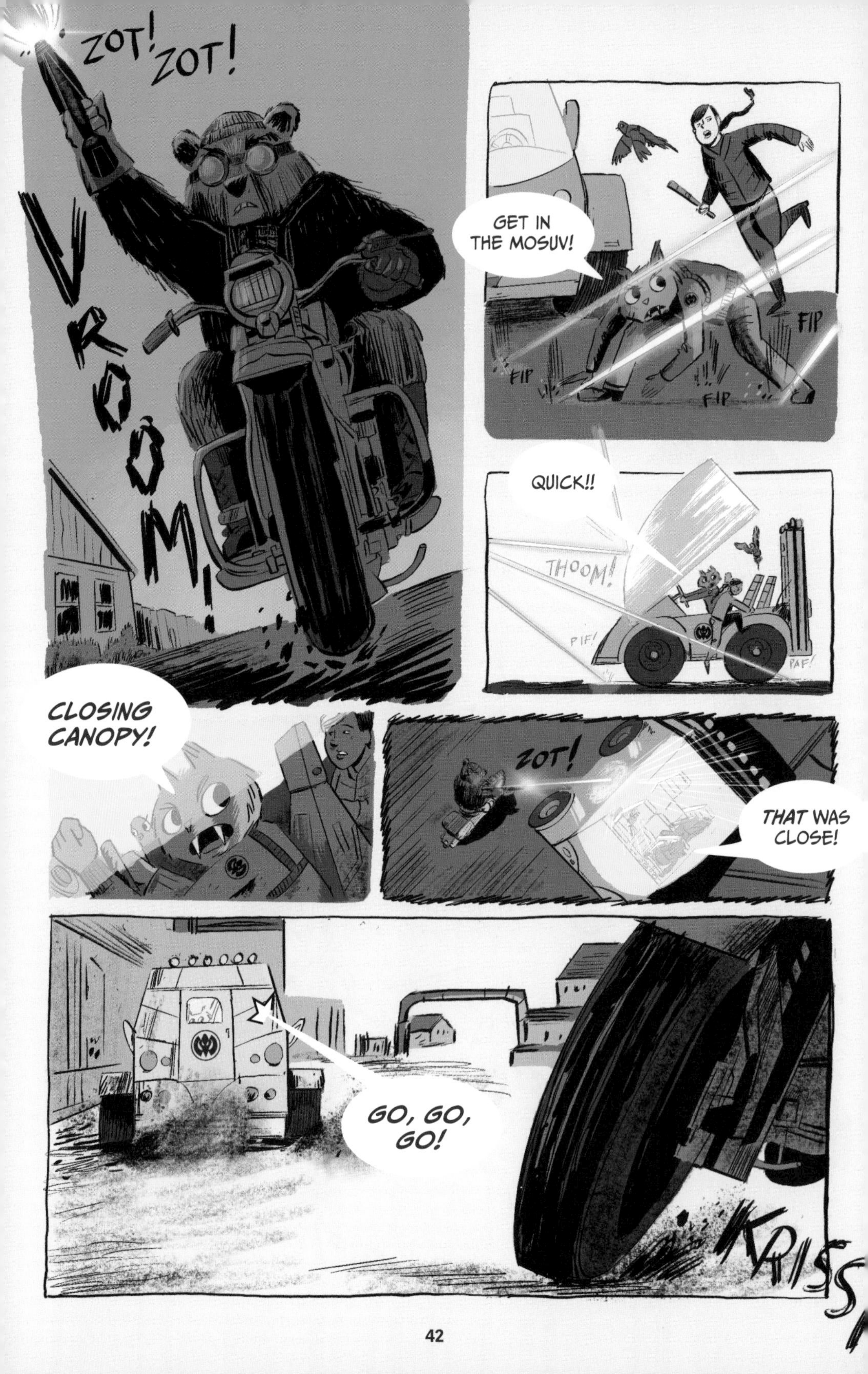
ZOT! ZOT!
VROOM!
GET IN THE MOSUV!
FIP
FIP
FIP
QUICK!!
THOOM!
PIF!
PAF!
CLOSING CANOPY!
ZOT!
THAT WAS CLOSE!
GO, GO, GO!
KRISS

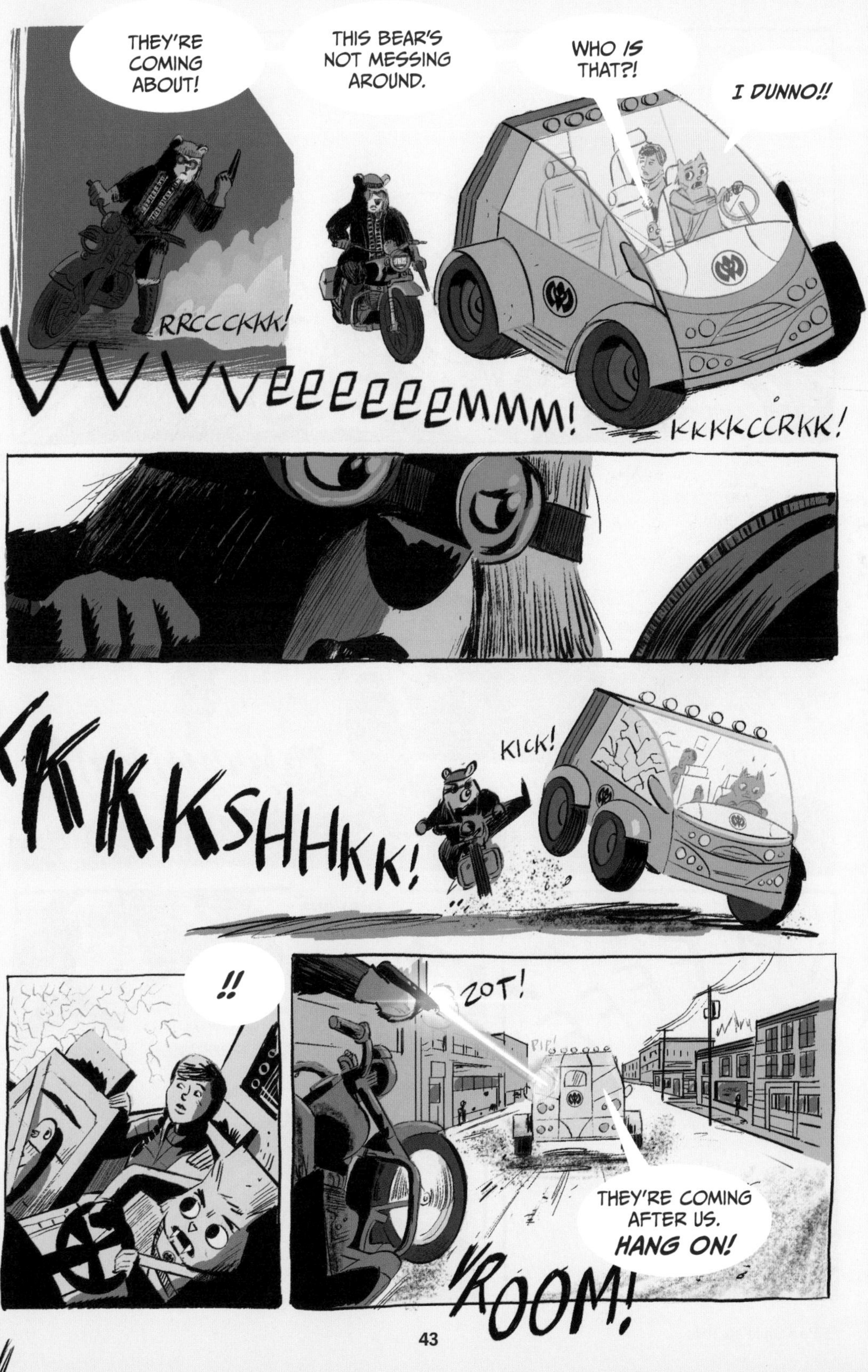
THEY'RE COMING ABOUT!
THIS BEAR'S NOT MESSING AROUND.
WHO *IS* THAT?!
I DUNNO!!
RRCCCKKK!
VVVVEEEEEEEMMMM!
KKKKCCRKK!
KKKKSHHKK!
KICK!
!!
ZOT!
PIP!
THEY'RE COMING AFTER US. **HANG ON!**
VROOM!

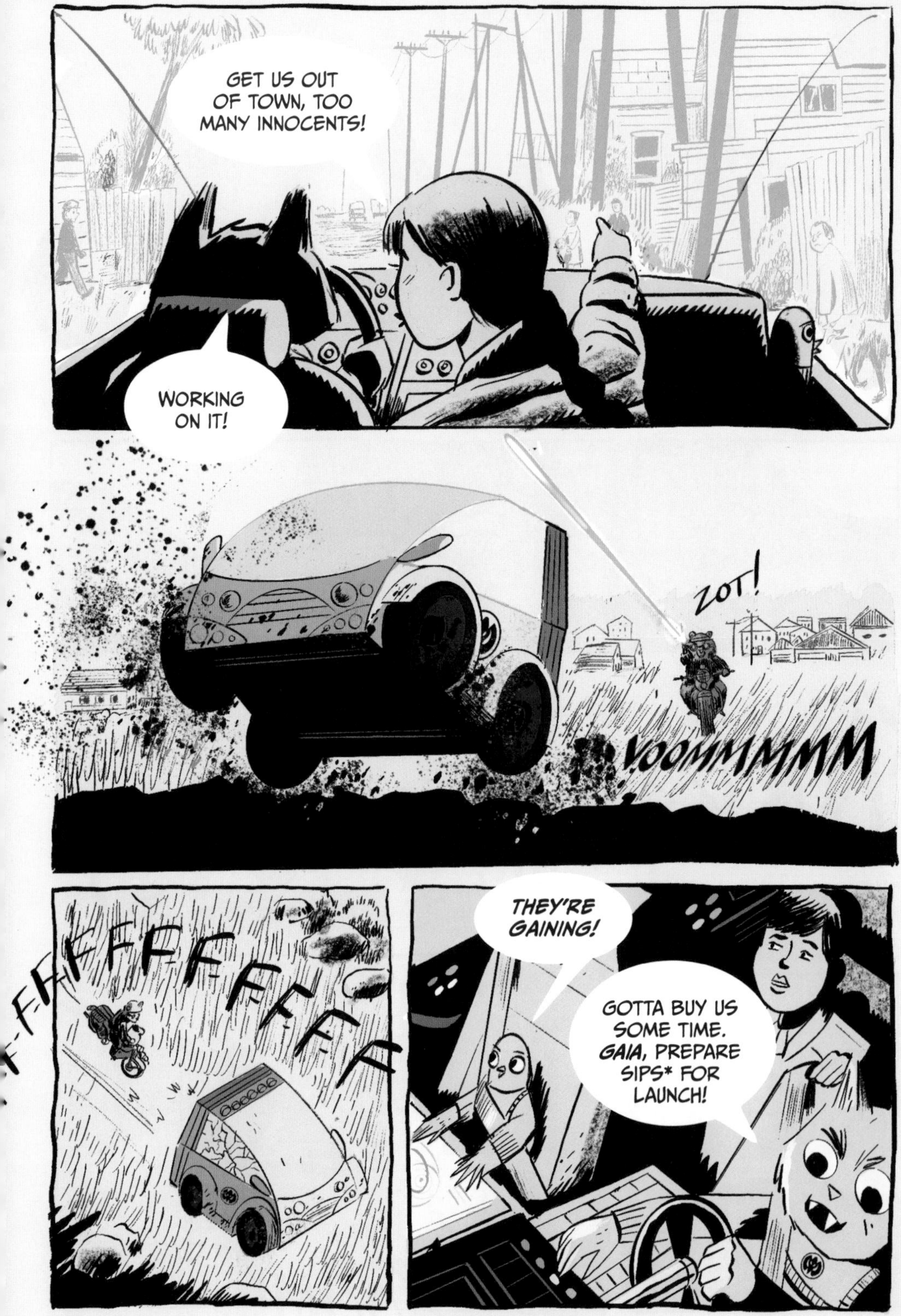
GET US OUT OF TOWN, TOO MANY INNOCENTS!
WORKING ON IT!
ZOT!
VOOMMMMM
F-F-FFFFFFFFFF
THEY'RE GAINING!
GOTTA BUY US SOME TIME. GAIA, PREPARE SIPS* FOR LAUNCH!

*SIPs = Squid Ink Pods

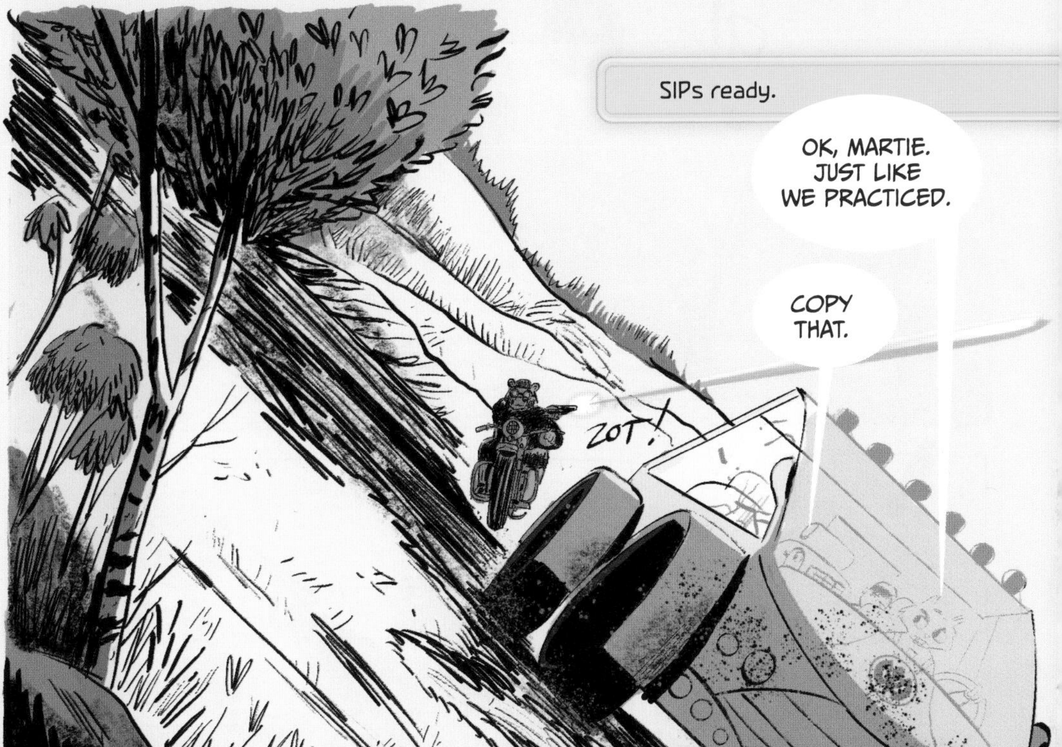
SIPs ready.
OK, MARTIE. JUST LIKE WE PRACTICED.
COPY THAT.
ZOT!

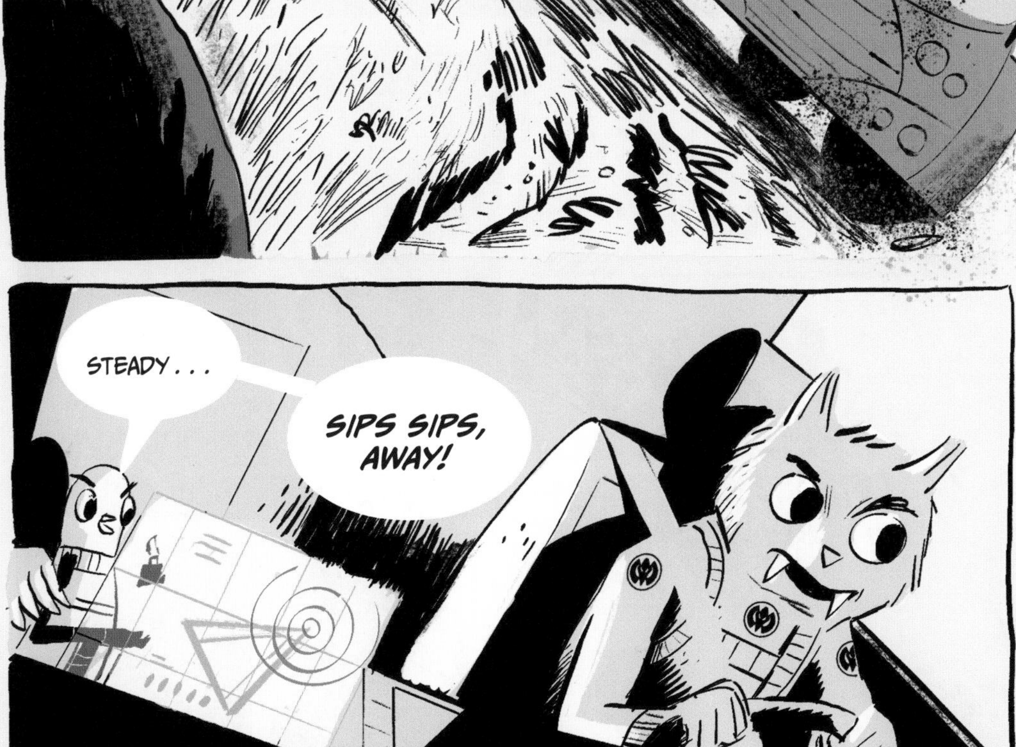
STEADY . . .
SIPS SIPS, AWAY!

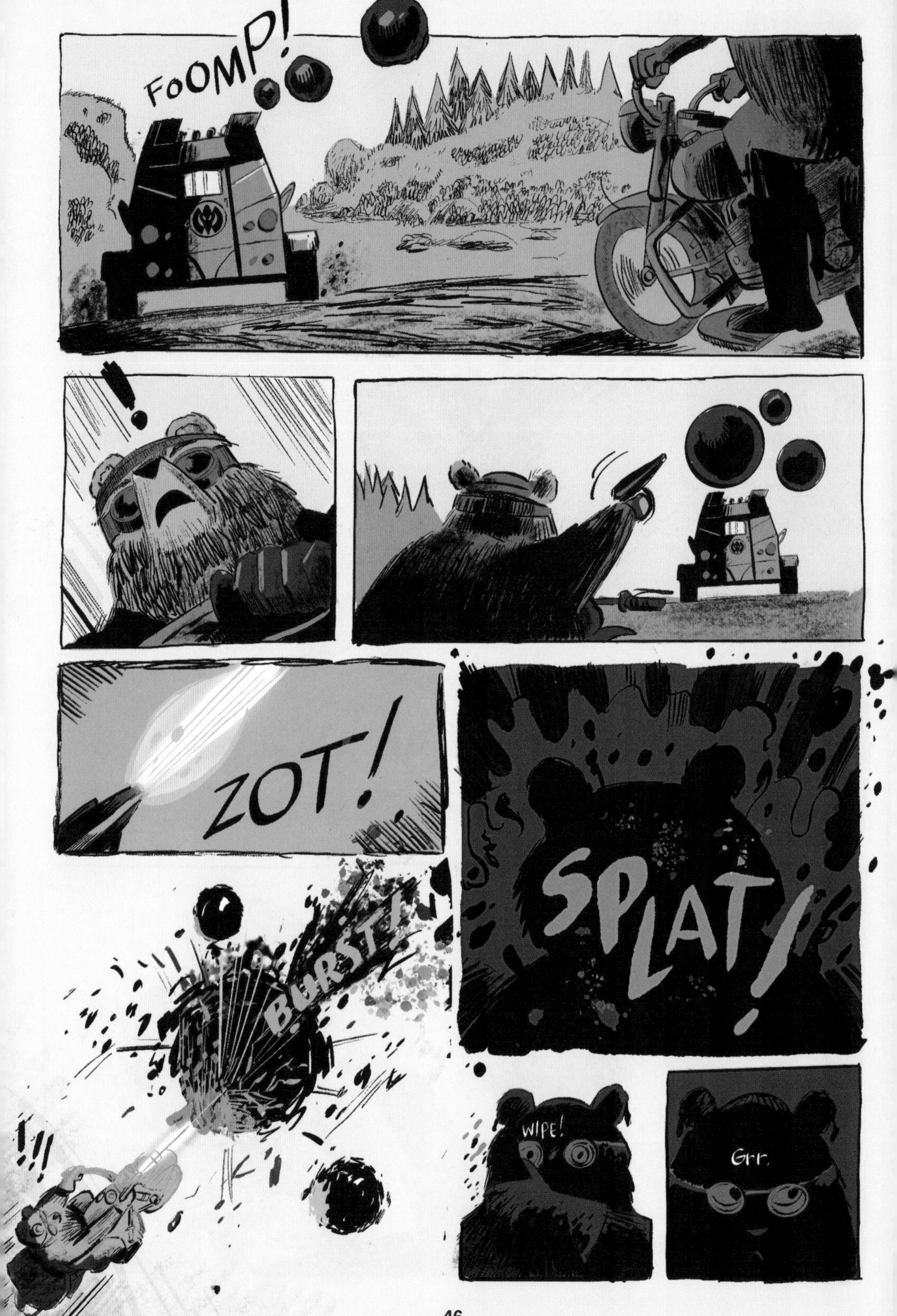
FOOMP!
!
ZOT!
SPLAT!
BURST!
!!!
WIPE!
Grr.

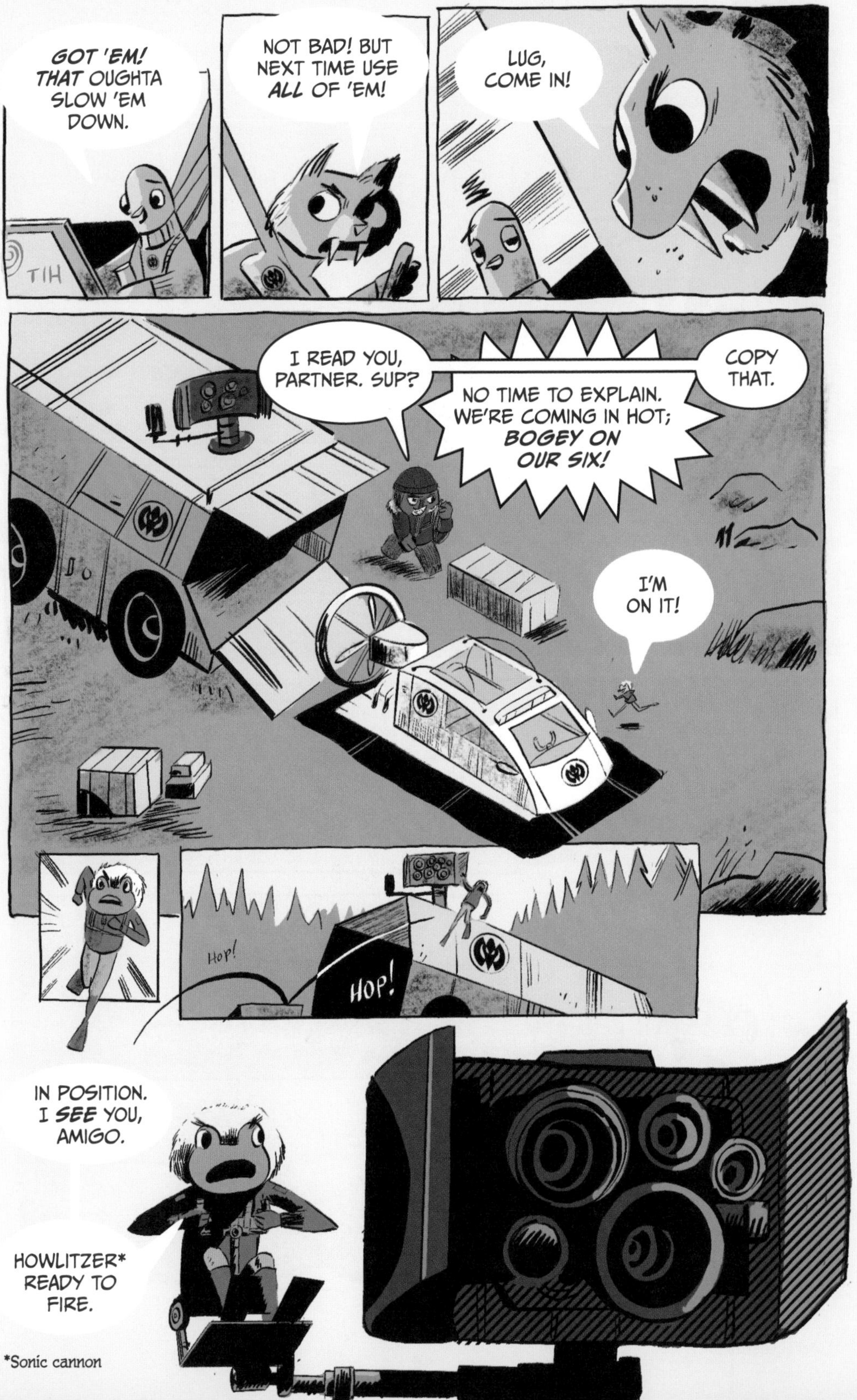
GOT 'EM! THAT OUGHTA SLOW 'EM DOWN.
TIH
NOT BAD! BUT NEXT TIME USE ALL OF 'EM!
LUG, COME IN!
I READ YOU, PARTNER. SUP?
NO TIME TO EXPLAIN. WE'RE COMING IN HOT; BOGEY ON OUR SIX!
COPY THAT.
I'M ON IT!
Hop!
HOP!
IN POSITION. I SEE YOU, AMIGO.
HOWLITZER* READY TO FIRE.

*Sonic cannon

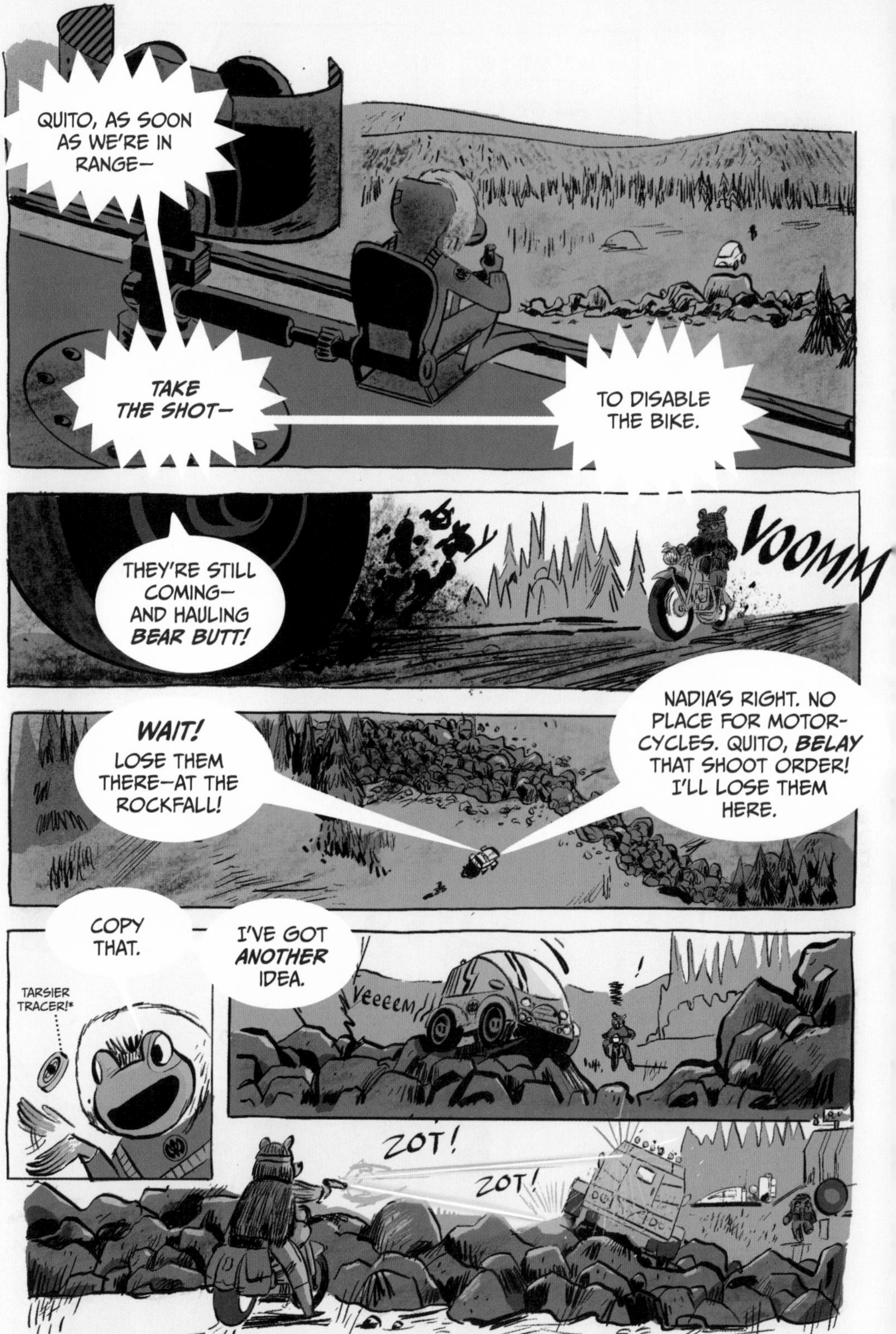
QUITO, AS SOON AS WE'RE IN RANGE—
TAKE THE SHOT—
TO DISABLE THE BIKE.
THEY'RE STILL COMING— AND HAULING BEAR BUTT!
VOOMM
WAIT! LOSE THEM THERE—AT THE ROCKFALL!
NADIA'S RIGHT. NO PLACE FOR MOTOR-CYCLES. QUITO, BELAY THAT SHOOT ORDER! I'LL LOSE THEM HERE.
COPY THAT.
I'VE GOT ANOTHER IDEA.
TARSIER TRACER!*
Veeeem
ZOT!
ZOT!
SLLLKT

*Tracking device

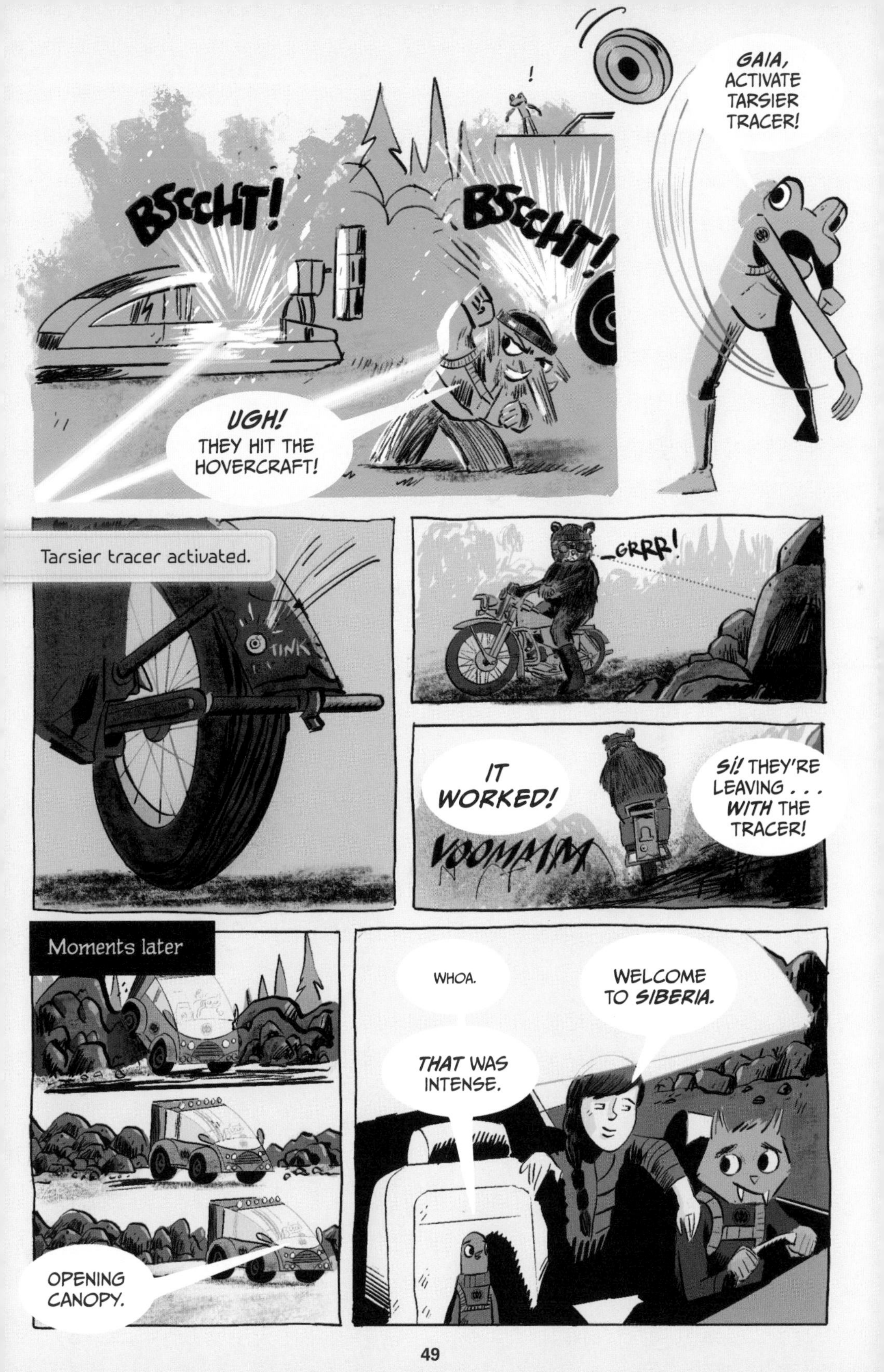
GAIA, ACTIVATE TARSIER TRACER!
BSCCHT!
BSCCHT!
UGH! THEY HIT THE HOVERCRAFT!
Tarsier tracer activated.
TINK
GRRR!
IT WORKED!
VOOMMM
SÍ! THEY'RE LEAVING . . . WITH THE TRACER!
Moments later
OPENING CANOPY.
WHOA.
WELCOME TO SIBERIA.
THAT WAS INTENSE.

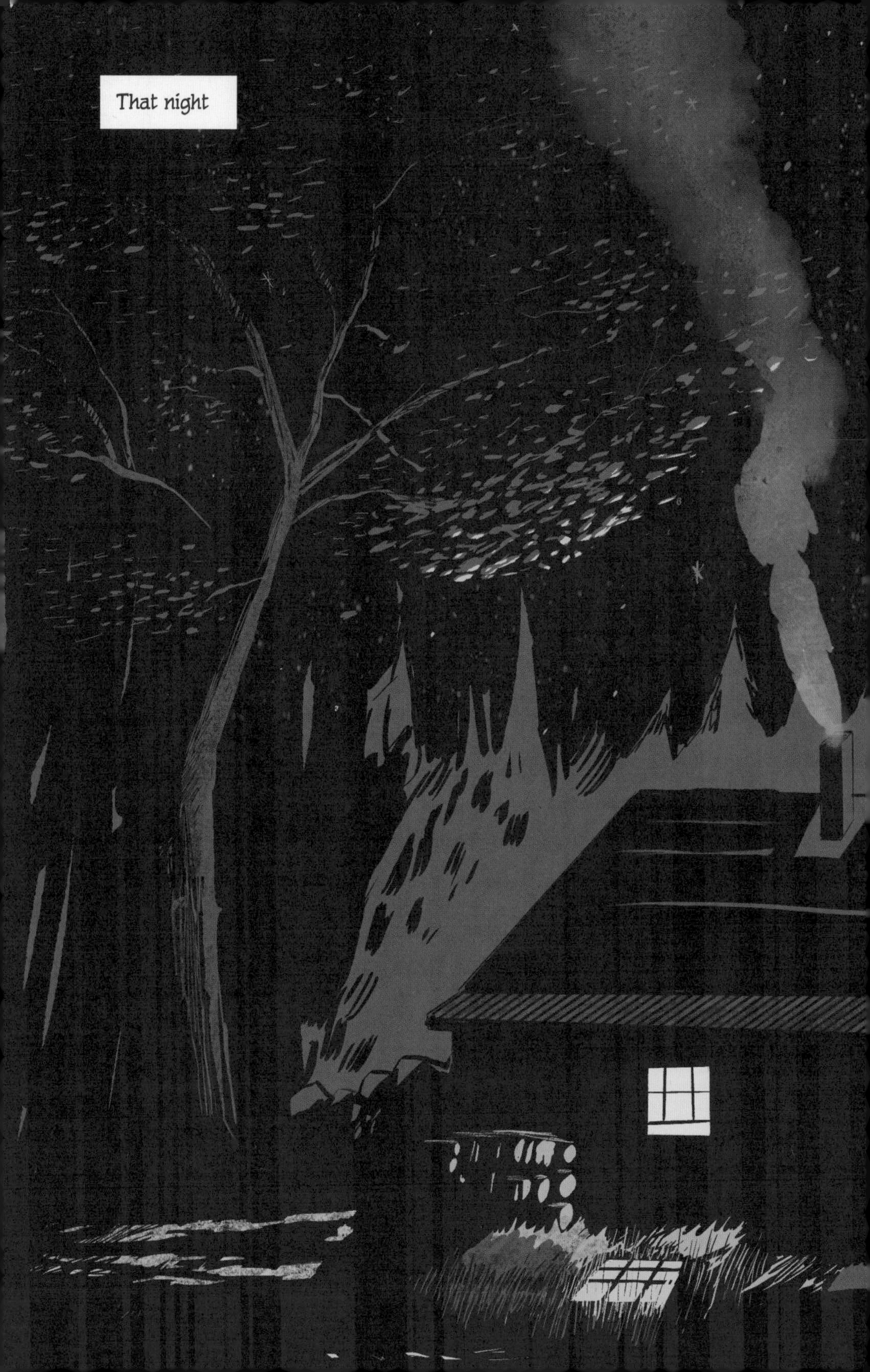
That night

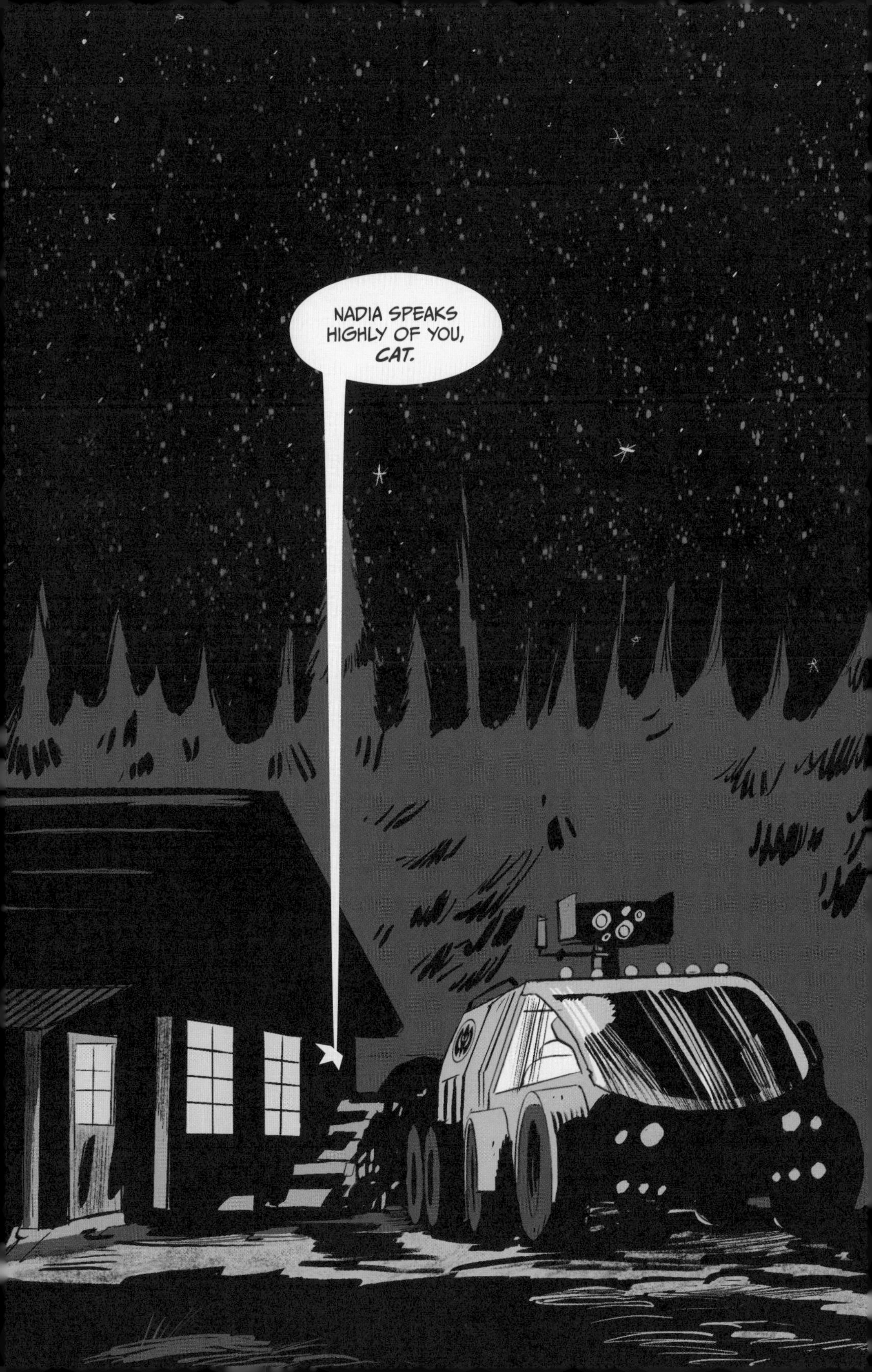
NADIA SPEAKS HIGHLY OF YOU, CAT.

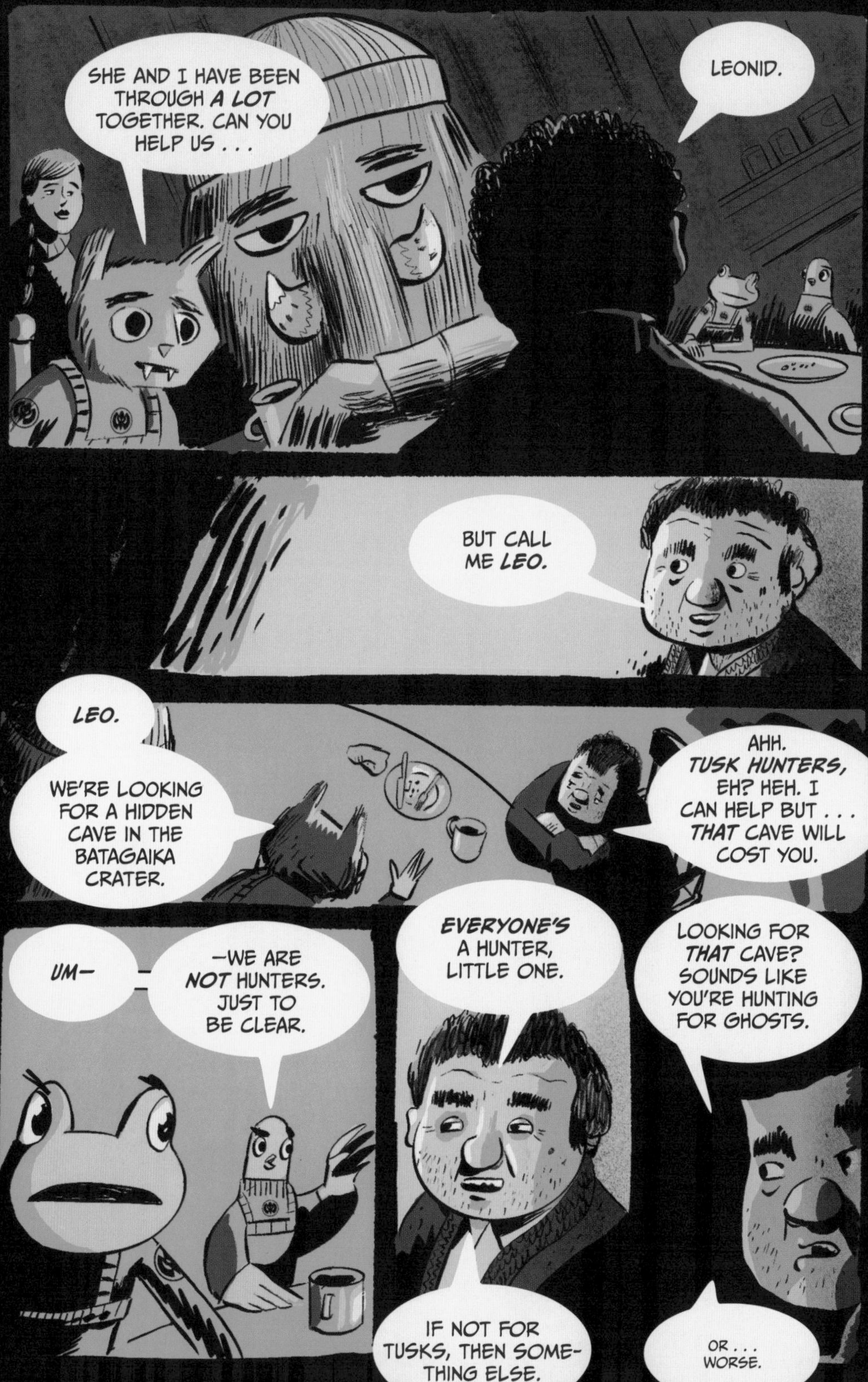
SHE AND I HAVE BEEN THROUGH *A LOT* TOGETHER. CAN YOU HELP US . . .
LEONID.
BUT CALL ME *LEO.*
LEO.
WE'RE LOOKING FOR A HIDDEN CAVE IN THE BATAGAIKA CRATER.
AHH. *TUSK HUNTERS,* EH? HEH. I CAN HELP BUT . . . *THAT* CAVE WILL COST YOU.
UM—
—WE ARE *NOT* HUNTERS. JUST TO BE CLEAR.
EVERYONE'S A HUNTER, LITTLE ONE.
IF NOT FOR TUSKS, THEN SOME-THING ELSE.
LOOKING FOR *THAT* CAVE? SOUNDS LIKE YOU'RE HUNTING FOR GHOSTS.
OR . . . WORSE.

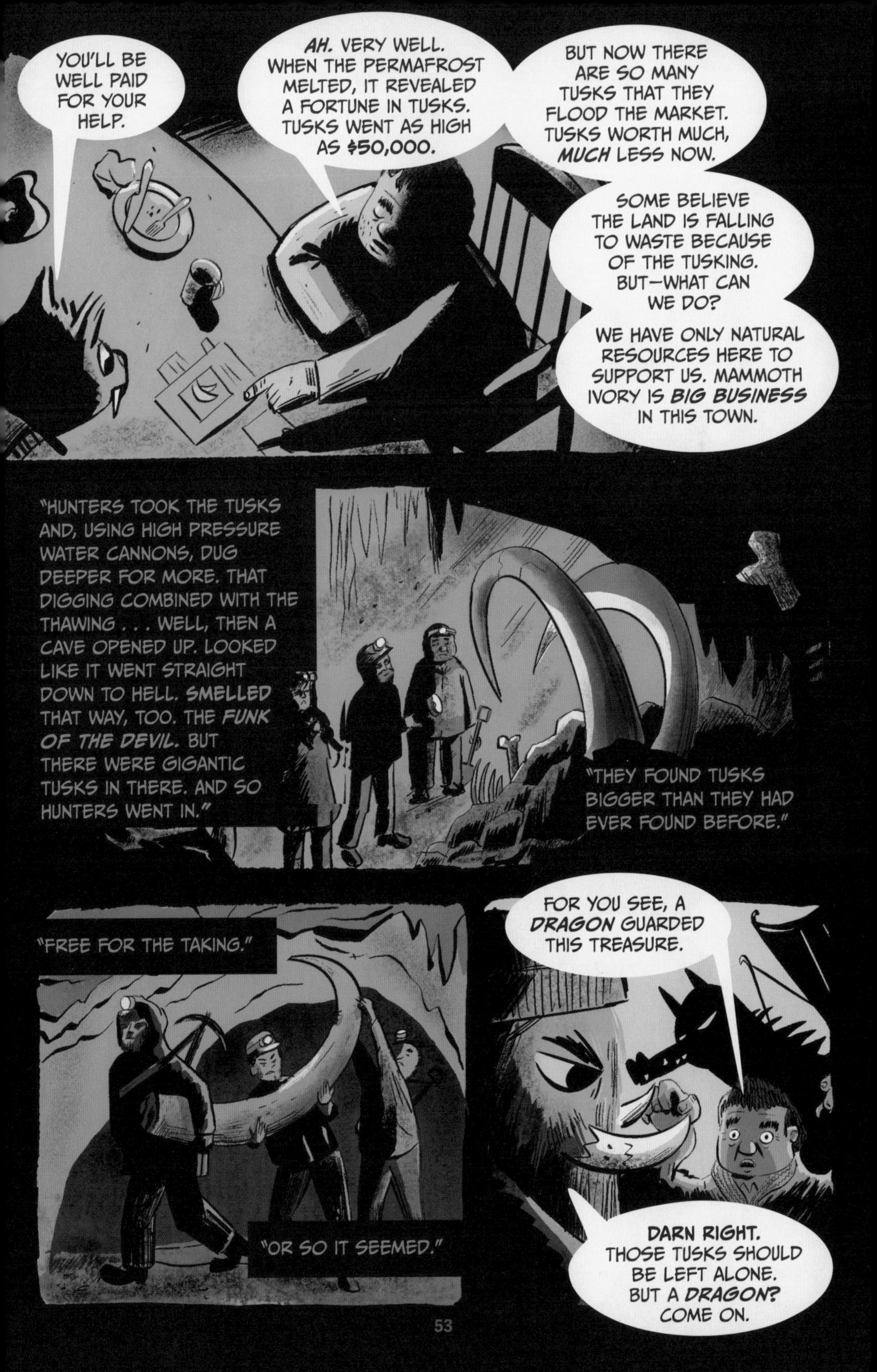
YOU'LL BE WELL PAID FOR YOUR HELP.
AH. VERY WELL. WHEN THE PERMAFROST MELTED, IT REVEALED A FORTUNE IN TUSKS. TUSKS WENT AS HIGH AS $50,000.
BUT NOW THERE ARE SO MANY TUSKS THAT THEY FLOOD THE MARKET. TUSKS WORTH MUCH, MUCH LESS NOW.
SOME BELIEVE THE LAND IS FALLING TO WASTE BECAUSE OF THE TUSKING. BUT—WHAT CAN WE DO?
WE HAVE ONLY NATURAL RESOURCES HERE TO SUPPORT US. MAMMOTH IVORY IS BIG BUSINESS IN THIS TOWN.
"HUNTERS TOOK THE TUSKS AND, USING HIGH PRESSURE WATER CANNONS, DUG DEEPER FOR MORE. THAT DIGGING COMBINED WITH THE THAWING . . . WELL, THEN A CAVE OPENED UP. LOOKED LIKE IT WENT STRAIGHT DOWN TO HELL. SMELLED THAT WAY, TOO. THE FUNK OF THE DEVIL. BUT THERE WERE GIGANTIC TUSKS IN THERE. AND SO HUNTERS WENT IN."
"THEY FOUND TUSKS BIGGER THAN THEY HAD EVER FOUND BEFORE."
"FREE FOR THE TAKING."
"OR SO IT SEEMED."
FOR YOU SEE, A DRAGON GUARDED THIS TREASURE.
DARN RIGHT. THOSE TUSKS SHOULD BE LEFT ALONE. BUT A DRAGON? COME ON.

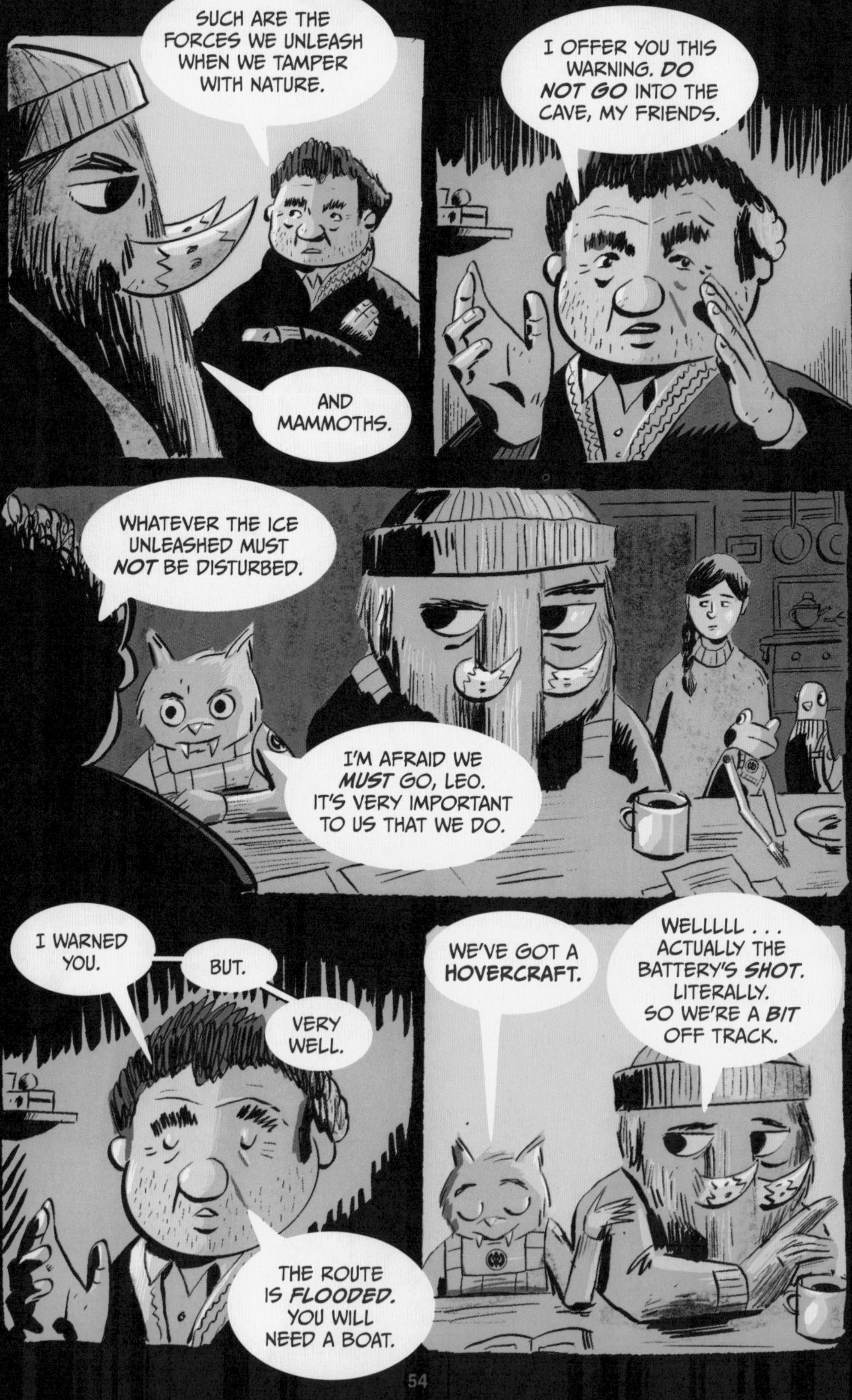
SUCH ARE THE FORCES WE UNLEASH WHEN WE TAMPER WITH NATURE.
AND MAMMOTHS.
I OFFER YOU THIS WARNING. *DO NOT GO* INTO THE CAVE, MY FRIENDS.
WHATEVER THE ICE UNLEASHED MUST *NOT* BE DISTURBED.
I'M AFRAID WE *MUST* GO, LEO. IT'S VERY IMPORTANT TO US THAT WE DO.
I WARNED YOU.
BUT.
VERY WELL.
THE ROUTE IS *FLOODED.* YOU WILL NEED A BOAT.
WE'VE GOT A **HOVERCRAFT.**
WELLLLL . . . ACTUALLY THE BATTERY'S *SHOT.* LITERALLY. SO WE'RE A *BIT* OFF TRACK.

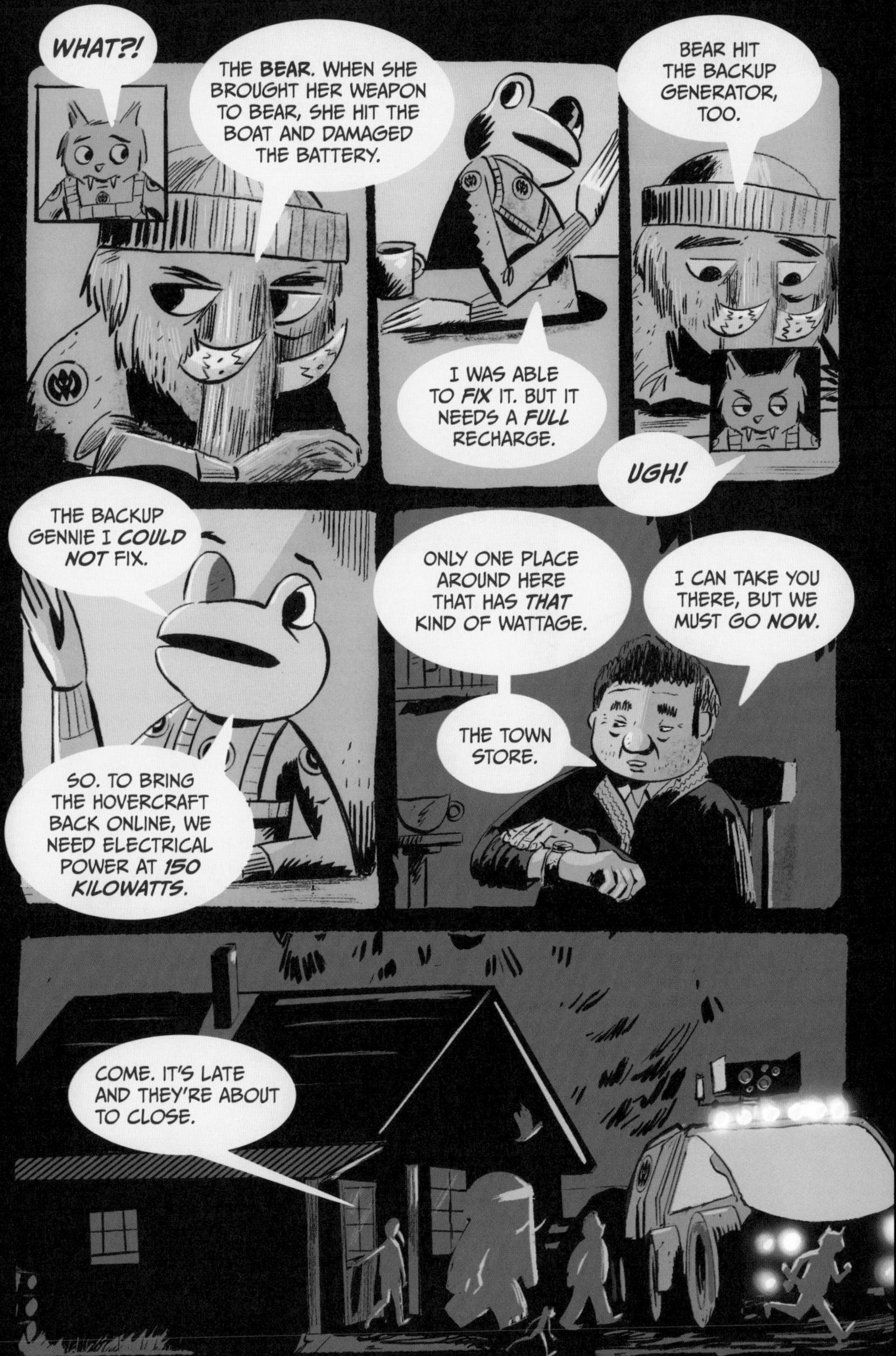
WHAT?!
THE BEAR. WHEN SHE BROUGHT HER WEAPON TO BEAR, SHE HIT THE BOAT AND DAMAGED THE BATTERY.
I WAS ABLE TO FIX IT. BUT IT NEEDS A FULL RECHARGE.
BEAR HIT THE BACKUP GENERATOR, TOO.
UGH!
THE BACKUP GENNIE I COULD NOT FIX.
SO. TO BRING THE HOVERCRAFT BACK ONLINE, WE NEED ELECTRICAL POWER AT 150 KILOWATTS.
ONLY ONE PLACE AROUND HERE THAT HAS THAT KIND OF WATTAGE.
THE TOWN STORE.
I CAN TAKE YOU THERE, BUT WE MUST GO NOW.
COME. IT'S LATE AND THEY'RE ABOUT TO CLOSE.

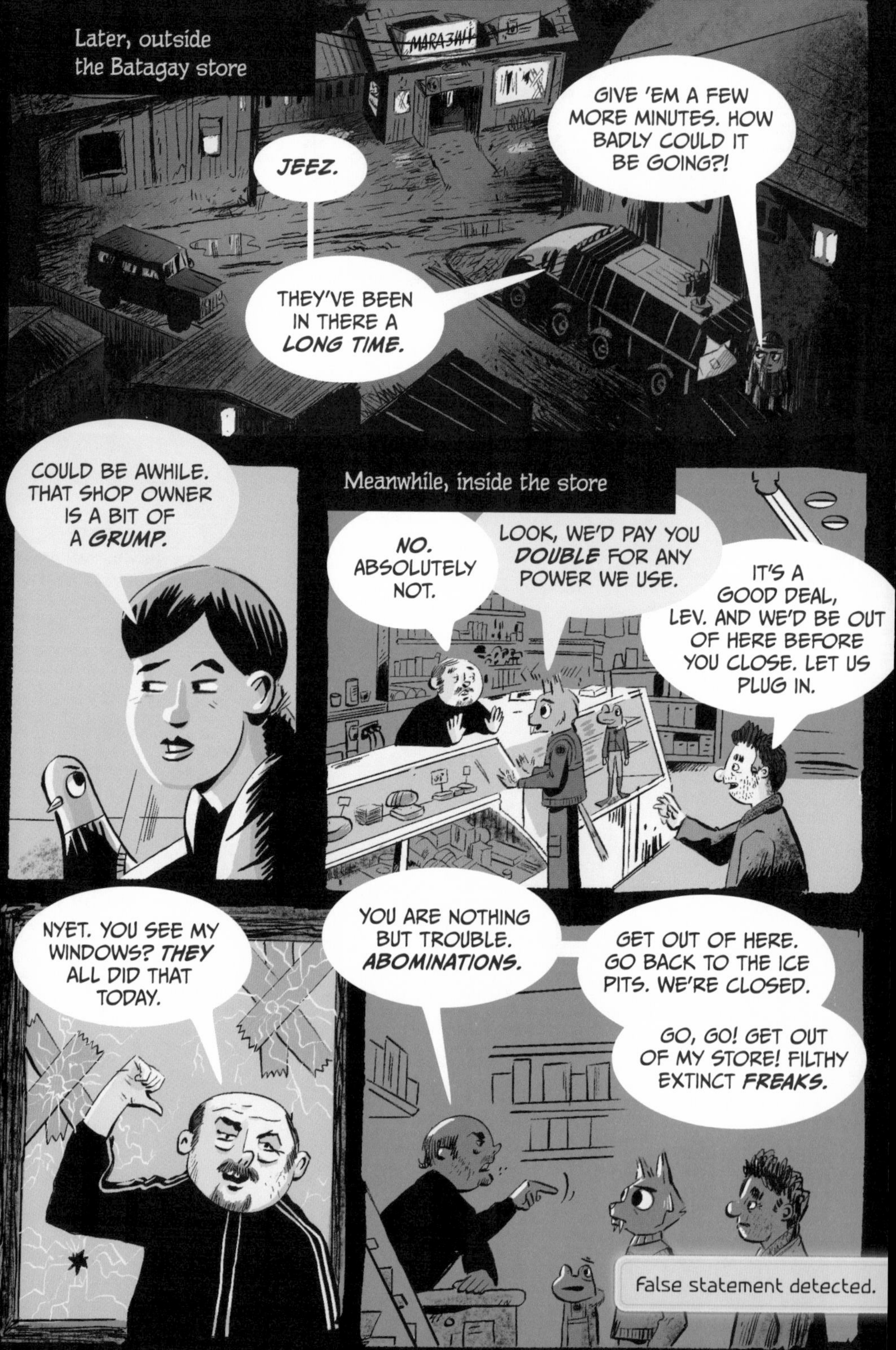
Later, outside the Batagay store
МАГАЗИН
JEEZ.
THEY'VE BEEN IN THERE A LONG TIME.
GIVE 'EM A FEW MORE MINUTES. HOW BADLY COULD IT BE GOING?!
COULD BE AWHILE. THAT SHOP OWNER IS A BIT OF A GRUMP.
Meanwhile, inside the store
NO. ABSOLUTELY NOT.
LOOK, WE'D PAY YOU DOUBLE FOR ANY POWER WE USE.
IT'S A GOOD DEAL, LEV. AND WE'D BE OUT OF HERE BEFORE YOU CLOSE. LET US PLUG IN.
NYET. YOU SEE MY WINDOWS? THEY ALL DID THAT TODAY.
YOU ARE NOTHING BUT TROUBLE. ABOMINATIONS.
GET OUT OF HERE. GO BACK TO THE ICE PITS. WE'RE CLOSED.
GO, GO! GET OUT OF MY STORE! FILTHY EXTINCT FREAKS.
False statement detected.

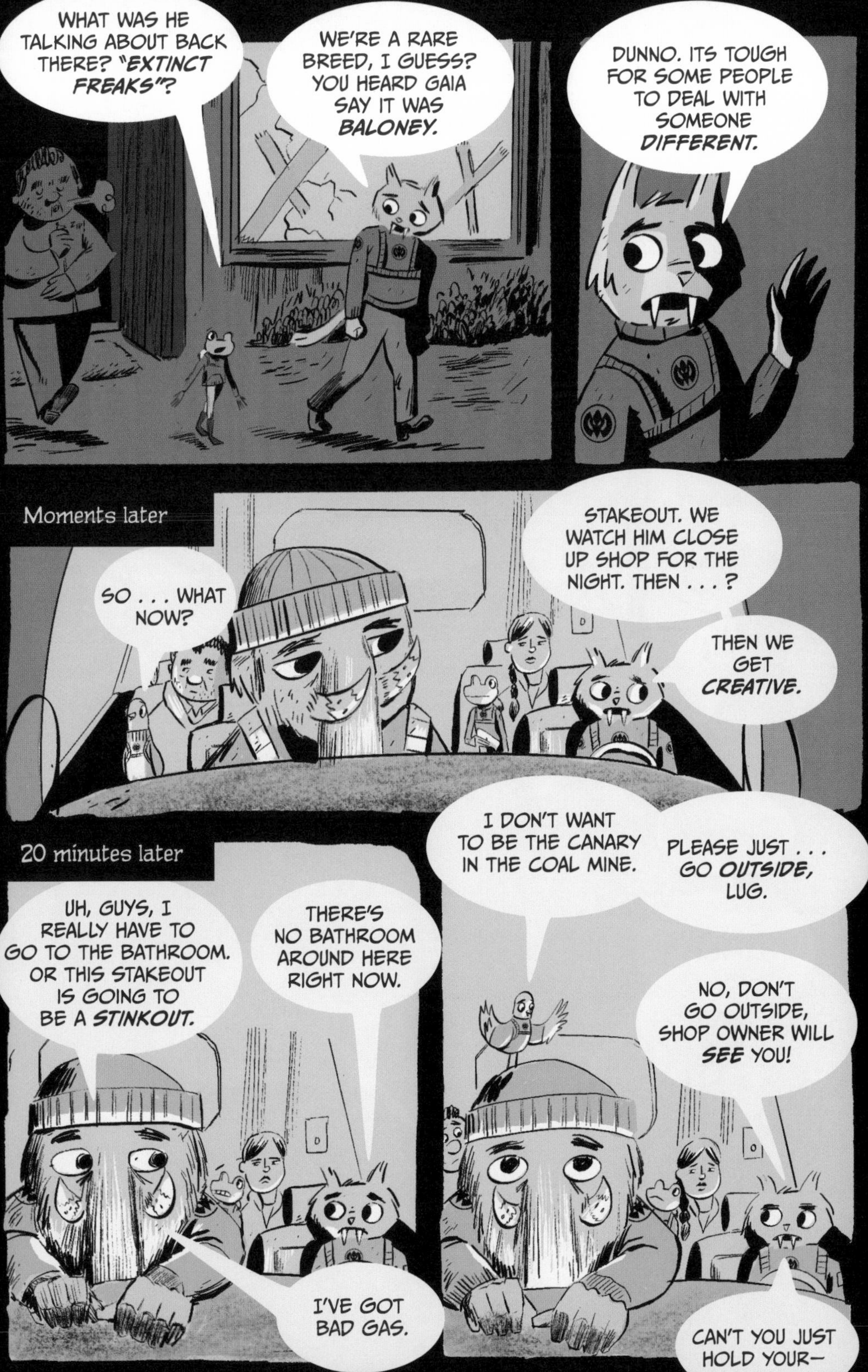
WHAT WAS HE TALKING ABOUT BACK THERE? "EXTINCT FREAKS"?
WE'RE A RARE BREED, I GUESS? YOU HEARD GAIA SAY IT WAS BALONEY.
DUNNO. ITS TOUGH FOR SOME PEOPLE TO DEAL WITH SOMEONE DIFFERENT.
Moments later
SO . . . WHAT NOW?
STAKEOUT. WE WATCH HIM CLOSE UP SHOP FOR THE NIGHT. THEN . . . ?
THEN WE GET CREATIVE.
20 minutes later
UH, GUYS, I REALLY HAVE TO GO TO THE BATHROOM. OR THIS STAKEOUT IS GOING TO BE A STINKOUT.
THERE'S NO BATHROOM AROUND HERE RIGHT NOW.
I'VE GOT BAD GAS.
I DON'T WANT TO BE THE CANARY IN THE COAL MINE.
PLEASE JUST . . . GO OUTSIDE, LUG.
NO, DON'T GO OUTSIDE, SHOP OWNER WILL SEE YOU!
CAN'T YOU JUST HOLD YOUR—

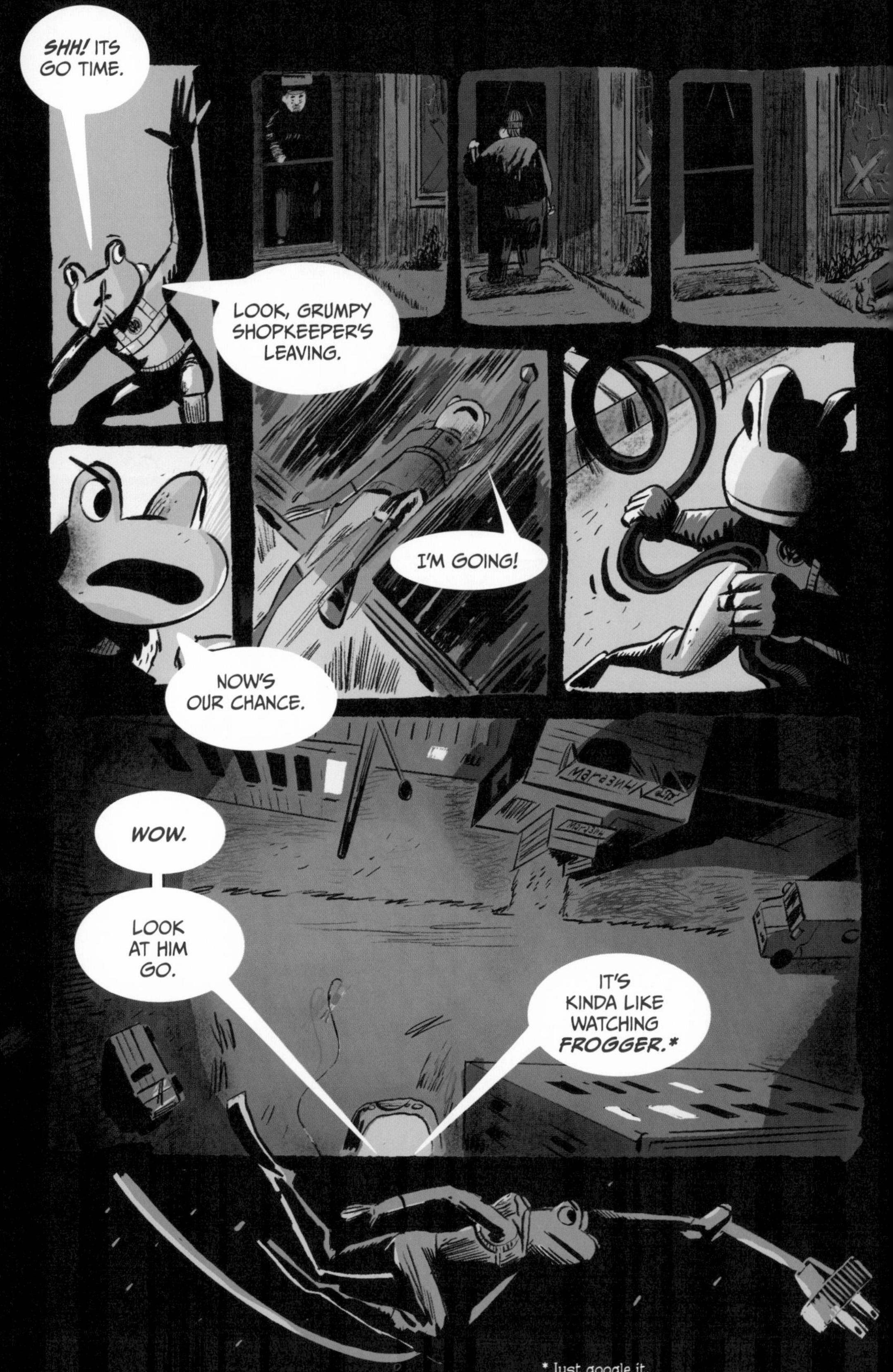
SHH! ITS GO TIME.
LOOK, GRUMPY SHOPKEEPER'S LEAVING.
NOW'S OUR CHANCE.
I'M GOING!
WOW.
LOOK AT HIM GO.
IT'S KINDA LIKE WATCHING FROGGER.*

* Just google it.

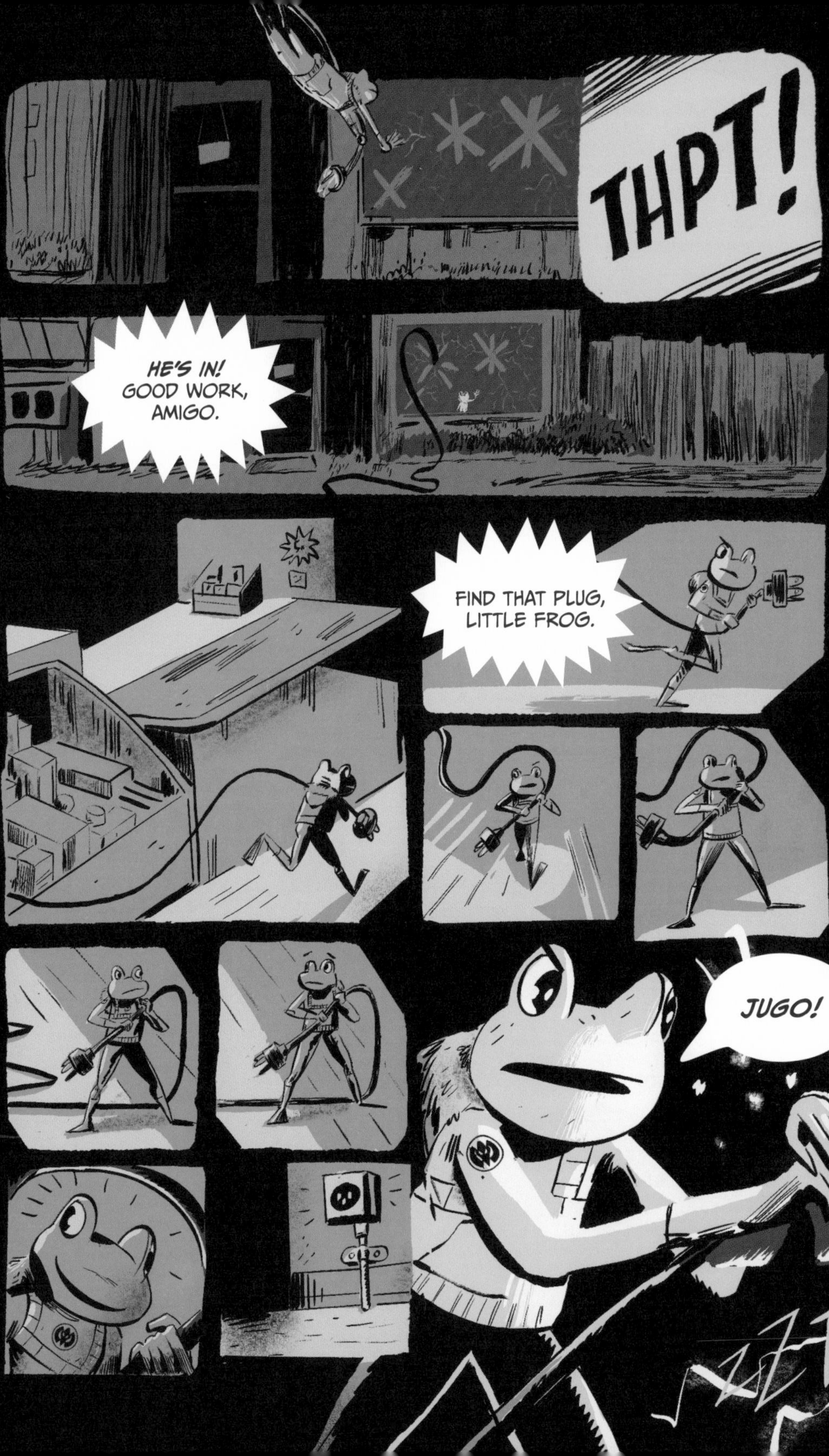
THPT!
HE'S IN! GOOD WORK, AMIGO.
FIND THAT PLUG, LITTLE FROG.
JUGO!
ZZT

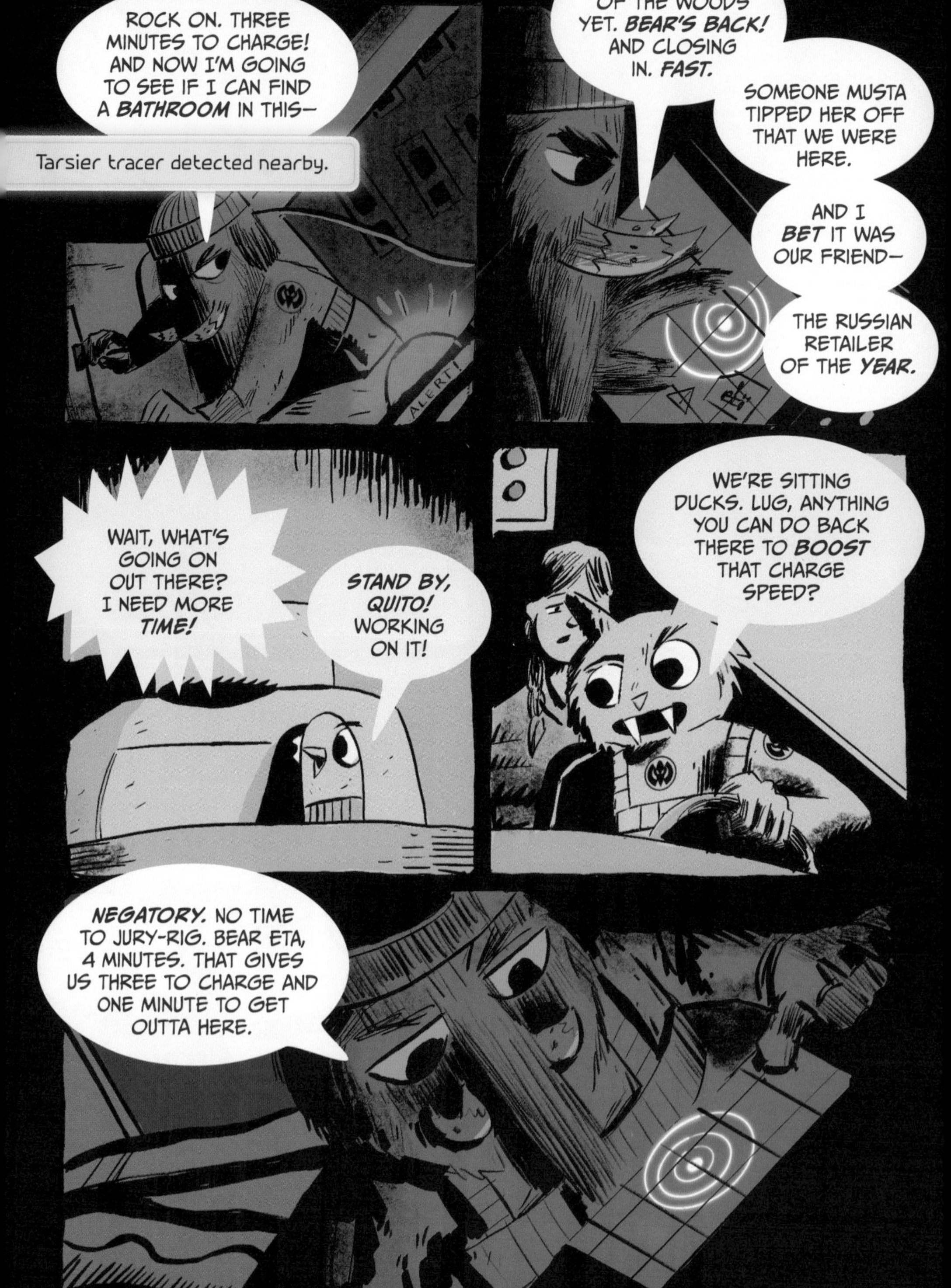
ROCK ON. THREE MINUTES TO CHARGE! AND NOW I'M GOING TO SEE IF I CAN FIND A BATHROOM IN THIS—
Tarsier tracer detected nearby.
ALERT!
NUTS!! NOT OUT OF THE WOODS YET. BEAR'S BACK! AND CLOSING IN. FAST.
SOMEONE MUSTA TIPPED HER OFF THAT WE WERE HERE.
AND I BET IT WAS OUR FRIEND—
THE RUSSIAN RETAILER OF THE YEAR.
WAIT, WHAT'S GOING ON OUT THERE? I NEED MORE TIME!
STAND BY, QUITO! WORKING ON IT!
WE'RE SITTING DUCKS. LUG, ANYTHING YOU CAN DO BACK THERE TO BOOST THAT CHARGE SPEED?
NEGATORY. NO TIME TO JURY-RIG. BEAR ETA, 4 MINUTES. THAT GIVES US THREE TO CHARGE AND ONE MINUTE TO GET OUTTA HERE.

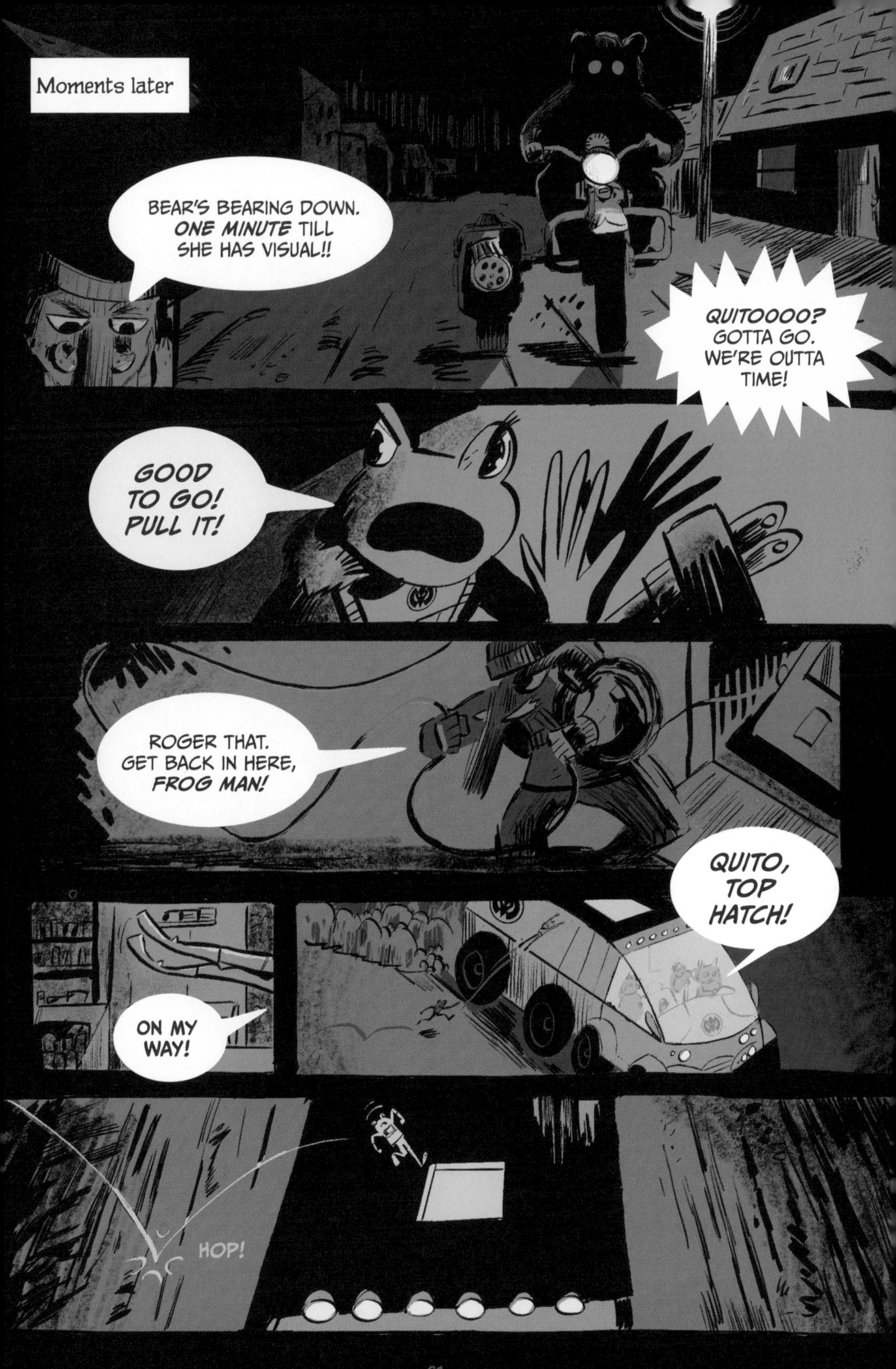
Moments later
BEAR'S BEARING DOWN. ONE MINUTE TILL SHE HAS VISUAL!!
QUITOOOO? GOTTA GO. WE'RE OUTTA TIME!
GOOD TO GO! PULL IT!
ROGER THAT. GET BACK IN HERE, FROG MAN!
QUITO, TOP HATCH!
ON MY WAY!
HOP!

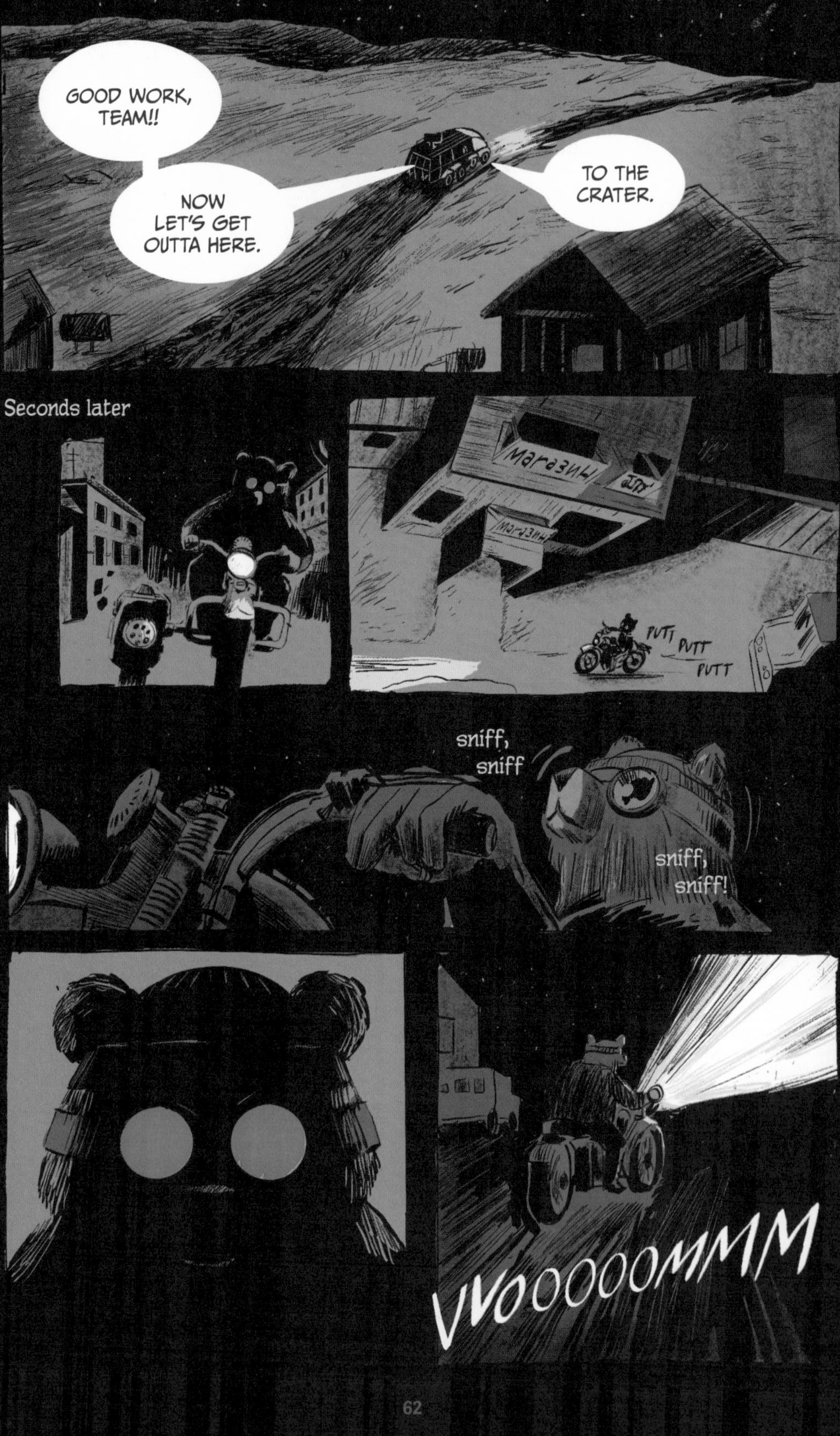
GOOD WORK, TEAM!!
NOW LET'S GET OUTTA HERE.
TO THE CRATER.
Seconds later
PUTT
PUTT
PUTT
sniff, sniff
sniff, sniff!
VVOOOOOMMM

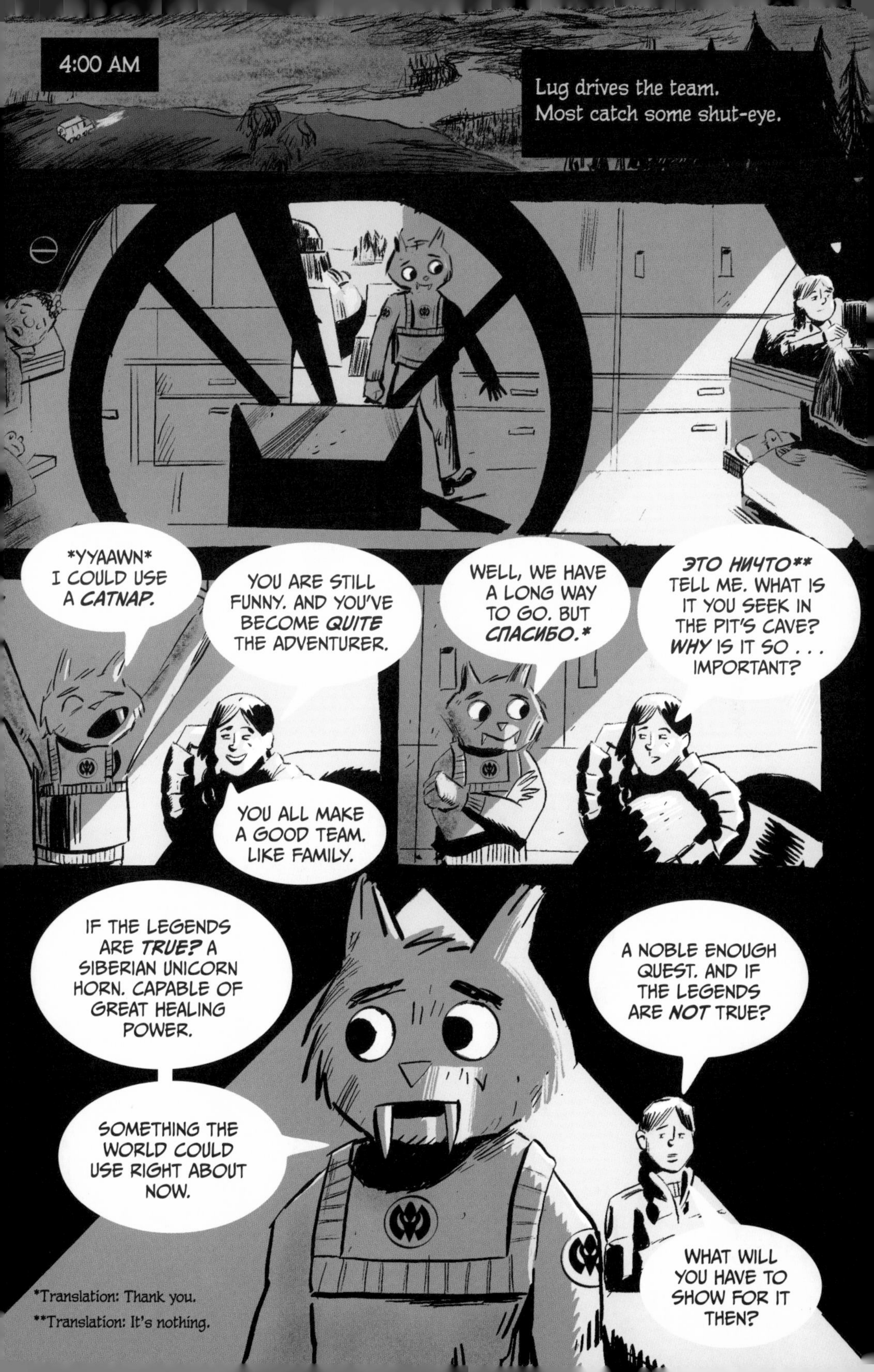
4:00 AM
Lug drives the team. Most catch some shut-eye.
YYAAWN I COULD USE A CATNAP.
YOU ARE STILL FUNNY. AND YOU'VE BECOME QUITE THE ADVENTURER.
YOU ALL MAKE A GOOD TEAM. LIKE FAMILY.
WELL, WE HAVE A LONG WAY TO GO. BUT СПАСИБО.*
ЭТО НИЧТО** TELL ME. WHAT IS IT YOU SEEK IN THE PIT'S CAVE? WHY IS IT SO . . . IMPORTANT?
IF THE LEGENDS ARE TRUE? A SIBERIAN UNICORN HORN. CAPABLE OF GREAT HEALING POWER.
SOMETHING THE WORLD COULD USE RIGHT ABOUT NOW.
A NOBLE ENOUGH QUEST. AND IF THE LEGENDS ARE NOT TRUE?
WHAT WILL YOU HAVE TO SHOW FOR IT THEN?
*Translation: Thank you.
**Translation: It's nothing.

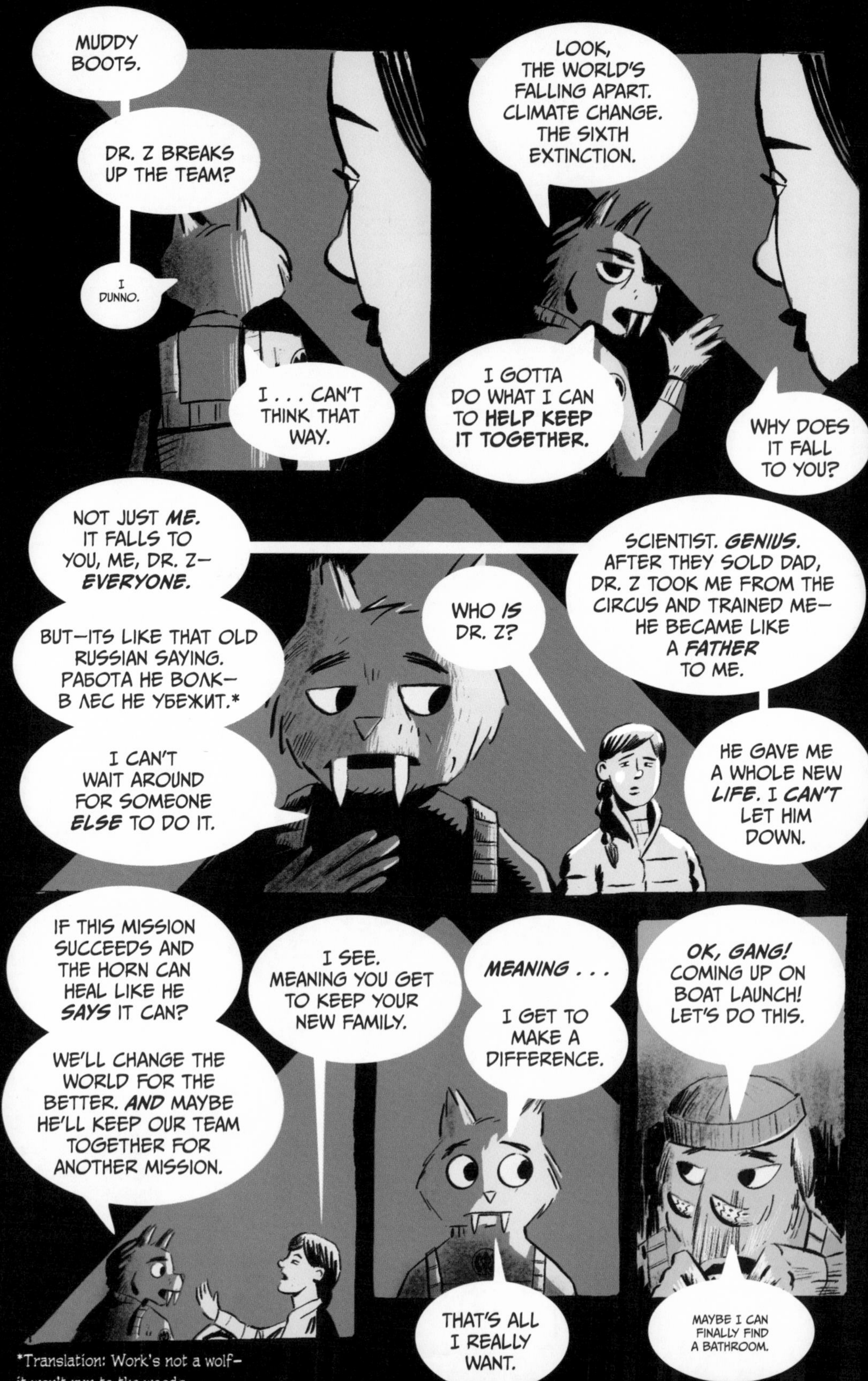
MUDDY BOOTS.
DR. Z BREAKS UP THE TEAM?
I DUNNO.
I . . . CAN'T THINK THAT WAY.
LOOK, THE WORLD'S FALLING APART. CLIMATE CHANGE. THE SIXTH EXTINCTION.
I GOTTA DO WHAT I CAN TO HELP KEEP IT TOGETHER.
WHY DOES IT FALL TO YOU?
NOT JUST ME. IT FALLS TO YOU, ME, DR. Z—EVERYONE.
BUT—ITS LIKE THAT OLD RUSSIAN SAYING. РАБОТА НЕ ВОЛК—В ЛЕС НЕ УБЕЖИТ.*
I CAN'T WAIT AROUND FOR SOMEONE ELSE TO DO IT.
WHO IS DR. Z?
SCIENTIST. GENIUS. AFTER THEY SOLD DAD, DR. Z TOOK ME FROM THE CIRCUS AND TRAINED ME—HE BECAME LIKE A FATHER TO ME.
HE GAVE ME A WHOLE NEW LIFE. I CAN'T LET HIM DOWN.
IF THIS MISSION SUCCEEDS AND THE HORN CAN HEAL LIKE HE SAYS IT CAN?
WE'LL CHANGE THE WORLD FOR THE BETTER. AND MAYBE HE'LL KEEP OUR TEAM TOGETHER FOR ANOTHER MISSION.
I SEE. MEANING YOU GET TO KEEP YOUR NEW FAMILY.
MEANING . . .
I GET TO MAKE A DIFFERENCE.
THAT'S ALL I REALLY WANT.
OK, GANG! COMING UP ON BOAT LAUNCH! LET'S DO THIS.
MAYBE I CAN FINALLY FIND A BATHROOM.

*Translation: Work's not a wolf—it won't run to the woods.

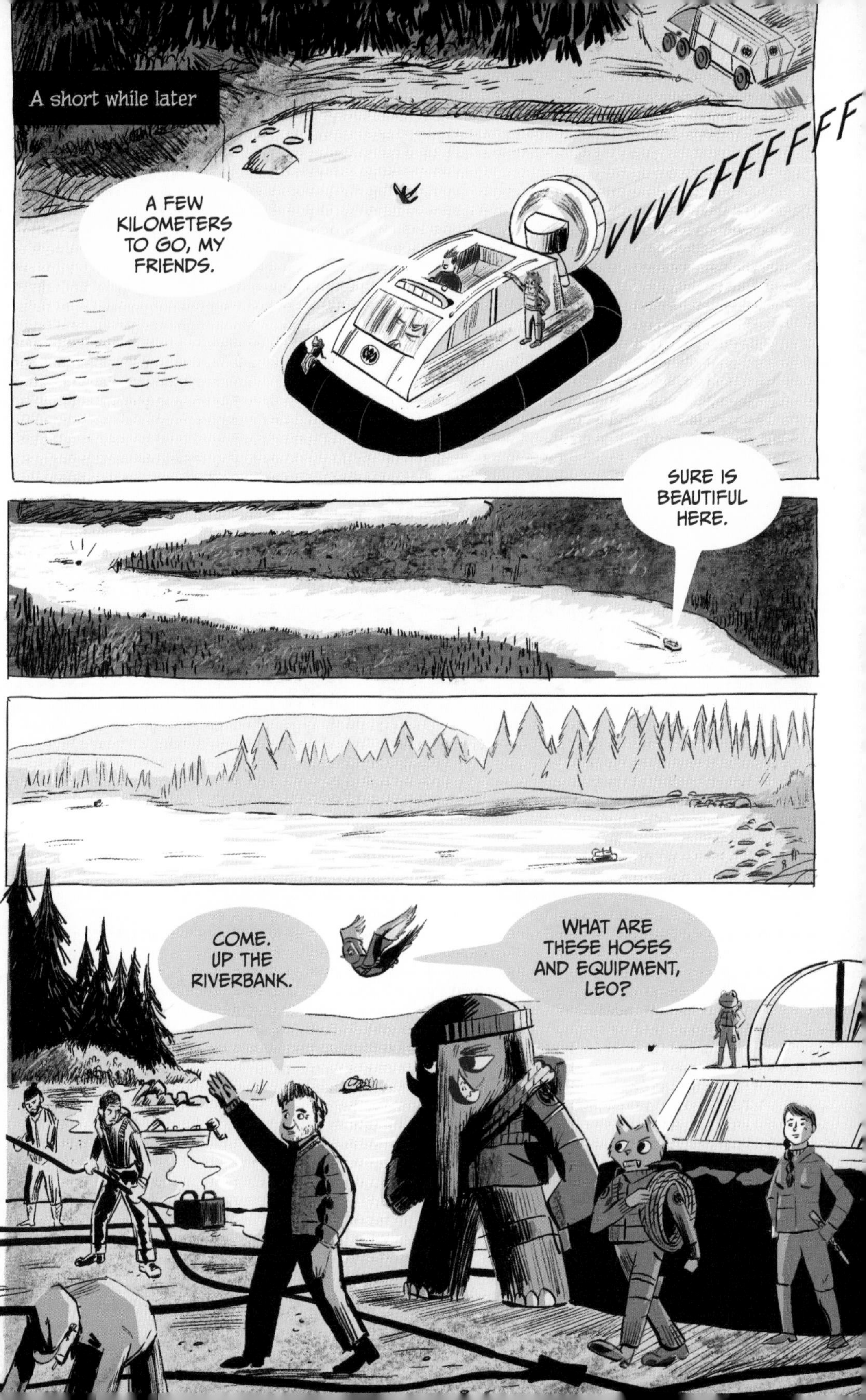
A short while later
A FEW KILOMETERS TO GO, MY FRIENDS.
VVVVFFFFFFFF
SURE IS BEAUTIFUL HERE.
COME. UP THE RIVERBANK.
WHAT ARE THESE HOSES AND EQUIPMENT, LEO?

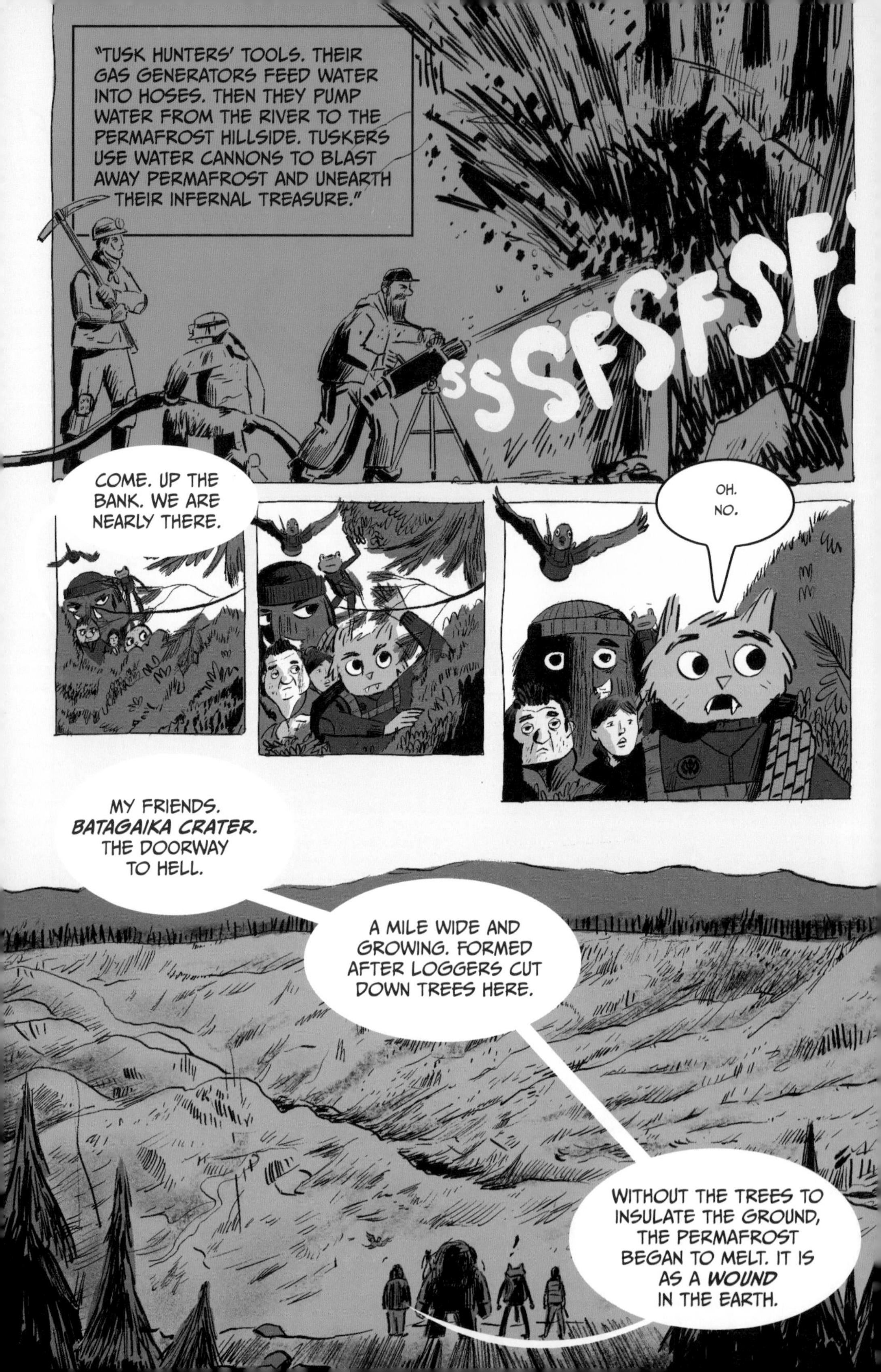
"TUSK HUNTERS' TOOLS. THEIR GAS GENERATORS FEED WATER INTO HOSES. THEN THEY PUMP WATER FROM THE RIVER TO THE PERMAFROST HILLSIDE. TUSKERS USE WATER CANNONS TO BLAST AWAY PERMAFROST AND UNEARTH THEIR INFERNAL TREASURE."
SSSFSFSF
COME. UP THE BANK. WE ARE NEARLY THERE.
OH. NO.
MY FRIENDS. *BATAGAIKA CRATER.* THE DOORWAY TO HELL.
A MILE WIDE AND GROWING. FORMED AFTER LOGGERS CUT DOWN TREES HERE.
WITHOUT THE TREES TO INSULATE THE GROUND, THE PERMAFROST BEGAN TO MELT. IT IS AS A *WOUND* IN THE EARTH.

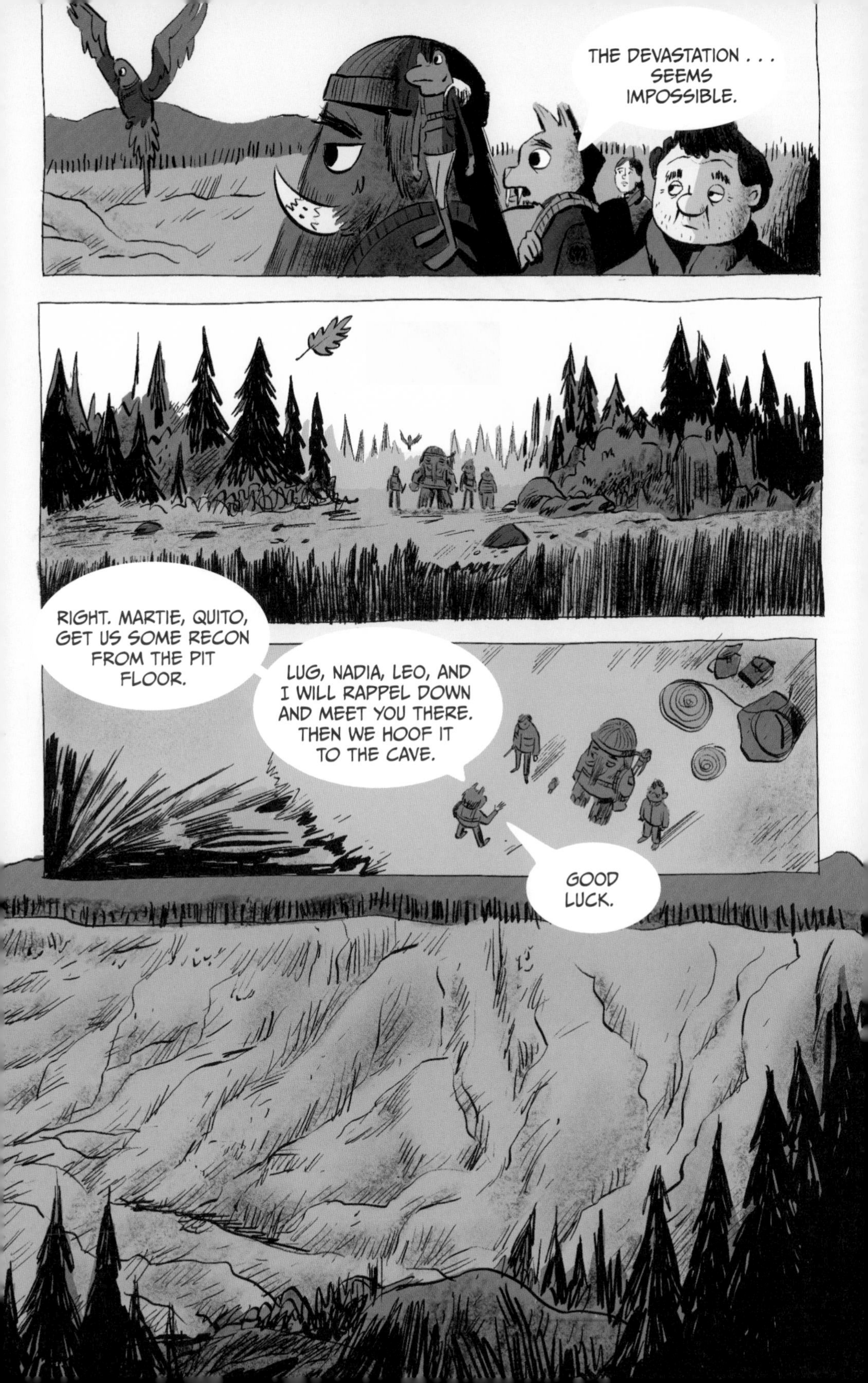
THE DEVASTATION . . . SEEMS IMPOSSIBLE.
RIGHT. MARTIE, QUITO, GET US SOME RECON FROM THE PIT FLOOR.
LUG, NADIA, LEO, AND I WILL RAPPEL DOWN AND MEET YOU THERE. THEN WE HOOF IT TO THE CAVE.
GOOD LUCK.

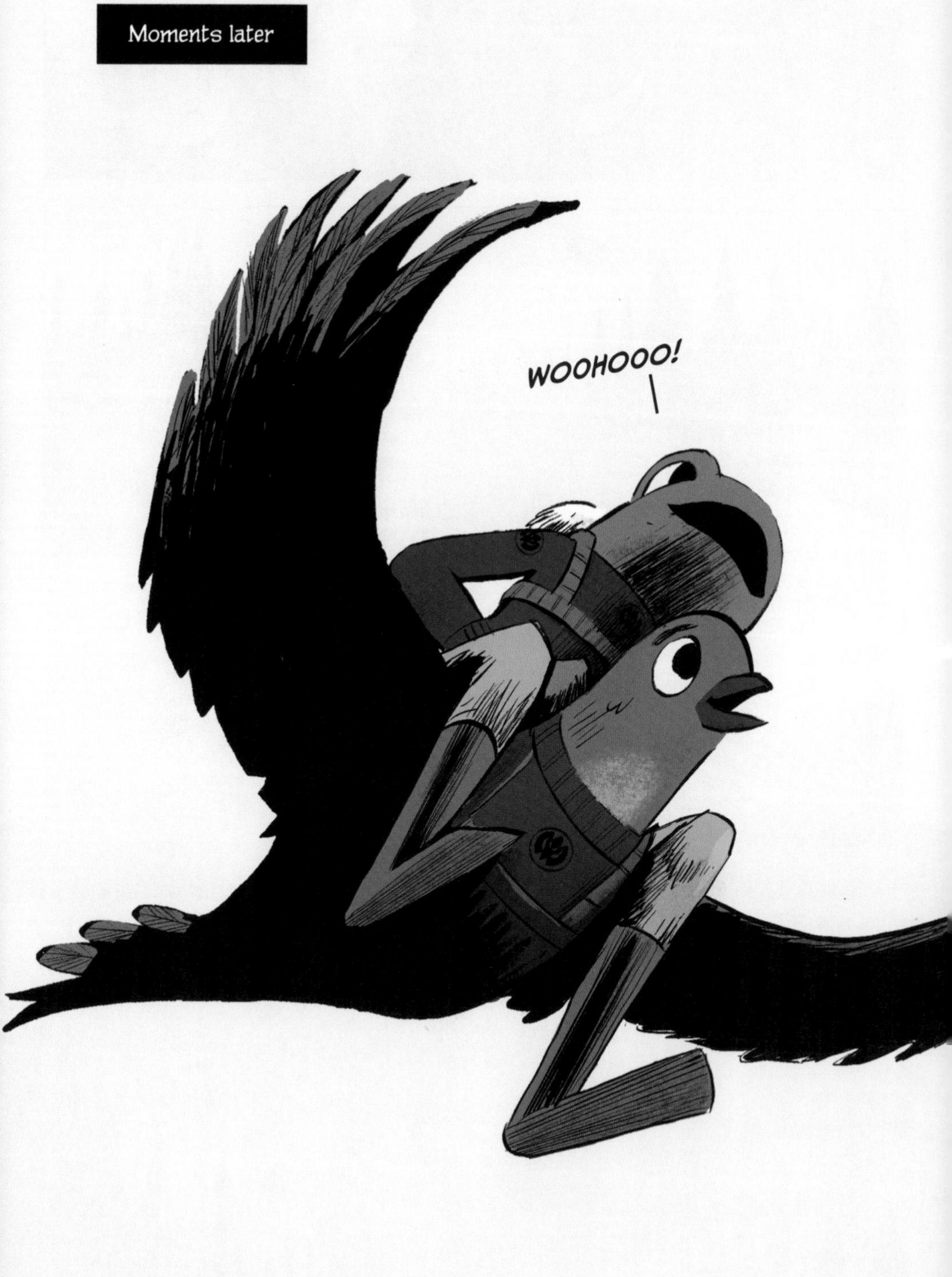
Moments later
WOOHOOO!

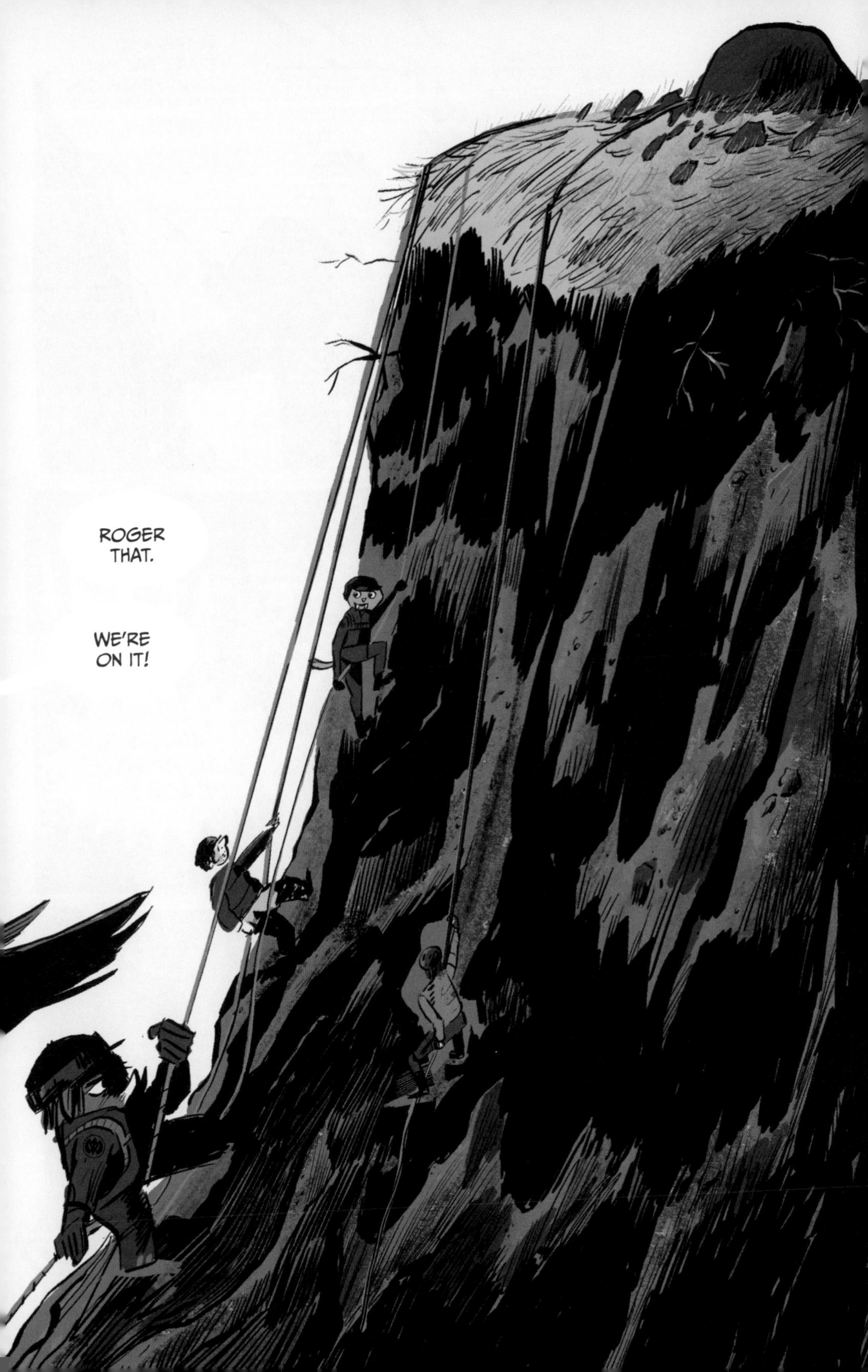
ROGER THAT.
WE'RE ON IT!

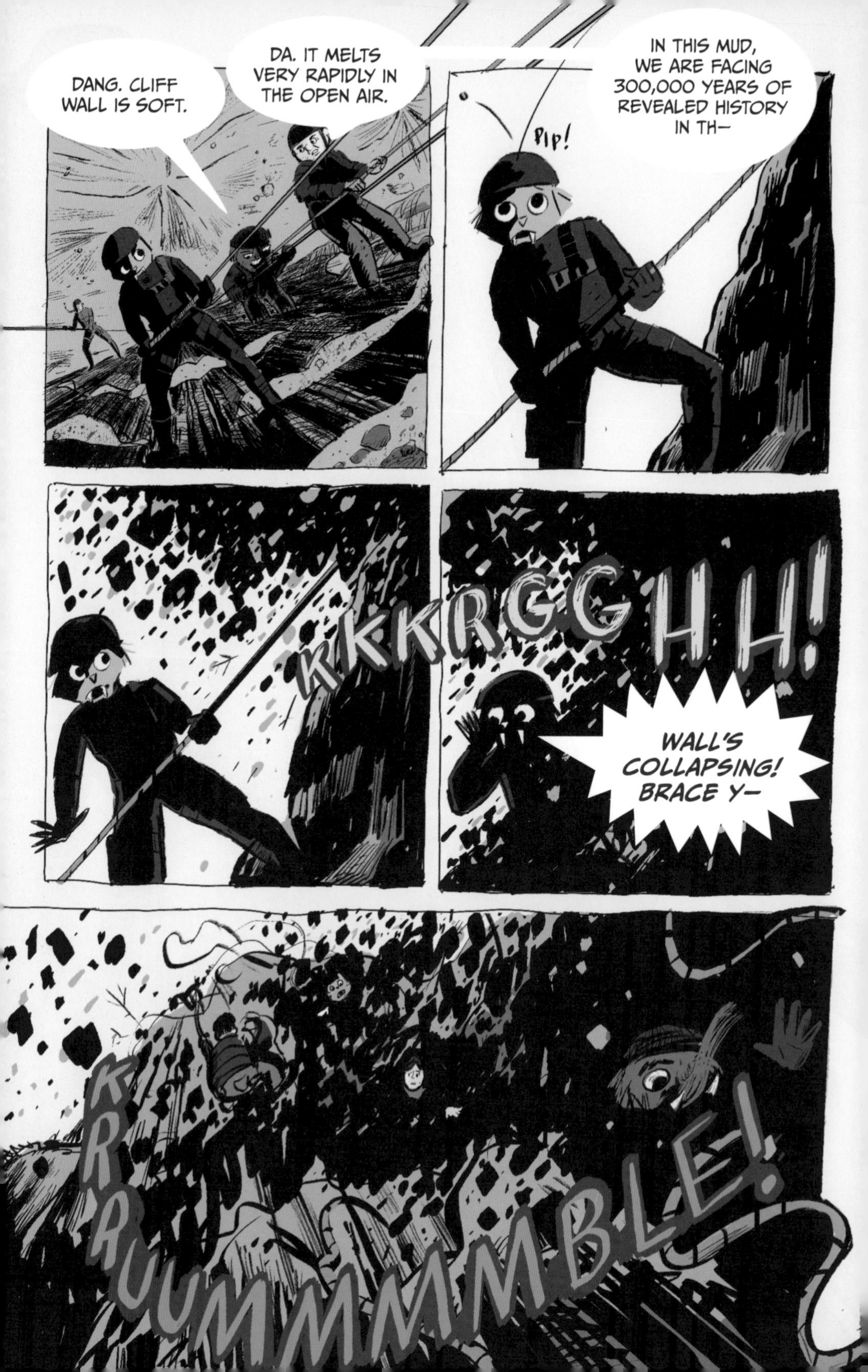
DANG. CLIFF WALL IS SOFT.
DA. IT MELTS VERY RAPIDLY IN THE OPEN AIR.
IN THIS MUD, WE ARE FACING 300,000 YEARS OF REVEALED HISTORY IN TH—
PIP!
KKKRGGHH!
WALL'S COLLAPSING! BRACE Y—
KRRUMMMMBLE!

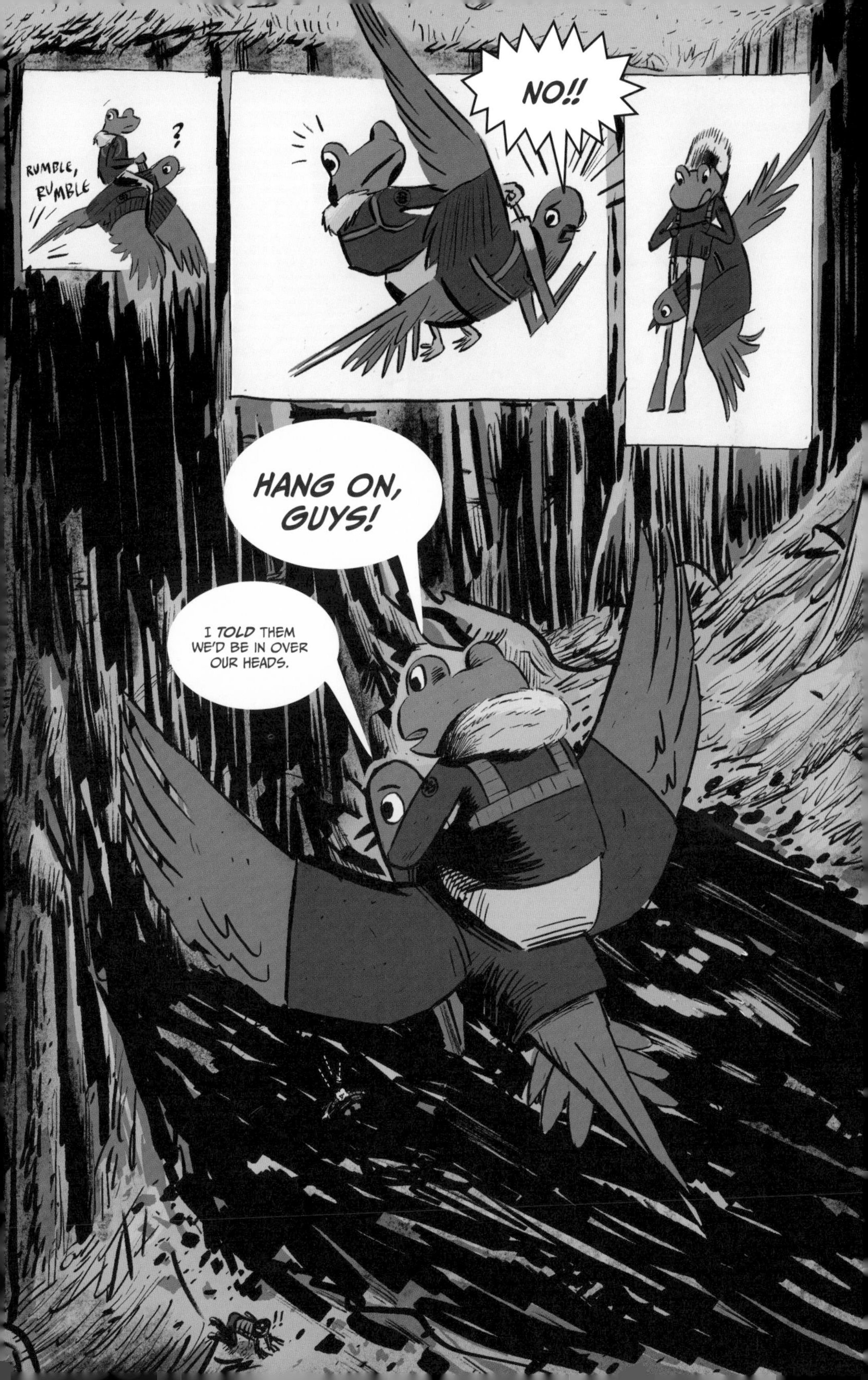
RUMBLE, RUMBLE
?
NO!!
HANG ON, GUYS!
I *TOLD* THEM WE'D BE IN OVER OUR HEADS.

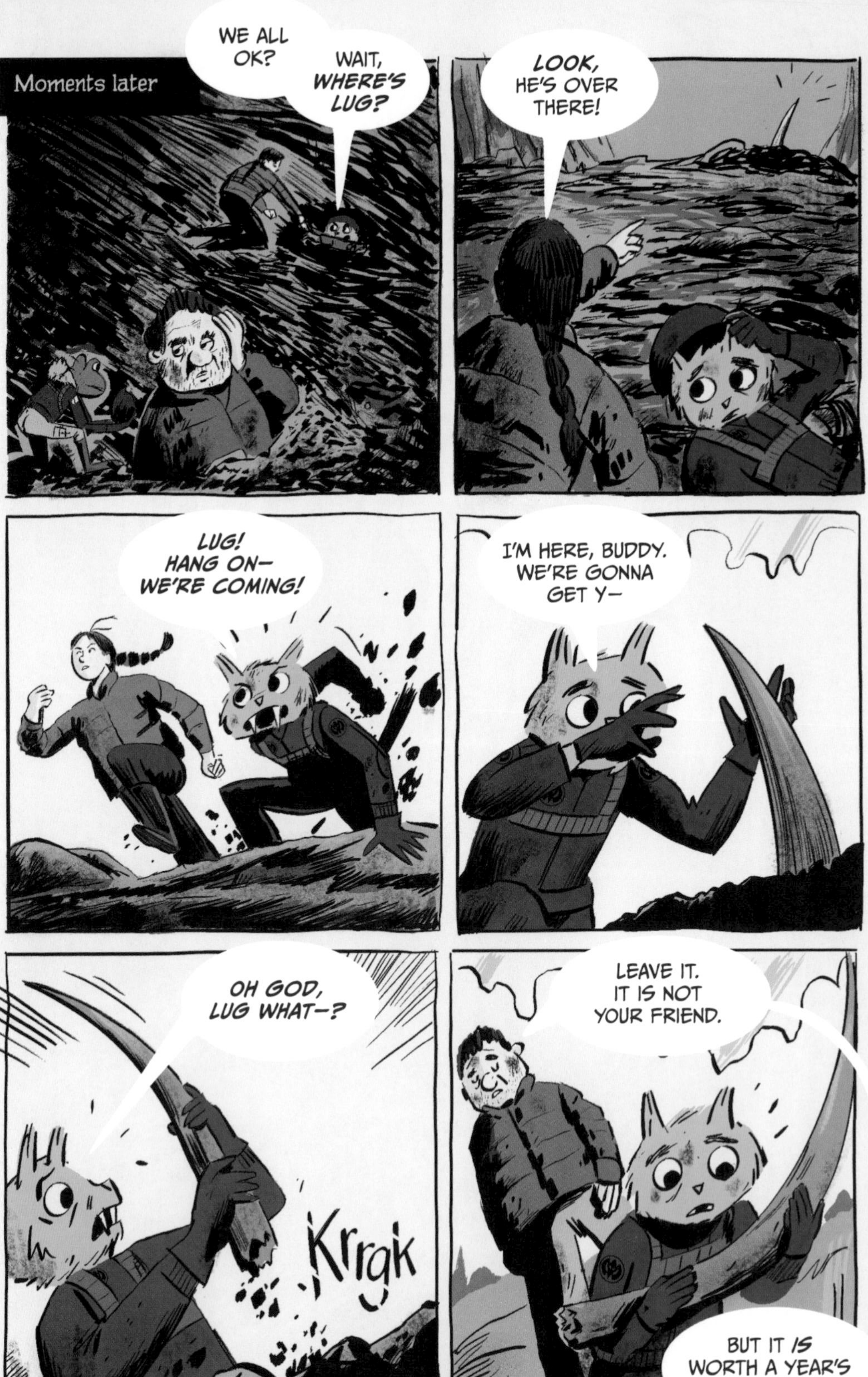
Moments later
WE ALL OK?
WAIT, *WHERE'S LUG?*
LOOK, HE'S OVER THERE!
LUG! HANG ON— WE'RE COMING!
I'M HERE, BUDDY. WE'RE GONNA GET Y—
OH GOD, LUG WHAT—?
Krrgk
LEAVE IT. IT IS NOT YOUR FRIEND.
BUT IT *IS* WORTH A YEAR'S SALARY.

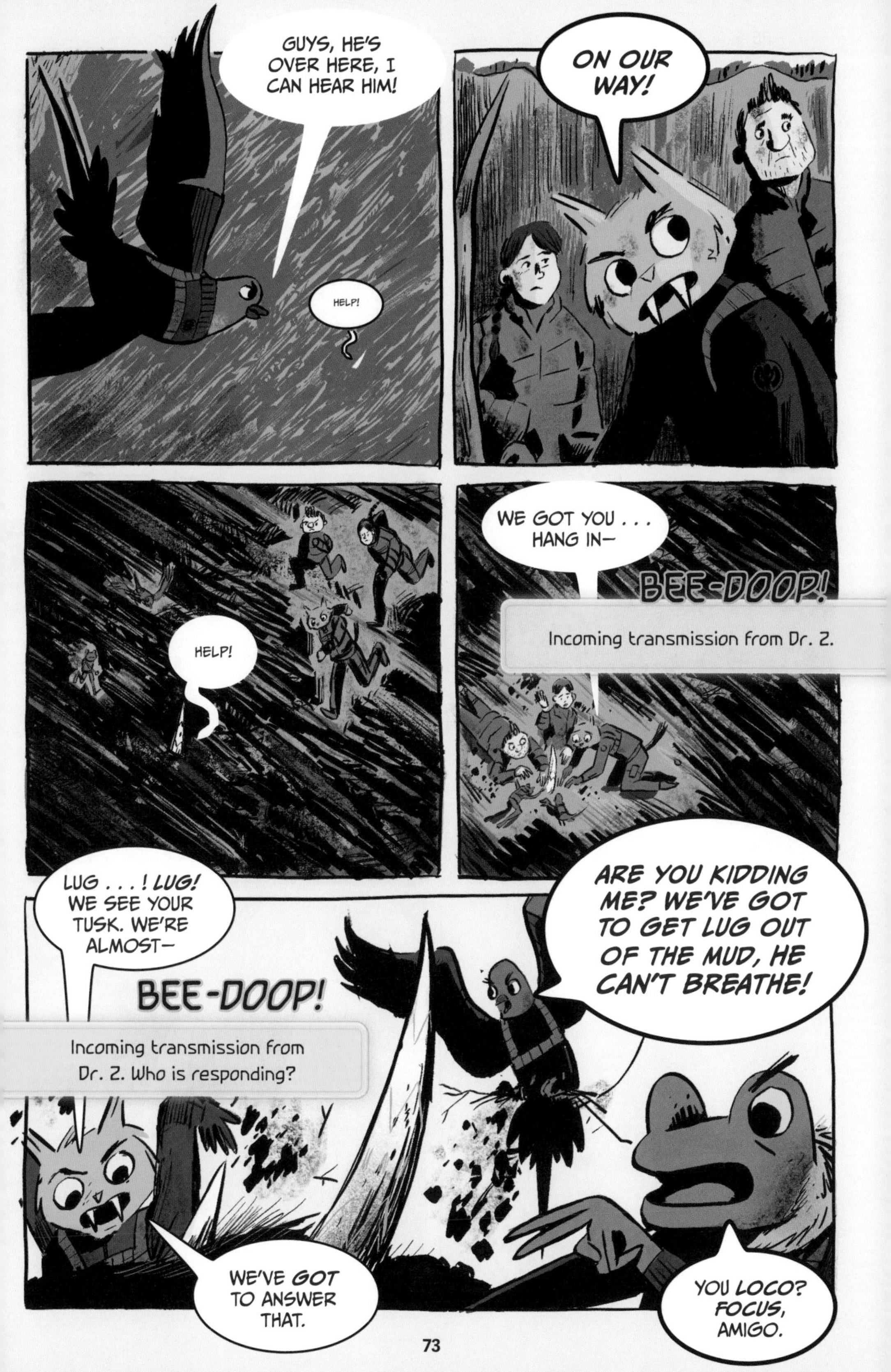
GUYS, HE'S OVER HERE, I CAN HEAR HIM!
HELP!
ON OUR WAY!
HELP!
WE GOT YOU . . . HANG IN—
BEE-DOOP!
Incoming transmission from Dr. Z.
LUG . . . ! LUG! WE SEE YOUR TUSK. WE'RE ALMOST—
BEE-DOOP!
Incoming transmission from Dr. Z. Who is responding?
ARE YOU KIDDING ME? WE'VE GOT TO GET LUG OUT OF THE MUD, HE CAN'T BREATHE!
WE'VE GOT TO ANSWER THAT.
YOU LOCO? FOCUS, AMIGO.

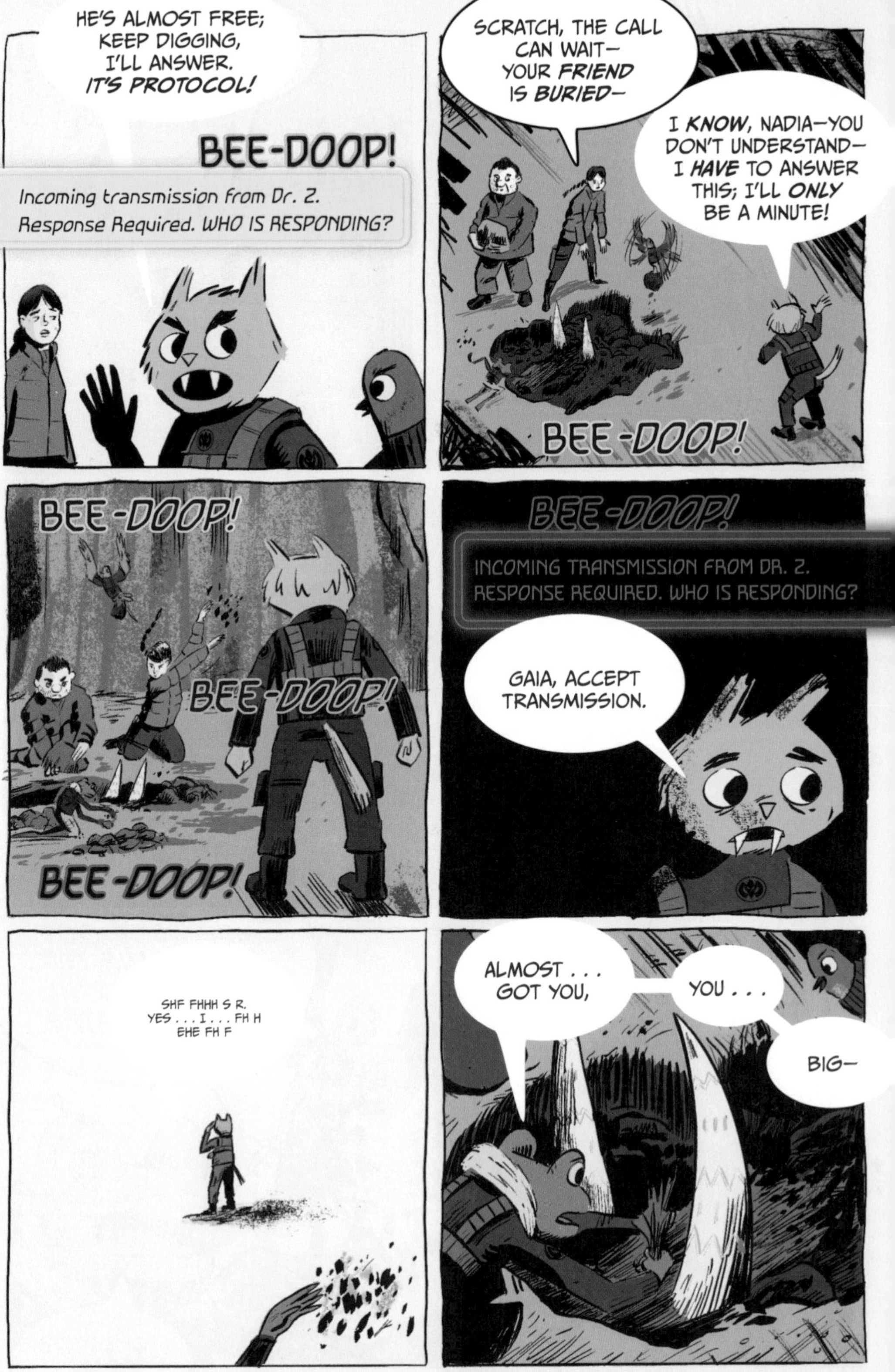
HE'S ALMOST FREE; KEEP DIGGING, I'LL ANSWER. IT'S PROTOCOL!
BEE-DOOP!
Incoming transmission from Dr. Z.
Response Required. WHO IS RESPONDING?
SCRATCH, THE CALL CAN WAIT— YOUR FRIEND IS BURIED—
I KNOW, NADIA—YOU DON'T UNDERSTAND— I HAVE TO ANSWER THIS; I'LL ONLY BE A MINUTE!
BEE-DOOP!
BEE-DOOP!
BEE-DOOP!
BEE-DOOP!
BEE-DOOP!
INCOMING TRANSMISSION FROM DR. Z.
RESPONSE REQUIRED. WHO IS RESPONDING?
GAIA, ACCEPT TRANSMISSION.
SHF FHHH S R.
YES . . . I . . . FH H
EHE FH F
ALMOST . . . GOT YOU,
YOU . . .
BIG—

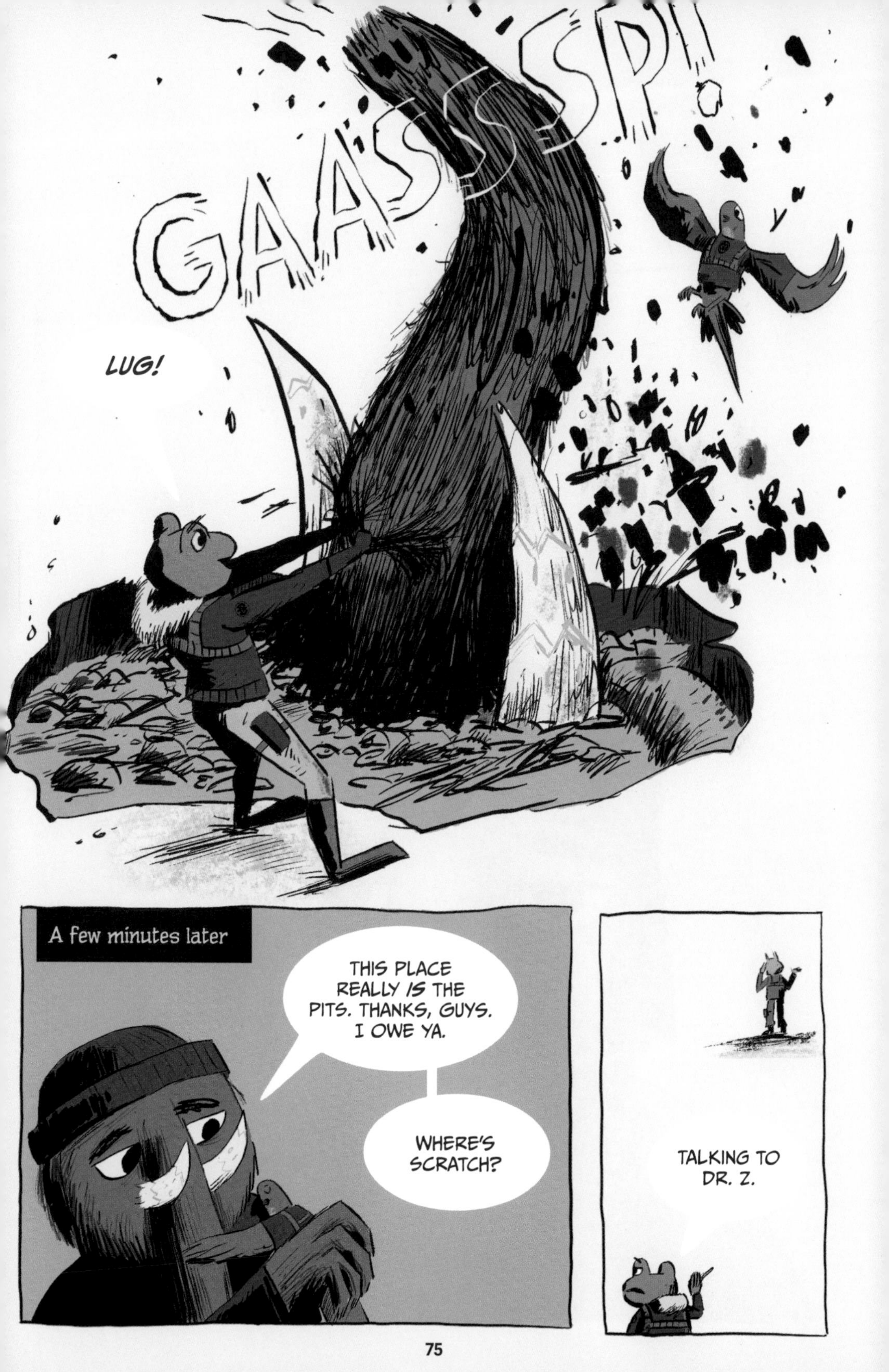
GAASSSP!!
LUG!
A few minutes later
THIS PLACE REALLY *IS* THE PITS. THANKS, GUYS. I OWE YA.
WHERE'S SCRATCH?
TALKING TO DR. Z.

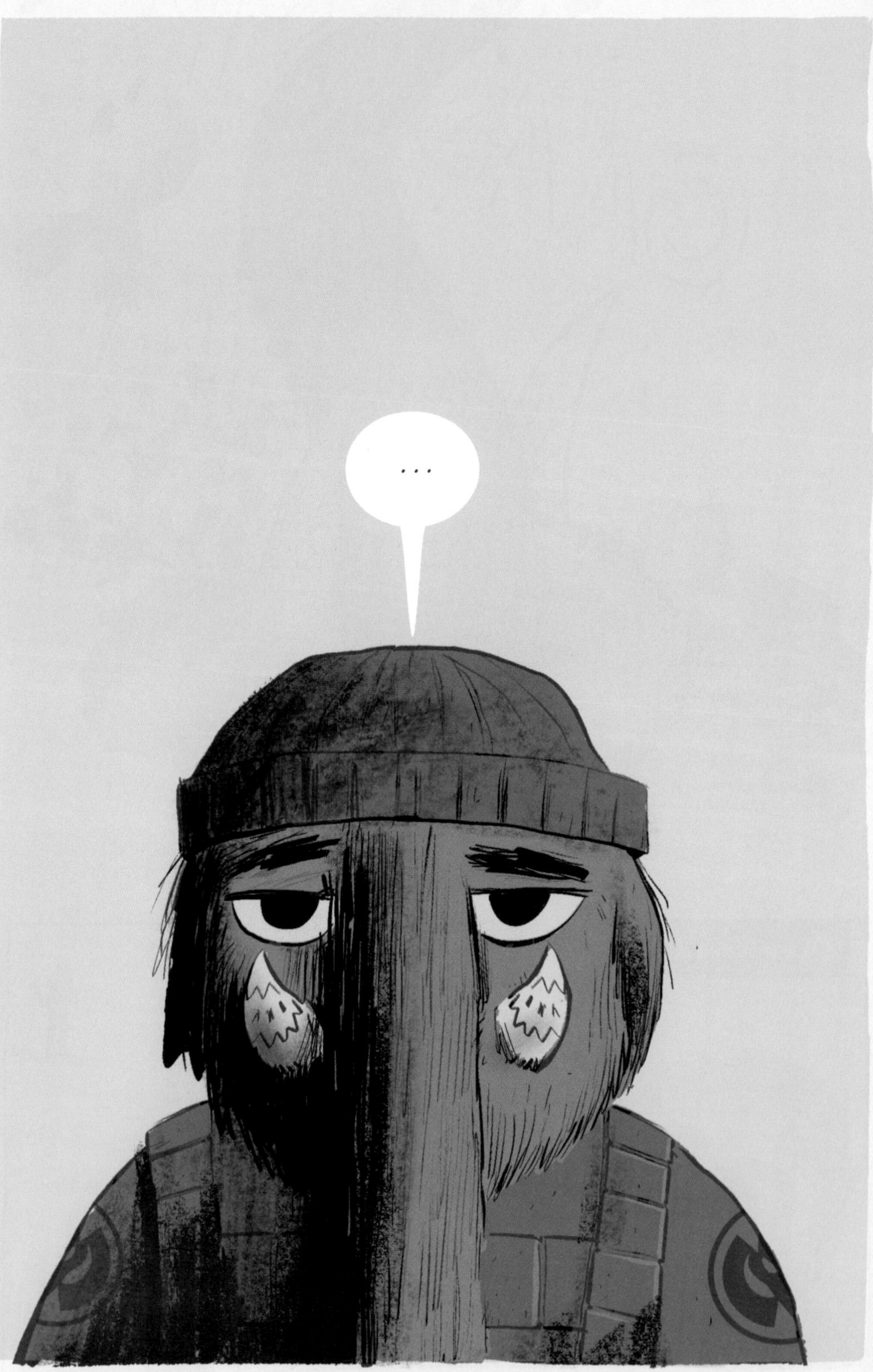
...

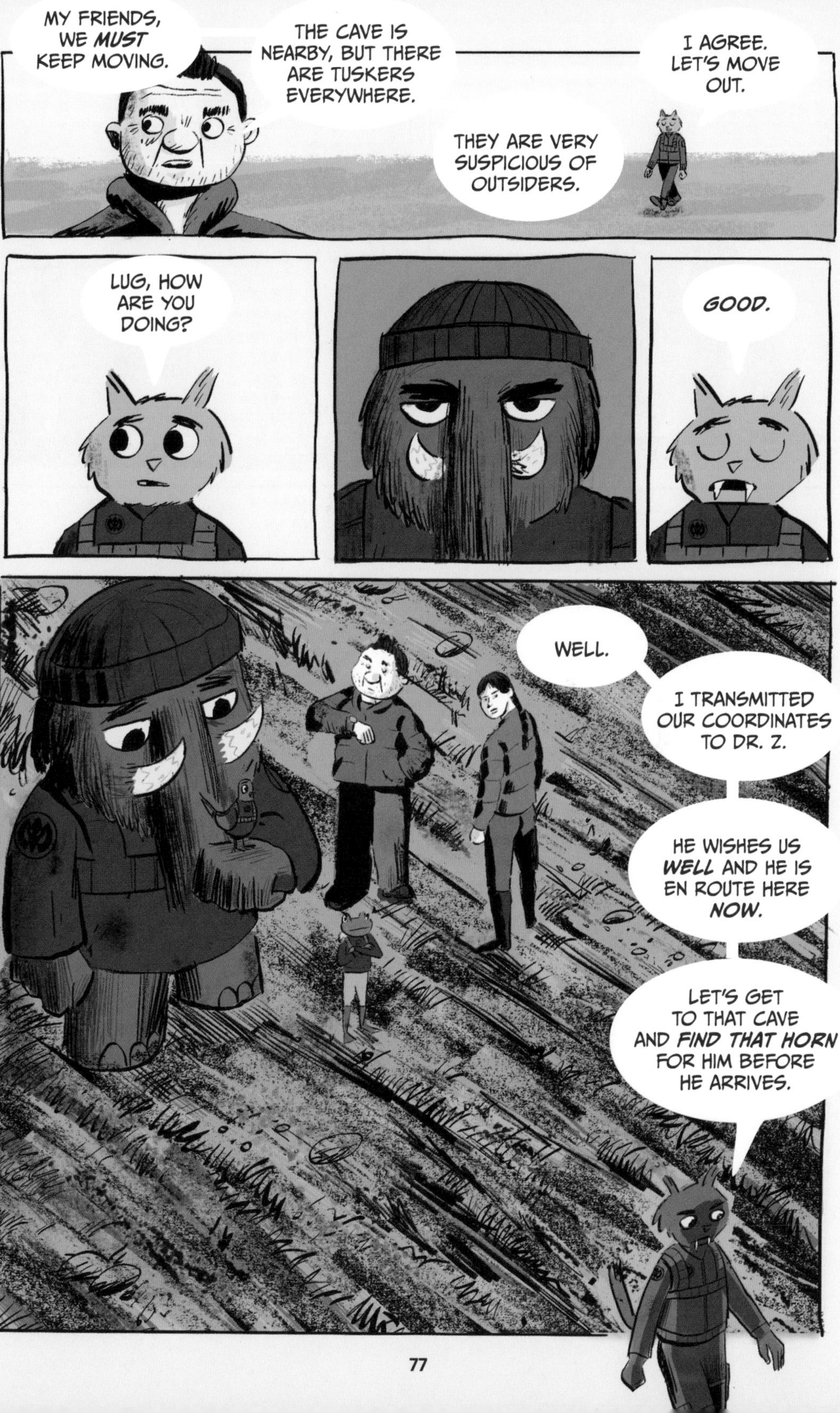
MY FRIENDS, WE *MUST* KEEP MOVING.
THE CAVE IS NEARBY, BUT THERE ARE TUSKERS EVERYWHERE.
THEY ARE VERY SUSPICIOUS OF OUTSIDERS.
I AGREE. LET'S MOVE OUT.
LUG, HOW ARE YOU DOING?
GOOD.
WELL.
I TRANSMITTED OUR COORDINATES TO DR. Z.
HE WISHES US *WELL* AND HE IS EN ROUTE HERE *NOW.*
LET'S GET TO THAT CAVE AND *FIND THAT HORN* FOR HIM BEFORE HE ARRIVES.

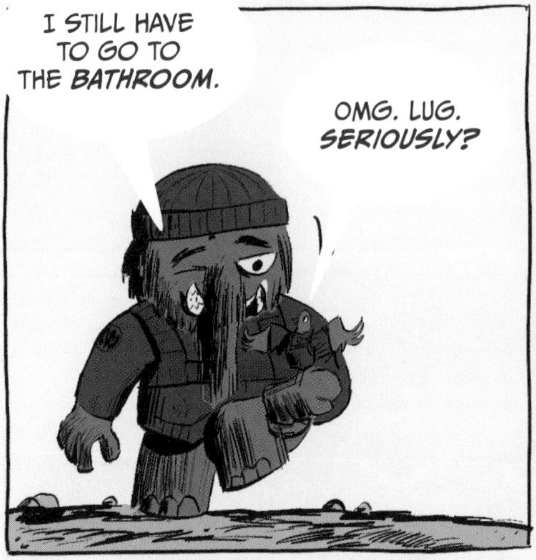
I STILL HAVE TO GO TO THE **BATHROOM**.
OMG. LUG. **SERIOUSLY?**

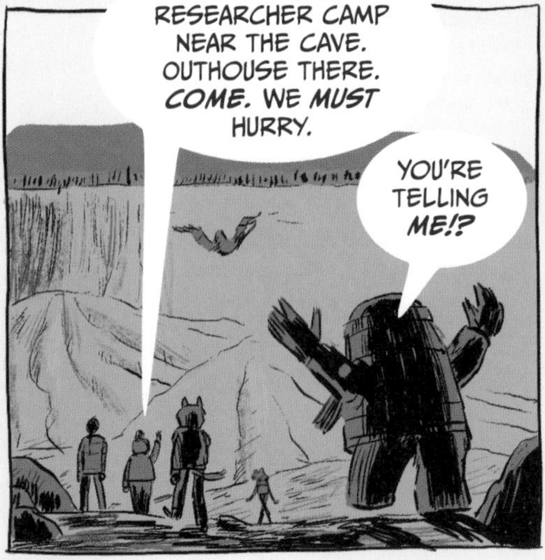
THERE IS A RESEARCHER CAMP NEAR THE CAVE. OUTHOUSE THERE. **COME**. WE **MUST** HURRY.
YOU'RE TELLING **ME!?**

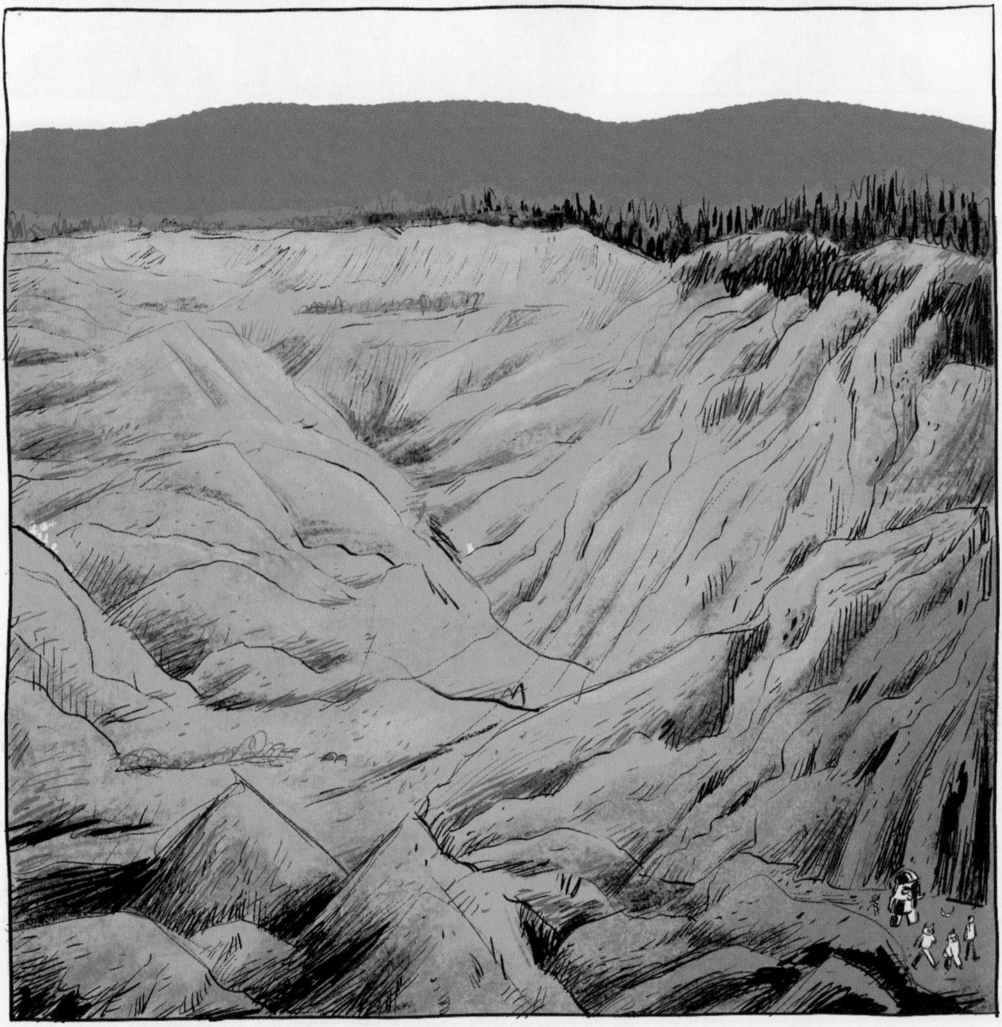

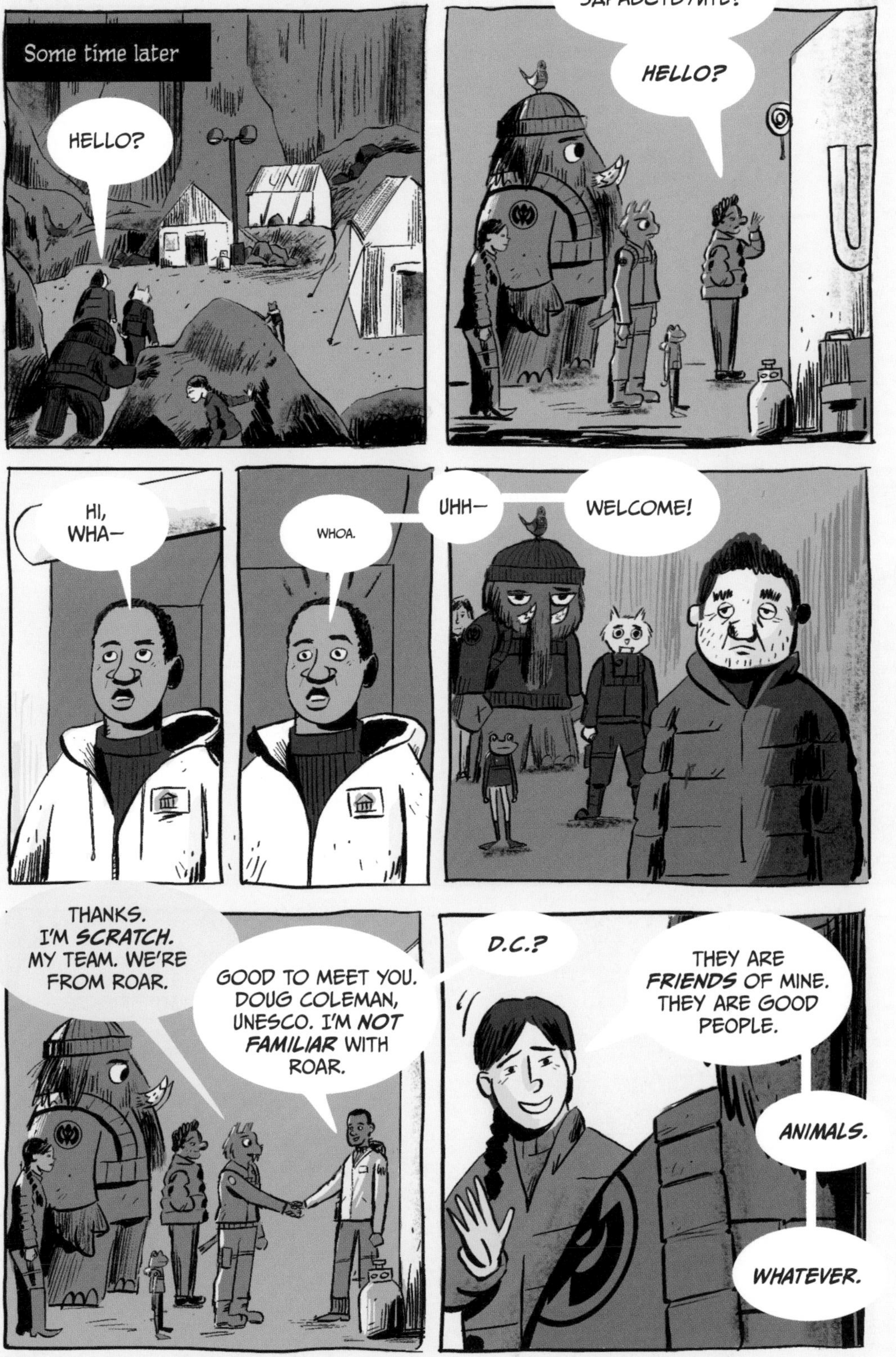
Some time later
HELLO?
ЗДРАВСТВУЙТЕ?*
HELLO?
HI, WHA—
WHOA.
UHH—
WELCOME!
THANKS. I'M SCRATCH. MY TEAM. WE'RE FROM ROAR.
GOOD TO MEET YOU. DOUG COLEMAN, UNESCO. I'M NOT FAMILIAR WITH ROAR.
D.C.?
THEY ARE FRIENDS OF MINE. THEY ARE GOOD PEOPLE.
ANIMALS.
WHATEVER.

*Translation: Hello?

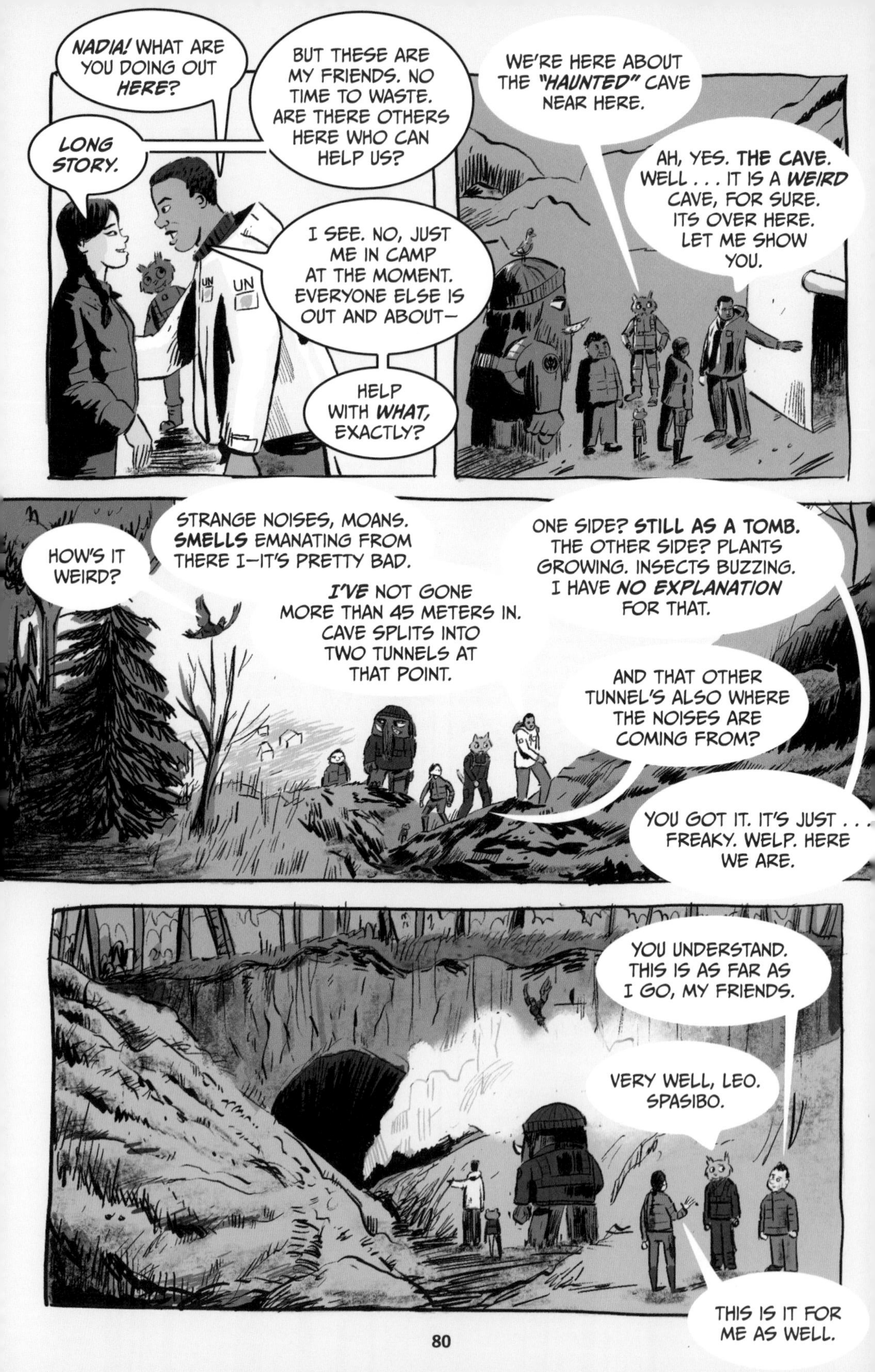
NADIA! WHAT ARE YOU DOING OUT HERE?
LONG STORY.
BUT THESE ARE MY FRIENDS. NO TIME TO WASTE. ARE THERE OTHERS HERE WHO CAN HELP US?
I SEE. NO, JUST ME IN CAMP AT THE MOMENT. EVERYONE ELSE IS OUT AND ABOUT—
HELP WITH WHAT, EXACTLY?
UN
UN
WE'RE HERE ABOUT THE "HAUNTED" CAVE NEAR HERE.
AH, YES. THE CAVE. WELL . . . IT IS A WEIRD CAVE, FOR SURE. ITS OVER HERE. LET ME SHOW YOU.
HOW'S IT WEIRD?
STRANGE NOISES, MOANS. SMELLS EMANATING FROM THERE I—IT'S PRETTY BAD.
I'VE NOT GONE MORE THAN 45 METERS IN. CAVE SPLITS INTO TWO TUNNELS AT THAT POINT.
ONE SIDE? STILL AS A TOMB. THE OTHER SIDE? PLANTS GROWING. INSECTS BUZZING. I HAVE NO EXPLANATION FOR THAT.
AND THAT OTHER TUNNEL'S ALSO WHERE THE NOISES ARE COMING FROM?
YOU GOT IT. IT'S JUST . . . FREAKY. WELP. HERE WE ARE.
YOU UNDERSTAND. THIS IS AS FAR AS I GO, MY FRIENDS.
VERY WELL, LEO. SPASIBO.
THIS IS IT FOR ME AS WELL.

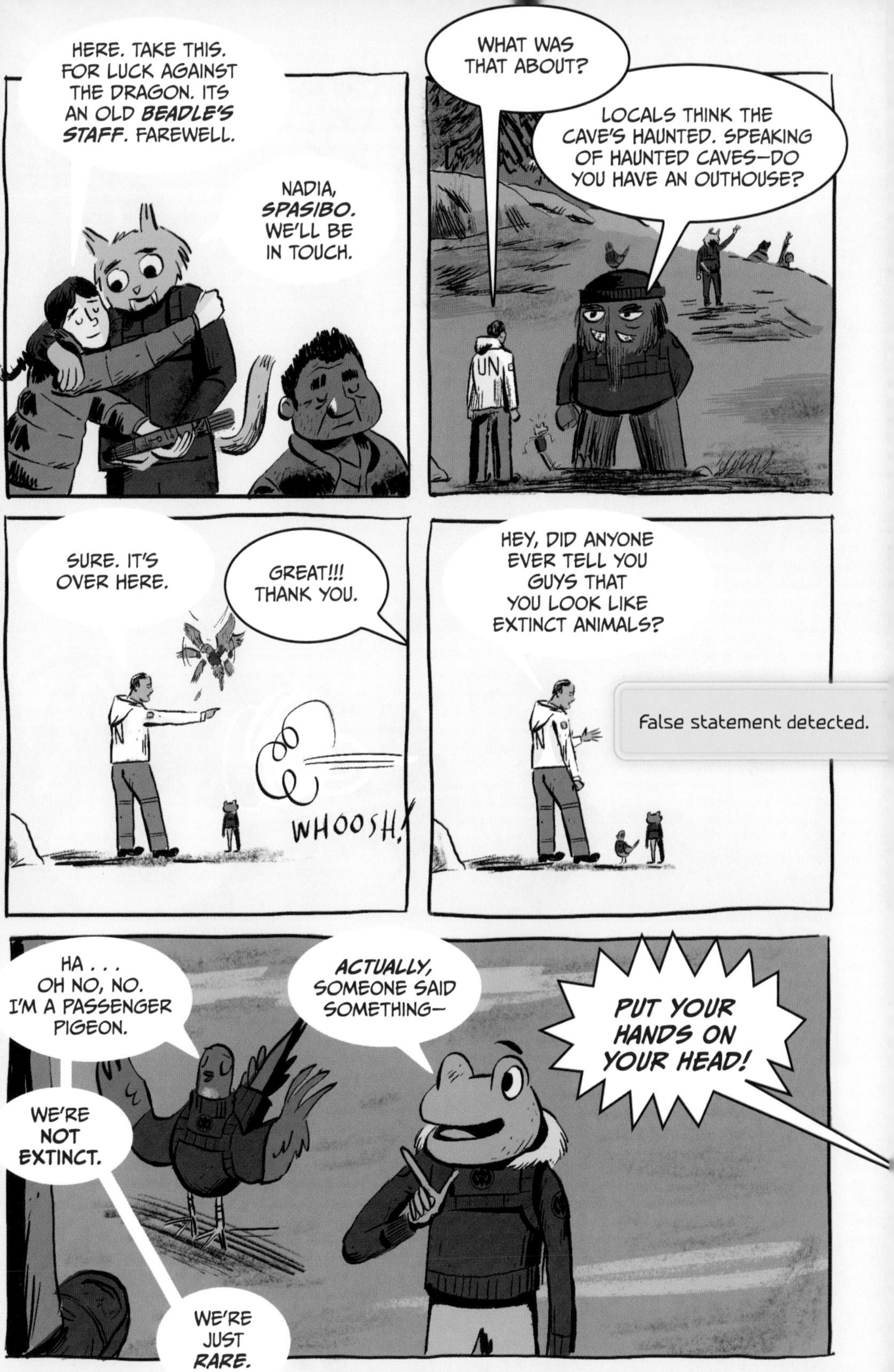

HERE. TAKE THIS. FOR LUCK AGAINST THE DRAGON. ITS AN OLD BEADLE'S STAFF. FAREWELL.
NADIA, SPASIBO. WE'LL BE IN TOUCH.
WHAT WAS THAT ABOUT?
LOCALS THINK THE CAVE'S HAUNTED. SPEAKING OF HAUNTED CAVES—DO YOU HAVE AN OUTHOUSE?
UN
SURE. IT'S OVER HERE.
GREAT!!! THANK YOU.
WHOOSH!
HEY, DID ANYONE EVER TELL YOU GUYS THAT YOU LOOK LIKE EXTINCT ANIMALS?
False statement detected.
HA . . . OH NO, NO. I'M A PASSENGER PIGEON.
WE'RE NOT EXTINCT.
WE'RE JUST RARE.
ACTUALLY, SOMEONE SAID SOMETHING—
PUT YOUR HANDS ON YOUR HEAD!

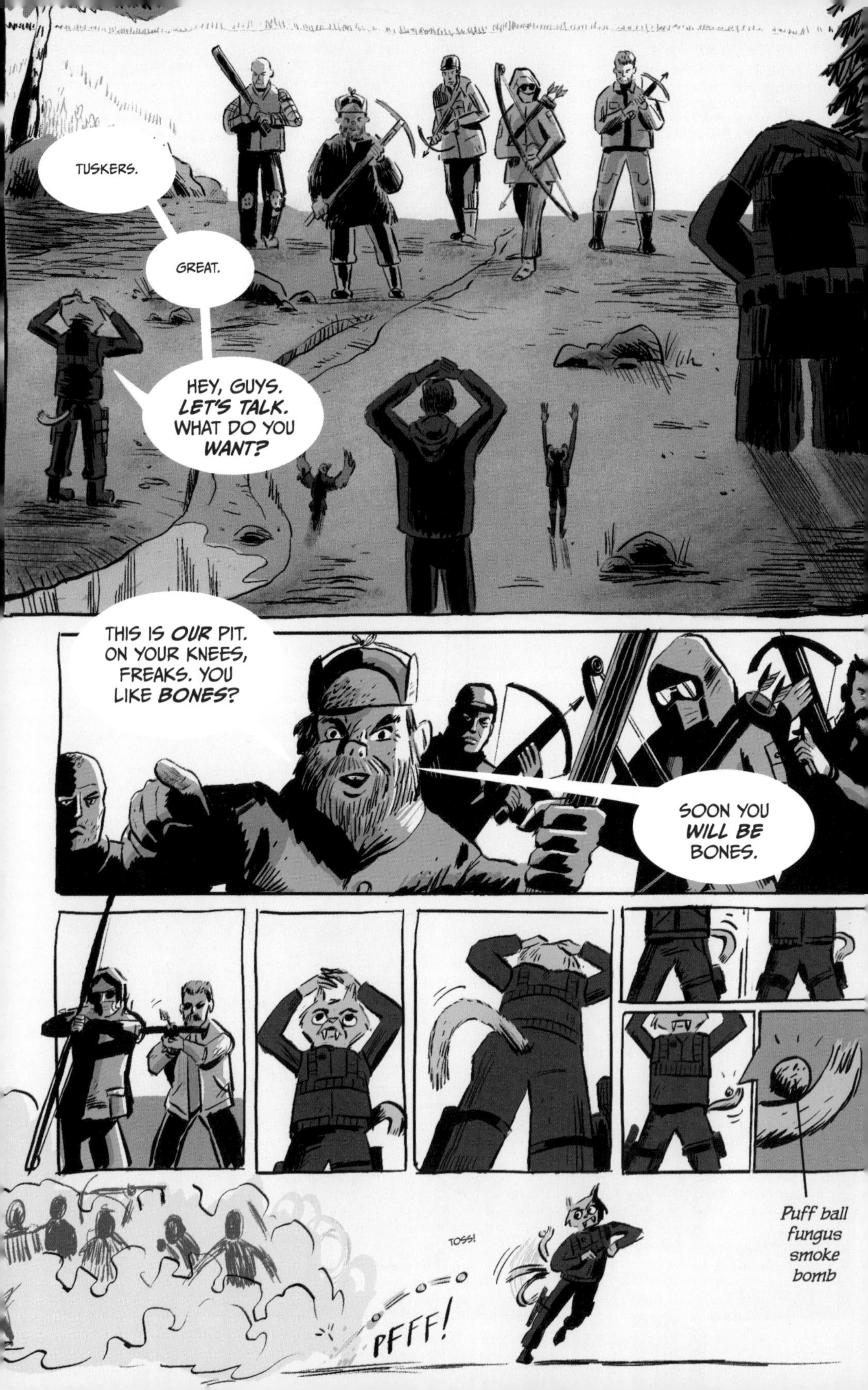
TUSKERS.
GREAT.
HEY, GUYS. LET'S TALK. WHAT DO YOU WANT?
THIS IS OUR PIT. ON YOUR KNEES, FREAKS. YOU LIKE BONES?
SOON YOU WILL BE BONES.
Puff ball fungus smoke bomb
TOSS!
PFFF!

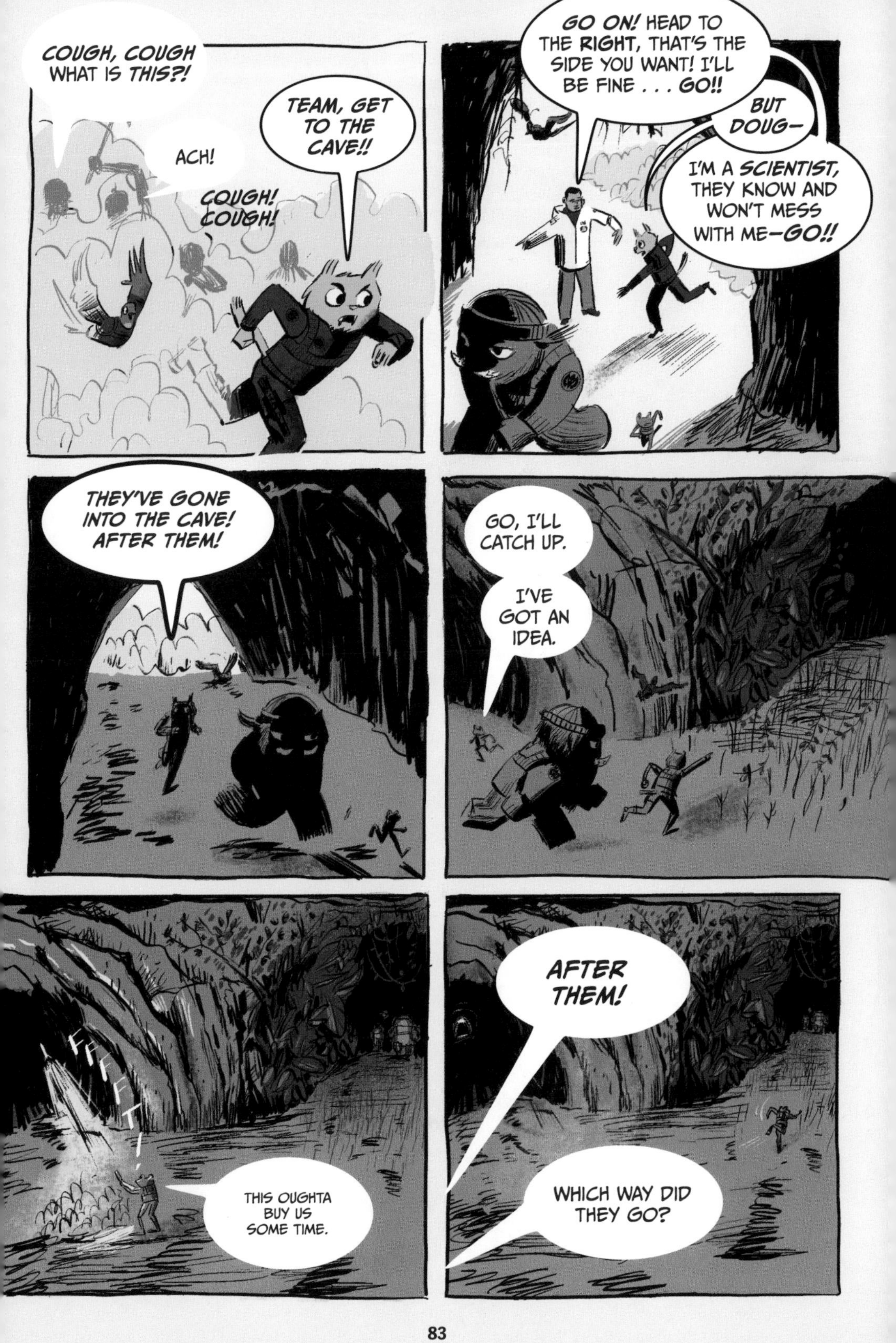
COUGH, COUGH WHAT IS THIS?!
ACH!
COUGH! COUGH!
TEAM, GET TO THE CAVE!!
GO ON! HEAD TO THE RIGHT, THAT'S THE SIDE YOU WANT! I'LL BE FINE . . . GO!!
BUT DOUG—
I'M A SCIENTIST, THEY KNOW AND WON'T MESS WITH ME—GO!!
THEY'VE GONE INTO THE CAVE! AFTER THEM!
GO, I'LL CATCH UP.
I'VE GOT AN IDEA.
FFFFT!
THIS OUGHTA BUY US SOME TIME.
AFTER THEM!
WHICH WAY DID THEY GO?

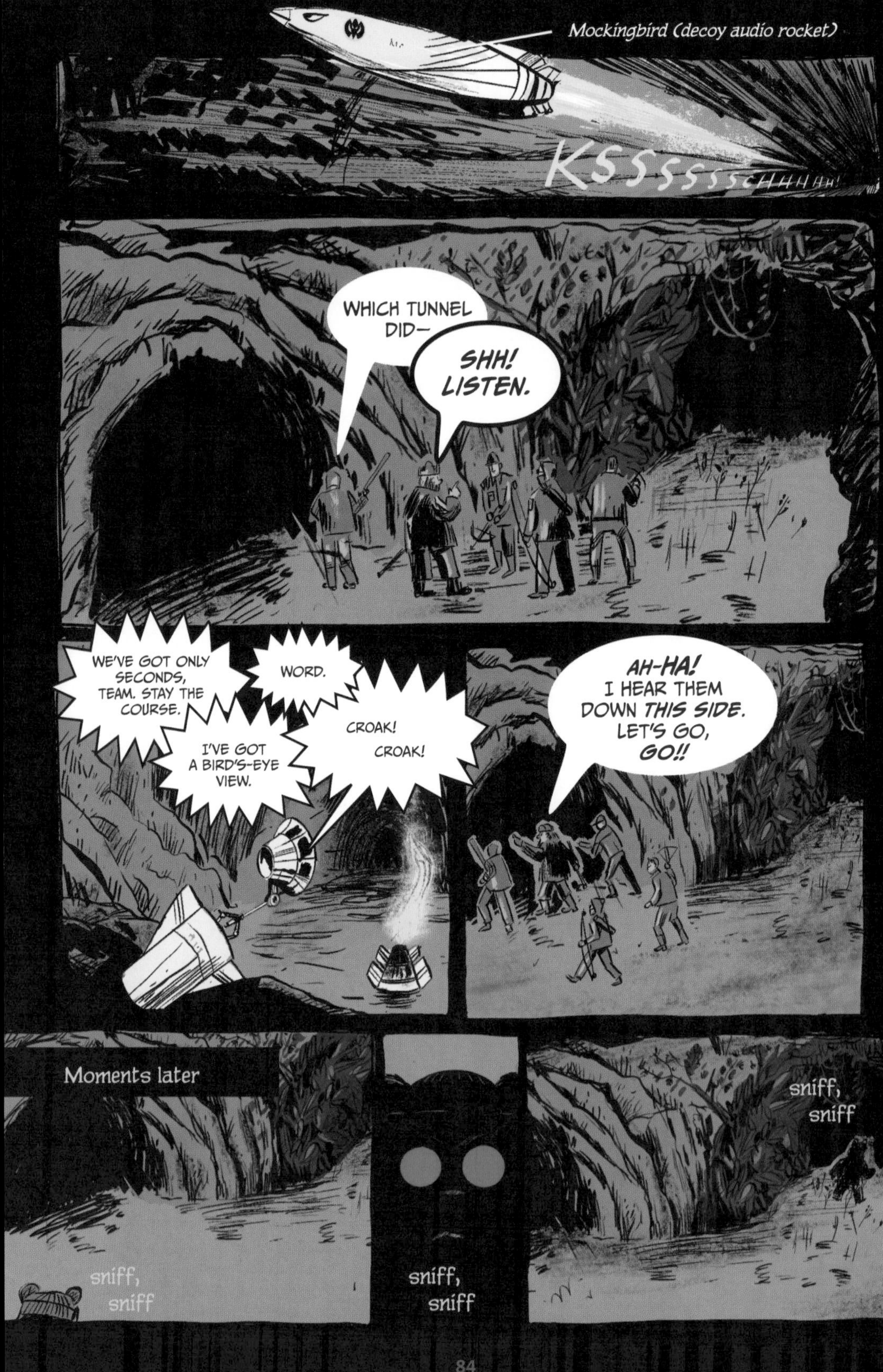
Mockingbird (decoy audio rocket)
KSSSSSSSCHHHHH!
WHICH TUNNEL DID—
SHH! LISTEN.
WE'VE GOT ONLY SECONDS, TEAM. STAY THE COURSE.
WORD.
I'VE GOT A BIRD'S-EYE VIEW.
CROAK!
CROAK!
AH-HA! I HEAR THEM DOWN THIS SIDE. LET'S GO, GO!!
Moments later
sniff, sniff
sniff, sniff
sniff, sniff

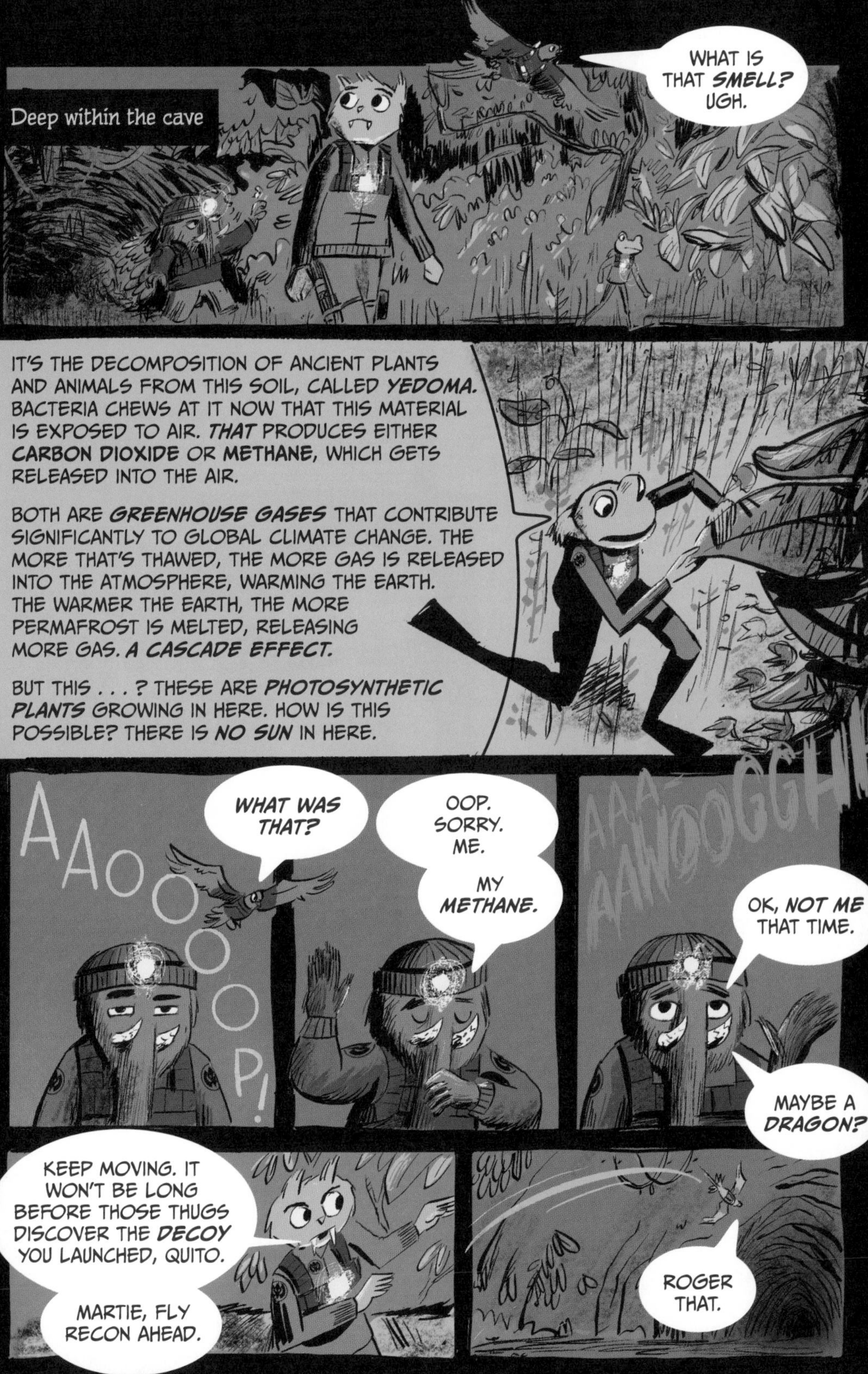
Deep within the cave
WHAT IS THAT SMELL? UGH.
IT'S THE DECOMPOSITION OF ANCIENT PLANTS AND ANIMALS FROM THIS SOIL, CALLED YEDOMA. BACTERIA CHEWS AT IT NOW THAT THIS MATERIAL IS EXPOSED TO AIR. THAT PRODUCES EITHER CARBON DIOXIDE OR METHANE, WHICH GETS RELEASED INTO THE AIR.
BOTH ARE GREENHOUSE GASES THAT CONTRIBUTE SIGNIFICANTLY TO GLOBAL CLIMATE CHANGE. THE MORE THAT'S THAWED, THE MORE GAS IS RELEASED INTO THE ATMOSPHERE, WARMING THE EARTH. THE WARMER THE EARTH, THE MORE PERMAFROST IS MELTED, RELEASING MORE GAS. A CASCADE EFFECT.
BUT THIS . . . ? THESE ARE PHOTOSYNTHETIC PLANTS GROWING IN HERE. HOW IS THIS POSSIBLE? THERE IS NO SUN IN HERE.
AAOOOOOP!
WHAT WAS THAT?
OOP. SORRY. ME.
MY METHANE.
AAA-AAWOOGGHH
OK, NOT ME THAT TIME.
MAYBE A DRAGON?
KEEP MOVING. IT WON'T BE LONG BEFORE THOSE THUGS DISCOVER THE DECOY YOU LAUNCHED, QUITO.
MARTIE, FLY RECON AHEAD.
ROGER THAT.

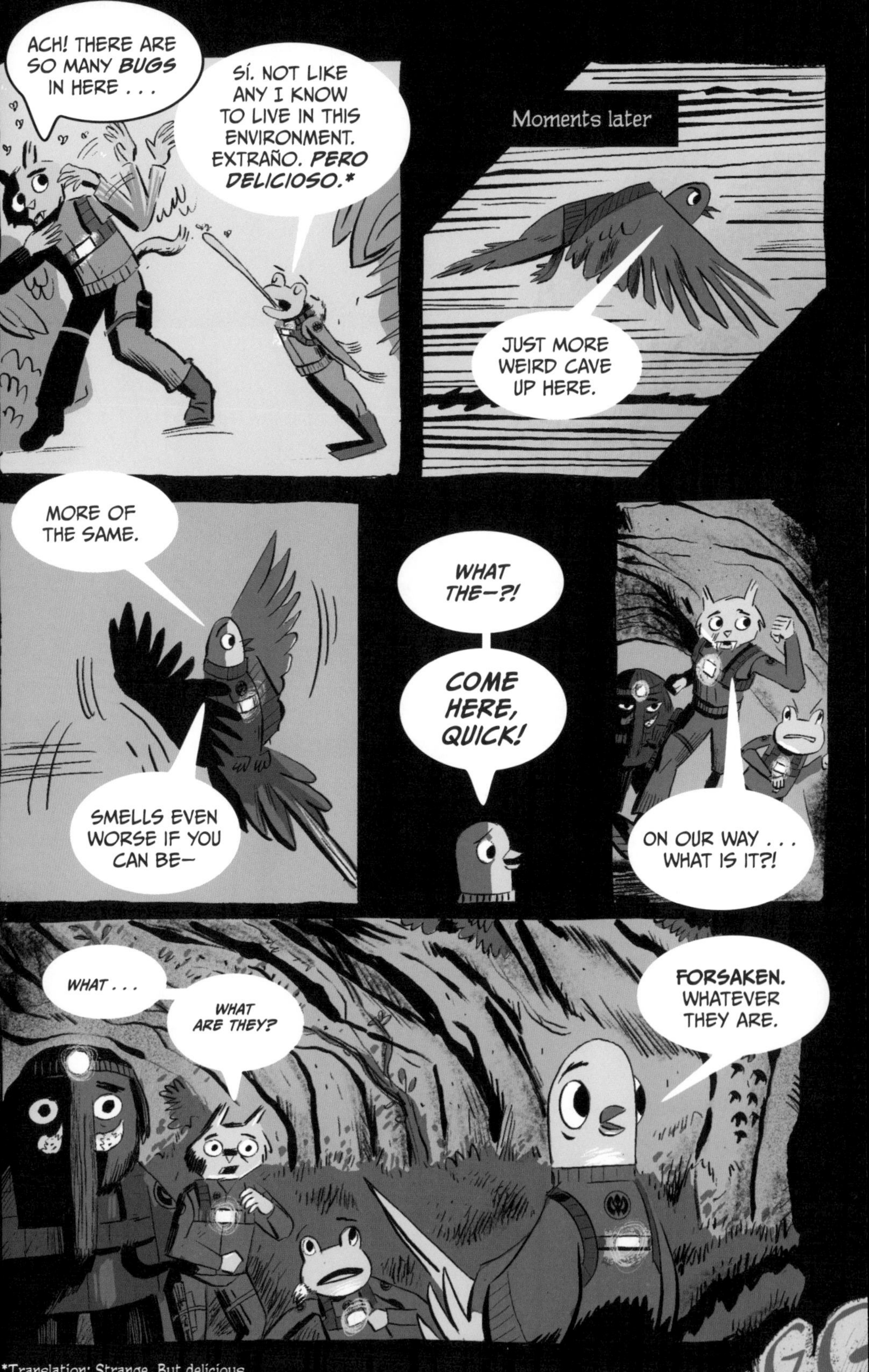
ACH! THERE ARE SO MANY BUGS IN HERE . . .
SÍ. NOT LIKE ANY I KNOW TO LIVE IN THIS ENVIRONMENT. EXTRAÑO. PERO DELICIOSO.*
Moments later
JUST MORE WEIRD CAVE UP HERE.
MORE OF THE SAME.
SMELLS EVEN WORSE IF YOU CAN BE—
WHAT THE—?!
COME HERE, QUICK!
ON OUR WAY . . . WHAT IS IT?!
WHAT . . .
WHAT ARE THEY?
FORSAKEN. WHATEVER THEY ARE.

*Translation: Strange. But delicious.

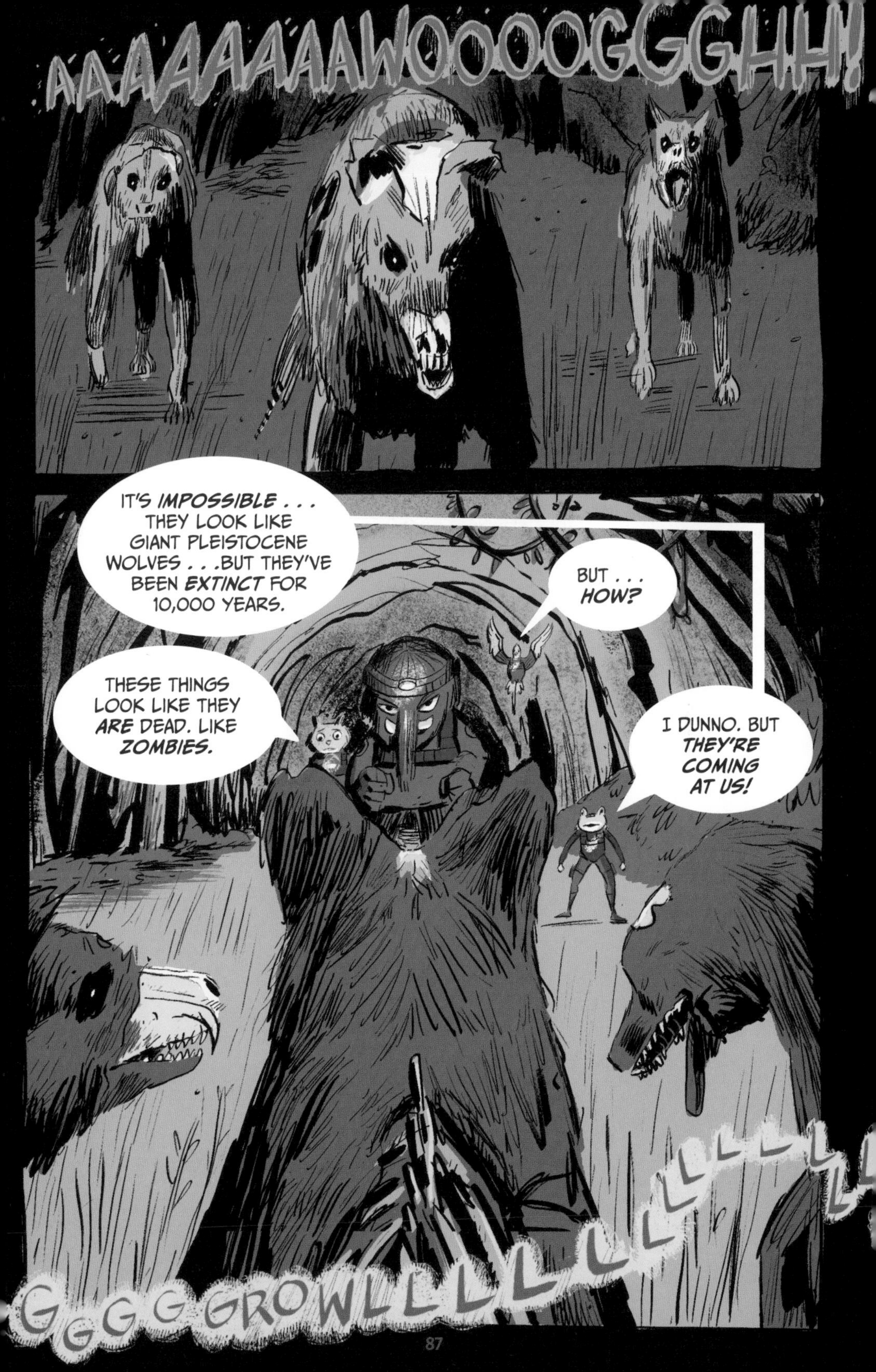
AAAAAAAAWOOOOGGGHH!
IT'S *IMPOSSIBLE* . . . THEY LOOK LIKE GIANT PLEISTOCENE WOLVES . . .BUT THEY'VE BEEN *EXTINCT* FOR 10,000 YEARS.
BUT . . . *HOW?*
THESE THINGS LOOK LIKE THEY *ARE* DEAD. LIKE *ZOMBIES.*
I DUNNO. BUT *THEY'RE COMING AT US!*
GGGGGROWLLLLLLLLLLLLLLLL

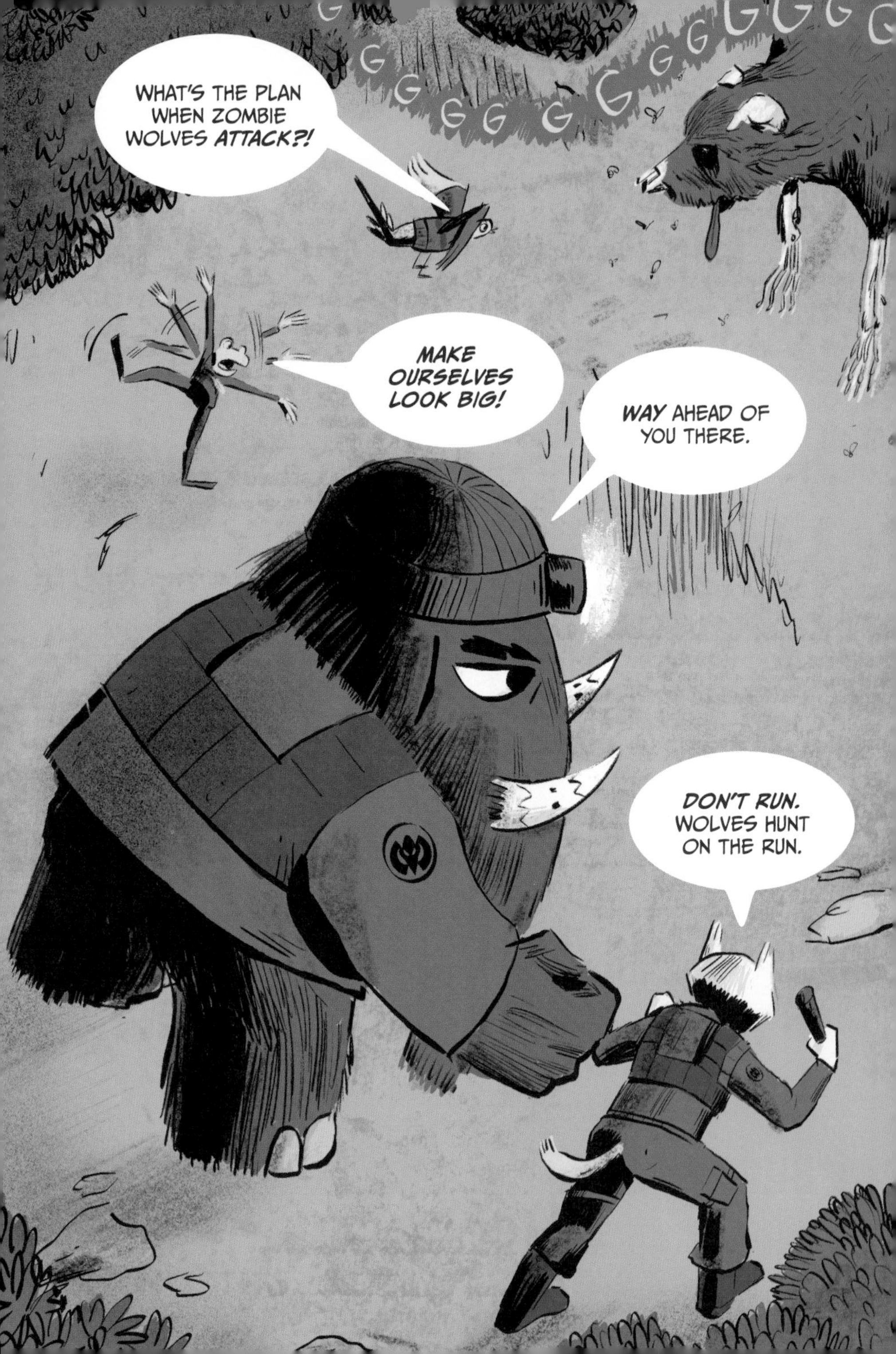
GGGGGGGGGGGGGG
WHAT'S THE PLAN WHEN ZOMBIE WOLVES ATTACK?!
MAKE OURSELVES LOOK BIG!
WAY AHEAD OF YOU THERE.
DON'T RUN. WOLVES HUNT ON THE RUN.

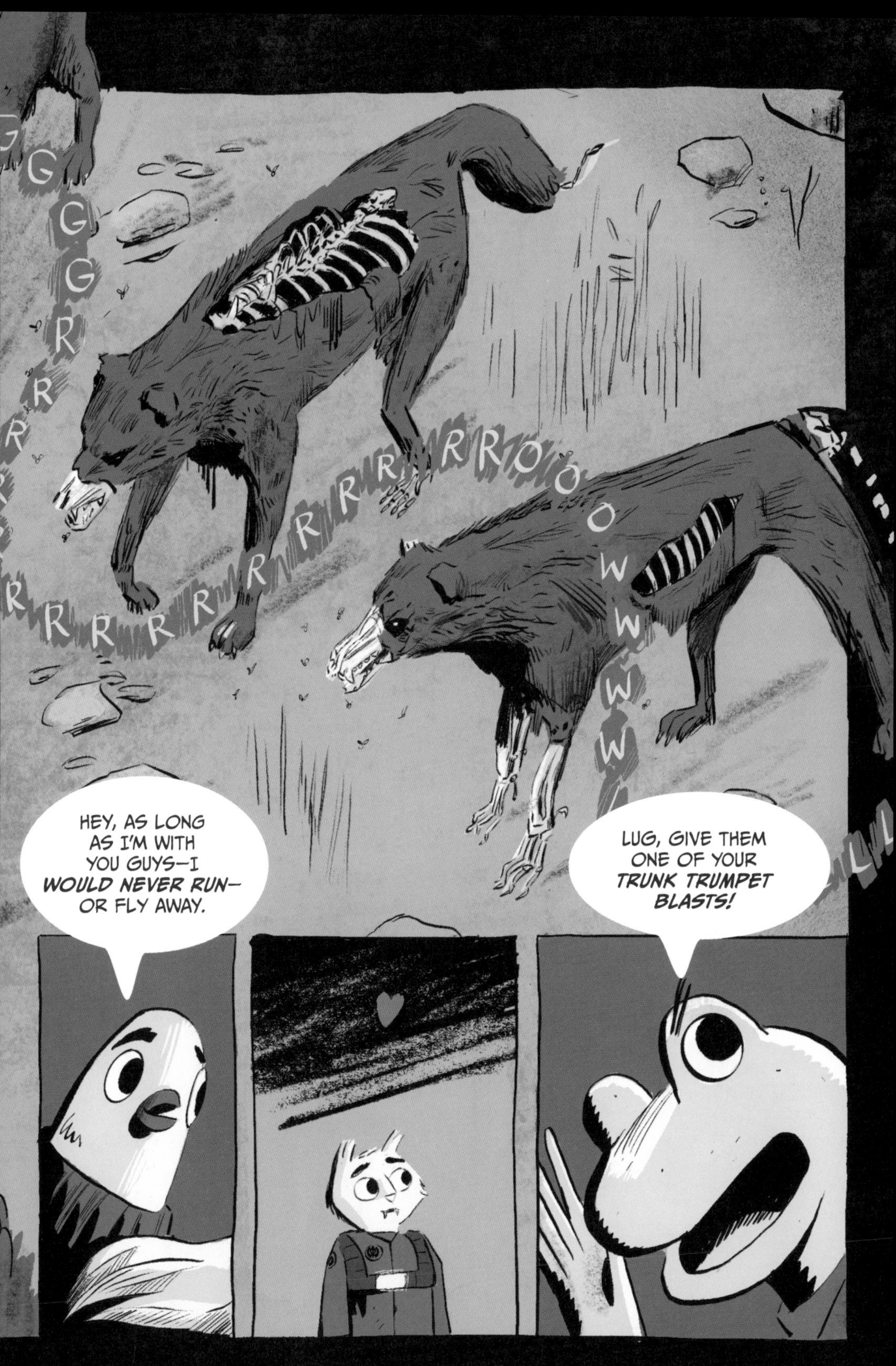
GGGRRRRRRRRRRRRRRRRRROOOWWWWWW
HEY, AS LONG AS I'M WITH YOU GUYS—I ***WOULD NEVER RUN***—OR FLY AWAY.
LUG, GIVE THEM ONE OF YOUR ***TRUNK TRUMPET BLASTS!***

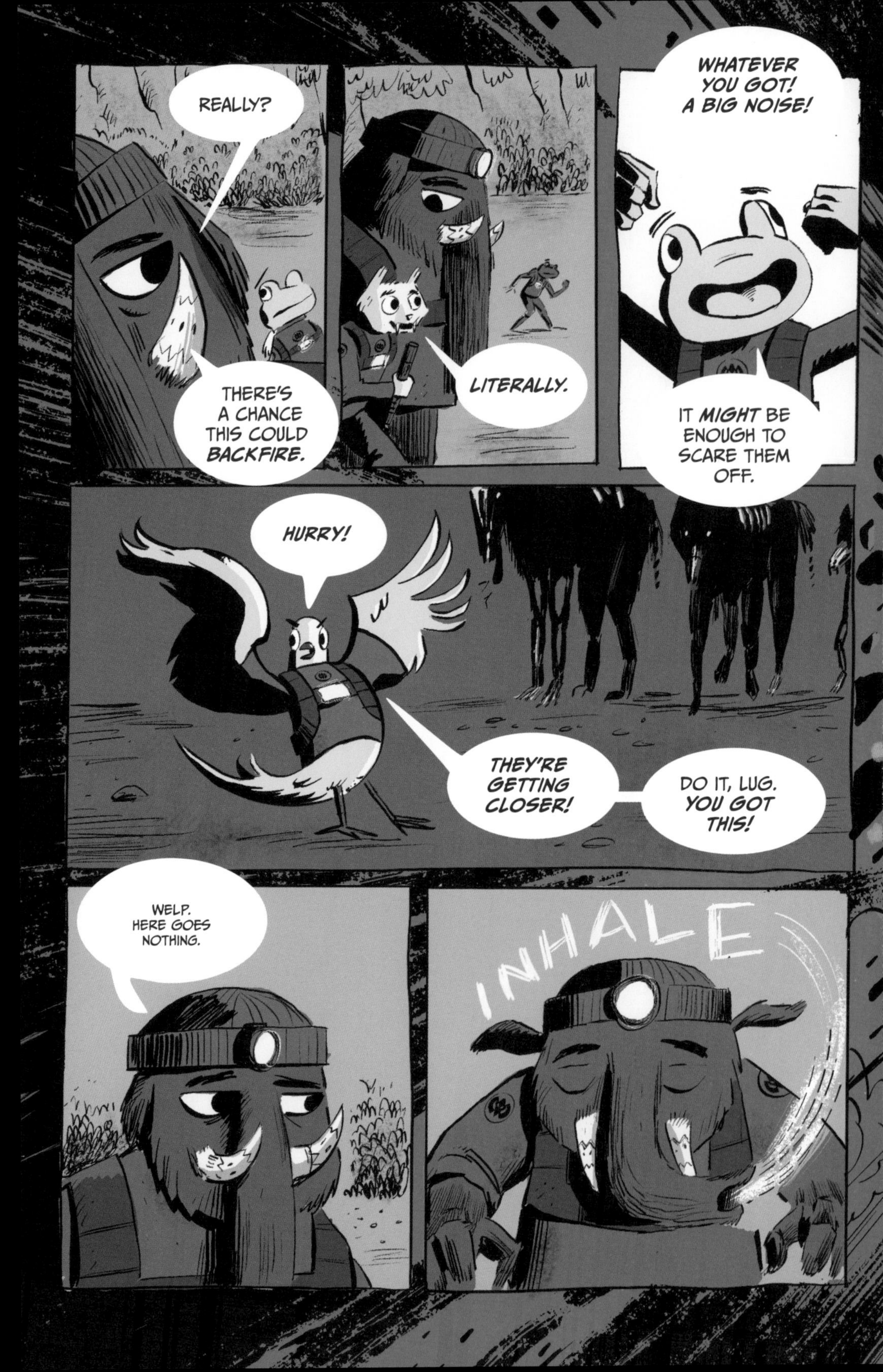
REALLY?
THERE'S A CHANCE THIS COULD BACKFIRE.
LITERALLY.
WHATEVER YOU GOT! A BIG NOISE!
IT MIGHT BE ENOUGH TO SCARE THEM OFF.
HURRY!
THEY'RE GETTING CLOSER!
DO IT, LUG. YOU GOT THIS!
WELP. HERE GOES NOTHING.
INHALE

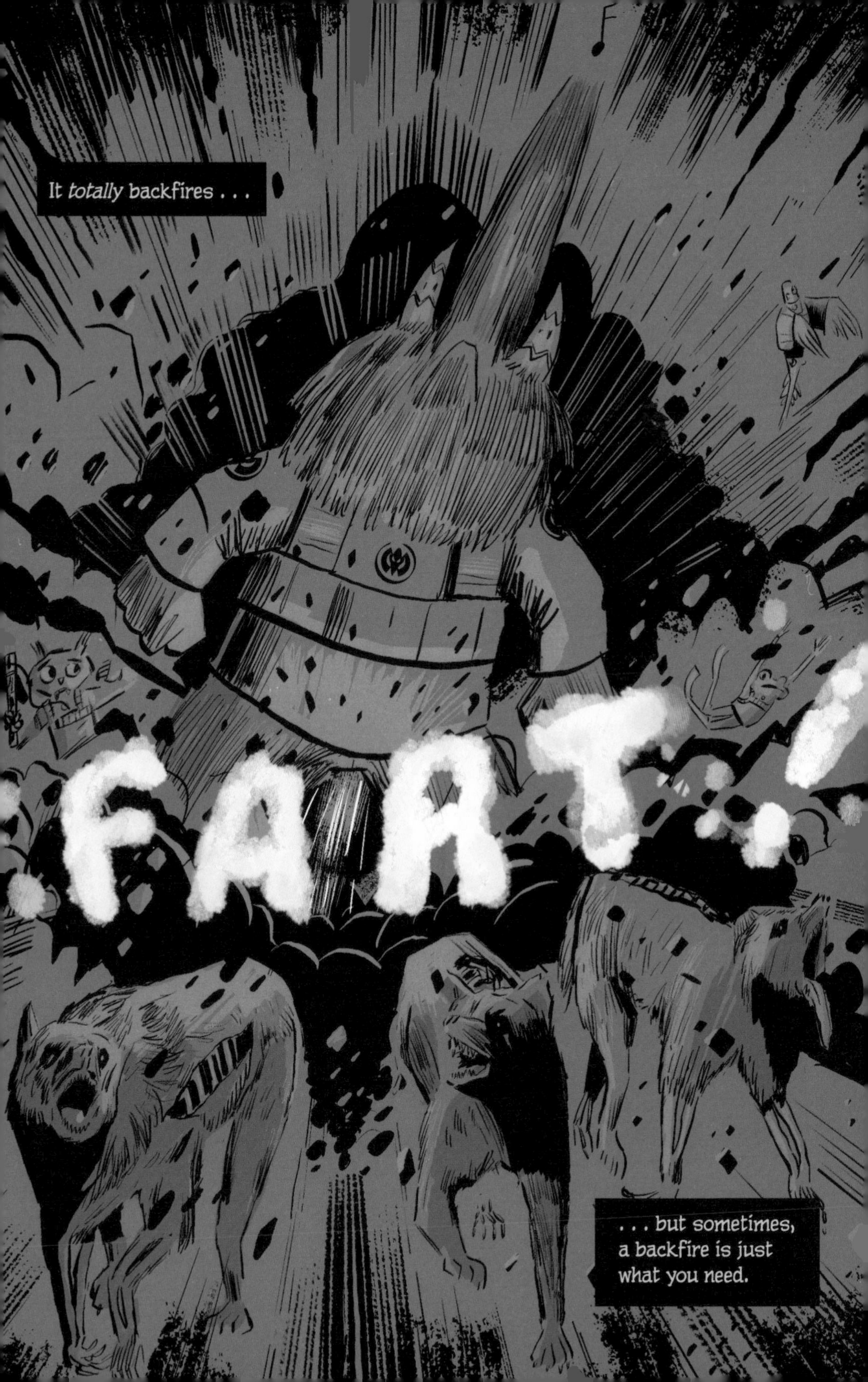
It *totally* backfires . . .
FART!
. . . but sometimes, a backfire is just what you need.

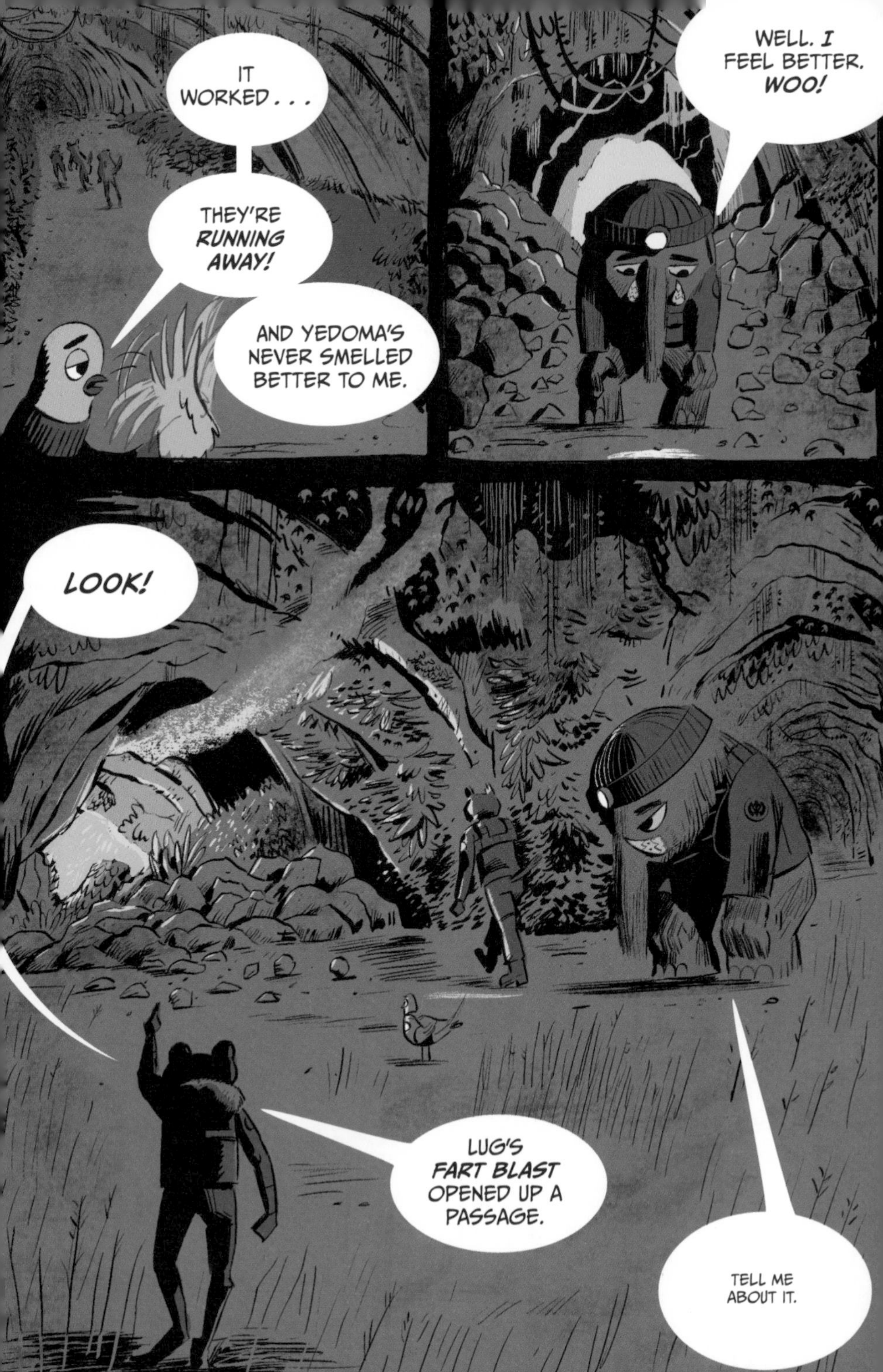
IT WORKED . . .
THEY'RE RUNNING AWAY!
AND YEDOMA'S NEVER SMELLED BETTER TO ME.
WELL. I FEEL BETTER. WOO!
LOOK!
LUG'S FART BLAST OPENED UP A PASSAGE.
TELL ME ABOUT IT.

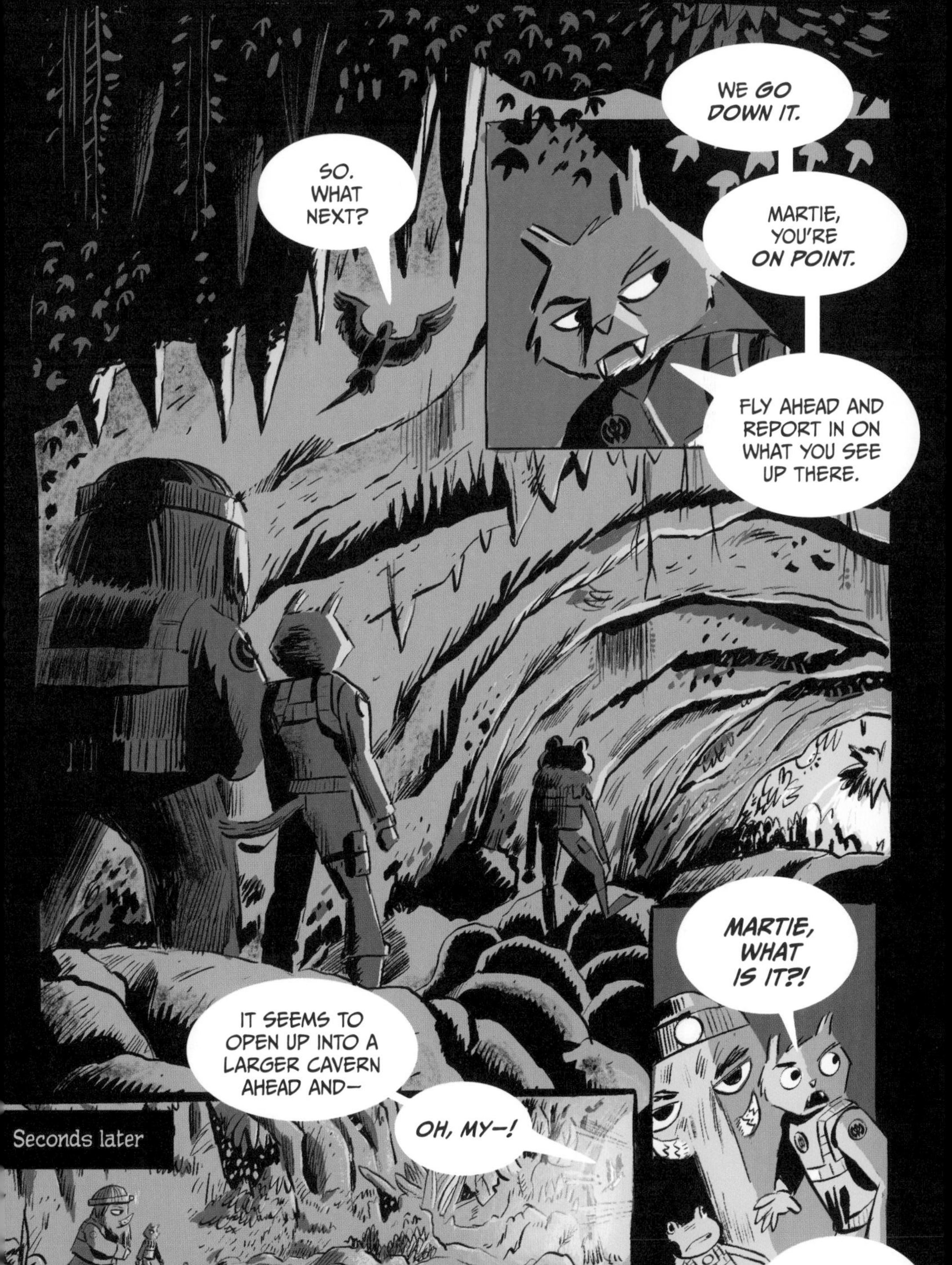
SO. WHAT NEXT?
WE GO DOWN IT.
MARTIE, YOU'RE ON POINT.
FLY AHEAD AND REPORT IN ON WHAT YOU SEE UP THERE.
IT SEEMS TO OPEN UP INTO A LARGER CAVERN AHEAD AND—
Seconds later
OH, MY—!
MARTIE, WHAT IS IT?!
IT CAN'T BE— CAN IT?

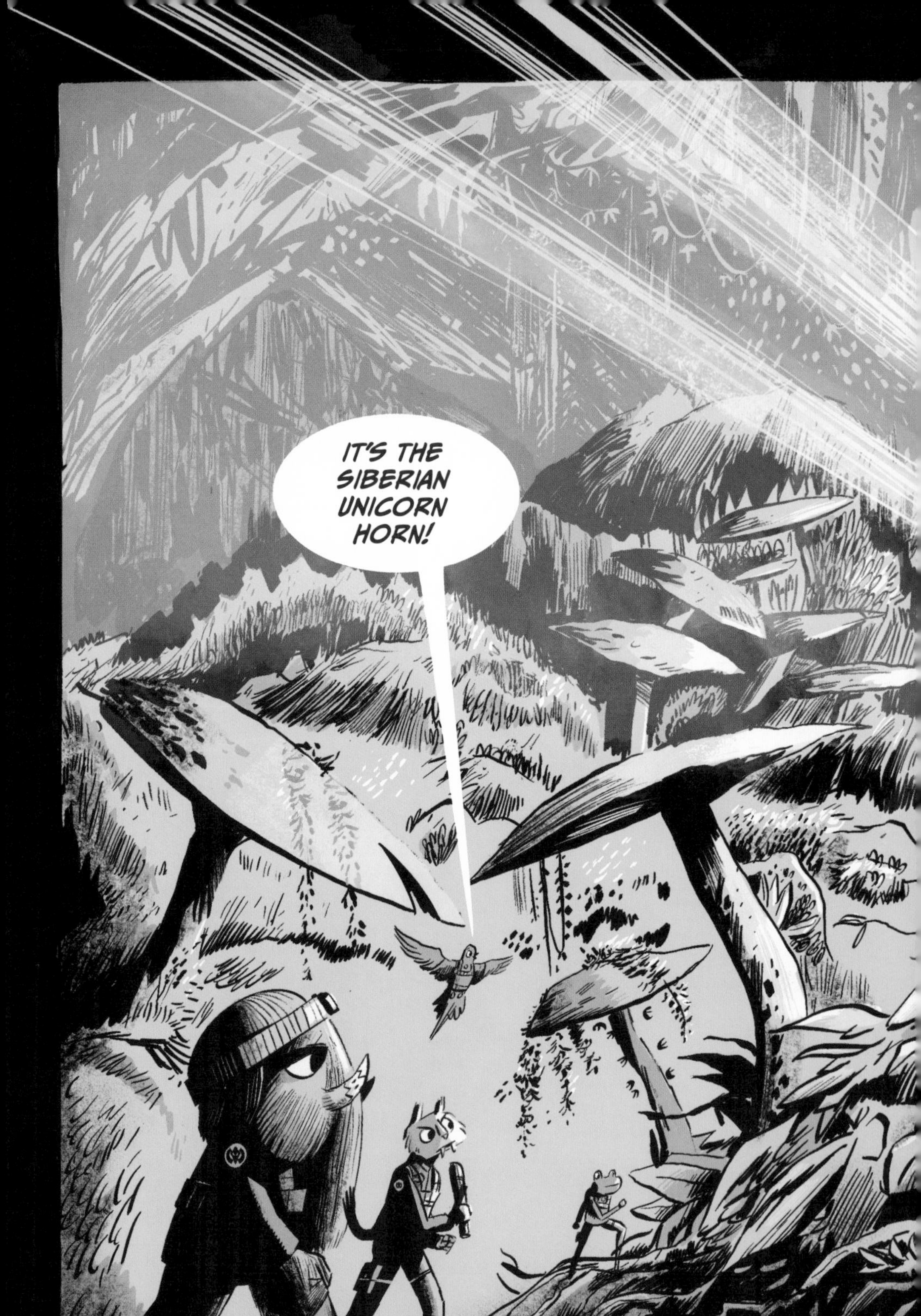
IT'S THE SIBERIAN UNICORN HORN!

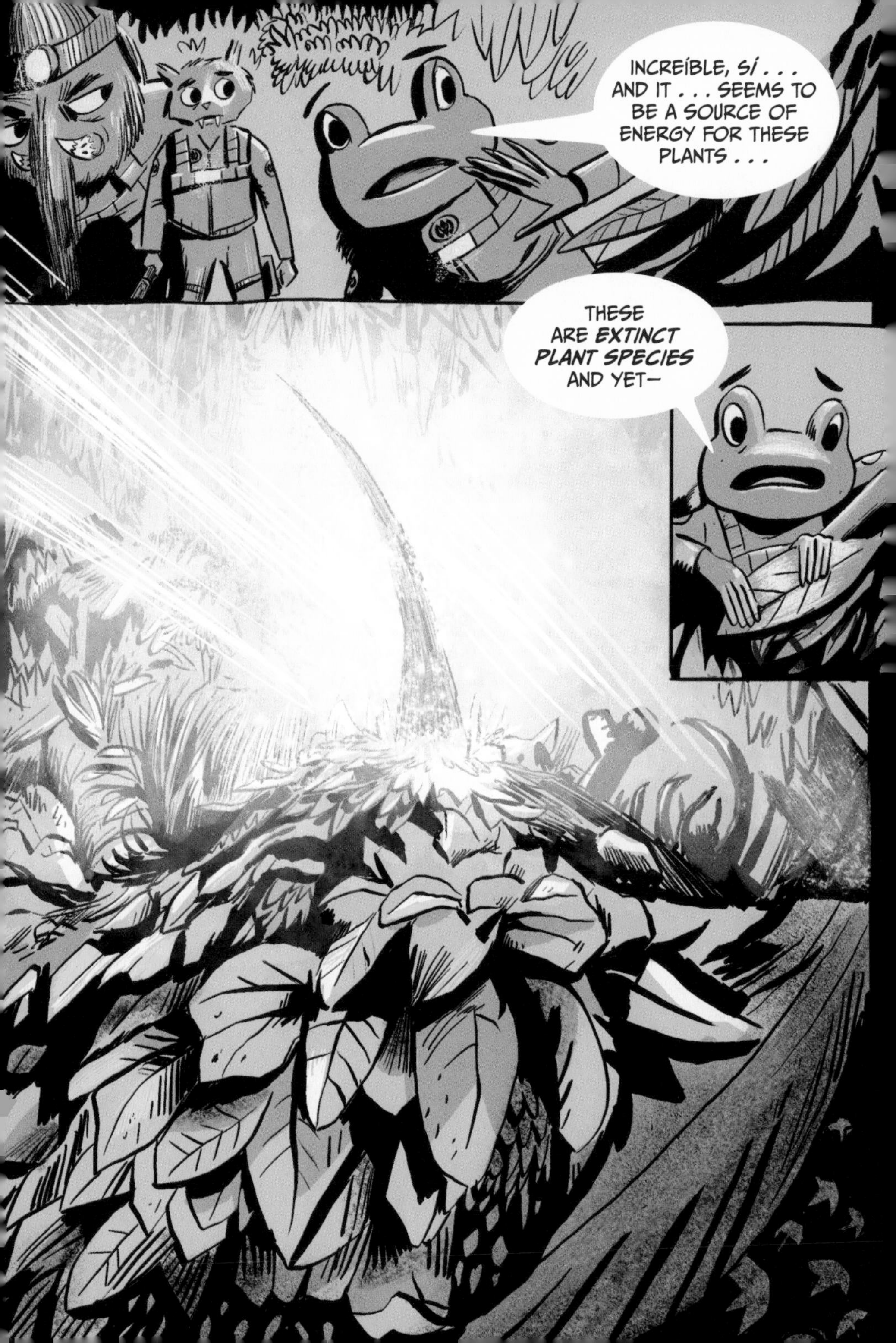
INCREÍBLE, SÍ . . . AND IT . . . SEEMS TO BE A SOURCE OF ENERGY FOR THESE PLANTS . . .
THESE ARE *EXTINCT PLANT SPECIES* AND YET—

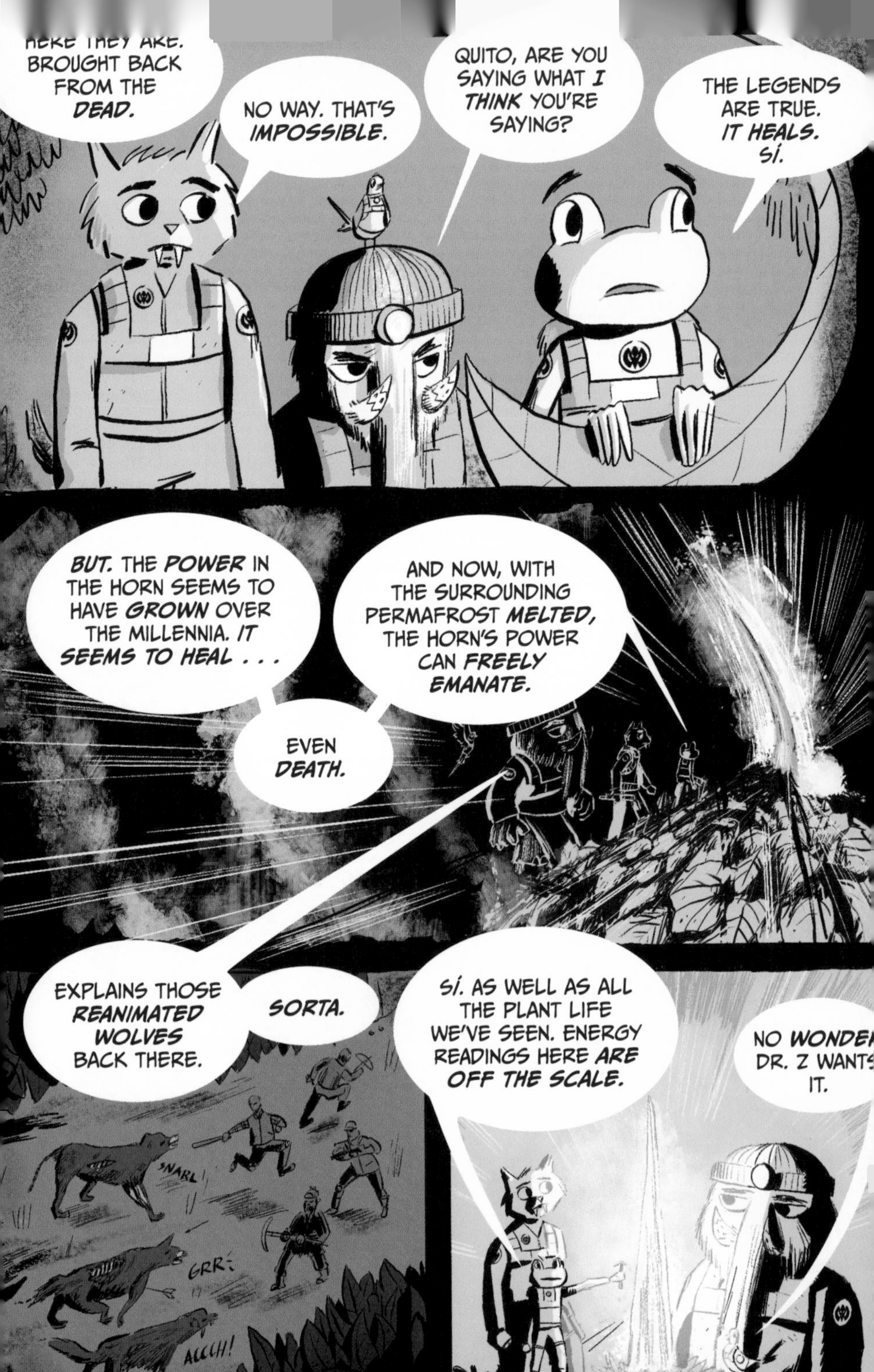
HERE THEY ARE. BROUGHT BACK FROM THE DEAD.
NO WAY. THAT'S IMPOSSIBLE.
QUITO, ARE YOU SAYING WHAT I THINK YOU'RE SAYING?
THE LEGENDS ARE TRUE. IT HEALS. SÍ.
BUT. THE POWER IN THE HORN SEEMS TO HAVE GROWN OVER THE MILLENNIA. IT SEEMS TO HEAL . . .
EVEN DEATH.
AND NOW, WITH THE SURROUNDING PERMAFROST MELTED, THE HORN'S POWER CAN FREELY EMANATE.
EXPLAINS THOSE REANIMATED WOLVES BACK THERE.
SORTA.
SNARL
GRR
ACCCH!
SÍ. AS WELL AS ALL THE PLANT LIFE WE'VE SEEN. ENERGY READINGS HERE ARE OFF THE SCALE.
NO WONDE DR. Z WANTS IT.

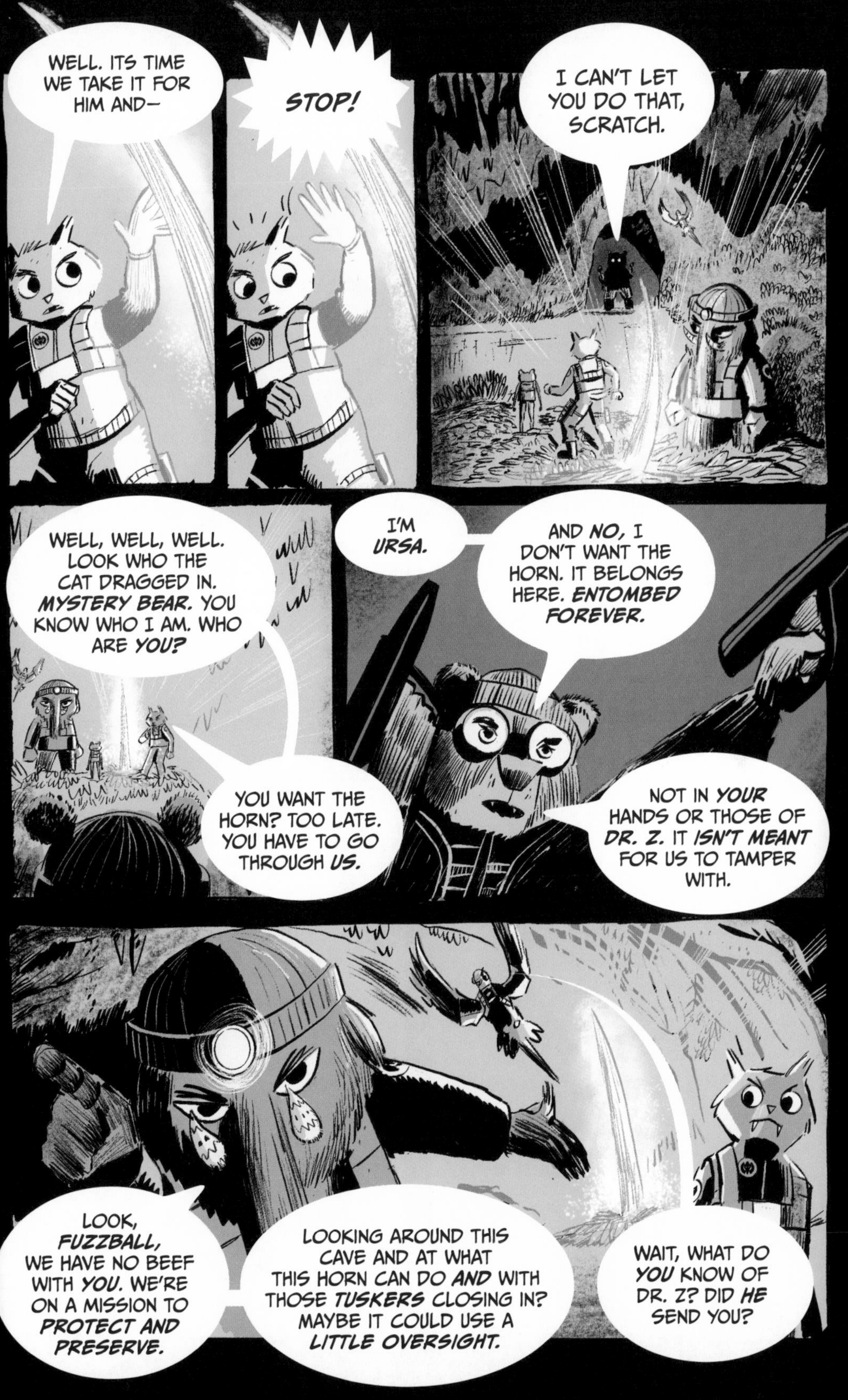
WELL. ITS TIME WE TAKE IT FOR HIM AND—
STOP!
I CAN'T LET YOU DO THAT, SCRATCH.
WELL, WELL, WELL. LOOK WHO THE CAT DRAGGED IN. MYSTERY BEAR. YOU KNOW WHO I AM. WHO ARE YOU?
YOU WANT THE HORN? TOO LATE. YOU HAVE TO GO THROUGH US.
I'M URSA.
AND NO, I DON'T WANT THE HORN. IT BELONGS HERE. ENTOMBED FOREVER.
NOT IN YOUR HANDS OR THOSE OF DR. Z. IT ISN'T MEANT FOR US TO TAMPER WITH.
LOOK, FUZZBALL, WE HAVE NO BEEF WITH YOU. WE'RE ON A MISSION TO PROTECT AND PRESERVE.
LOOKING AROUND THIS CAVE AND AT WHAT THIS HORN CAN DO AND WITH THOSE TUSKERS CLOSING IN? MAYBE IT COULD USE A LITTLE OVERSIGHT.
WAIT, WHAT DO YOU KNOW OF DR. Z? DID HE SEND YOU?

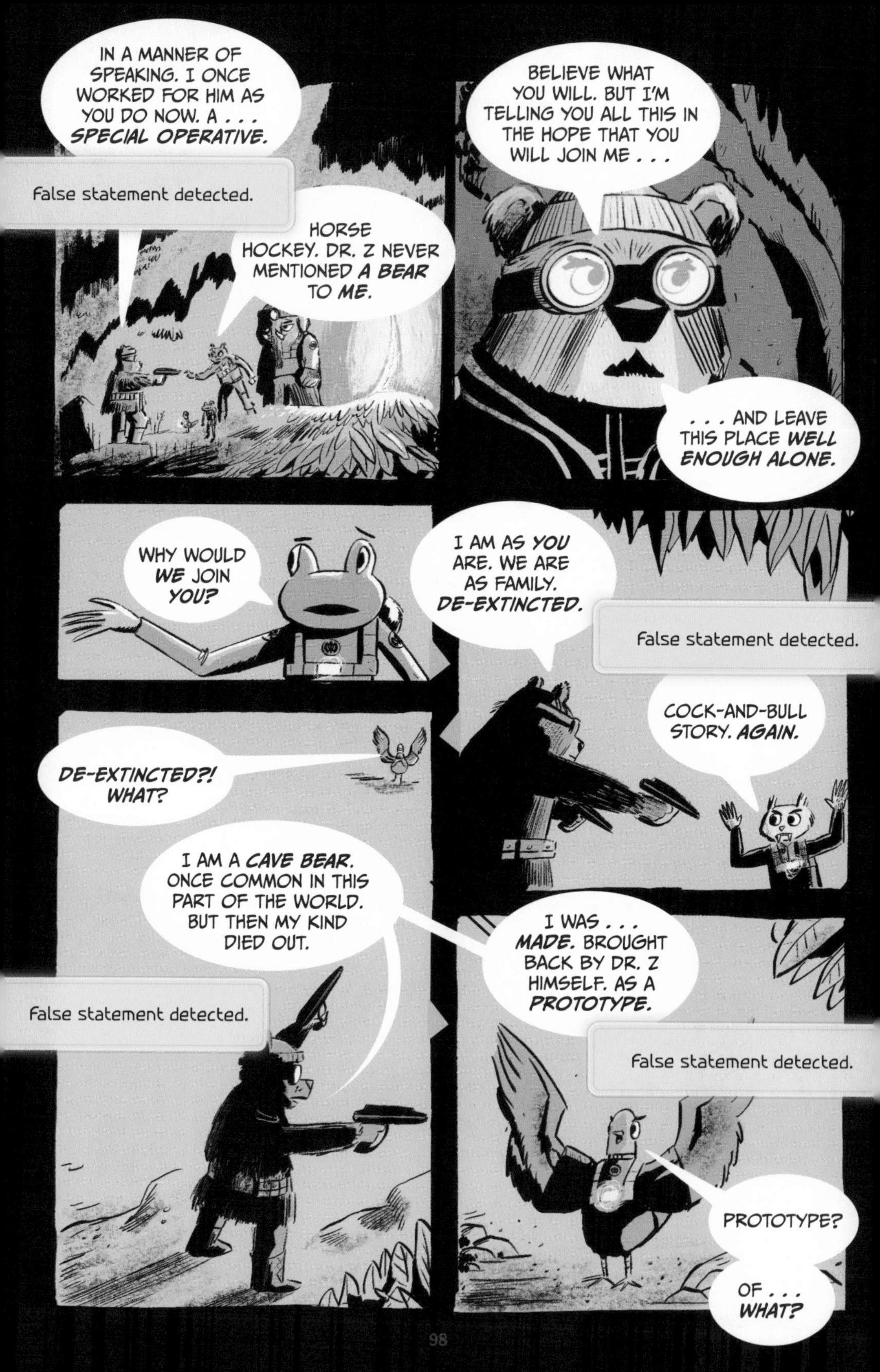
IN A MANNER OF SPEAKING. I ONCE WORKED FOR HIM AS YOU DO NOW. A . . . SPECIAL OPERATIVE.
False statement detected.
HORSE HOCKEY. DR. Z NEVER MENTIONED A BEAR TO ME.
BELIEVE WHAT YOU WILL. BUT I'M TELLING YOU ALL THIS IN THE HOPE THAT YOU WILL JOIN ME . . .
. . . AND LEAVE THIS PLACE WELL ENOUGH ALONE.
WHY WOULD WE JOIN YOU?
I AM AS YOU ARE. WE ARE AS FAMILY. DE-EXTINCTED.
False statement detected.
COCK-AND-BULL STORY. AGAIN.
DE-EXTINCTED?! WHAT?
I AM A CAVE BEAR. ONCE COMMON IN THIS PART OF THE WORLD. BUT THEN MY KIND DIED OUT.
False statement detected.
I WAS . . . MADE. BROUGHT BACK BY DR. Z HIMSELF. AS A PROTOTYPE.
False statement detected.
PROTOTYPE?
OF . . . WHAT?

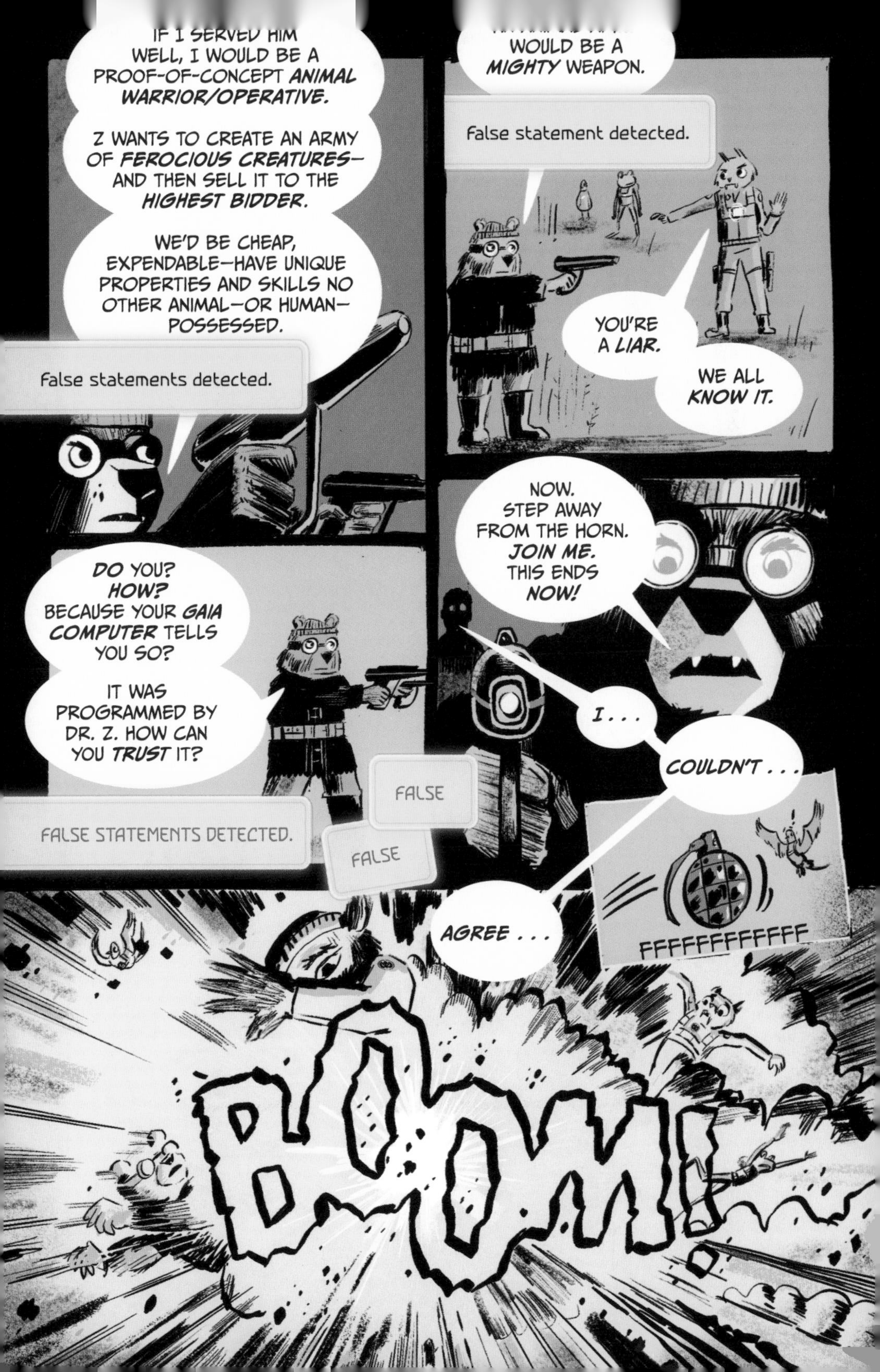
IF I SERVED HIM WELL, I WOULD BE A PROOF-OF-CONCEPT ANIMAL WARRIOR/OPERATIVE.
Z WANTS TO CREATE AN ARMY OF FEROCIOUS CREATURES—AND THEN SELL IT TO THE HIGHEST BIDDER.
WE'D BE CHEAP, EXPENDABLE—HAVE UNIQUE PROPERTIES AND SKILLS NO OTHER ANIMAL—OR HUMAN—POSSESSED.
False statements detected.
WOULD BE A MIGHTY WEAPON.
False statement detected.
YOU'RE A LIAR.
WE ALL KNOW IT.
DO YOU? HOW? BECAUSE YOUR GAIA COMPUTER TELLS YOU SO?
IT WAS PROGRAMMED BY DR. Z. HOW CAN YOU TRUST IT?
FALSE STATEMENTS DETECTED.
FALSE
FALSE
NOW. STEP AWAY FROM THE HORN. JOIN ME. THIS ENDS NOW!
I . . .
COULDN'T . . .
AGREE . . .
FFFFFFFFFFFF
BOOM!

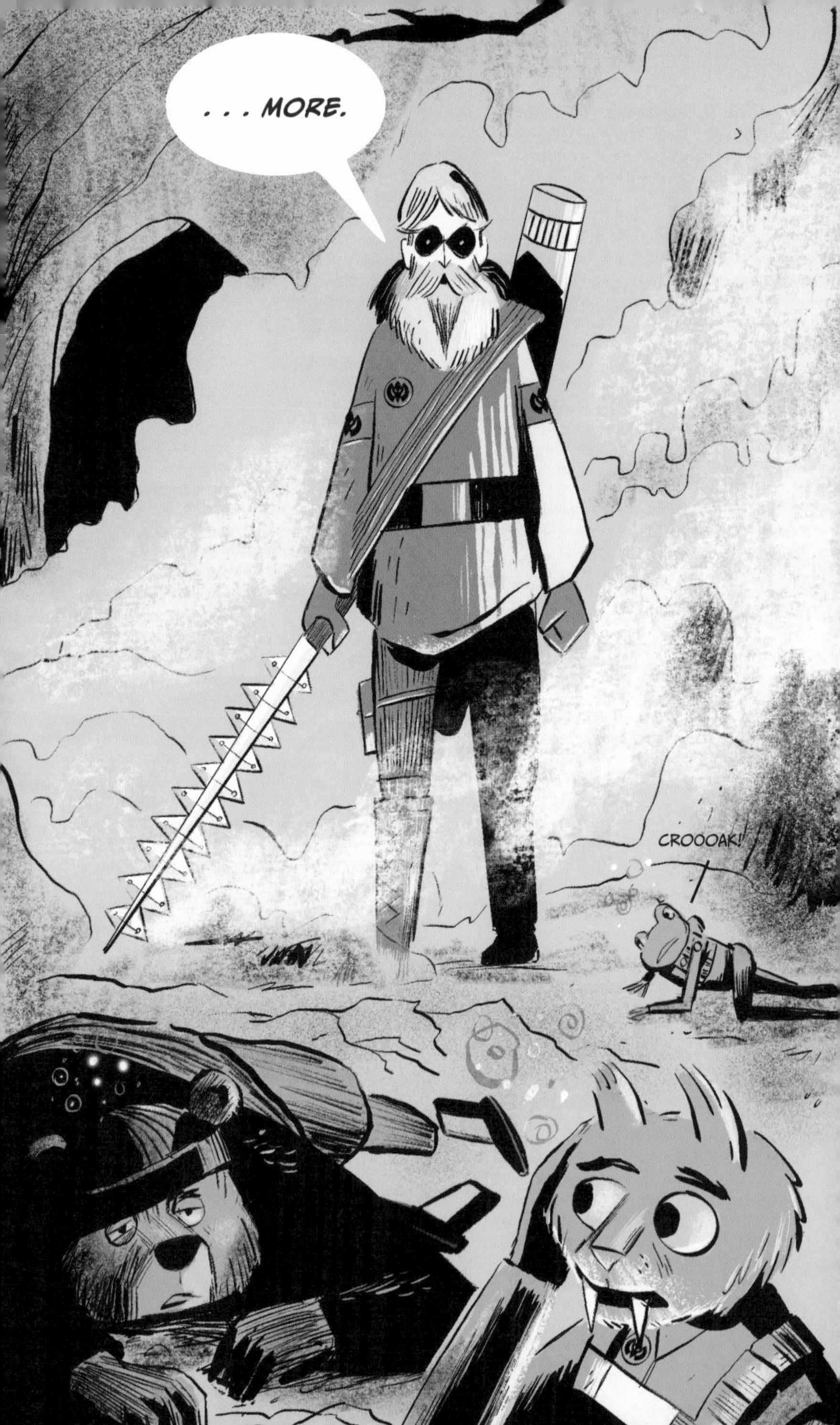
. . . MORE.
CROOOAK!

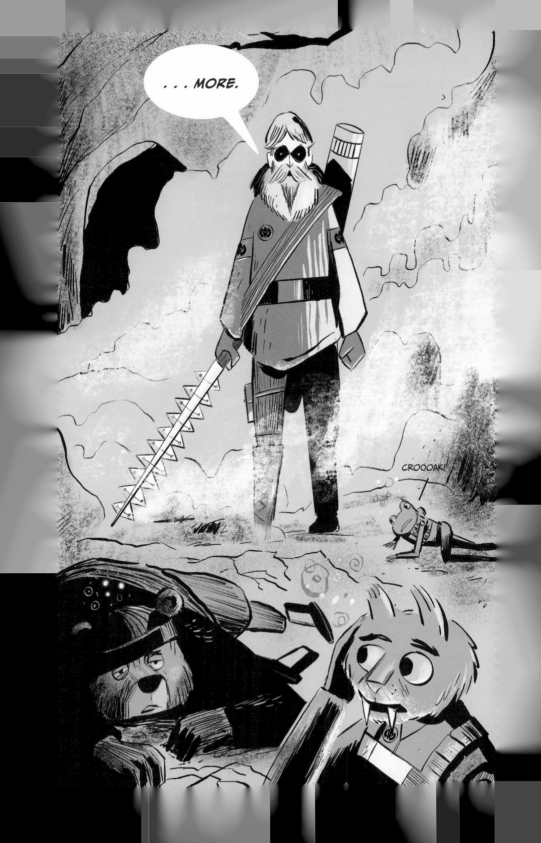

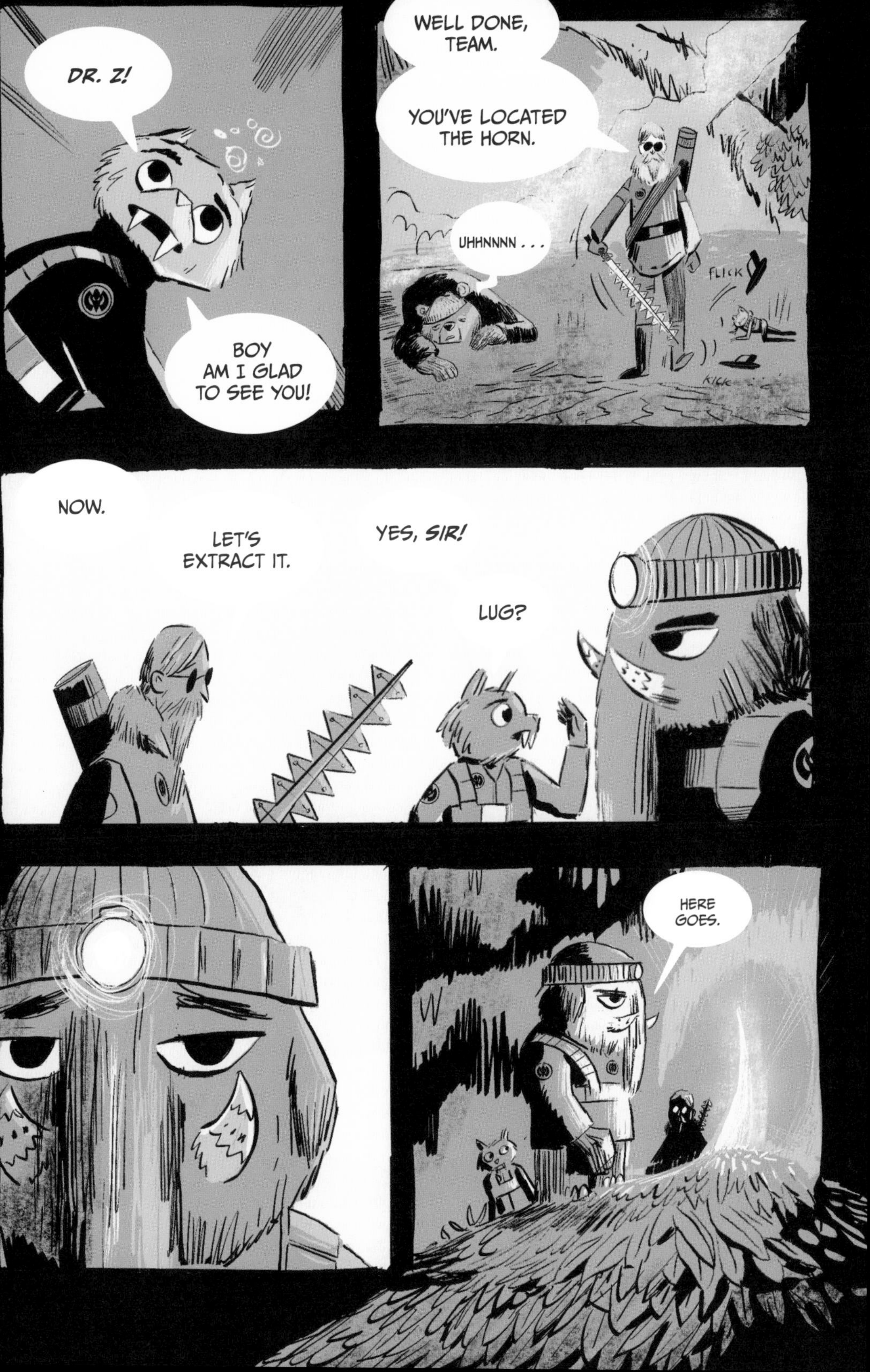
DR. Z!
BOY AM I GLAD TO SEE YOU!
WELL DONE, TEAM.
YOU'VE LOCATED THE HORN.
UHHNNNN . . .
FLICK
KICK
NOW.
LET'S EXTRACT IT.
YES, SIR!
LUG?
HERE GOES.

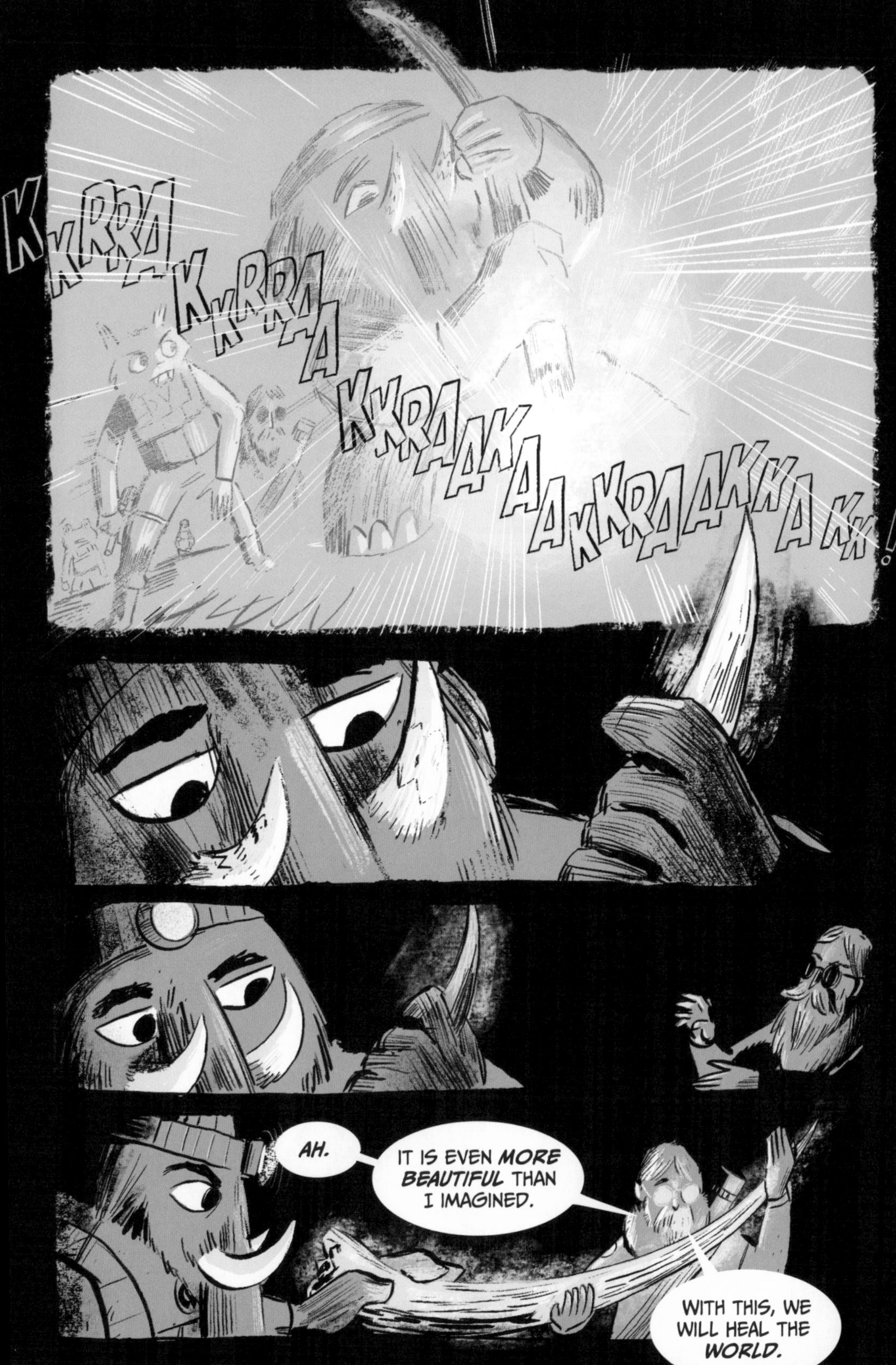
KKRRAKKRRAA
KKRAAKAAKKRAAKKAKK!
AH.
IT IS EVEN MORE BEAUTIFUL THAN I IMAGINED.
WITH THIS, WE WILL HEAL THE WORLD.

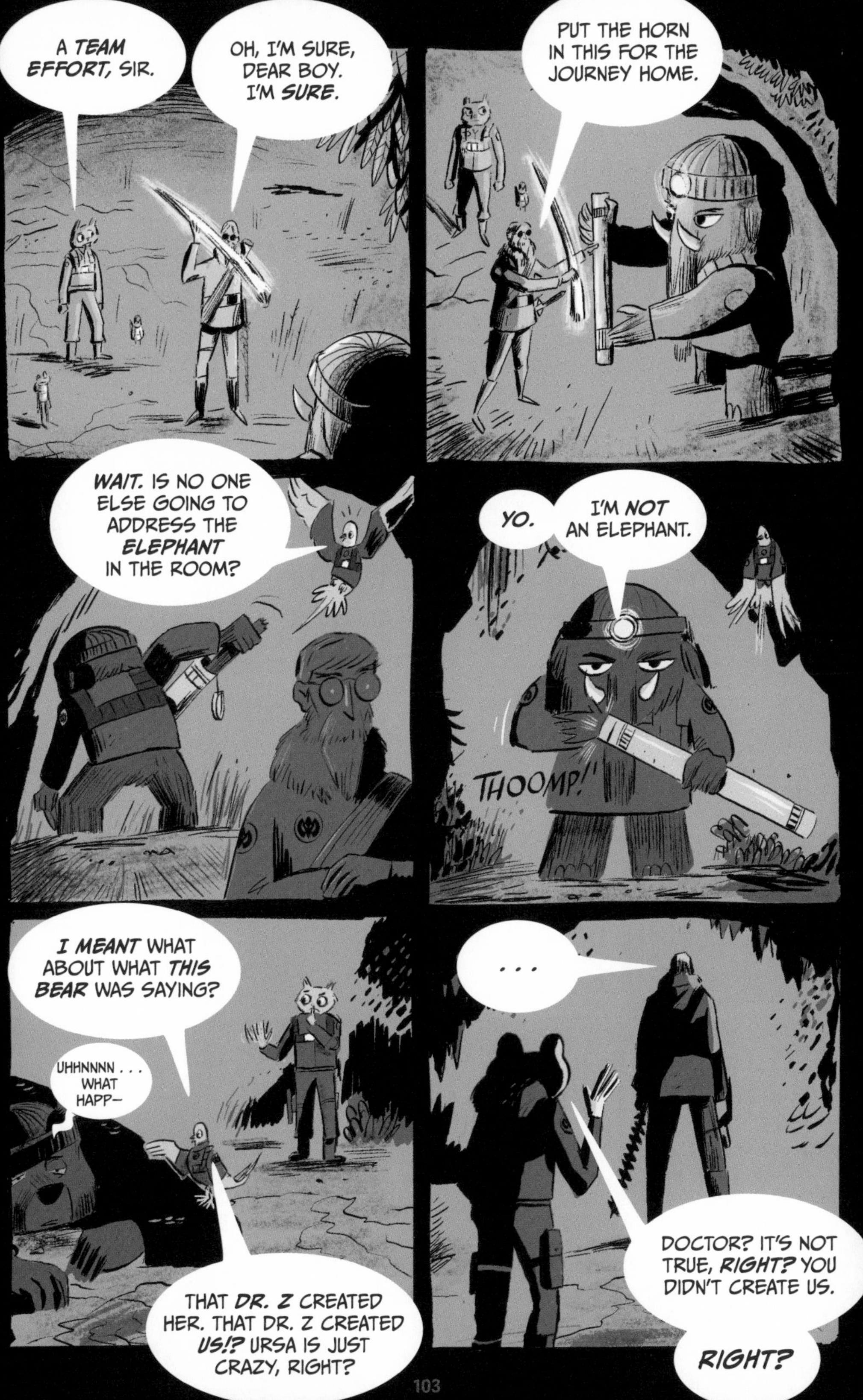
A TEAM EFFORT, SIR.
OH, I'M SURE, DEAR BOY. I'M SURE.
PUT THE HORN IN THIS FOR THE JOURNEY HOME.
WAIT. IS NO ONE ELSE GOING TO ADDRESS THE ELEPHANT IN THE ROOM?
YO.
I'M NOT AN ELEPHANT.
THOOMP!
I MEANT WHAT ABOUT WHAT THIS BEAR WAS SAYING?
UHHNNNN . . . WHAT HAPP—
THAT DR. Z CREATED HER. THAT DR. Z CREATED US!? URSA IS JUST CRAZY, RIGHT?
. . .
DOCTOR? IT'S NOT TRUE, RIGHT? YOU DIDN'T CREATE US.
RIGHT?

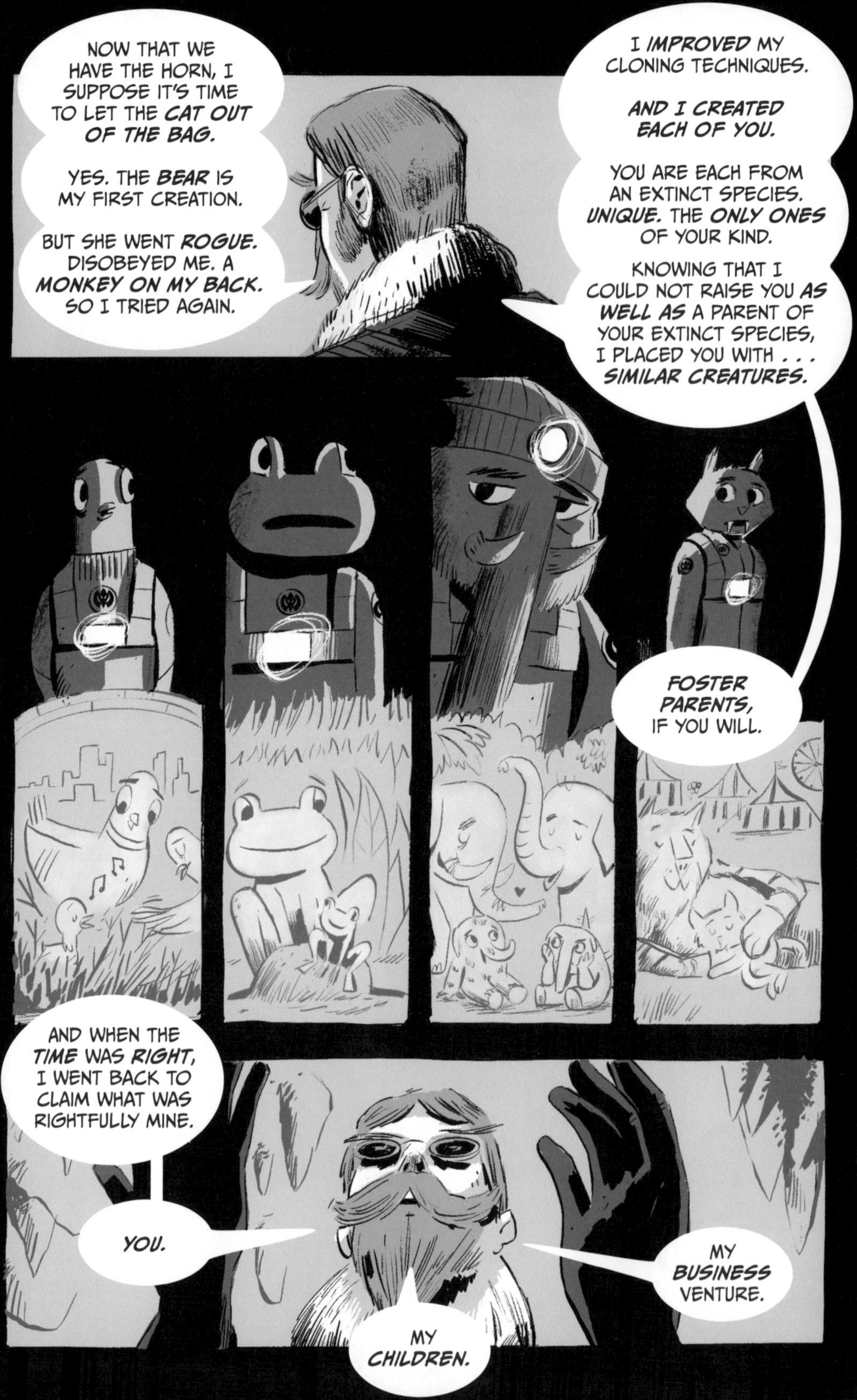
NOW THAT WE HAVE THE HORN, I SUPPOSE IT'S TIME TO LET THE *CAT OUT OF THE BAG.*
YES. THE *BEAR* IS MY FIRST CREATION.
BUT SHE WENT *ROGUE.* DISOBEYED ME. A *MONKEY ON MY BACK.* SO I TRIED AGAIN.
I *IMPROVED* MY CLONING TECHNIQUES.
AND I CREATED EACH OF YOU.
YOU ARE EACH FROM AN EXTINCT SPECIES. *UNIQUE.* THE *ONLY ONES* OF YOUR KIND.
KNOWING THAT I COULD NOT RAISE YOU *AS WELL AS* A PARENT OF YOUR EXTINCT SPECIES, I PLACED YOU WITH . . . *SIMILAR CREATURES.*
FOSTER PARENTS, IF YOU WILL.
AND WHEN THE *TIME* WAS *RIGHT,* I WENT BACK TO CLAIM WHAT WAS RIGHTFULLY MINE.
YOU.
MY *CHILDREN.*
MY *BUSINESS* VENTURE.

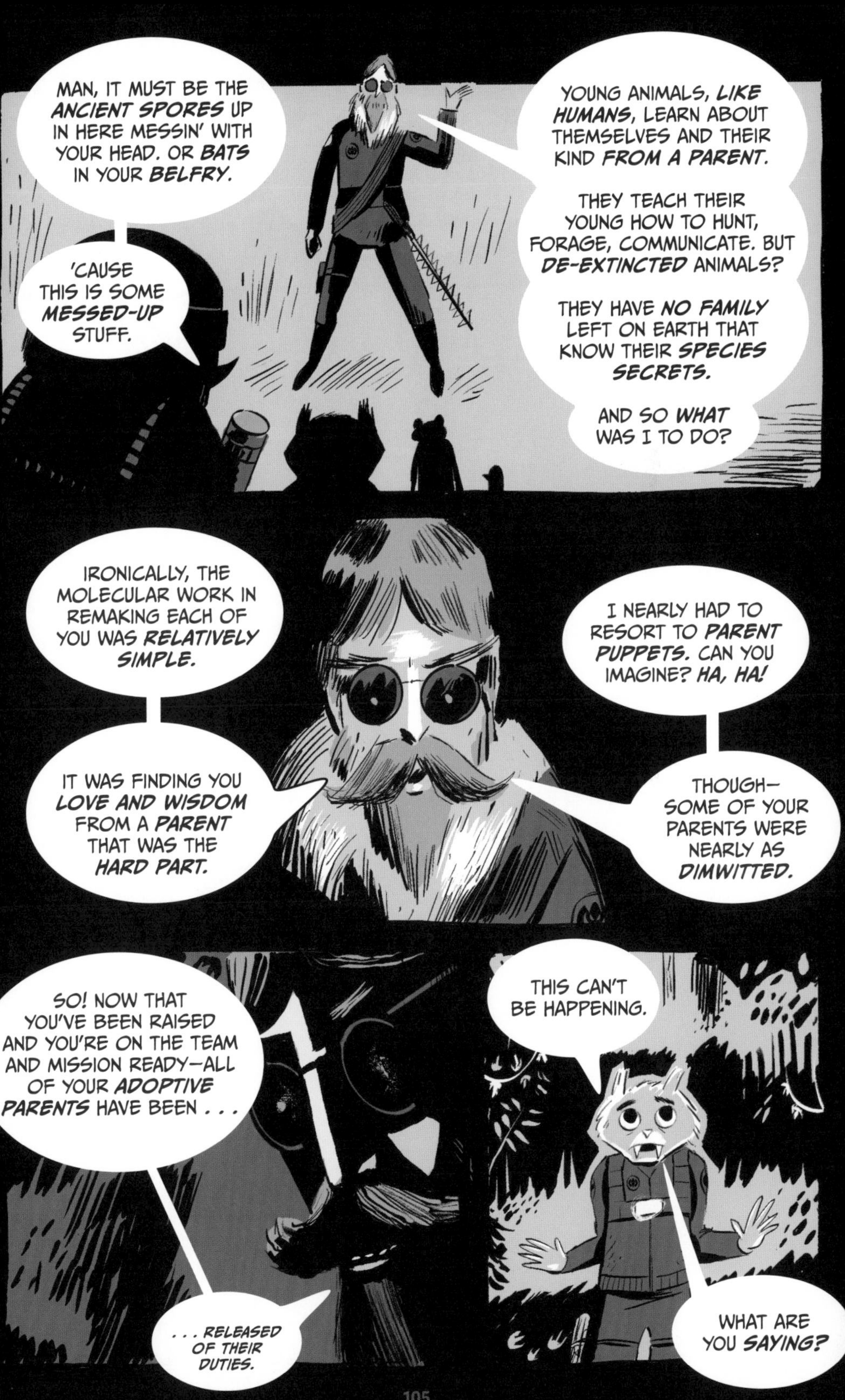
MAN, IT MUST BE THE ANCIENT SPORES UP IN HERE MESSIN' WITH YOUR HEAD. OR BATS IN YOUR BELFRY.
'CAUSE THIS IS SOME MESSED-UP STUFF.
YOUNG ANIMALS, LIKE HUMANS, LEARN ABOUT THEMSELVES AND THEIR KIND FROM A PARENT.
THEY TEACH THEIR YOUNG HOW TO HUNT, FORAGE, COMMUNICATE. BUT DE-EXTINCTED ANIMALS?
THEY HAVE NO FAMILY LEFT ON EARTH THAT KNOW THEIR SPECIES SECRETS.
AND SO WHAT WAS I TO DO?
IRONICALLY, THE MOLECULAR WORK IN REMAKING EACH OF YOU WAS RELATIVELY SIMPLE.
IT WAS FINDING YOU LOVE AND WISDOM FROM A PARENT THAT WAS THE HARD PART.
I NEARLY HAD TO RESORT TO PARENT PUPPETS. CAN YOU IMAGINE? HA, HA!
THOUGH— SOME OF YOUR PARENTS WERE NEARLY AS DIMWITTED.
SO! NOW THAT YOU'VE BEEN RAISED AND YOU'RE ON THE TEAM AND MISSION READY—ALL OF YOUR ADOPTIVE PARENTS HAVE BEEN . . .
. . . RELEASED OF THEIR DUTIES.
THIS CAN'T BE HAPPENING.
WHAT ARE YOU SAYING?

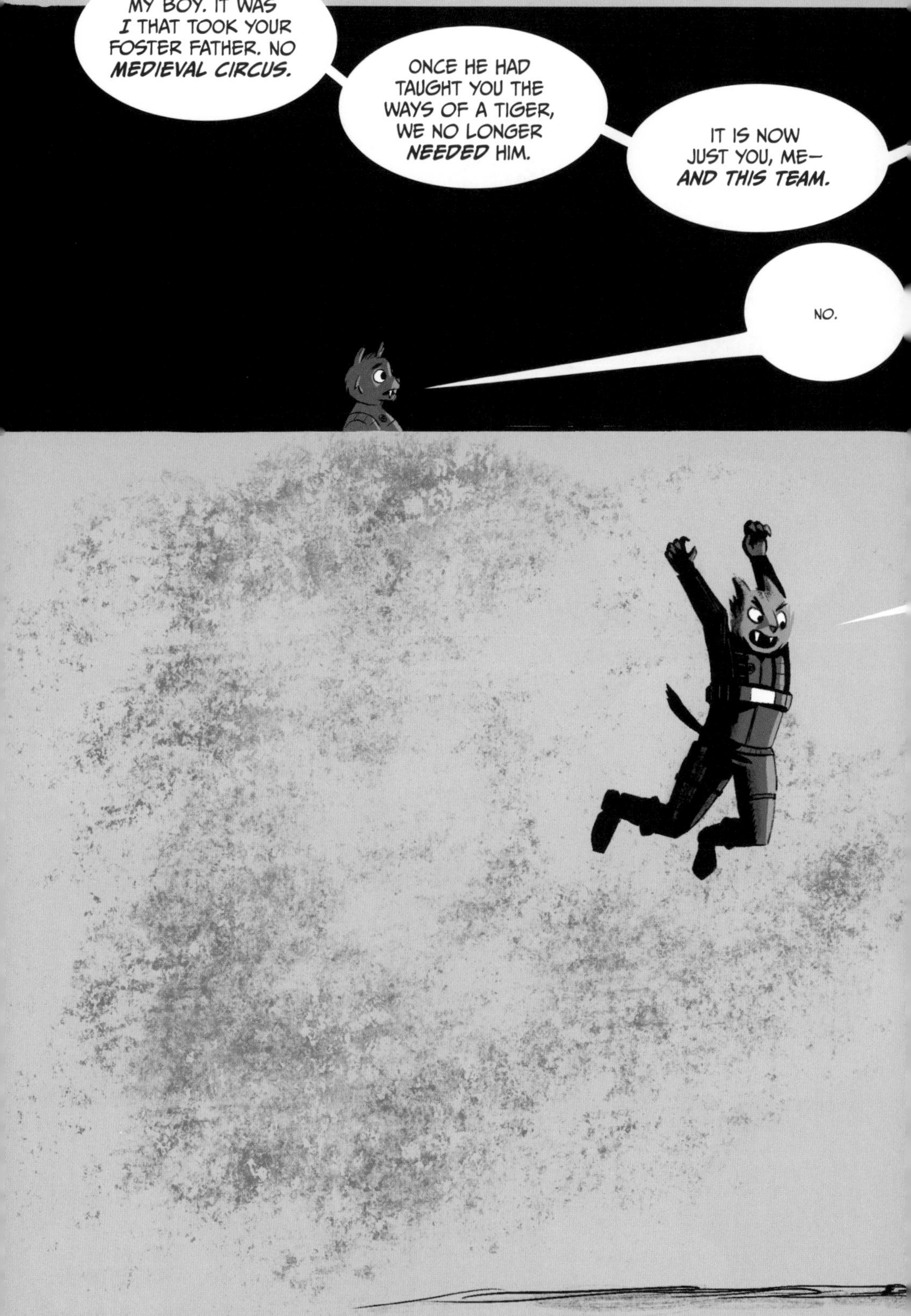
MY BOY. IT WAS *I* THAT TOOK YOUR FOSTER FATHER. NO ***MEDIEVAL CIRCUS.***
ONCE HE HAD TAUGHT YOU THE WAYS OF A TIGER, WE NO LONGER ***NEEDED*** HIM.
IT IS NOW JUST YOU, ME— ***AND THIS TEAM.***
NO.

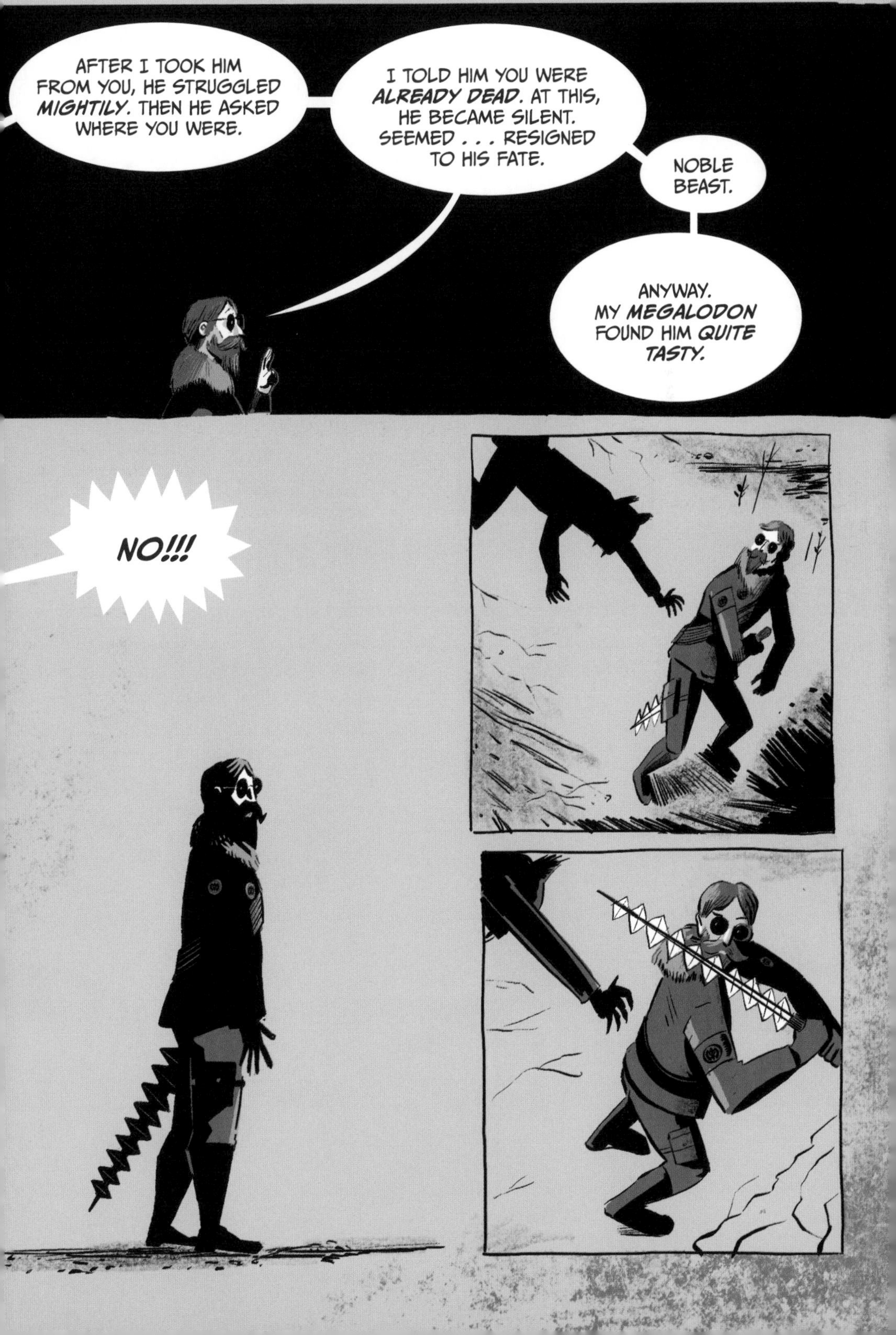
AFTER I TOOK HIM FROM YOU, HE STRUGGLED MIGHTILY. THEN HE ASKED WHERE YOU WERE.
I TOLD HIM YOU WERE ALREADY DEAD. AT THIS, HE BECAME SILENT. SEEMED . . . RESIGNED TO HIS FATE.
NOBLE BEAST.
ANYWAY. MY MEGALODON FOUND HIM QUITE TASTY.
NO!!!

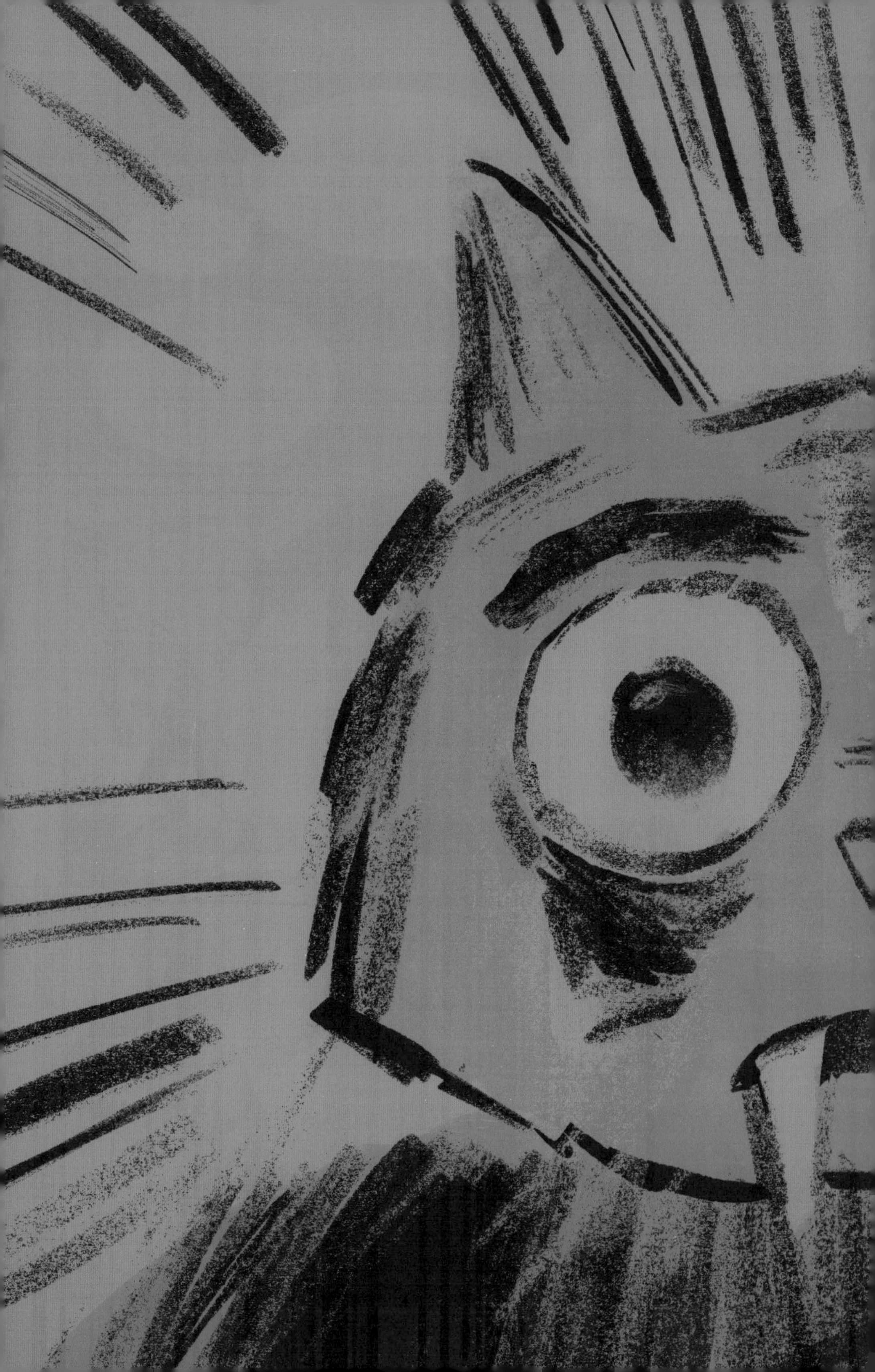

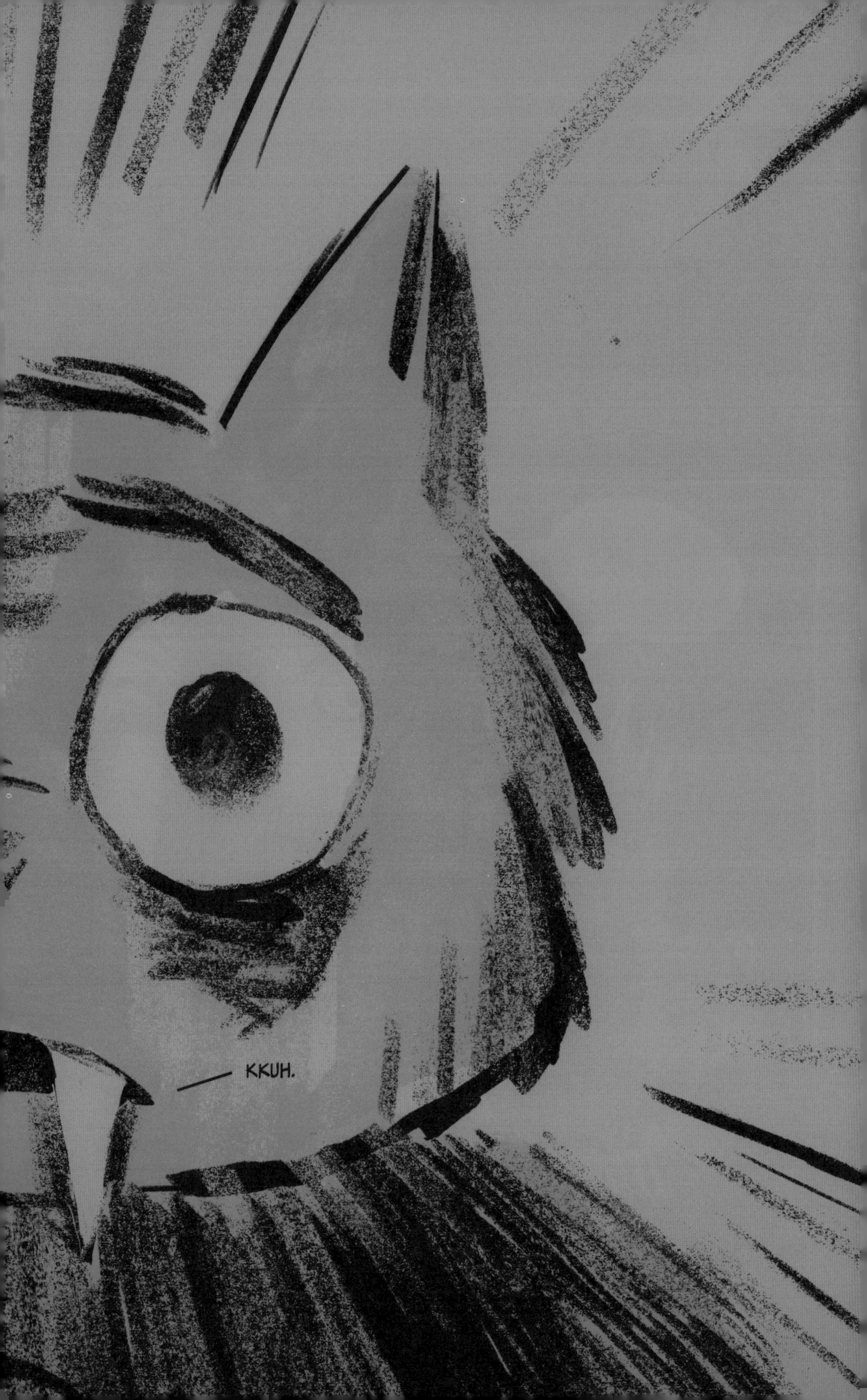
—KKUH.

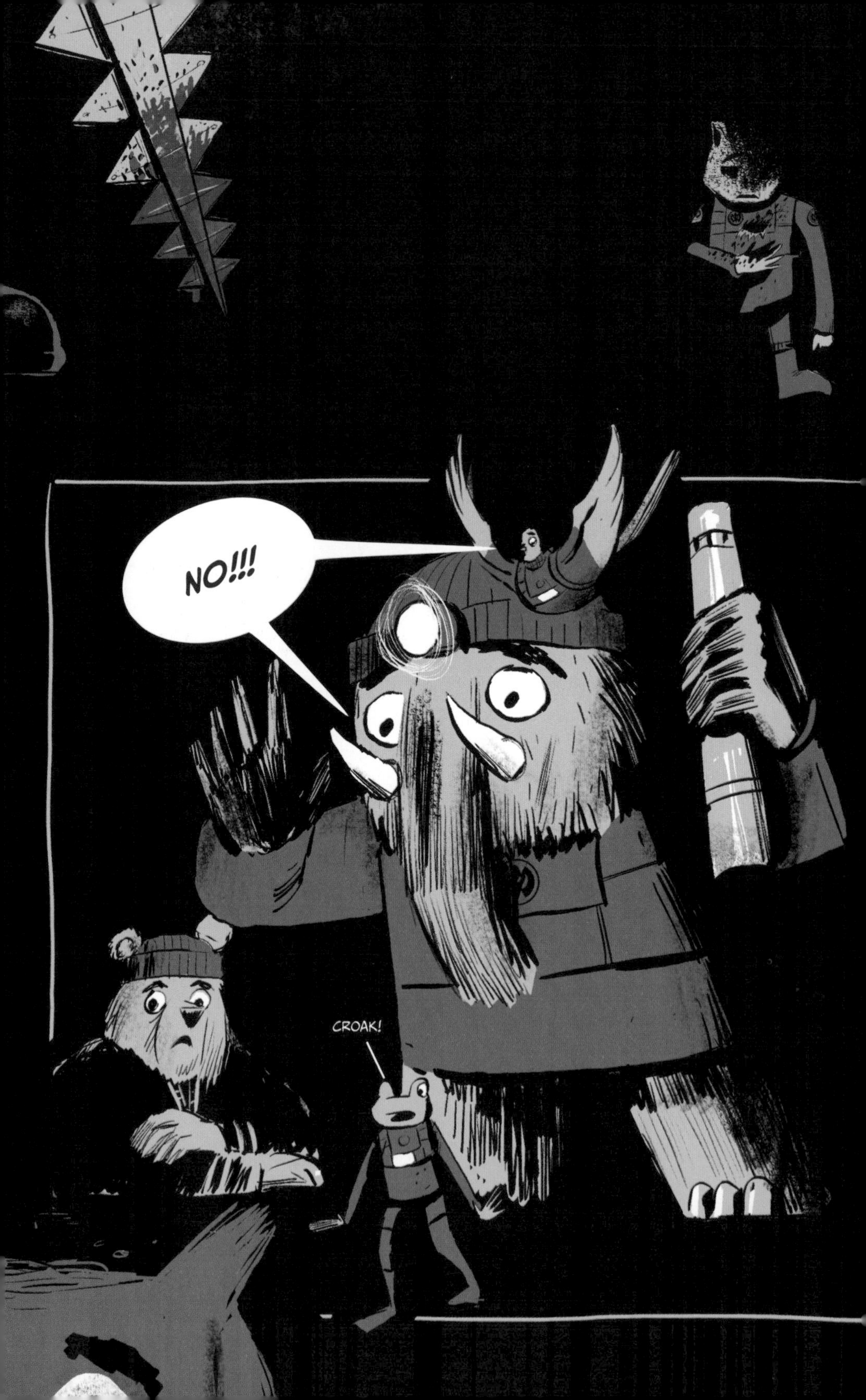
NO!!!
CROAK!

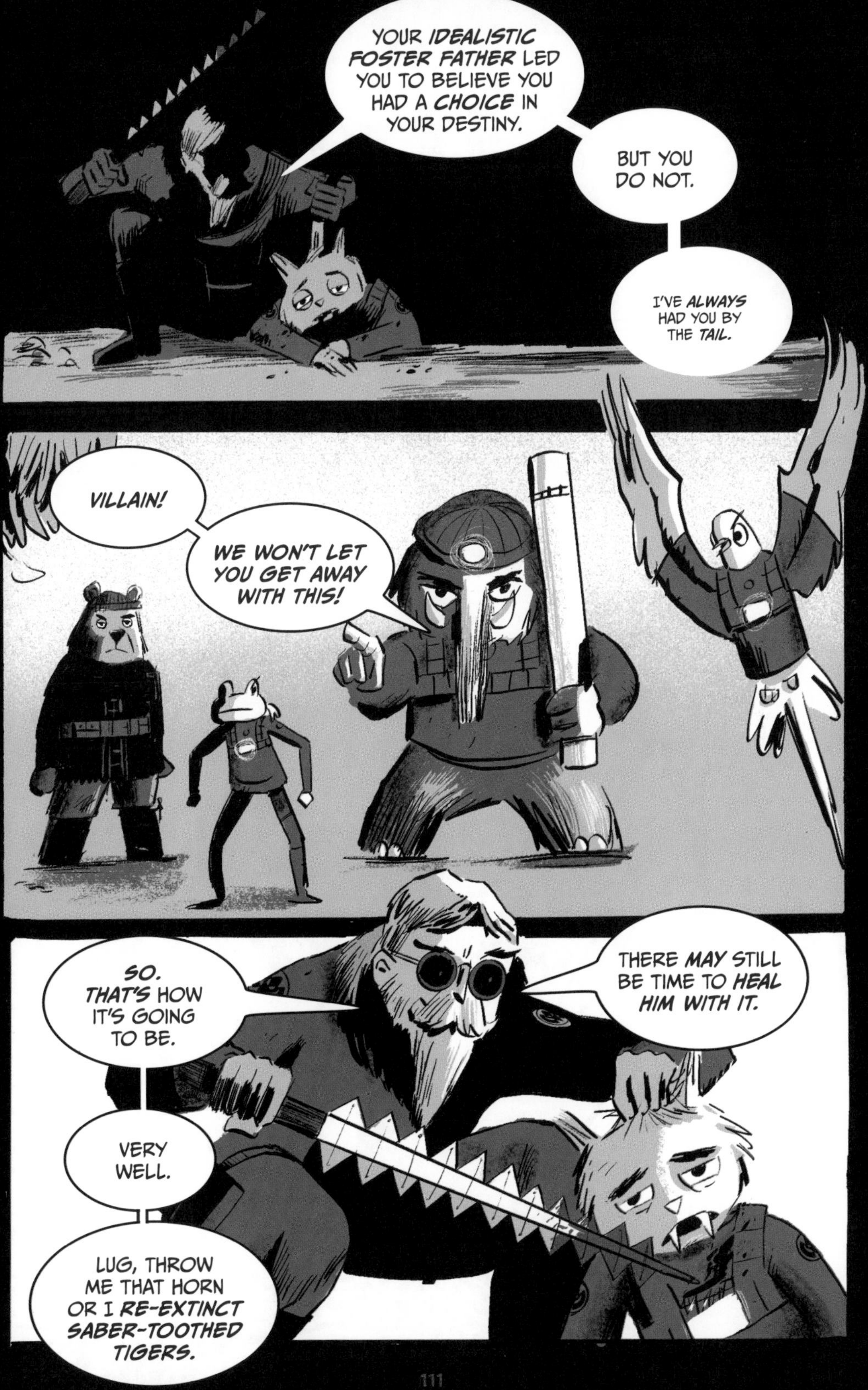
YOUR IDEALISTIC FOSTER FATHER LED YOU TO BELIEVE YOU HAD A CHOICE IN YOUR DESTINY.
BUT YOU DO NOT.
I'VE ALWAYS HAD YOU BY THE TAIL.
VILLAIN!
WE WON'T LET YOU GET AWAY WITH THIS!
SO. THAT'S HOW IT'S GOING TO BE.
THERE MAY STILL BE TIME TO HEAL HIM WITH IT.
VERY WELL.
LUG, THROW ME THAT HORN OR I RE-EXTINCT SABER-TOOTHED TIGERS.

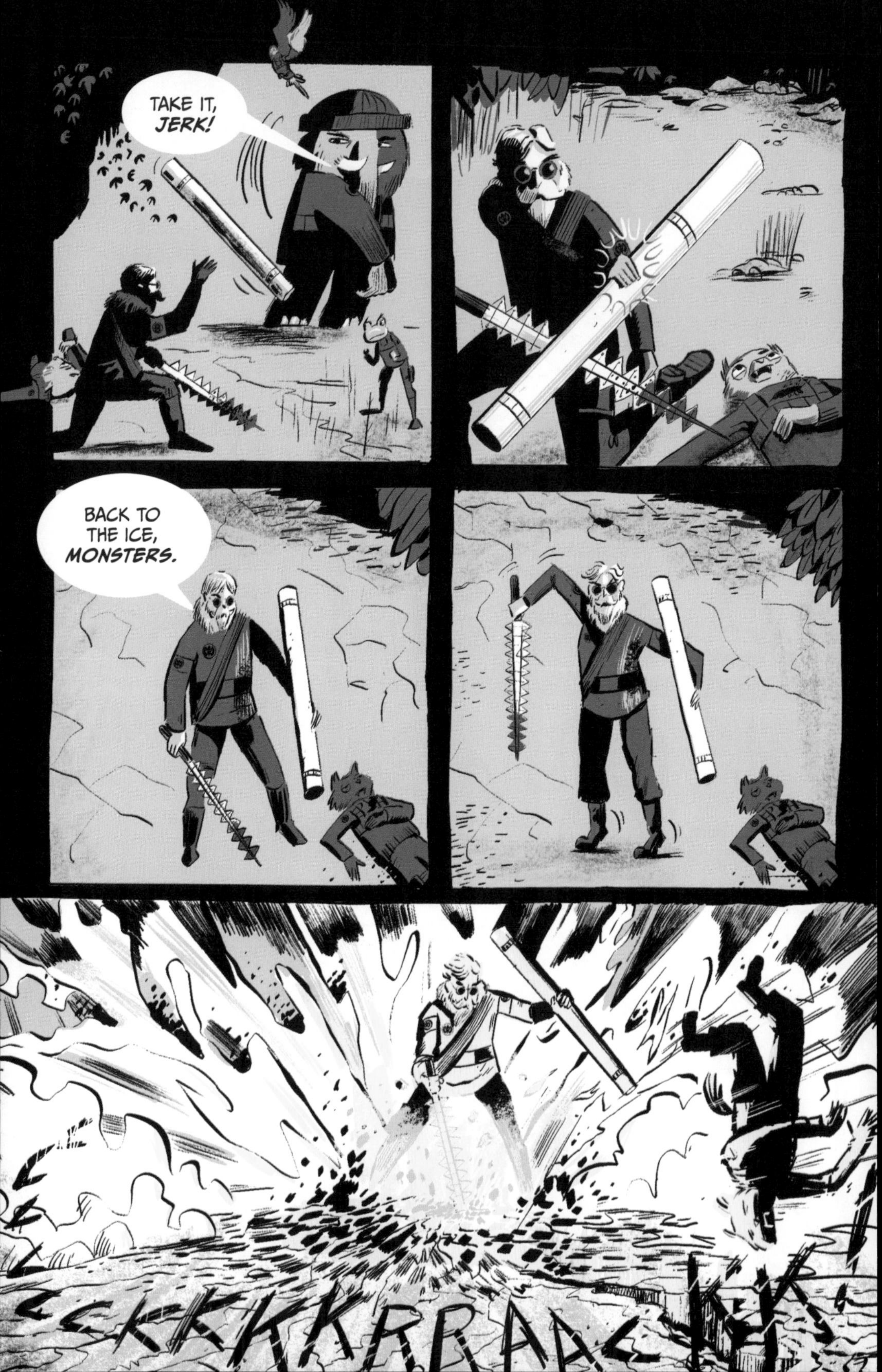
TAKE IT, JERK!
BACK TO THE ICE, MONSTERS.
CKKKKRRAACK

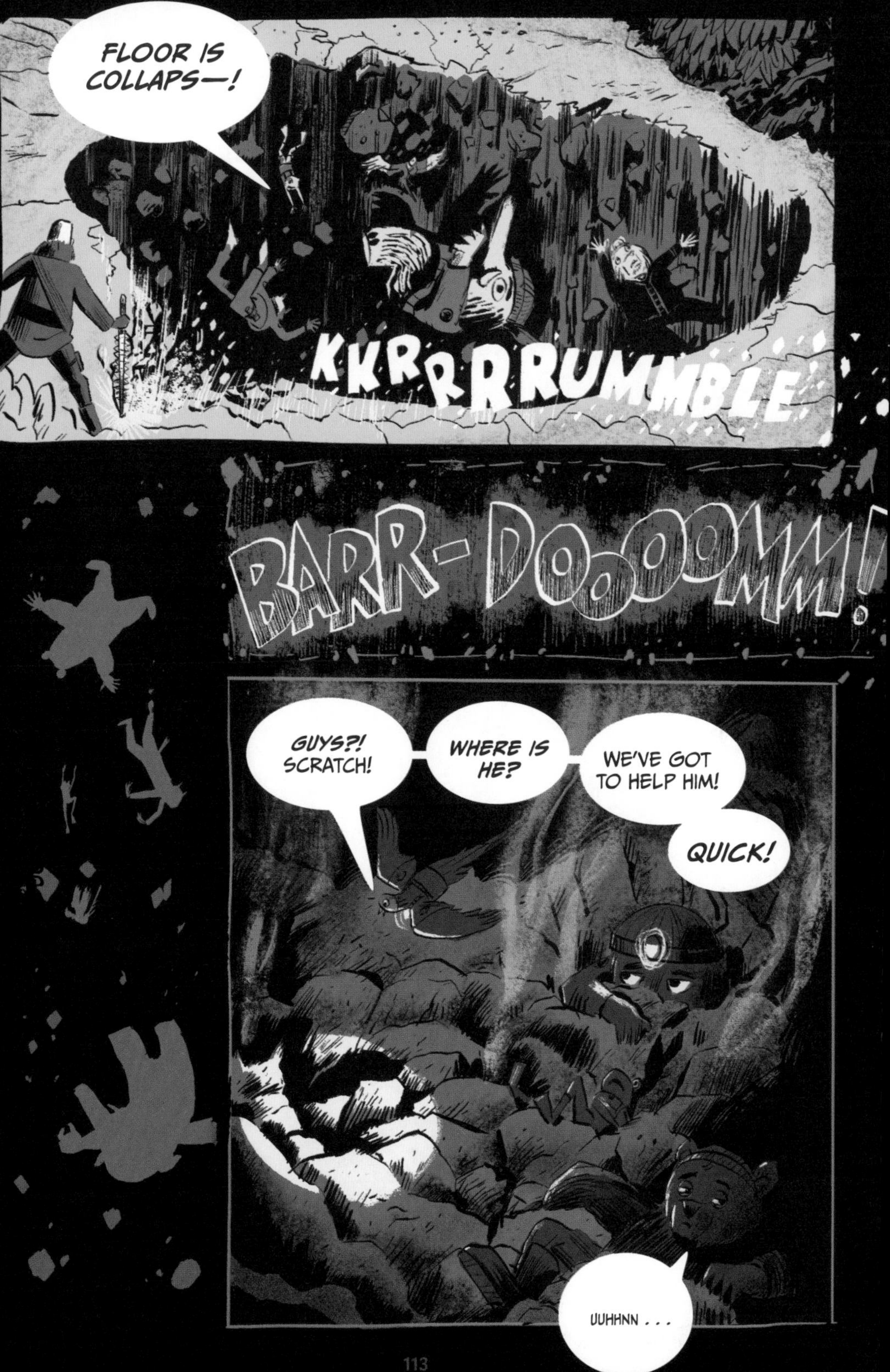
FLOOR IS COLLAPS—!
KKRRRRUMMBLE
BARR-DOOOOMM!
GUYS?! SCRATCH!
WHERE IS HE?
WE'VE GOT TO HELP HIM!
QUICK!
UUHHNN . . .

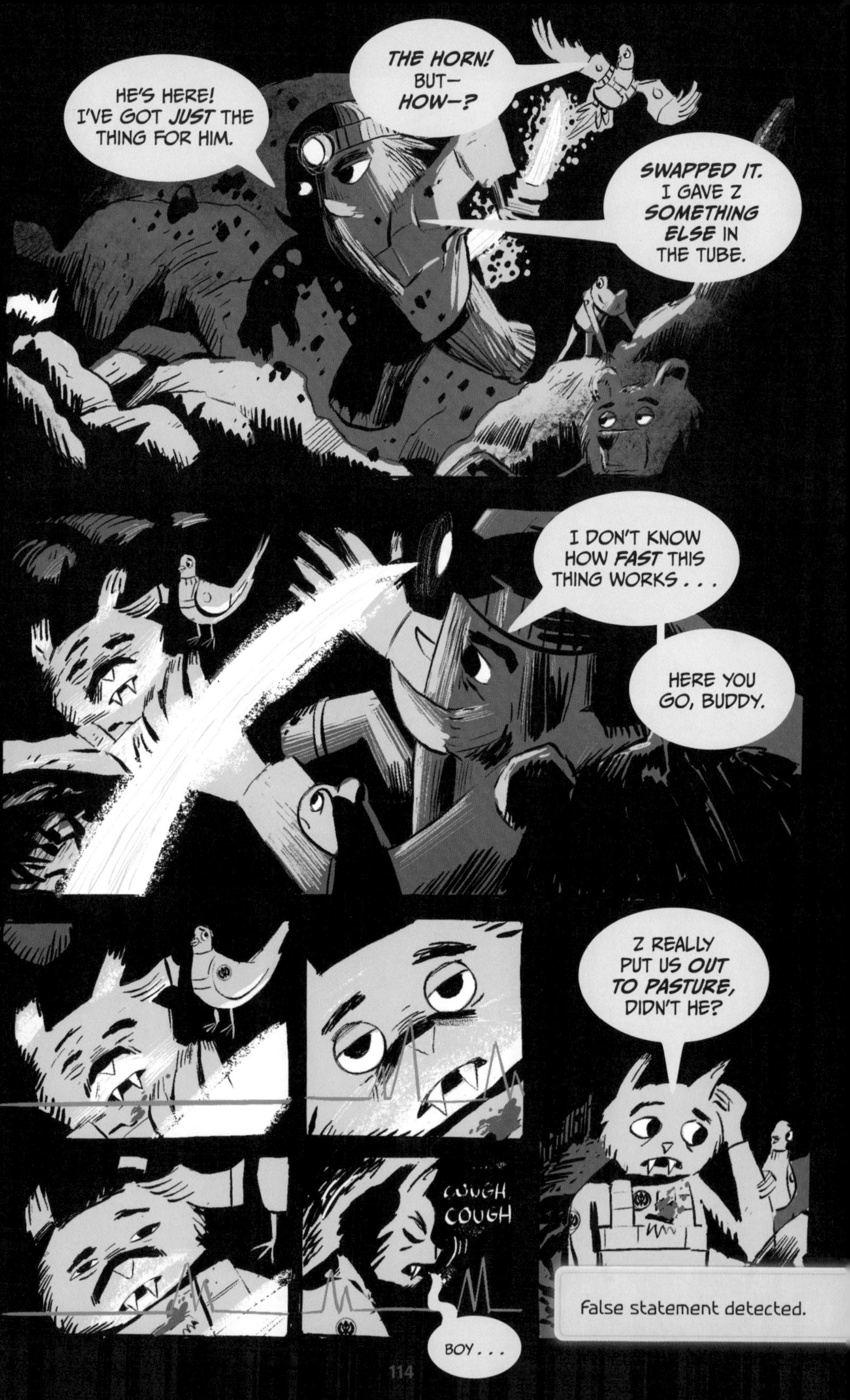
HE'S HERE! I'VE GOT *JUST* THE THING FOR HIM.
THE HORN! BUT— *HOW—?*
SWAPPED IT. I GAVE Z *SOMETHING ELSE* IN THE TUBE.
I DON'T KNOW HOW *FAST* THIS THING WORKS . . .
HERE YOU GO, BUDDY.
Z REALLY PUT US *OUT TO PASTURE,* DIDN'T HE?
COUGH COUGH
BOY . . .
False statement detected.

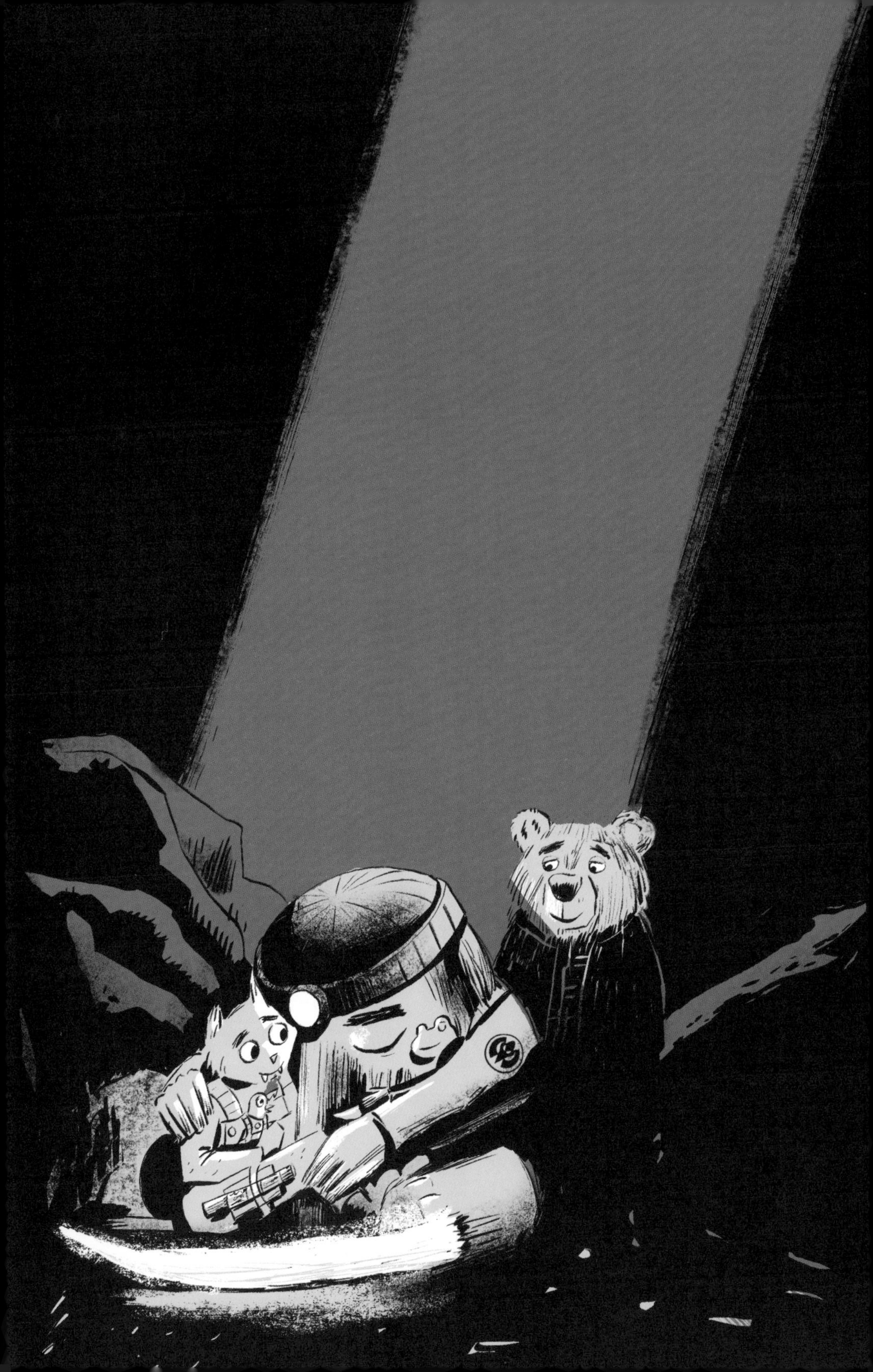

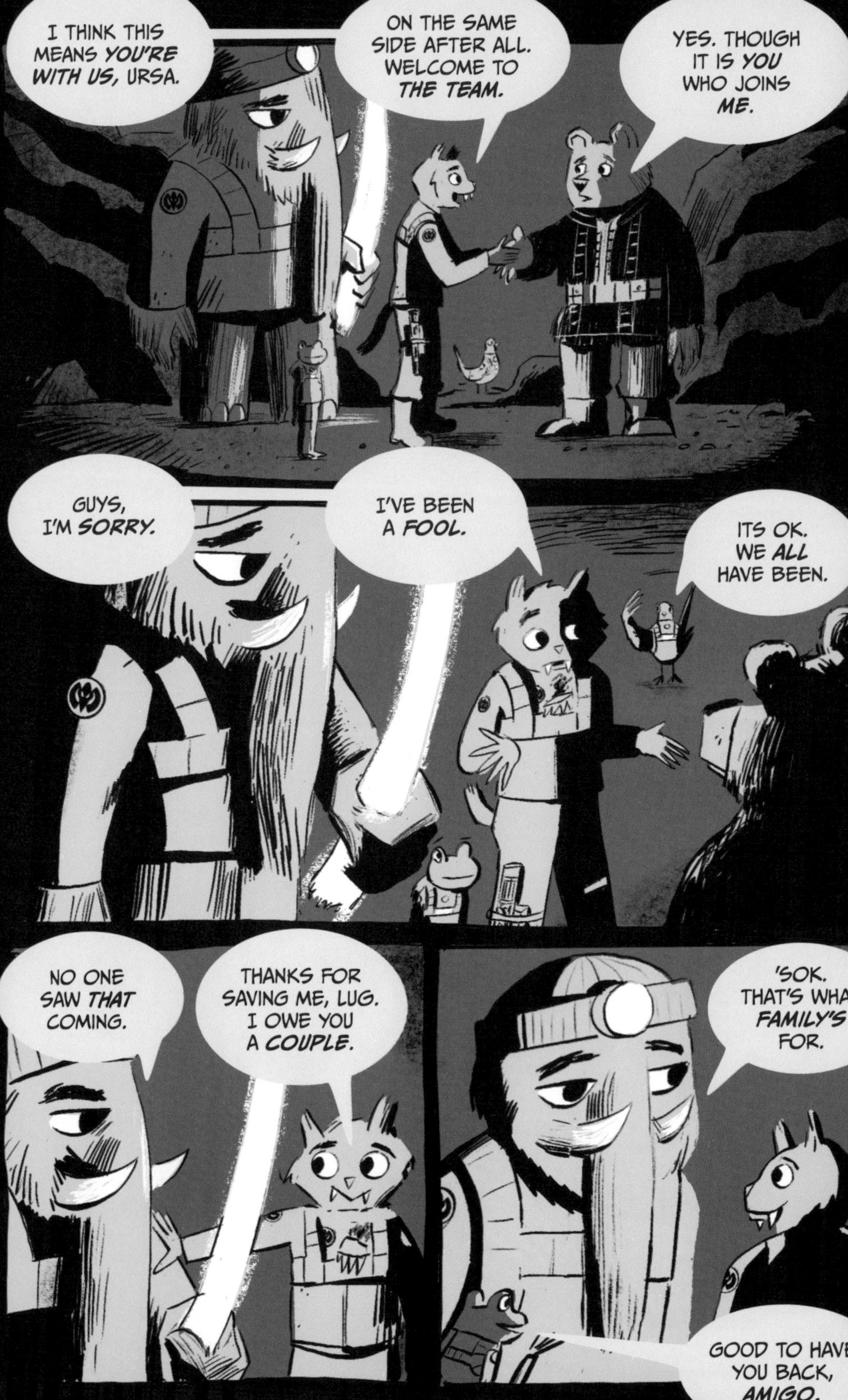
I THINK THIS MEANS *YOU'RE WITH US,* URSA.
ON THE SAME SIDE AFTER ALL. WELCOME TO *THE TEAM.*
YES. THOUGH IT IS *YOU* WHO JOINS *ME.*
GUYS, I'M *SORRY.*
I'VE BEEN A *FOOL.*
ITS OK. WE *ALL* HAVE BEEN.
NO ONE SAW *THAT* COMING.
THANKS FOR SAVING ME, LUG. I OWE YOU A *COUPLE.*
'SOK. THAT'S WHAT *FAMILY'S* FOR.
GOOD TO HAVE YOU BACK, *AMIGO.*

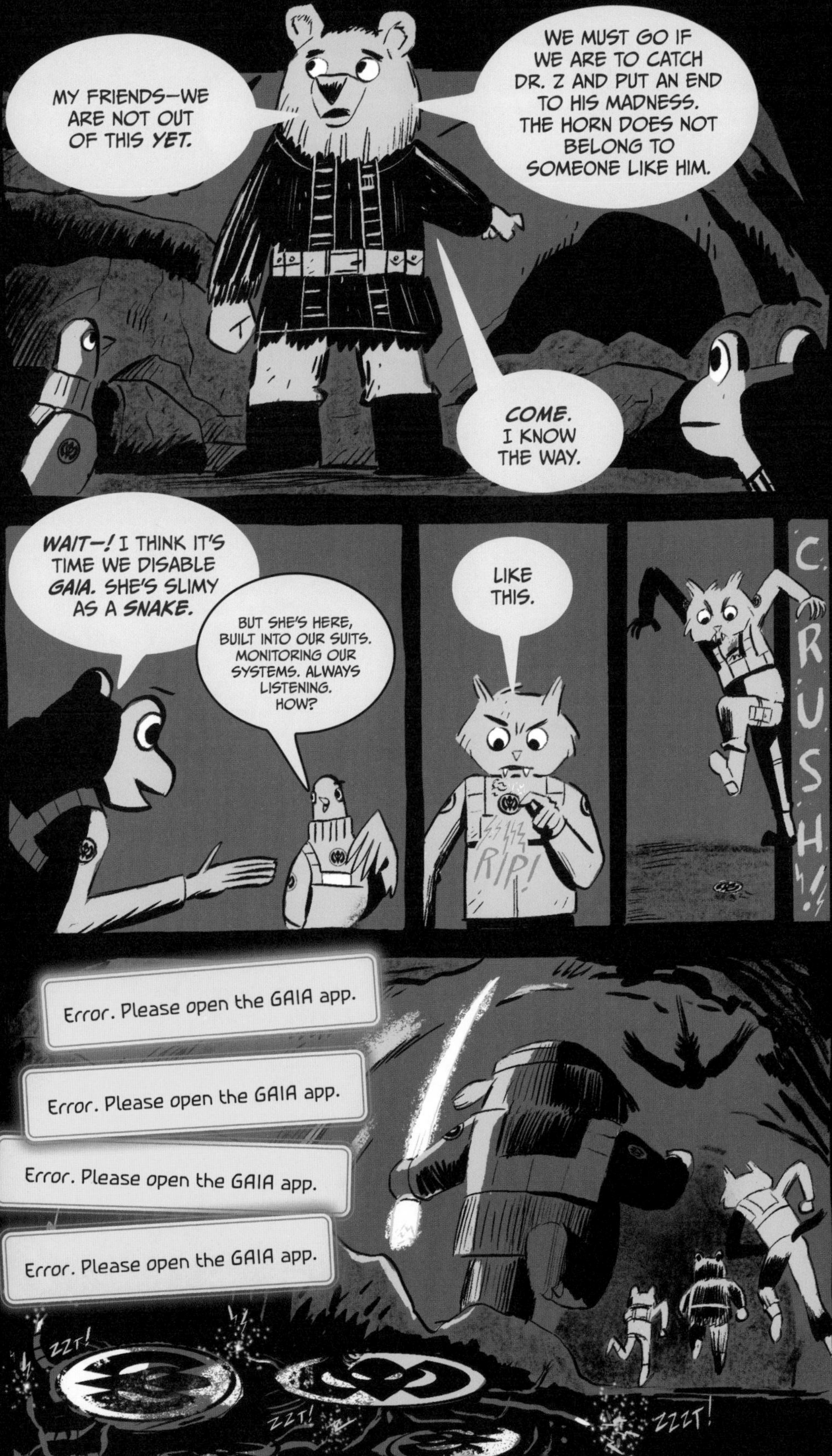
MY FRIENDS—WE ARE NOT OUT OF THIS *YET.*
WE MUST GO IF WE ARE TO CATCH DR. Z AND PUT AN END TO HIS MADNESS. THE HORN DOES NOT BELONG TO SOMEONE LIKE HIM.
COME. I KNOW THE WAY.
WAIT—! I THINK IT'S TIME WE DISABLE *GAIA.* SHE'S SLIMY AS A *SNAKE.*
BUT SHE'S HERE, BUILT INTO OUR SUITS. MONITORING OUR SYSTEMS. ALWAYS LISTENING. HOW?
LIKE THIS.
RIP!
CRUSH!
Error. Please open the GAIA app.
Error. Please open the GAIA app.
Error. Please open the GAIA app.
Error. Please open the GAIA app.
ZZT!
ZZT!
ZZZT!

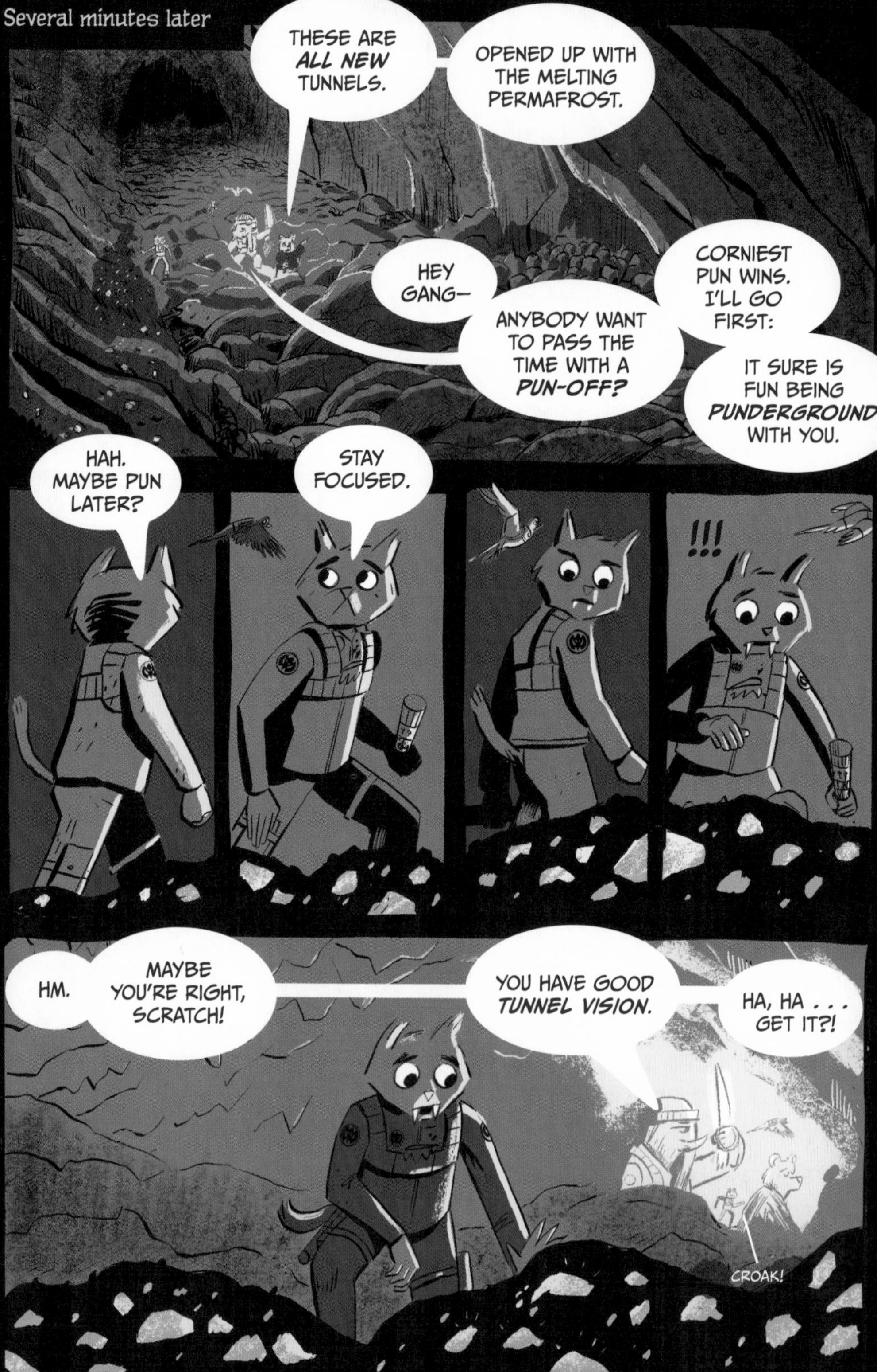
Several minutes later
THESE ARE ALL NEW TUNNELS.
OPENED UP WITH THE MELTING PERMAFROST.
HEY GANG—
ANYBODY WANT TO PASS THE TIME WITH A PUN-OFF?
CORNIEST PUN WINS. I'LL GO FIRST:
IT SURE IS FUN BEING PUNDERGROUND WITH YOU.
HAH. MAYBE PUN LATER?
STAY FOCUSED.
!!!
HM.
MAYBE YOU'RE RIGHT, SCRATCH!
YOU HAVE GOOD TUNNEL VISION.
HA, HA . . . GET IT?!
CROAK!

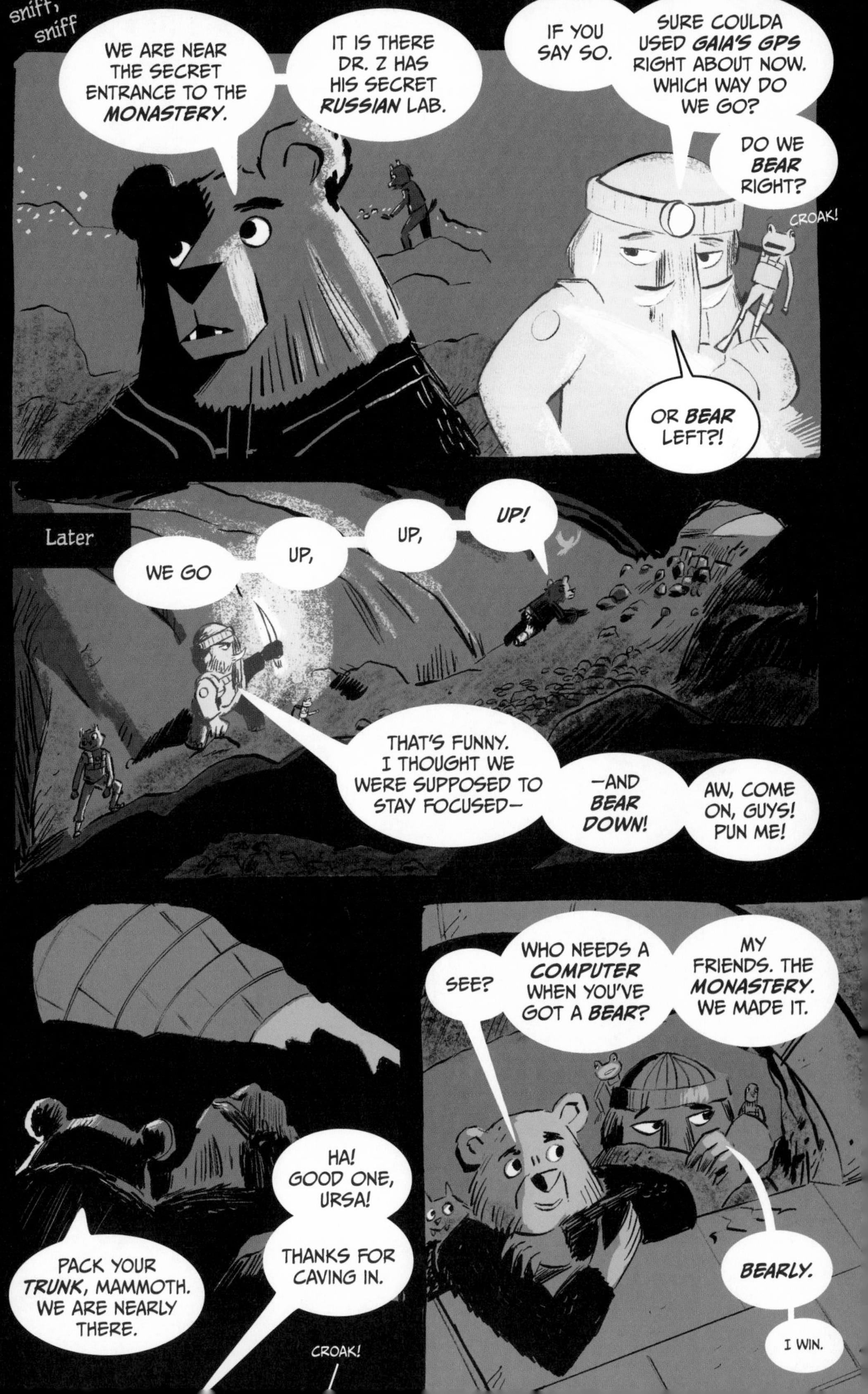
sniff, sniff
WE ARE NEAR THE SECRET ENTRANCE TO THE MONASTERY.
IT IS THERE DR. Z HAS HIS SECRET RUSSIAN LAB.
IF YOU SAY SO.
SURE COULDA USED GAIA'S GPS RIGHT ABOUT NOW. WHICH WAY DO WE GO?
DO WE BEAR RIGHT?
CROAK!
OR BEAR LEFT?!
Later
WE GO
UP,
UP,
UP!
THAT'S FUNNY. I THOUGHT WE WERE SUPPOSED TO STAY FOCUSED—
—AND BEAR DOWN!
AW, COME ON, GUYS! PUN ME!
PACK YOUR TRUNK, MAMMOTH. WE ARE NEARLY THERE.
HA! GOOD ONE, URSA!
THANKS FOR CAVING IN.
CROAK!
SEE?
WHO NEEDS A COMPUTER WHEN YOU'VE GOT A BEAR?
MY FRIENDS. THE MONASTERY. WE MADE IT.
BEARLY.
I WIN.

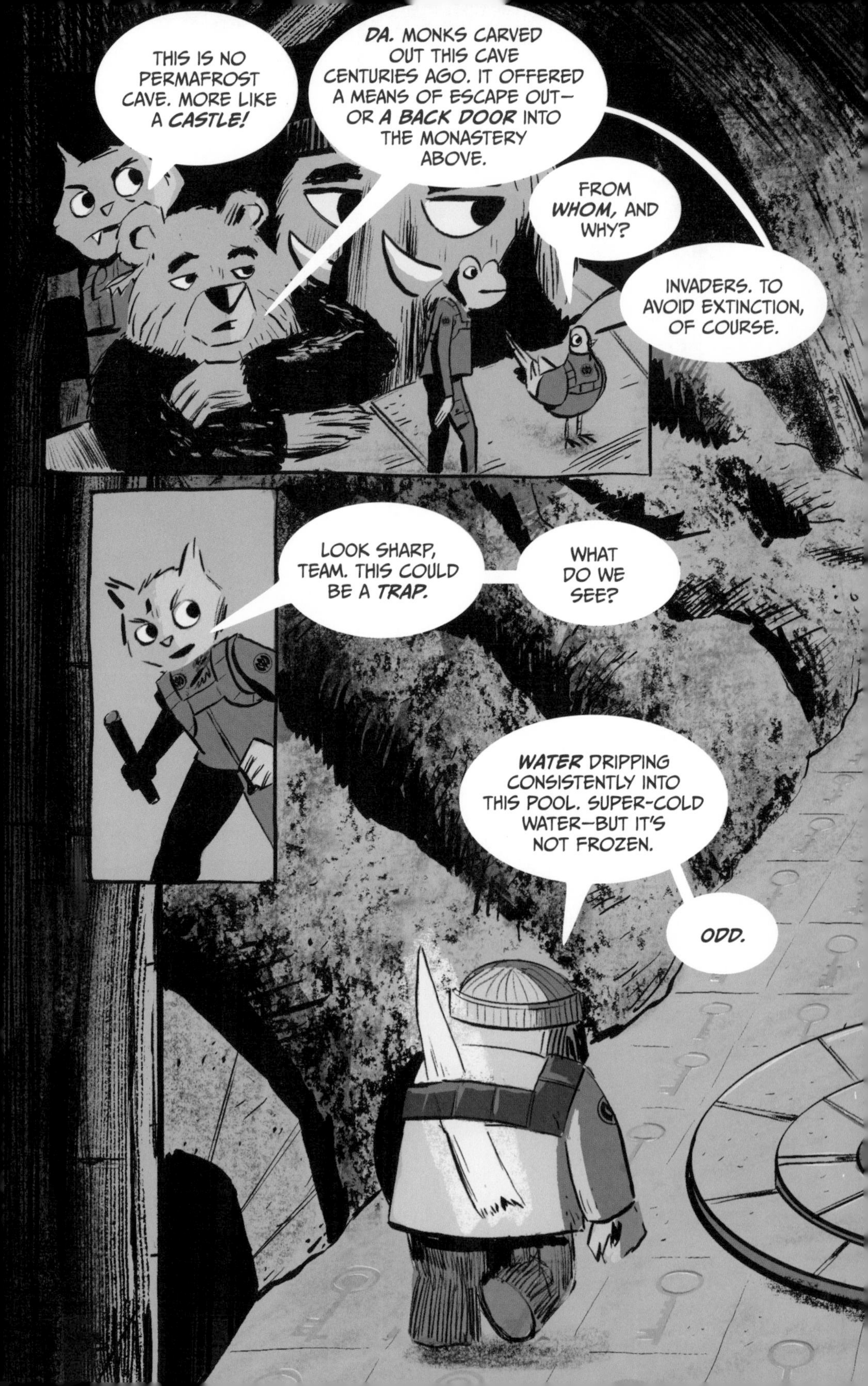

THIS IS NO PERMAFROST CAVE. MORE LIKE A CASTLE!
DA. MONKS CARVED OUT THIS CAVE CENTURIES AGO. IT OFFERED A MEANS OF ESCAPE OUT—OR A BACK DOOR INTO THE MONASTERY ABOVE.
FROM WHOM, AND WHY?
INVADERS. TO AVOID EXTINCTION, OF COURSE.
LOOK SHARP, TEAM. THIS COULD BE A TRAP.
WHAT DO WE SEE?
WATER DRIPPING CONSISTENTLY INTO THIS POOL. SUPER-COLD WATER—BUT IT'S NOT FROZEN.
ODD.

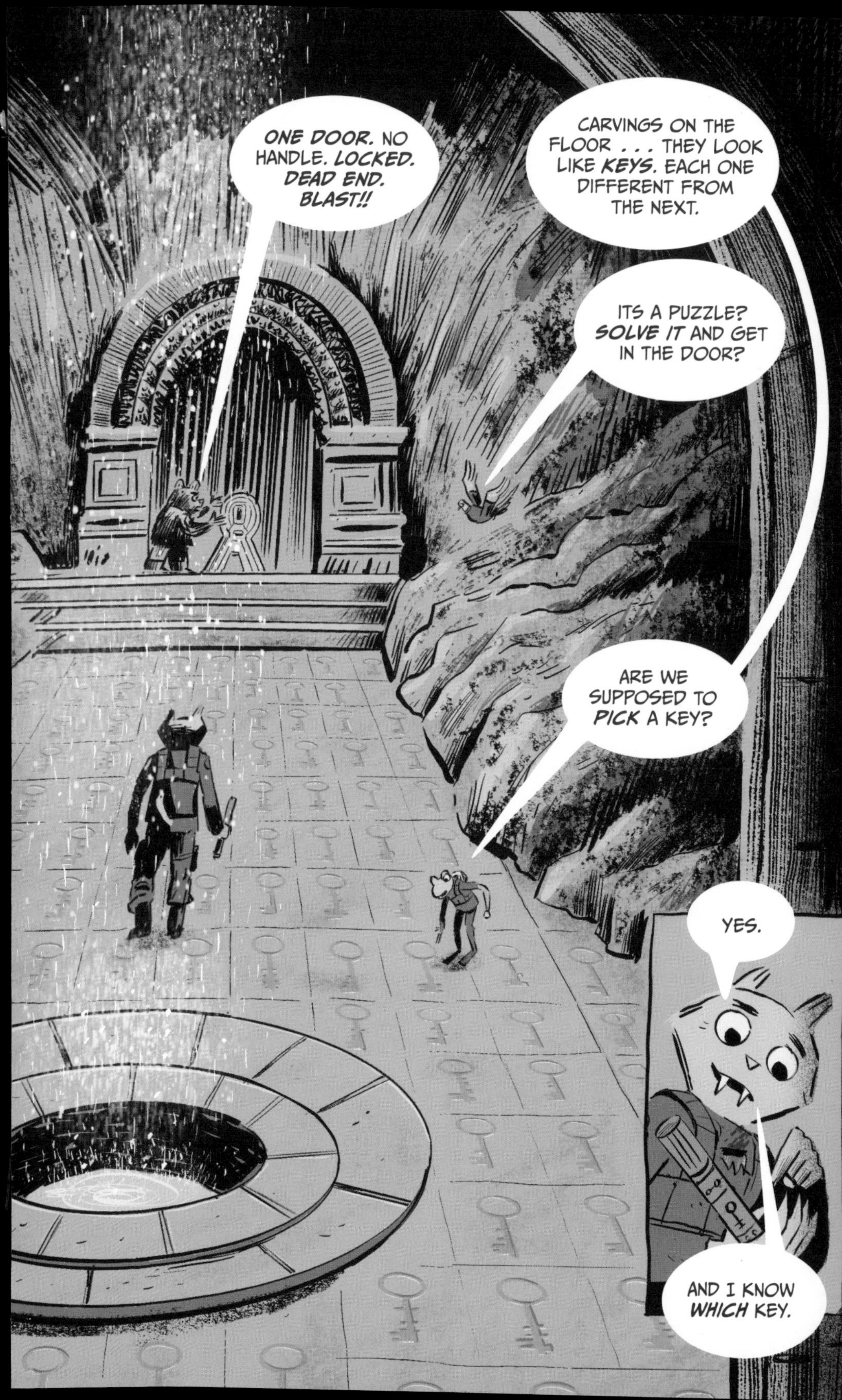
ONE DOOR. NO HANDLE. LOCKED. DEAD END. BLAST!!
CARVINGS ON THE FLOOR . . . THEY LOOK LIKE KEYS. EACH ONE DIFFERENT FROM THE NEXT.
ITS A PUZZLE? SOLVE IT AND GET IN THE DOOR?
ARE WE SUPPOSED TO PICK A KEY?
YES.
AND I KNOW WHICH KEY.

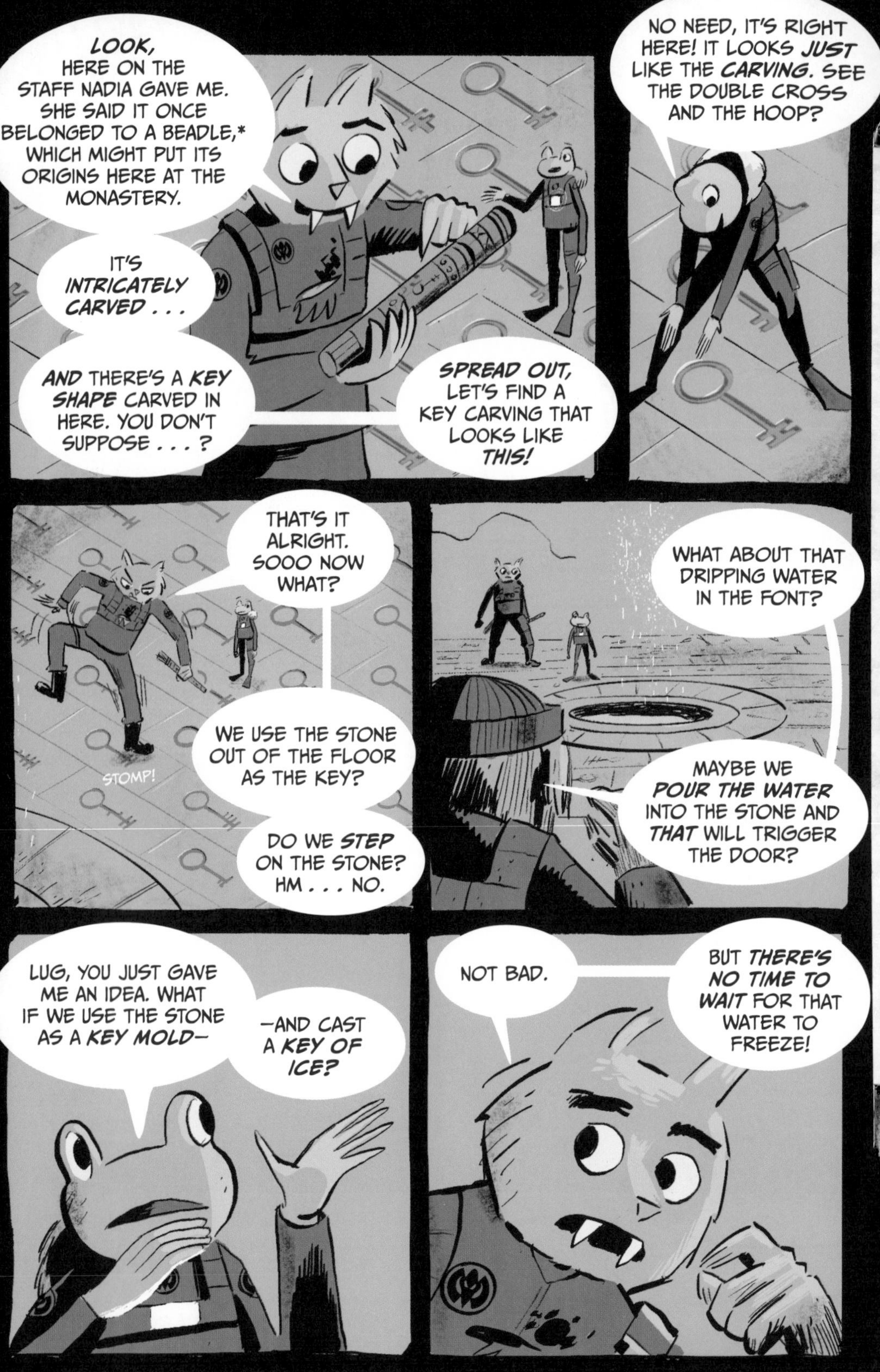
LOOK, HERE ON THE STAFF NADIA GAVE ME. SHE SAID IT ONCE BELONGED TO A BEADLE,* WHICH MIGHT PUT ITS ORIGINS HERE AT THE MONASTERY.
IT'S INTRICATELY CARVED . . .
AND THERE'S A KEY SHAPE CARVED IN HERE. YOU DON'T SUPPOSE . . . ?
SPREAD OUT, LET'S FIND A KEY CARVING THAT LOOKS LIKE THIS!
NO NEED, IT'S RIGHT HERE! IT LOOKS JUST LIKE THE CARVING. SEE THE DOUBLE CROSS AND THE HOOP?
THAT'S IT ALRIGHT. SOOO NOW WHAT?
WE USE THE STONE OUT OF THE FLOOR AS THE KEY?
DO WE STEP ON THE STONE? HM . . . NO.
STOMP!
WHAT ABOUT THAT DRIPPING WATER IN THE FONT?
MAYBE WE POUR THE WATER INTO THE STONE AND THAT WILL TRIGGER THE DOOR?
LUG, YOU JUST GAVE ME AN IDEA. WHAT IF WE USE THE STONE AS A KEY MOLD—
—AND CAST A KEY OF ICE?
NOT BAD.
BUT THERE'S NO TIME TO WAIT FOR THAT WATER TO FREEZE!

*A church official whose duties include preserving order at services.

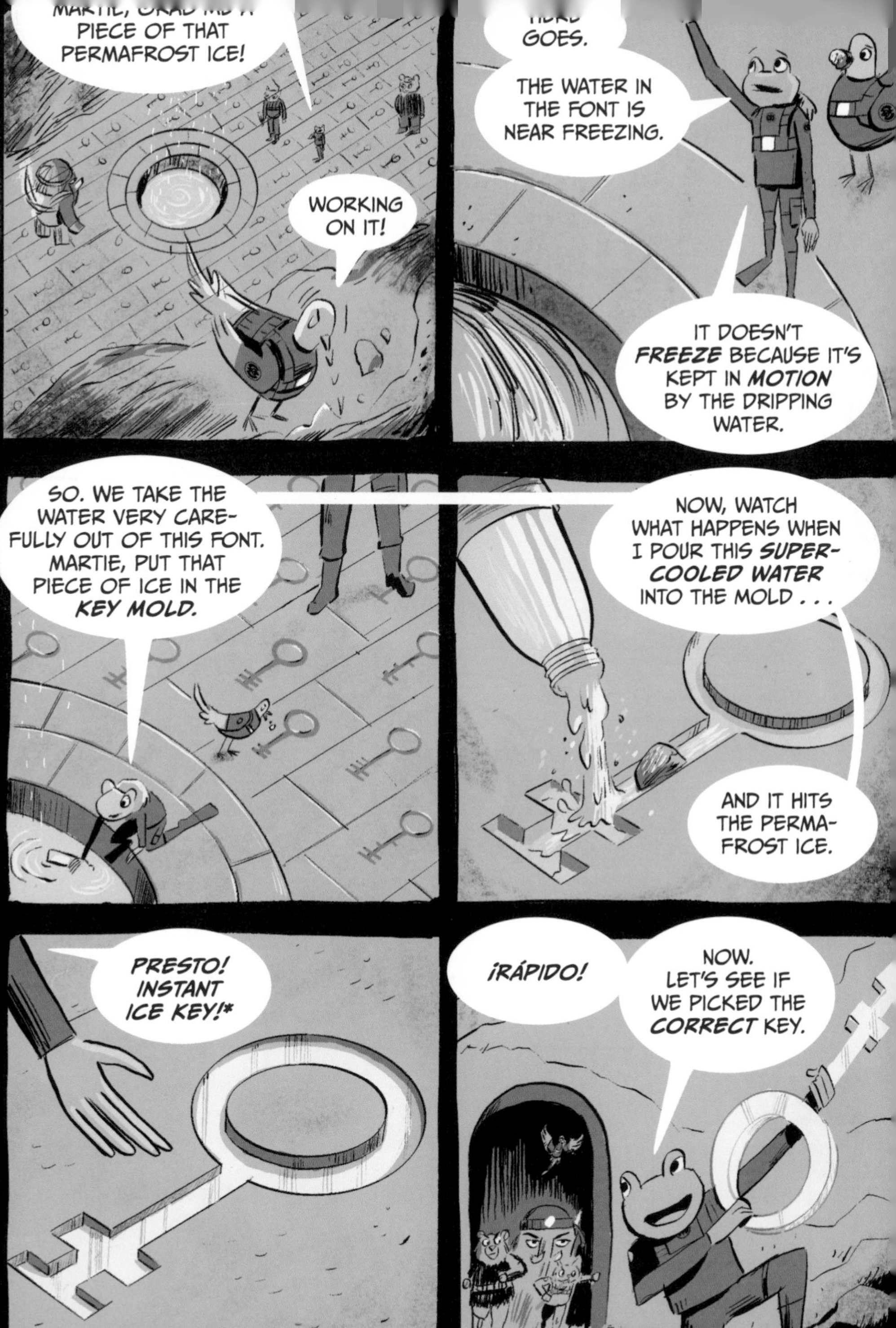

PIECE OF THAT PERMAFROST ICE!
WORKING ON IT!
GOES.
THE WATER IN THE FONT IS NEAR FREEZING.
IT DOESN'T *FREEZE* BECAUSE IT'S KEPT IN *MOTION* BY THE DRIPPING WATER.
SO. WE TAKE THE WATER VERY CARE-FULLY OUT OF THIS FONT. MARTIE, PUT THAT PIECE OF ICE IN THE *KEY MOLD.*
NOW, WATCH WHAT HAPPENS WHEN I POUR THIS *SUPER-COOLED WATER* INTO THE MOLD . . .
AND IT HITS THE PERMA-FROST ICE.
*PRESTO! INSTANT ICE KEY!**
¡RÁPIDO!
NOW. LET'S SEE IF WE PICKED THE *CORRECT* KEY.

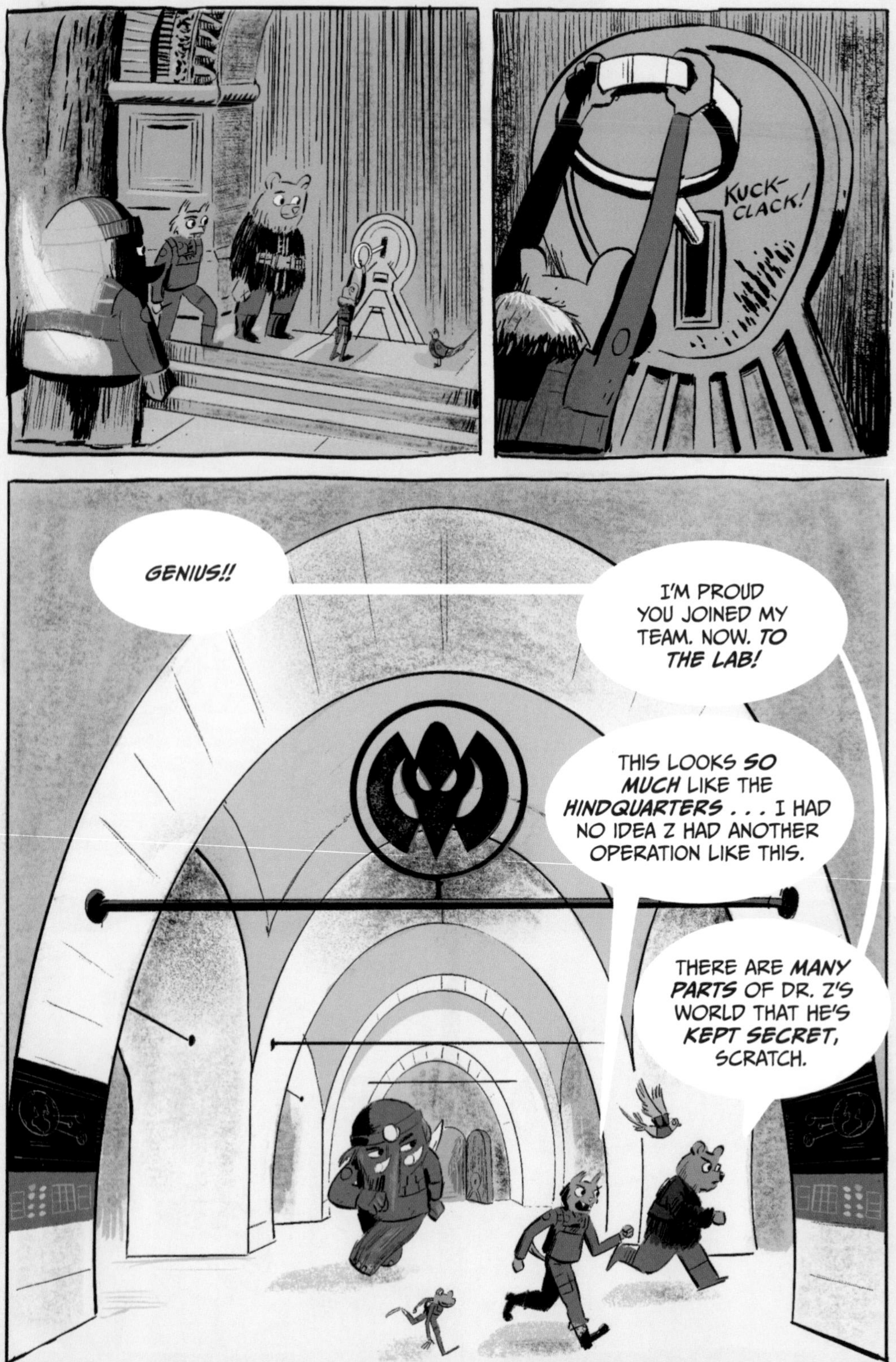
KUCK-CLACK!
GENIUS!!
I'M PROUD YOU JOINED MY TEAM. NOW. TO THE LAB!
THIS LOOKS SO MUCH LIKE THE HINDQUARTERS . . . I HAD NO IDEA Z HAD ANOTHER OPERATION LIKE THIS.
THERE ARE MANY PARTS OF DR. Z'S WORLD THAT HE'S KEPT SECRET, SCRATCH.

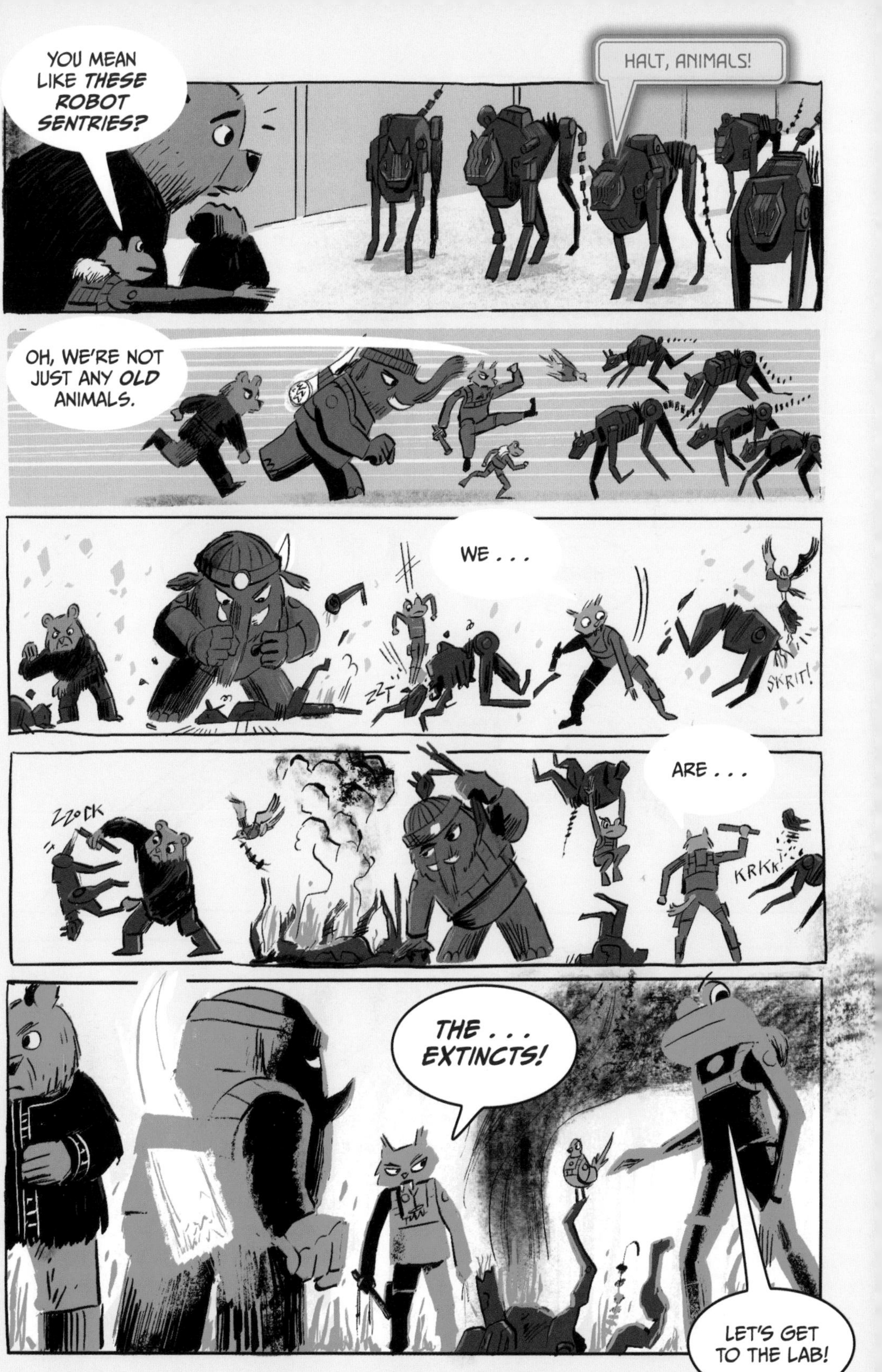
YOU MEAN LIKE THESE ROBOT SENTRIES?
HALT, ANIMALS!
OH, WE'RE NOT JUST ANY OLD ANIMALS.
WE . . .
ZZT
SKRIT!
ZZOCK
ARE . . .
KRKK!
THE . . . EXTINCTS!
LET'S GET TO THE LAB!

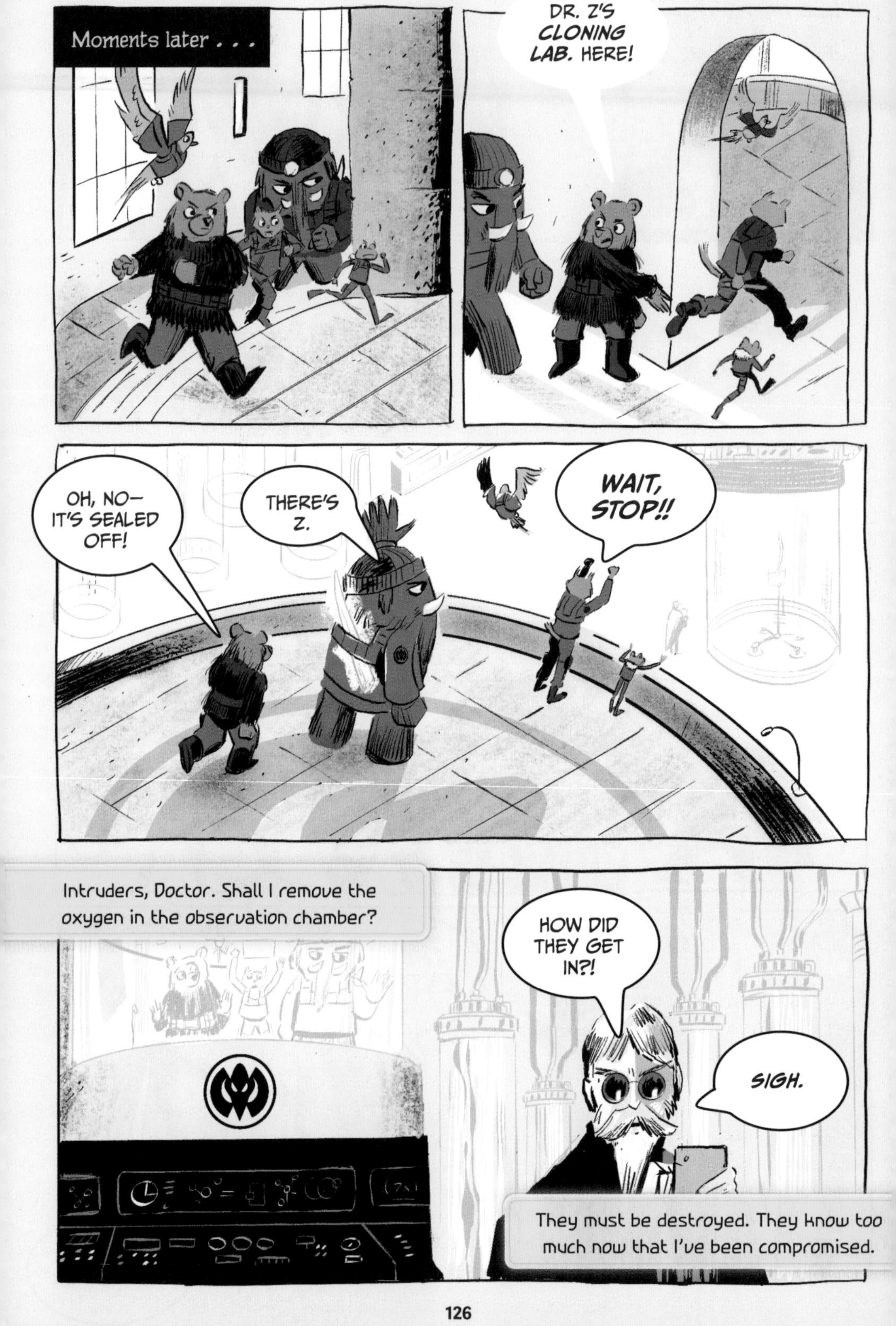
Moments later . . .
DR. Z'S CLONING LAB. HERE!
OH, NO— IT'S SEALED OFF!
THERE'S Z.
WAIT, STOP!!
Intruders, Doctor. Shall I remove the oxygen in the observation chamber?
HOW DID THEY GET IN?!
SIGH.
They must be destroyed. They know too much now that I've been compromised.

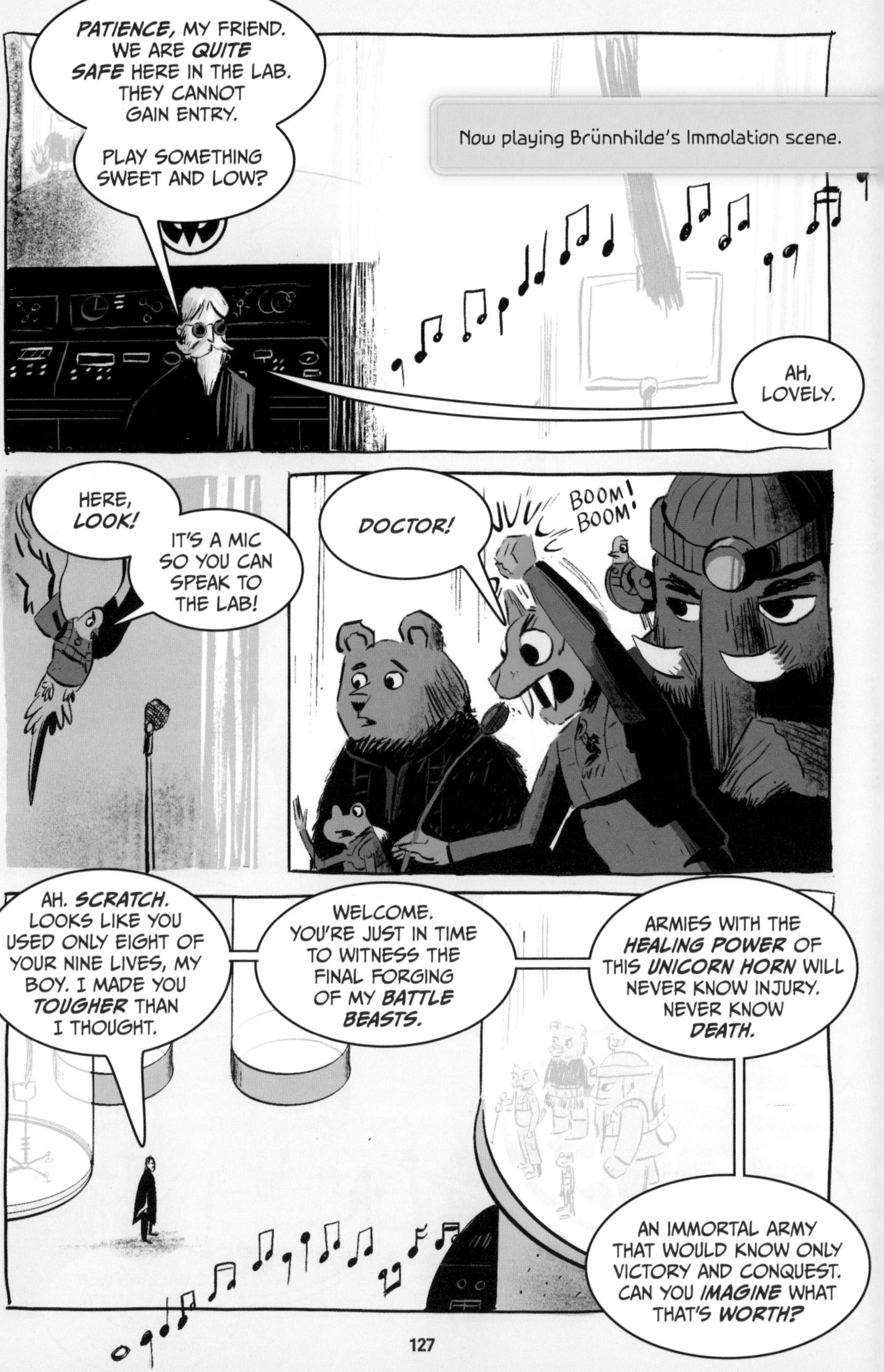
PATIENCE, MY FRIEND. WE ARE QUITE SAFE HERE IN THE LAB. THEY CANNOT GAIN ENTRY.
PLAY SOMETHING SWEET AND LOW?
Now playing Brünnhilde's Immolation scene.
AH, LOVELY.
HERE, LOOK!
IT'S A MIC SO YOU CAN SPEAK TO THE LAB!
DOCTOR!
BOOM! BOOM!
AH. SCRATCH. LOOKS LIKE YOU USED ONLY EIGHT OF YOUR NINE LIVES, MY BOY. I MADE YOU TOUGHER THAN I THOUGHT.
WELCOME. YOU'RE JUST IN TIME TO WITNESS THE FINAL FORGING OF MY BATTLE BEASTS.
ARMIES WITH THE HEALING POWER OF THIS UNICORN HORN WILL NEVER KNOW INJURY. NEVER KNOW DEATH.
AN IMMORTAL ARMY THAT WOULD KNOW ONLY VICTORY AND CONQUEST. CAN YOU IMAGINE WHAT THAT'S WORTH?

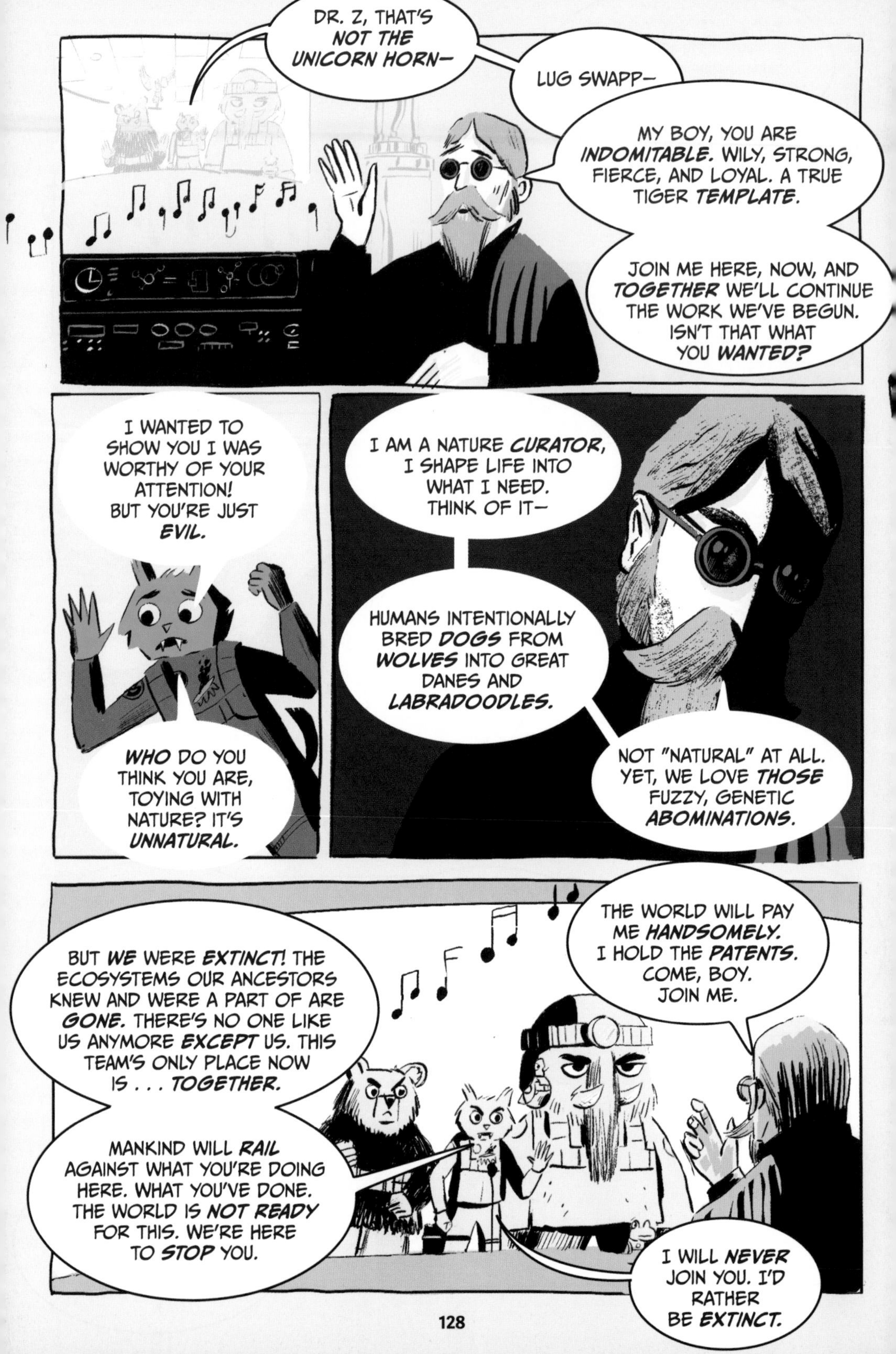
DR. Z, THAT'S NOT THE UNICORN HORN—
LUG SWAPP—
MY BOY, YOU ARE INDOMITABLE. WILY, STRONG, FIERCE, AND LOYAL. A TRUE TIGER TEMPLATE.
JOIN ME HERE, NOW, AND TOGETHER WE'LL CONTINUE THE WORK WE'VE BEGUN. ISN'T THAT WHAT YOU WANTED?
I WANTED TO SHOW YOU I WAS WORTHY OF YOUR ATTENTION! BUT YOU'RE JUST EVIL.
WHO DO YOU THINK YOU ARE, TOYING WITH NATURE? IT'S UNNATURAL.
I AM A NATURE CURATOR, I SHAPE LIFE INTO WHAT I NEED. THINK OF IT—
HUMANS INTENTIONALLY BRED DOGS FROM WOLVES INTO GREAT DANES AND LABRADOODLES.
NOT "NATURAL" AT ALL. YET, WE LOVE THOSE FUZZY, GENETIC ABOMINATIONS.
BUT WE WERE EXTINCT! THE ECOSYSTEMS OUR ANCESTORS KNEW AND WERE A PART OF ARE GONE. THERE'S NO ONE LIKE US ANYMORE EXCEPT US. THIS TEAM'S ONLY PLACE NOW IS . . . TOGETHER.
MANKIND WILL RAIL AGAINST WHAT YOU'RE DOING HERE. WHAT YOU'VE DONE. THE WORLD IS NOT READY FOR THIS. WE'RE HERE TO STOP YOU.
THE WORLD WILL PAY ME HANDSOMELY. I HOLD THE PATENTS. COME, BOY. JOIN ME.
I WILL NEVER JOIN YOU. I'D RATHER BE EXTINCT.

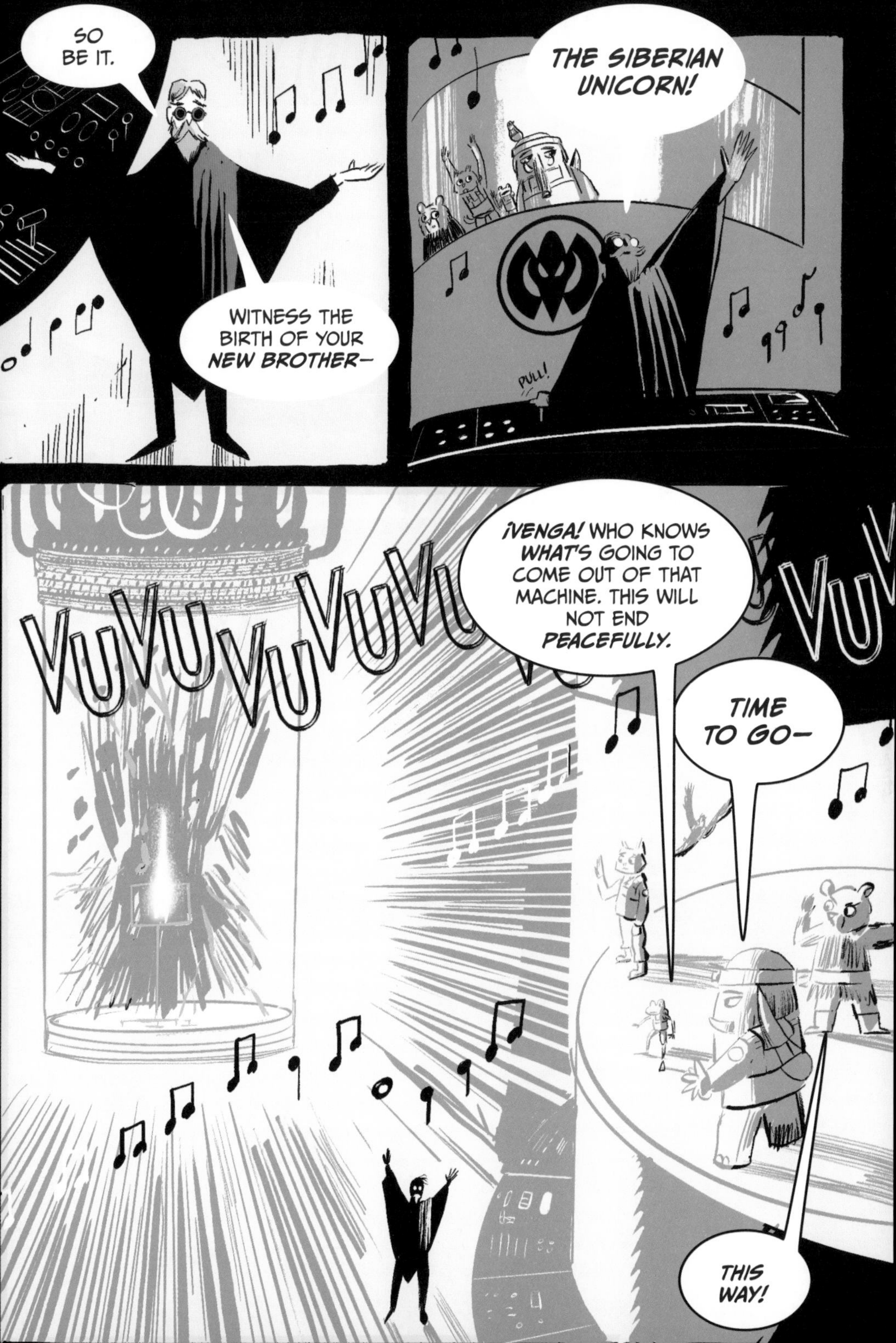
SO BE IT.
WITNESS THE BIRTH OF YOUR *NEW BROTHER*—
THE SIBERIAN UNICORN!
PULL!
VUVUVUVUVUVUVU
¡VENGA! WHO KNOWS *WHAT'S* GOING TO COME OUT OF THAT MACHINE. THIS WILL NOT END *PEACEFULLY.*
TIME TO GO—
THIS WAY!

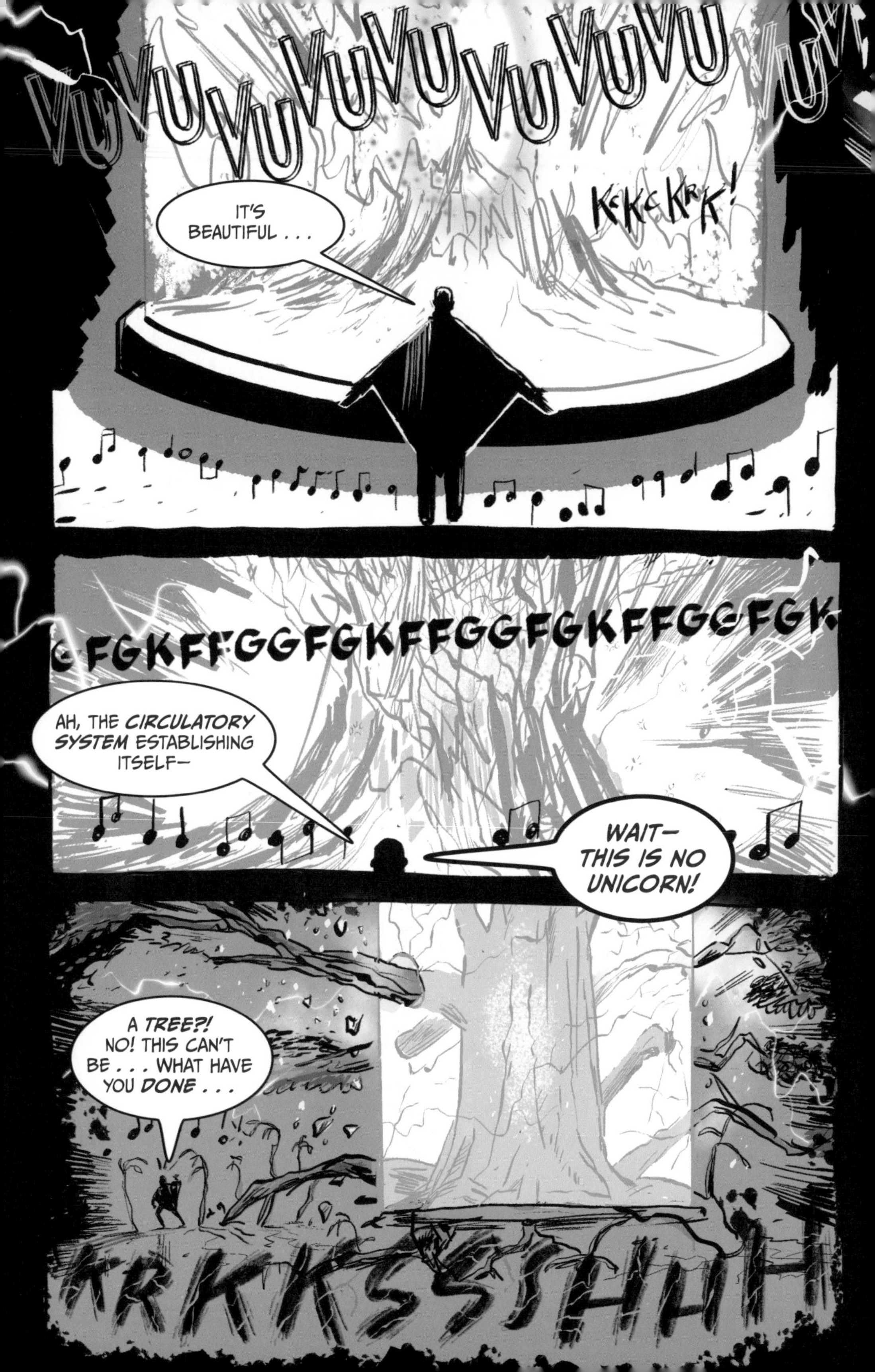
VUVUVUVUVUVUVUVUVUVUVU
IT'S BEAUTIFUL . . .
KKKKRK!
GFGKFFGGFGKFFGGFGKFFGGFGK
AH, THE *CIRCULATORY SYSTEM* ESTABLISHING ITSELF—
WAIT— THIS IS NO UNICORN!
A *TREE?!* NO! THIS CAN'T BE . . . WHAT HAVE YOU *DONE* . . .
KRKKSSSHHH

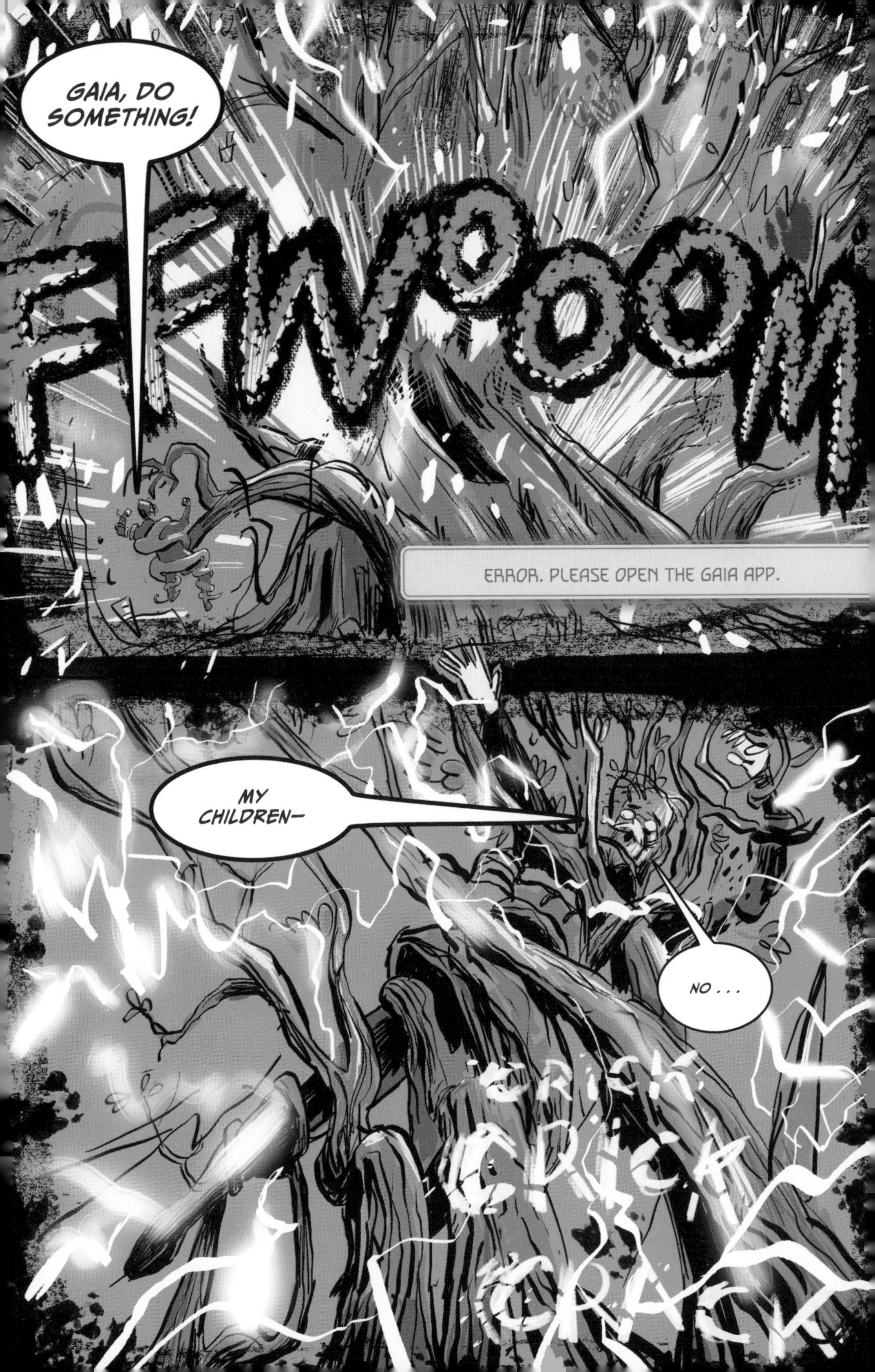
GAIA, DO SOMETHING!
FWOOOM
ERROR. PLEASE OPEN THE GAIA APP.
MY CHILDREN—
NO . . .
CRICK
CRICK
CRACK

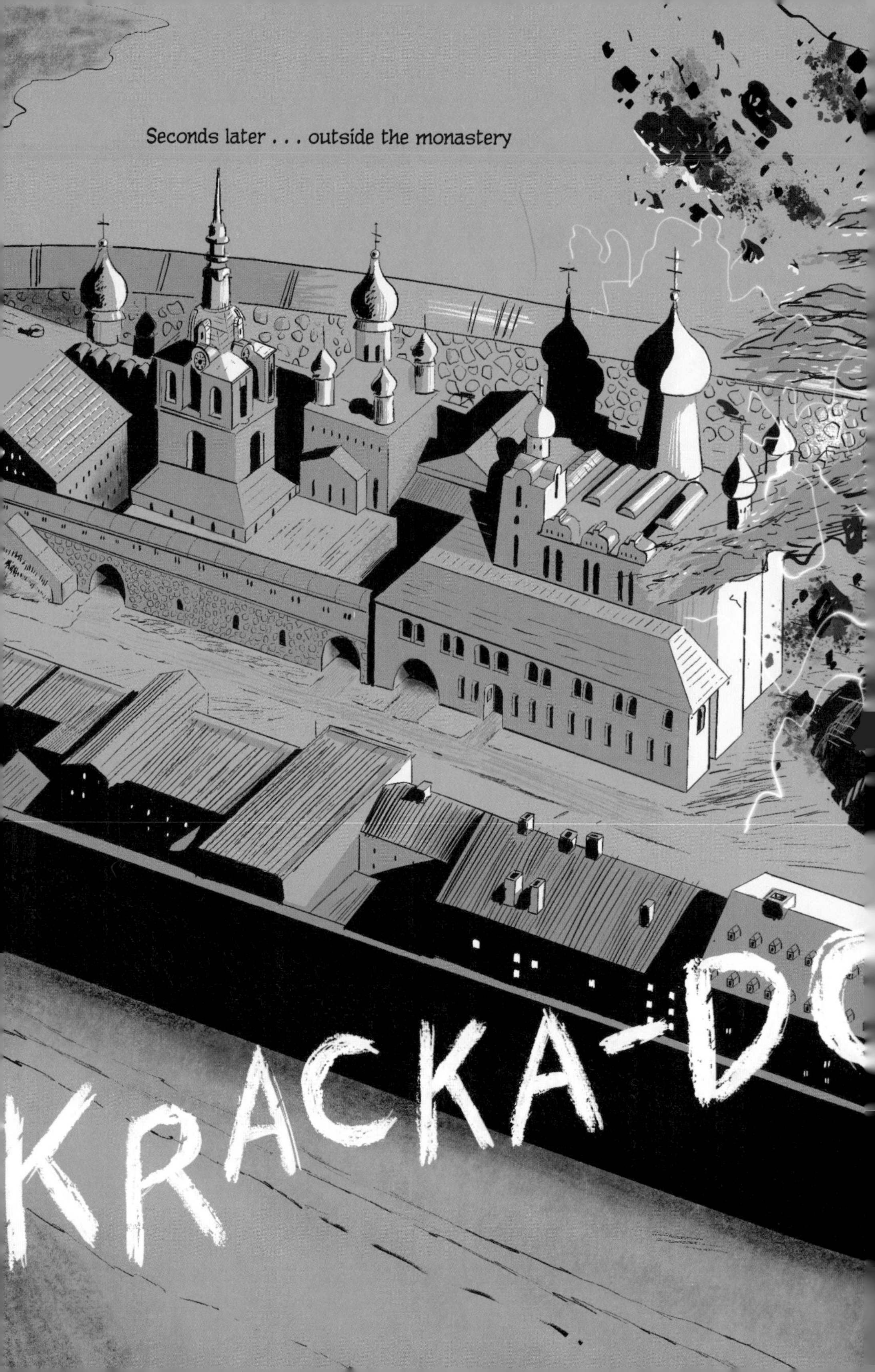
Seconds later . . . outside the monastery
KRACKA-DO

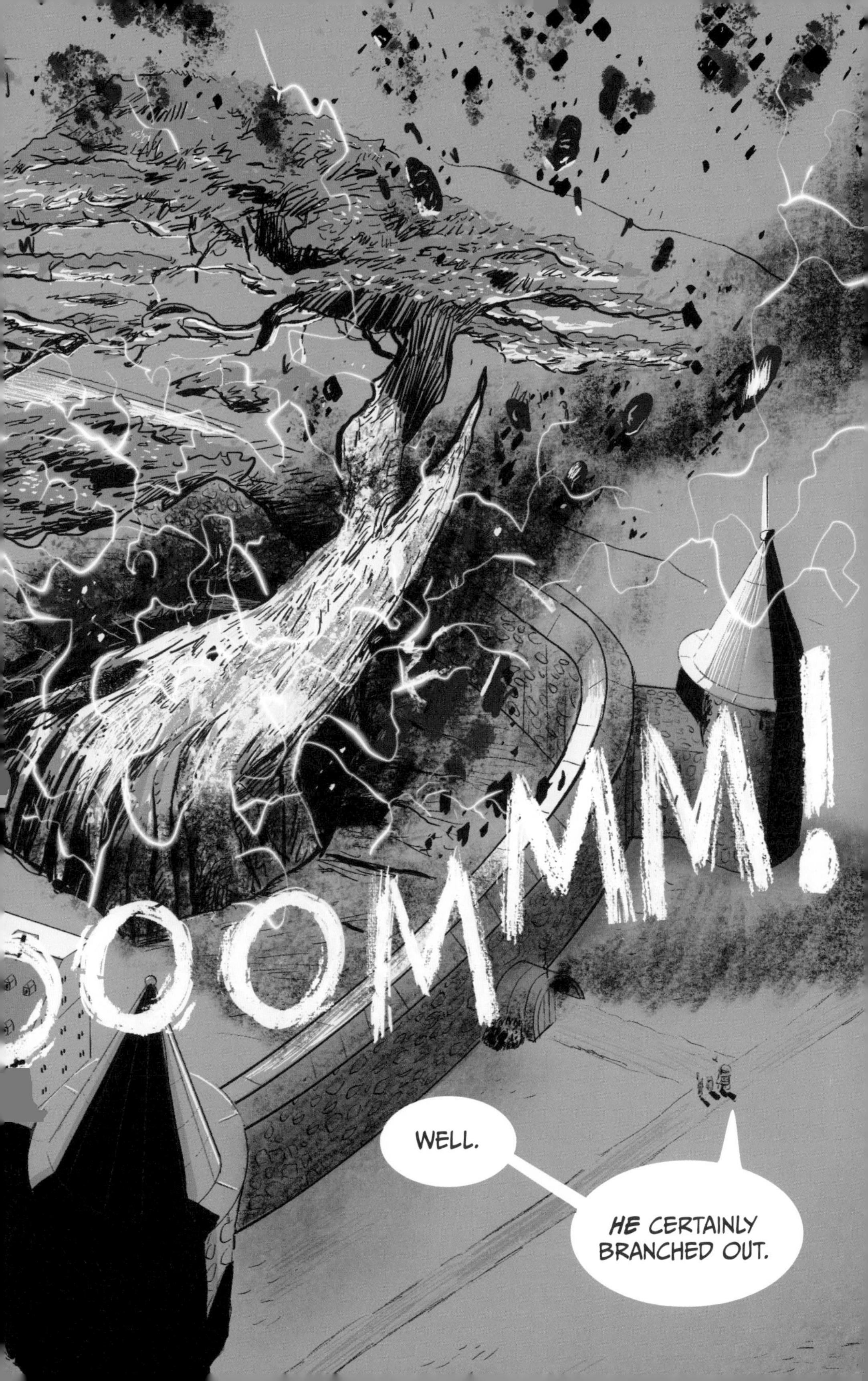
OOOMMM!
WELL.
HE CERTAINLY BRANCHED OUT.

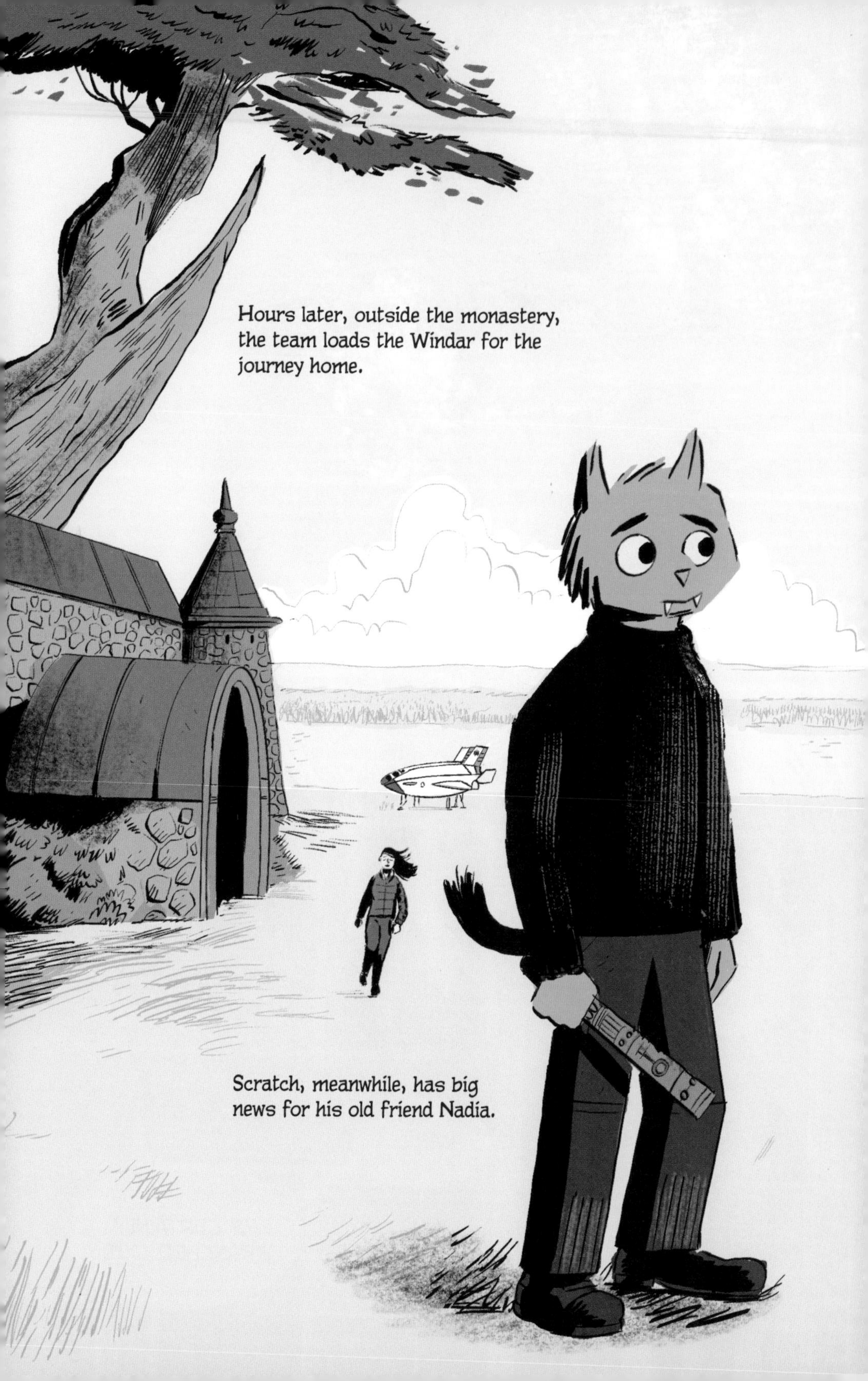
Hours later, outside the monastery, the team loads the Windar for the journey home.
Scratch, meanwhile, has big news for his old friend Nadia.

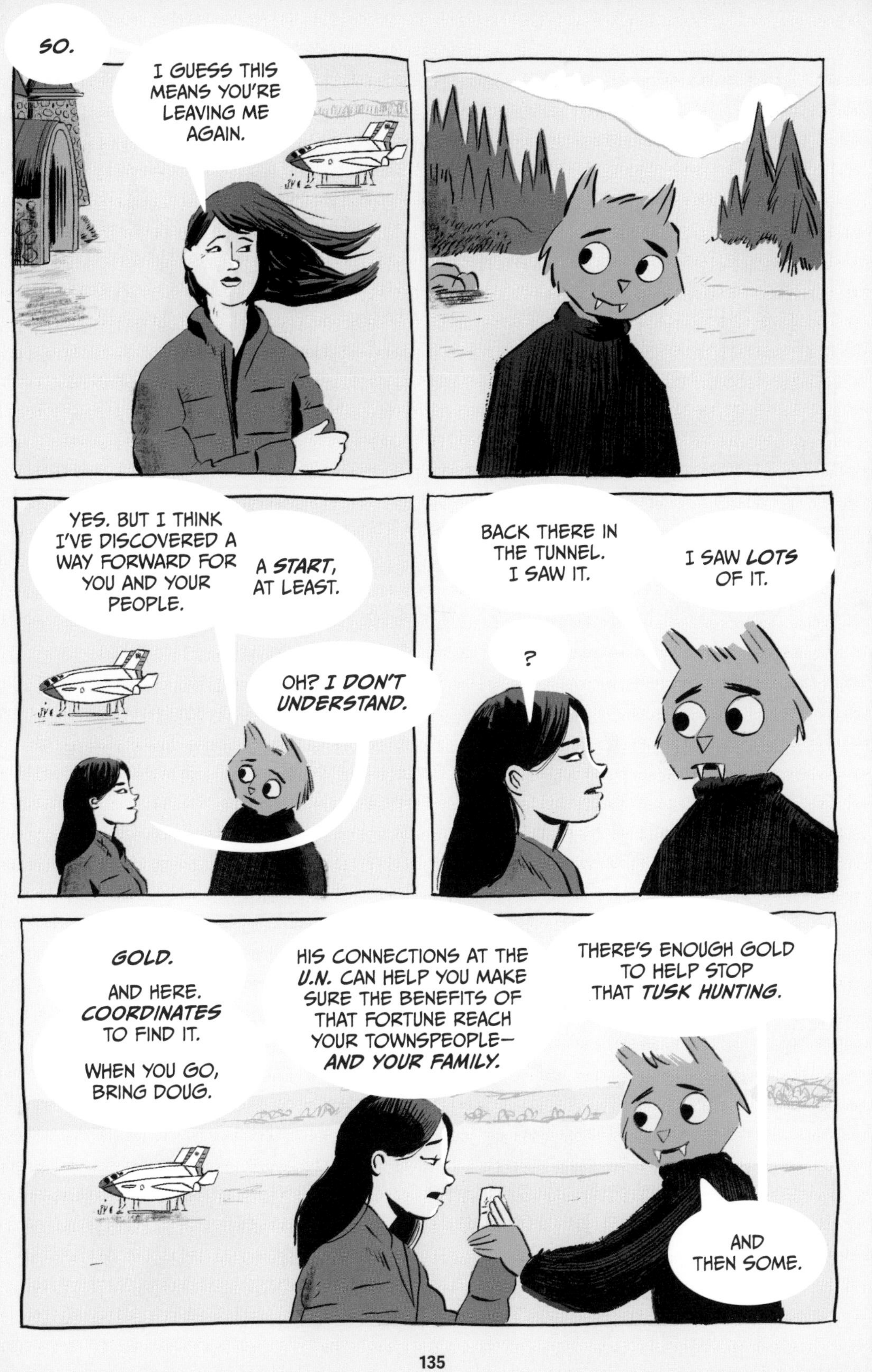
SO.
I GUESS THIS MEANS YOU'RE LEAVING ME AGAIN.
YES. BUT I THINK I'VE DISCOVERED A WAY FORWARD FOR YOU AND YOUR PEOPLE.
A *START*, AT LEAST.
OH? *I DON'T UNDERSTAND.*
BACK THERE IN THE TUNNEL. I SAW IT.
I SAW *LOTS* OF IT.
?
GOLD.
AND HERE. *COORDINATES* TO FIND IT.
WHEN YOU GO, BRING DOUG.
HIS CONNECTIONS AT THE *U.N.* CAN HELP YOU MAKE SURE THE BENEFITS OF THAT FORTUNE REACH YOUR TOWNSPEOPLE— *AND YOUR FAMILY.*
THERE'S ENOUGH GOLD TO HELP STOP THAT *TUSK HUNTING*.
AND THEN SOME.

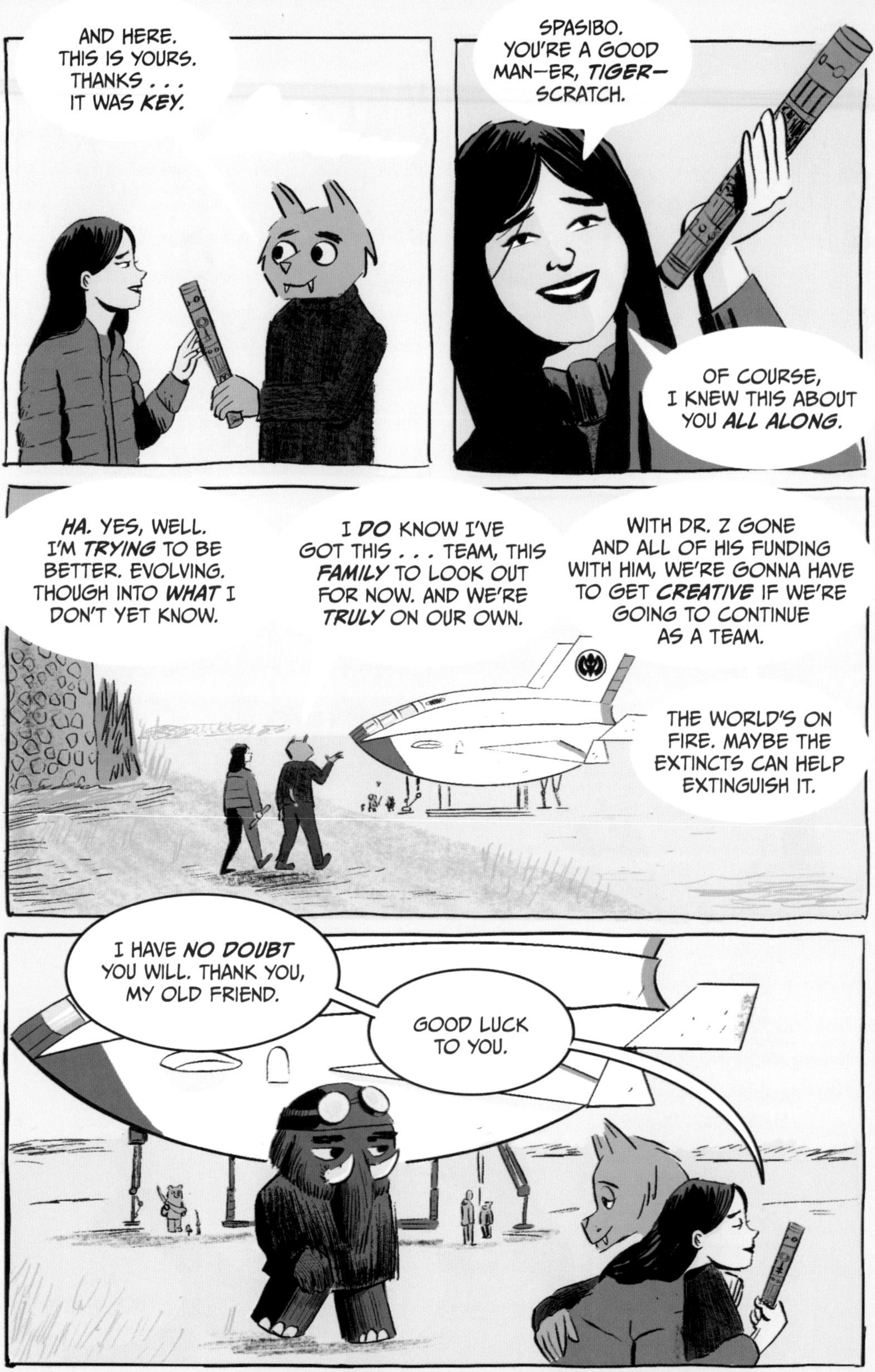
AND HERE. THIS IS YOURS. THANKS . . . IT WAS KEY.
SPASIBO. YOU'RE A GOOD MAN—ER, TIGER—SCRATCH.
OF COURSE, I KNEW THIS ABOUT YOU ALL ALONG.
HA. YES, WELL. I'M TRYING TO BE BETTER. EVOLVING. THOUGH INTO WHAT I DON'T YET KNOW.
I DO KNOW I'VE GOT THIS . . . TEAM, THIS FAMILY TO LOOK OUT FOR NOW. AND WE'RE TRULY ON OUR OWN.
WITH DR. Z GONE AND ALL OF HIS FUNDING WITH HIM, WE'RE GONNA HAVE TO GET CREATIVE IF WE'RE GOING TO CONTINUE AS A TEAM.
THE WORLD'S ON FIRE. MAYBE THE EXTINCTS CAN HELP EXTINGUISH IT.
I HAVE NO DOUBT YOU WILL. THANK YOU, MY OLD FRIEND.
GOOD LUCK TO YOU.

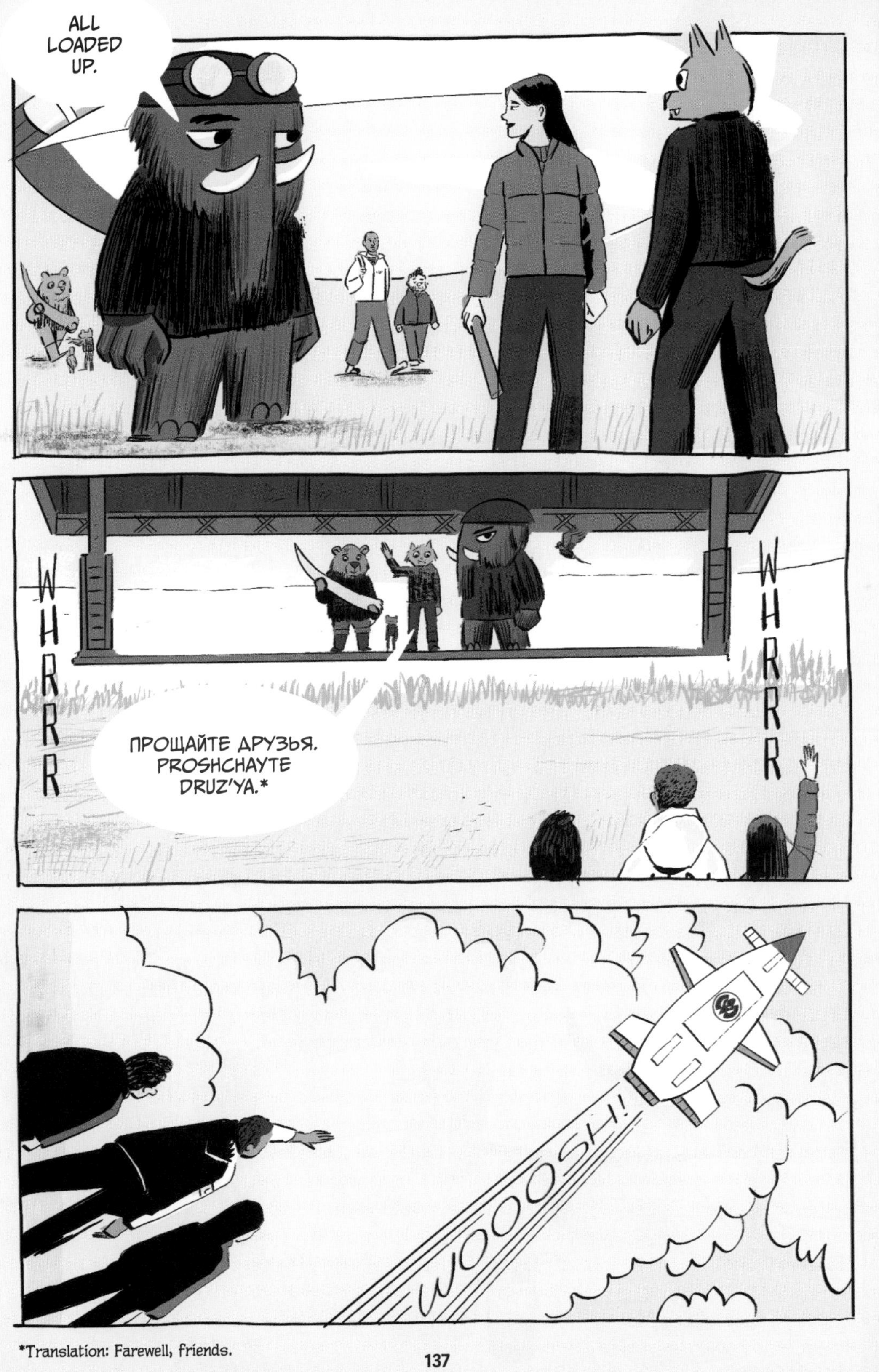
ALL LOADED UP.
WHRRR
WHRRR
ПРОЩАЙТЕ ДРУЗЬЯ. PROSHCHAYTE DRUZ'YA.*
WOOOSH!

*Translation: Farewell, friends.

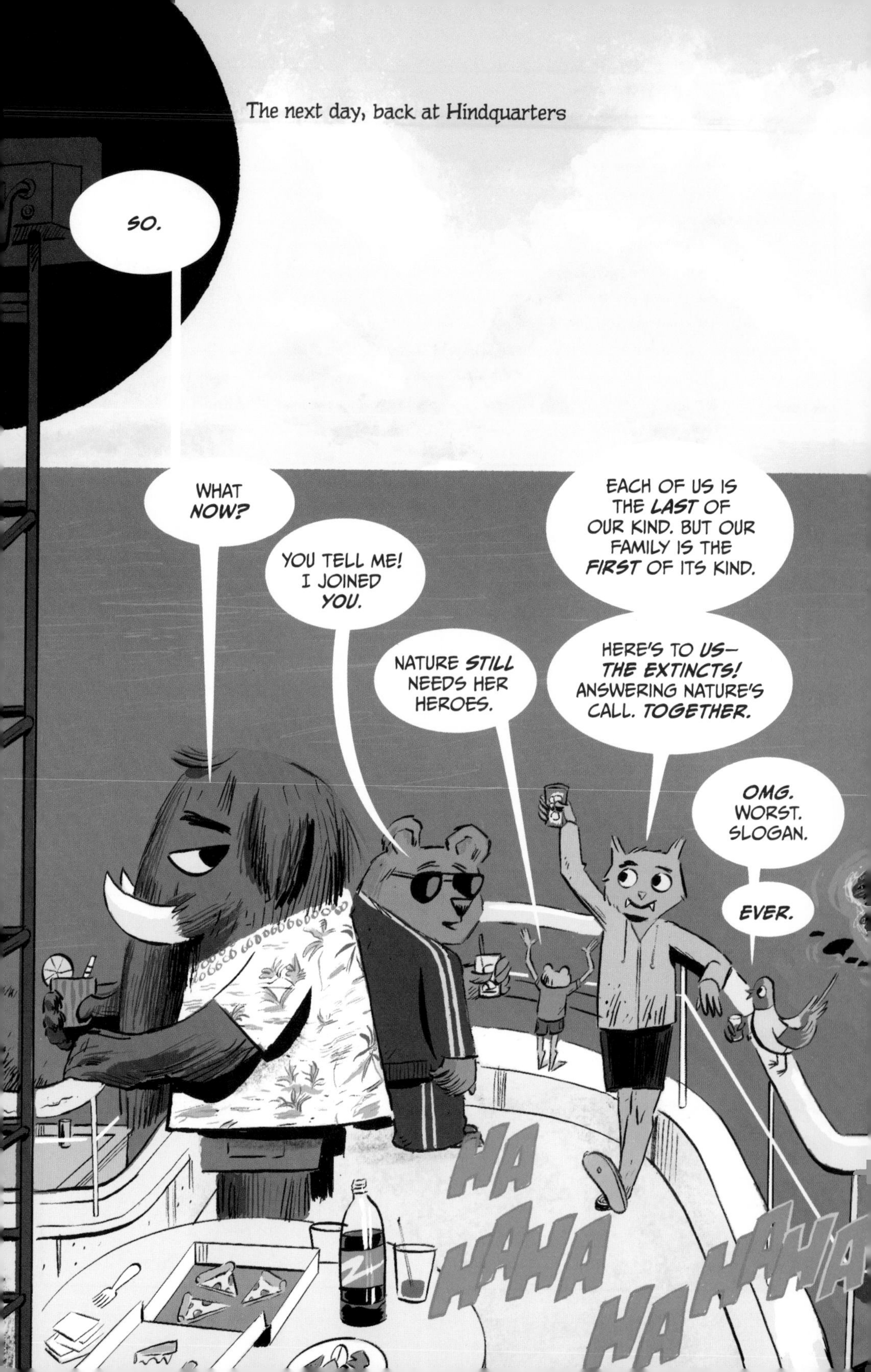
The next day, back at Hindquarters
SO.
WHAT NOW?
YOU TELL ME! I JOINED YOU.
NATURE STILL NEEDS HER HEROES.
EACH OF US IS THE LAST OF OUR KIND. BUT OUR FAMILY IS THE FIRST OF ITS KIND.
HERE'S TO US— THE EXTINCTS! ANSWERING NATURE'S CALL. TOGETHER.
OMG. WORST. SLOGAN.
EVER.
HA HAHA HA HAHAHAHA

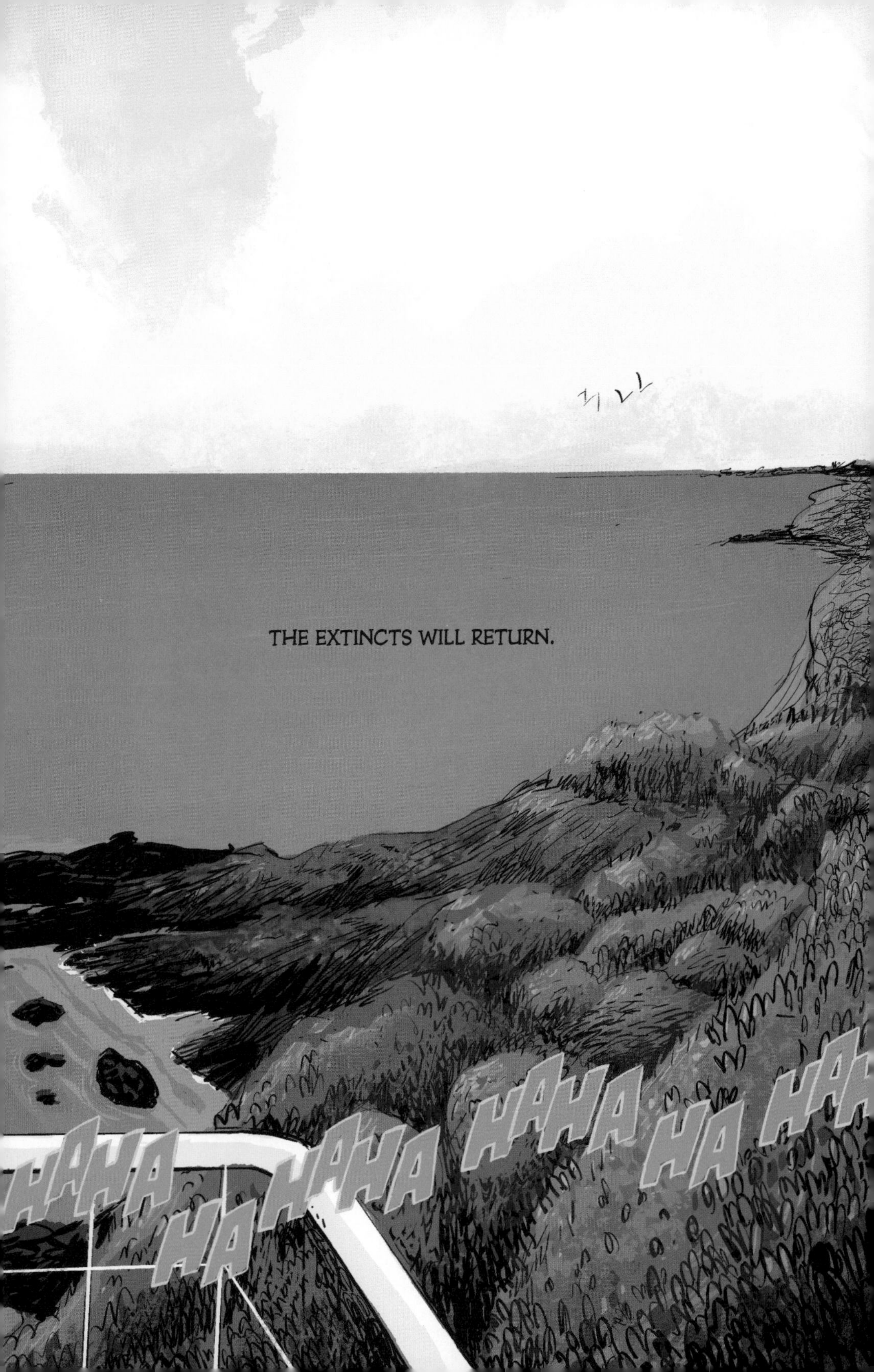
THE EXTINCTS WILL RETURN.
HAHA
HA
HAHA
HAHA
HA
HAH

THE EXTINCTIARY

Your field guide to the extinct creatures & concepts featured in this book*

* Don't worry, GAIA didn't write it.

CAVE BEAR *Ursus spelaeus*

HABITAT: Forested low mountainous areas
DISTRIBUTION: Europe and parts of Eurasia
TEMPORAL RANGE: Chibanian to Upper Pleistocene (129,000–11,000 years ago)
SIZE: 11.5' standing on hind legs, 5.5' at shoulder on all fours, up to 1500 lbs
LIFESPAN: Probably fewer than 20 years
EXTINCTION CAUSE: Food loss due to climate change and competition with humans for caves in which to hibernate
FUN FACT: A 1917–23 excavacation of the Drachenloch cave in Switzerland uncovered more than 30,000 cave bear skeletons.

NONE SHALL BEAR WITNESS

Thousands of winters ago, as cave bears hibernated in their cave homes, cave lions snuck in to hunt them. A great idea—until the bears awoke to fight off the cats, their only predator. Explorers discovered the cats' bones in caves years later, and the creatures became known, ironically perhaps, as cave lions.

Still, dying during hibernation was common for the cave bears. If one was sick, old, or did not feast to prepare for the cold winters, then it wouldn't awaken in spring.

Like its modern Eurasian brown bear cousin, the cave bear was an omnivore, but it loved eating plants. Unfortunately, the ice age shortened or eliminated plant-growing seasons, likely starving the bears.

Cave bears were among the first megafauna to go extinct in the late Pleistocene era, around 27,000 years ago. Most other megafauna survived the ice age and died out 10 to 15,000 years ago.

For ages, people assumed the remains of cave bears were those of apes, large dogs, cats—even dragons. But by the end of the 19th century, scientists had identified the cave bear as a member of the ursine—or bear—family.

Today, scientists collect frozen and well-preserved cave bear DNA. In late 2020, Siberian reindeer herders unearthed a well-preserved frozen cave bear carcass. They turned it over to a local university that specializes in studying ancient megafauna. For the first time ever, scientists have been able to study the bear's soft tissues, inner organs—and even its nose.

SEE A SKELETON
American Museum of Natural History, New York, NY
Field Museum, Chicago, IL

FURTHER READING
Hehner, Barbara. *Ice Age Cave Bear. The Giant Beast That Terrified Ancient Humans.* New York, NY: Crown Books for Young Readers, 2002.
Kurtén, Björn. *The Cave Bear Story: Life and Death of a Vanished Animal.* New York, NY: Columbia University Press, 1995.

MEGAFAUNAL WOLF *Canis Cf. lupus* (where cf. in Latin means uncertain)

HABITAT: Multiple, across the Holarctic
DISTRIBUTION: Northern continents of the world
TEMPORAL RANGE: Upper Pleistocene to Holocene
(About 45,000–7,500 years ago)
SIZE: About 3.5'–5.3' in length and about 2.75' at
shoulder, up to 180 lbs
LIFESPAN: 6–8 years
EXTINCTION CAUSE: Loss of food
FUN FACT: All modern wolves descended from
a separate species, meaning this megafaunal
species died out completely.

ONE BIG BAD WOLF

The megafaunal wolf was similar to the gray wolf we know today, but there are subtle differences. The megafaunal wolf had a shorter and wider mouth with larger rear teeth in relation to the size of its skull. This adaptation allowed it to prey and scavenge on Pleistocene megafauna. Analysis of the isotopes in these wolves' bones has revealed that their diet included bison, horse, musk ox, and scavenged woolly mammoths.

Megafaunal wolf samples show moderately-to-heavily worn teeth, as well as frequent broken teeth. The place where the teeth broke is also different compared to gray wolves. Megafaunal wolves had more fractures of incisors, cheek teeth, and molars than gray wolves. Scientists have observed a similar pattern in hyenas' teeth, suggesting that increased fang and side teeth breaks meant these megafaunal wolves, like hyenas, often ate bone, because wolves gnaw bones with fangs and then crack them with their cheek teeth.

Scientists examined specimens of all of the carnivore species from the La Brea Tar Pits in California, including remains of dire wolves, which were also megafaunal hypercarnivores. That evidence suggests that these carnivores were well-fed just before they went extinct and that scavenging was less common than among large carnivores today. Tooth breaking was probably from the catching and eating of larger prey and not from scavenging.

In 2019, the head of the world's first adult Pleistocene-era wolf was unearthed in Siberia. The wolf had thick, mammoth-like fur and intact fangs and was two to four years old when it died. It was the first found with soft tissue preserved. Russian scientists will compare it to modern-day wolves to better understand its evolution and to reconstruct its appearance.

SEE A GRAY WOLF
Detroit Zoo, Detroit, MI
San Diego Zoo, San Diego, CA
Stone Zoo, Stoneham, MA

FURTHER READING
Dutcher, Jim, and Jamie Dutcher. *Living with Wolves!: True Stories of Adventures with Animals.*
    Washington, DC: National Geographic, 2016.
Marsh, Laura F. *Wolves.* Washington, DC: National Geographic, 2012.

COLLINS' POISON FROG *Andinobates abditus*

HABITAT: Dense, humid forests
DISTRIBUTION: Ecuador, in the eastern base of
the Reventador stratovolcano, in Napo Province
TEMPORAL RANGE: Cretaceous to Holocene
(100 million years–modern era)
SIZE: Approx. 0.4" to approx. 1.5" long, 0.2–0.14 oz
LIFESPAN: 4–6 years
EXTINCTION CAUSE: Habitat loss, possible fungal infection
FUN FACT: Its poison comes from a diet of poisonous insects.

HOPPED OUT

Andinobates abditus is a species of poison dart frog currently listed as extinct in its only known home. It may survive elsewhere in areas not surveyed.

Poison dart frogs are among the most toxic creatures on earth. We've come to know these creatures as "poison dart" frogs because Columbia's Emberá Chocó group of tribes from the Pacific slopes of the Andes reportedly rub the frogs and hunting darts together to infuse the darts with poison. However, scientists identified that only a few of the nearly 200 species are actually used for this purpose, including the golden poison frog. That species is the most toxic of all poison dart frogs, secreting enough poison to kill several humans! Some poison frogs secrete the alkaloid toxin batrachotoxin that medical researchers (very carefully) use in promising research into muscle relaxants, heart stimulants, and anesthetics.

These frogs do not create their own poison. Instead, like us, they are what they eat. Using sticky, retractable tongues, the frogs catch and eat poisonous insects that have eaten poisonous plants. The frogs digest the insects but keep the poison in their skin and use it to protect themselves from predators. By contrast, poison frogs in captivity that live on a diet of crickets and other nonpoisonous insects are not poisonous themselves.

Poison frogs' beautiful skin colorings are a visual warning to would-be predators. "Don't eat me!" the colors seem to shout. Indeed, if a predator tries to eat a colorful frog and it finds it unappetizing, it will then recognize that creature and not attack it in the future.

Scientists can identify species of poison frogs by their calls. Frogs use these calls to attract mates, mark their territories, and express distress.

SEE A POISON FROG
Smithsonian National Zoo, Washington, DC (green-and-black, tricolored, and blue poison frogs)
Detroit Zoo, Detroit, MI (Golfodulcean, green-and-black, dyeing, mimic, and yellow-headed poison frogs)
San Diego Zoo, San Diego, CA (green-and-black dyeing, splashback, and black-legged poison frogs)

FURTHER READING
Bredeson, Carmen. *Poison Dart Frogs Up Close.* Berkeley Heights, NJ: Enslow Elementary, 2012.
Carney, Elizabeth. *Frogs!* Washington, DC: National Geographic, 2009.
Davey, Owen. *Fanatical about Frogs.* London, UK: Flying Eye Books, 2019.
Owings, Lisa. *Poison Dart Frogs.* New York, NY: Bellweather Media, 2011.

MEGALODON *Carcharocles megalodon*

HABITAT: Warm coastal waters
DISTRIBUTION: Nearly worldwide,
with fossils found globally except Antarctica
TEMPORAL RANGE: Burdigalian to Zanclean
(About 20–3.6 million years ago)
SIZE: Average estimates 33' long, possibly larger,
up to 65 tons
LIFESPAN: Up to 25 years
EXTINCTION CAUSE: Climate change,
competition from Great White Shark
FUN FACT: Its name in Latin means "big tooth."

JAWESOME

The megalodon is thought by paleontologists to have been one of the largest and most powerful predators ever. Its bony jawbone and teeth preserved in fossil records give scientists scant clues as to what the megalodon looked like—and just how big it grew. There are theories that it resembled a massive great white shark, a large sand tiger shark, or even a basking shark. Scientists estimate the megalodon's size based on the size of its teeth and jaw. Maximum length estimates put the leviathan at 59 feet—longer than a tractor trailer!

Given their enormous size, the shark most likely preyed on large animals like whales, seals, and sea turtles—and maybe, given its 6-foot-wide jaws, several of them in a single bite. The long-standing uncertainty about sharks has led humans throughout history to make wild assumptions about them. People used shark teeth as jewelry and as medicine. In the Middle Ages, Europeans even thought shark teeth were petrified tongues of dragons and snakes.

Today, there are a number of theories about how the megalodon died out. A warmer water fish, the megalodon might have met its match in the cooling of oceans at the dawn of the ice age. With so much water freezing, sea levels worldwide lowered—and the resulting loss of acceptable areas to raise young could have contributed to the megalodon's extinction.

Their prey also began to disperse into cooler waters. Baleen whales moved into polar seas, which reduced the megalodon's main food source. Then there was the competition—the great white shark, smaller and more nimble, might have literally eaten the meg's lunch.

SEE A SPECIMEN

Jaws at the American Museum of Natural History, New York, NY
Life-size model at the Smithsonian Museum of Natural History, Washington, DC
Reconstructed skeleton at the Calvert Marine Museum, Solomons, MD

FURTHER READING

Skerry, Brian, Elizabeth Carney, and Sarah Wassner Flynn. *The Ultimate Book of Sharks: Your Guide to These Fierce and Fantastic Fish.* Washington, DC: National Geographic, 2018.
Harvey, Derek. *Super Shark Encyclopedia: And Other Creatures of the Deep.* New York, NY: DK Publishing, 2015.

PASSENGER PIGEON *Ectopistes migratorius*

HABITAT: Deciduous forests
DISTRIBUTION: Midwest & Eastern North America
TEMPORAL RANGE: Zanclean to Holocene
(3.6 million years ago–1914)
SIZE: 15–16" length, 7–8.5" wingspan, 9–12 oz.
LIFESPAN: 15 years in captivity, unknown in wild
EXTINCTION CAUSE: Hunting, loss of habitat
FUN FACT: They could fly at speeds up to 62 mph!

NO MORE PASSENGERS

Long ago, the passenger pigeon was one of the most common birds in North America. At 3–5 billion birds, their population was so large that gigantic flocks of them darkened the sky, sometimes taking days to pass by overhead. It must've seemed unbelievable at the time that humans could wipe out billions of birds. But we did—in less than a century.

Pigeon meat was tasty, and purveyors sold it as a cheap and plentiful food. Humans hunted the birds on a massive scale for many decades, enabled by new and emerging technology. The telegraph spread word about pigeon nestings to hunters, who would flock to the flocks. Trains carried tons of ice-packed barrels of dead birds to distant diners. Sportsmen shot at live pigeons in shooting competitions. There's at least one instance of them used as cannon fodder. Hunters chopped down trees full of nesting birds to net them before they could escape. Widespread deforestation also destroyed the pigeons' habitat. All of this reduced the large breeding population necessary for its species survival.

The decimation of the passenger pigeon and other species led to some of the nation's first natural conservation laws. But it was too little, too late. A hunter shot the last confirmed wild bird in 1901. The last passenger pigeon, Martha (for whom Martie in this book was named) died in captivity in the Cincinnati Zoo on September 1, 1914. It was the first time we witnessed the extinction of a species by our own hand. You can see the specimen made from Martha's remains at the Smithsonian in Washington, DC.

There are efforts underway to "de-extinct" a passenger pigeon—but some people believe resources would be better spent conserving existing endangered creatures. Indeed, today many of our extant birds are at risk. North America has lost nearly 3 billion birds belonging to hundreds of species over the past fifty years. It's an enormous loss that reveals an "overlooked biodiversity crisis," according to a study by scientists and government agencies.

SEE A SPECIMEN
Cleveland Museum of Natural History, Cleveland, OH
Harvard Natural History Museum, Cambridge, MA
Smithsonian Museum of Natural History, Washington, DC

FURTHER READING
Avery, Mark. *A Message from Martha: the Extinction of the Passenger Pigeon and Its Relevance Today*. London, UK: Bloomsbury, 2014.

Benchwick, Greg. *Martha: The Last Passenger Pigeon*. Castroville, TX: Black Rose Writing, 2019.

Greenberg, Joel. *A Feathered River Across the Sky: The Passenger Pigeon's Flight to Extinction*. New York, NY: Bloomsbury USA, 2014

Timberlake, Amy, and David Homer. *One Came Home*. New York, NY: Alfred A. Knopf, 2013.

SABER-TOOTHED TIGER *Smilodon*

HABITAT: Forests
DISTRIBUTION: The Americas
TEMPORAL RANGE: Early Pleistocene to
Early Holocene (About 2.5 million–10,000 years ago)
SIZE: Varied, depended on species:
- *S. gracilis*, 120–220 lbs, unknown height
  & weight, jaguar-sized
- *S. Fatalis*, 350–620 lbs., 3.25' tall,
  about 5.8' length, lion-sized
- *S. populator*, 490–880 lbs,
  4' shoulder height, unknown length

LIFESPAN: 20–40 years
EXTINCTION CAUSE: Loss of food
FUN FACT: *Smilodon*'s name comes
from the Greek words for "knife" and "tooth."

A REAL BIG MOUTH, LONG IN THE TOOTH

Its huge mouth made *Smilodon* the legendary apex predator of its age. It had a special jaw
that could open very wide, unleashing its 7-inch-long serrated fangs. The cat sank those
dagger-like fangs into a prey's neck or belly, causing it to bleed to death. Prey included
bison, horses, giant sloths, American camels, and mammoths.

Smilodon was probably not as fast as modern cats because it had somewhat bear-like legs
that were strong and heavy. It also had a very short tail that was only about 14 inches long.
Like modern cats, it had retractable claws to help it hold down large prey. Even though we
think of the fierce Sabertooth as a tiger, it was not closely related to tigers or even lions.
Instead, most species we know today descended from the jaguar-like *Megantereon*.

Smilodon's exact appearance and behavior remain something of a mystery. For instance,
we're not sure what the *Smilodon*'s coat looked like. Nor is it known for certain whether
Smilodon lived solitary lives or were more social creatures. Shedding some light on that
question are Smilodon fossils that show healed wounds. Such wounds, before they
healed, would have crippled the cat and kept it from hunting. Yet, somehow the creature
continued to eat while it recuperated. This could mean that other *Smilodons* provided food
for injured or old members of their pack. It could also mean that *Smilodons* raised their
young in packs and were more social than solitary.

SEE A SKELETON
Harvard Natural History Museum, Cambridge, MA
La Brea Tar Pits and Museum, Los Angeles, CA

FURTHER READING
Antón, Mauricio. *Sabertooth*. Bloomington, IN: Indiana University Press, 2013.
   Bailey, Gerry, and Trevor Reaveley. *Sabre-Tooth Tiger*. St. Catharines, ON: Crabtree Publishers,
   2011.
MacPhee, R. D. E., and Peter Schouten. *End of the Megafauna: The Fate of the World's Hugest,
   Fiercest, and Strangest Animals*. New York, NY: W. W. Norton & Company, 2018.
Zoehfeld, Kathleen Weidner, and Franco Tempesta. *Prehistoric Mammals*. Washington, DC:
   National Geographic Kids, 2015.

SIBERIAN UNICORN *Elasmotherium sibiricum*

HABITAT: Tundra
DISTRIBUTION: Siberia, Russian Federation
TEMPORAL RANGE: Late Pliocene to Late Pleistocene (About 2.5 million to about 10,000 years ago)
SIZE: 15' length, 6–7' at shoulder, 3.8 tons (7,716 lbs)
LIFESPAN: Unknown
EXTINCTION CAUSE: Climate change: fall in temperatures killed food source
FUN FACT: Also known as the giant rhinoceros, the steppe rhinoceros, and the giant Siberian rhinoceros.

YOU'RE NEVER GOING TO SEE NO UNICORN

Interestingly, none of the Siberian unicorn skeletons unearthed so far have included a preserved horn. Why? Part of the reason may be because the horn was probably made of keratin—the same softer material of which hair, nails, claws, and hooves are made—and likely decayed over thousands of years. Under the right conditions, though, paleontologists have found hair, horns, and claws of other ancient creatures. As more permafrost melts and reveals more megafaunal remains, it may be just a matter of time before a horn is discovered.

How do we know the unicorn even had a horn? By studying its skeleton. Paleozoologists look to a significant cranial vertebrae, hunched back, and a furrowed and domed skull. From this, they theorize that each of these features would have allowed for the creature to support a massive horn—estimated to be about 3 feet in diameter and 3 to 6 feet long.

The bones give us other clues. A genetic analysis of twenty-three specimens' DNA revealed that the Siberian unicorn was the last surviving member of a unique subset of rhinos. The bones also showed that the species survived much later than previously thought—39,000 years ago—which means they coexisted with modern humans and Neanderthals.

The Siberian unicorn had fallen on hard times by the start of the ice age in Eurasia, when a dramatic fall in temperature led to frozen ground, reducing the grasses it fed on and impacting herds of the creatures over an entire region.

Some theorize that modern man's collective unicorn myth-making might've stemmed from this creature, but the modern unicorn myth originated in India, far from the Siberian unicorn's known habitat or range. It's possible that the discovery of a narwhal's horn was the start of the unicorn myth.

SEE A SKELETON
Azov Museum-Reserve in Azov, Russia

FURTHER READING
Prothero, Donald R., and Mary Persis Williams. *The Princeton Field Guide to Prehistoric Mammals.* Princeton, NJ: Princeton University Press, 2017.

Zoehfeld, Kathleen Weidner, and Franco Tempesta. *Prehistoric Mammals.* Washington, DC: National Geographic Kids, 2015.

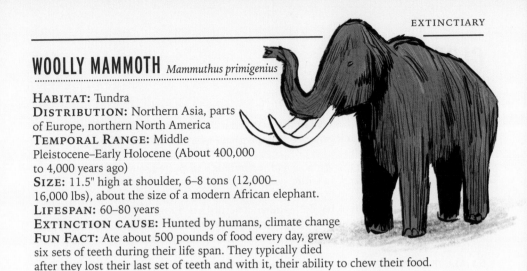

WOOLLY MAMMOTH *Mammuthus primigenius*

HABITAT: Tundra
DISTRIBUTION: Northern Asia, parts
of Europe, northern North America
TEMPORAL RANGE: Middle
Pleistocene–Early Holocene (About 400,000
to 4,000 years ago)
SIZE: 11.5" high at shoulder, 6–8 tons (12,000–
16,000 lbs), about the size of a modern African elephant.
LIFESPAN: 60–80 years
EXTINCTION CAUSE: Hunted by humans, climate change
FUN FACT: Ate about 500 pounds of food every day, grew
six sets of teeth during their life span. They typically died
after they lost their last set of teeth and with it, their ability to chew their food.

A TRUNCATED HISTORY

For eons, the woolly mammoth ruled the frozen tundra. A two-layer shaggy coat of hair
kept them warm while their 6-foot-long trunk and two massive 10-foot-long curved
tusks foraged for grasses under winter snow and ice. If food became scarce, they used
large humps of fat stored on their back as—quite literally—a backup source for energy.
They traveled in herds of matriarchal family units, caring for their young, sick, and old.
Mammoths were mammoth (some over 12 feet tall!) and, owing to this great size, had no
predator for thousands of years.

But then humans invented the spear. Emboldened by the weapon, hunters began to prey
upon the mammoth for meat and other resources. Traces of mammoths are found in
prehistoric art, tools, dwellings, and ancient ceremonial burial sites.

The last known population of mammoths died out around just 4,000 years ago, probably
hunted to extinction by humans. The woolly mammoth was the last of its kind of
mammoth. Its closest living relative is the Asian elephant.

Today, humans' exploitation of the woolly mammoth continues with efforts to clone the
creature, which, if successful, would bring it back to life. The scientists intent on this face
serious obstacles, however. A mammoth cannot be exactly recreated from DNA. Instead,
scientists work to create a mammoth-elephant hybrid using frozen mammoth DNA and
an Asian Elephant mother. The possibility of this has profound ethical, environmental,
and scientific implications. In addition, people question the need to de-extinct a species
when so many living species are currently threatened.

SEE A SKELETON
American Museum of Natural History, New York, NY
Field Museum, Chicago, IL
La Brea Tar Pits and Museum, Los Angeles, CA

FURTHER READING
Lister, Adrian, Paul G. Bahn, and Jean M. Auel. *Mammoths: Giants of the Ice Age*. New York,
    NY: Chartwell Books, 2015.
Shapiro, Beth. *How to Clone a Mammoth: The Science of De-Extinction*. Princeton, NJ:
    Princeton University Press, 2016.

GLOSSARY

CARBON DIOXIDE: An invisible, odorless gas produced by organic compounds, created by burning carbon, and breathing. It is about 0.03 percent naturally present in air. Plants absorb it in photosynthesis. See also *Greenhouse Gases, Photosynthesis*

CASCADE EFFECT: An unavoidable and sometimes unexpected sequence of events caused by one act that affects an entire system.

CLIMATE: The combined or regular weather conditions of a region. To determine climate, scientists measure air pressure, winds, temperature, precipitation, humidity, sunshine, and cloudiness for a year. Then that data is averaged over a series of years.

CLIMATE CHANGE: A long-term change in the average weather patterns of Earth's established local, regional, and global climates.

DE-EXTINCTION: The process of creating an organism of an extinct species or one that looks like an extinct species. Also known as species revivalism or resurrection biology.

ECOSYSTEM: A community of living organisms interacting with the nonliving components of their environment. These living and and nonliving components are connected by nutrient cycles and energy flows.

EXTINCTION: The death of the last member of a species or a group of species. Scientists consider the moment of extinction to be the death of the last individual of the species. However, the species may have lost the ability to reproduce and rebuild the species before that point.

GLOBAL WARMING: The ongoing rise of the average temperature of Earth's climate. It is a major aspect of climate change. In addition to rising global surface and atmosphere temperatures, global warming also includes its effects, like precipitation changes. See also *Climate Change*

GREENHOUSE EFFECT: The process by which radiation from the sun is absorbed and re-radiated by greenhouse gases. While some energy radiates back into space, some is sent toward the surface. This warms the planet's atmosphere and surface to a temperature higher than what it would be without this effect.

GREENHOUSE GASES: Like glass on a greenhouse, a greenhouse gas absorbs and then radiates energy within the thermal infrared range. Greenhouse gases cause the greenhouse effect on planets. The main greenhouse gases in Earth's atmosphere include water vapor, carbon dioxide, methane, nitrous oxide, and ozone.

MEGAFAUNA: The large mammals of a certain region, habitat, or geological era.

METHANE: An odorless, invisible, flammable gas, a principal component of marsh gas and the dangerous firedamp of coal mines. It is created commercially from natural gas. See also *Greenhouse Gases*

PALEOGENETICS: The examination of the past by studying preserved genetic material from the remains of ancient organisms.

PERMAFROST: A thick layer of subsurface soil that remains frozen throughout the year for at least two consecutive years, occurring primarily in polar regions.

PHOTOSYNTHESIS: The process by which green plants, algae, and certain bacteria convert carbon dioxide, water, and salts into carbohydrates using chlorophyll and energy from the sun.

RESURRECTION ECOLOGY: An evolutionary biology technique wherein researchers hatch old dormant eggs from lake sediments to study animals as they existed in the past. Others have used this technique to explore the evolutionary effects of a lake's excessive nutrients due to runoff from the land, predation, and contaminants.

SIXTH EXTINCTION: An ongoing extinction event of species during our present-day Holocene epoch as a result of human activity. Also known as the Holocene extinction, or Anthropocene extinction. See also *Extinction*

THERMOKARST: Terrain formed by the melting of the permafrost sublayer. The melting ice leaves small pits, marshes, valleys, hummocks, and uneven ground.

TUNDRA: A flat or gently rolling treeless plain, typical of arctic and subarctic regions. The soil is black and mucky with a permanently frozen subsoil called permafrost, and supports a dominant vegetation of herbs, mosses, lichens, and dwarf shrubs. See also *Permafrost*

WEATHER: A short-term (as in minutes, hours, or days) atmospheric change in conditions that occur in a local area. Examples include rain, snow, clouds, winds, floods, or thunderstorms. See also *Climate Change* and *Global Warming*

YEDOMA: An organic-rich Pleistocene-age permafrost with 50–90 percent ice content by volume. Yedoma is abundant in the regions of eastern Siberia, such as northern Yakutia of the Russian Federation, as well as in Alaska in the United States and Canada's Yukon Territory.

MORE ABOUT THE BATAGAIKA CRATER

We can learn a great deal from the Batagaika Crater. Certainly, this "megaslump" and others like it reveal well-preserved remains of ancient creatures for scientists to study. But more importantly—given climate change's urgency—scientists also study the pits for the impacts of our warming world.

The pit is both a result of a warming climate *and a cause* of more warming temperatures to come. Geologists estimate that up to 50 percent of the earth's methane gas may be locked up in Arctic permafrost. As it thaws, permafrost releases the greenhouse gas methane—and then microbes consume the dirt's unfrozen organic matter. After they eat, the microbes release methane and carbon dioxide as waste into the atmosphere, speeding up warming even more. In short, the megaslumps are huge greenhouse gas emitters.

Thanks in part to their Arctic research, scientists have a better idea of the ways permafrost changes can contribute to greenhouse gas emissions—and how large that contribution is. That work helps us to know what we're up against in our changing climate.

The Arctic may foretell global environmental changes to come. But it does so while we still have time to apply what we learn at Batagaika and places like it. The question is, then, will we take action in time? That's up to you and me.

HELP THE EXTINCTS SAVE THE WORLD

HERE ARE SOME WAYS YOU CAN GET INVOLVED TO HELP PROTECT THE ENVIRONMENT

ON YOUR OWN

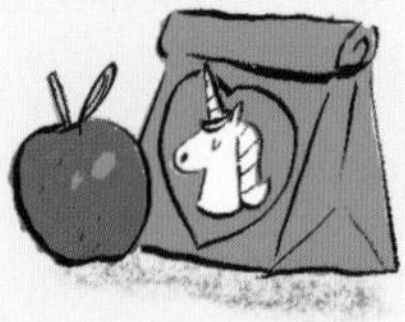

- Reduce trash. Take your lunch to school in a reusable container. Avoid using throw away containers.
- Conserve water. Turn off the faucet whenever you're not using the water—when you're brushing your teeth, for instance. Avoid long showers.
- Keep reusable resources out of the trash. Glass, aluminum, and plastics can be used again—recycle them.

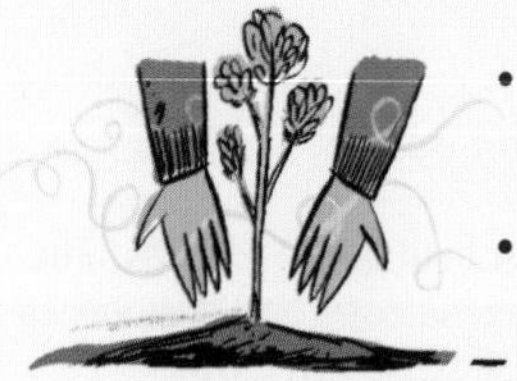

- Plant a tree to put more oxygen in the air and give birds a home.
- Use reusable drink containers instead of disposable ones.
- Save electricity! Turn off the lights and TV when you leave the room. Unplug chargers you're not using.
- Collect old books for a book drive.

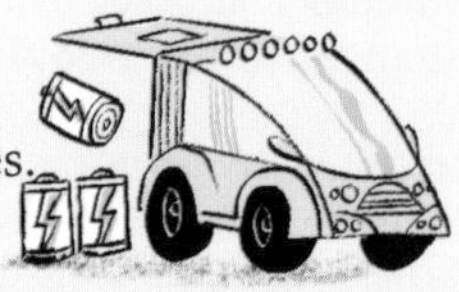

- Use rechargeable batteries in your devices, toys, and games.
- If possible, use paper straws instead of plastic ones.
- Use both sides of your paper or old newspapers and magazines for art projects.

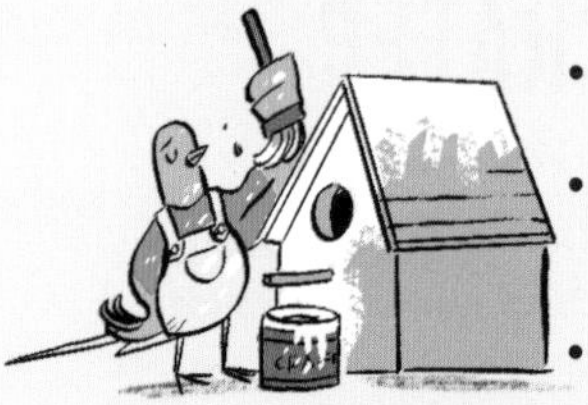

- Check out and read library books about the environment.
- Ask your teachers about starting a bottle recycling program at your school.
- Make gifts for others instead of buying them.
- Don't waste food—or anything, for that matter. Make maximum use of stuff.

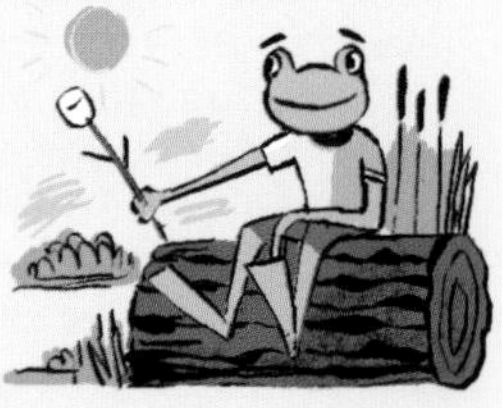

- Ask your teachers about your school "adopting" an endangered animal. They can contact your local zoo or visit the World Wildlife Fund's website for more info.
- Ask your school about hosting a "solar cookout." Cook s'mores with the sun with solar ovens you make.
- Ask your school about taking an environment-related field trip.
- Share these lists with your friends and family. They may have even more ideas!

WITH YOUR PARENTS

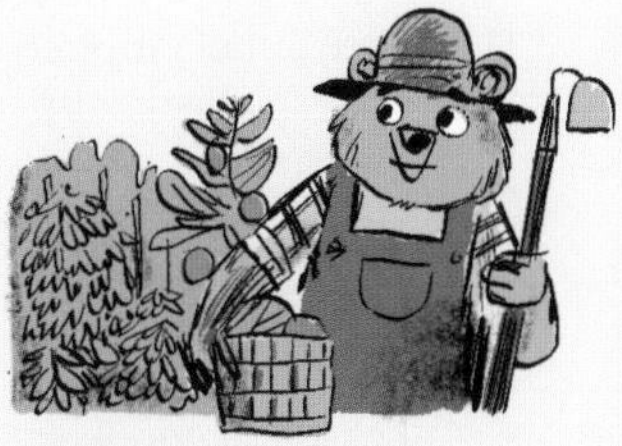

- Grow a vegetable garden or plant pollinator-friendly plants to help struggling butterflies and bees.
- Create a compost pile from table scraps and yard clippings. It'll make great fertilizer for that garden you just made!
- Write a letter to your member of Congress about environmental issues.

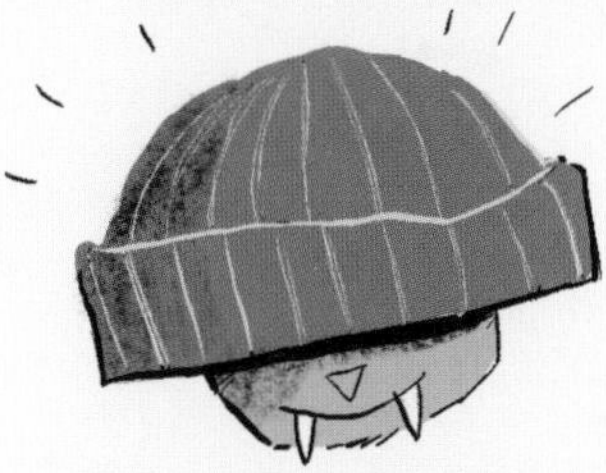

- Donate your old clothes so that they will be worn by someone else.
- Volunteer or organize a community cleanup or recycling drive.
- Carpool. Create a rideshare with friends and family.
- Spend time in nature. Try birdwatching or geocaching!

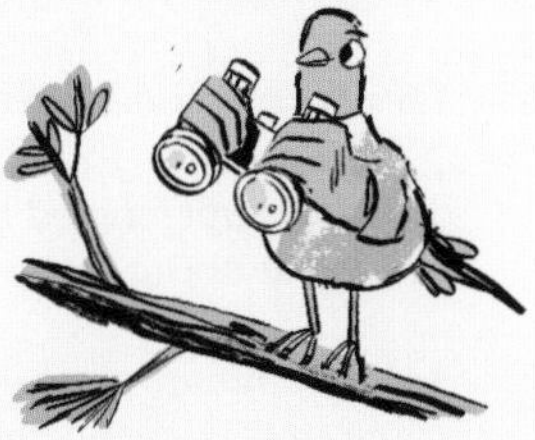

- Go electric! Ask your parents about solar panels for your home or an electric car to reduce greenhouse gas emissions.
- Replace incandescent lightbulbs with more energy-efficient LED ones.
- Walk or ride a bike whenever possible instead of driving.

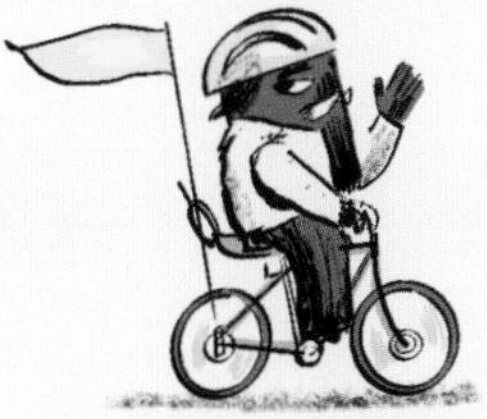

- Stay out of the fast food drive-through lane! Sitting in a car with the engine running pollutes the air. Ask your driver to park and go inside instead.
- Hang a bird feeder or birdbath in your backyard to help local bird species.
- Ask your parents to help you research your local endangered creatures—and what you can do to help conserve them. Many states have endangered species watchlists. Learn more at goextincts.com.

Further Reading on How You Can Help

French, Jess. *What a Waste: Trash, Recycling, and Protecting Our Planet*. New York, NY: DK Publishing, 2019.

EarthWorks Group, Michele Montez, and Lorraine Bodger. *The New 50 Simple Things Kids Can Do to Save the Earth*. Kansas City, MO: Andrews McMeel Publishers, 2009.

Siber, Kate, and Chris Turnham. *National Parks of the U.S.A.* London: Wide Eyed Editions, 2018.

TRY THE QUICK-FREEZE TRICK

WHAT YOU'LL NEED

- 3 or 4 17 oz. unopened spring water bottles
- 1 ice cube, chipped
- A clear plastic cup
- A freezer

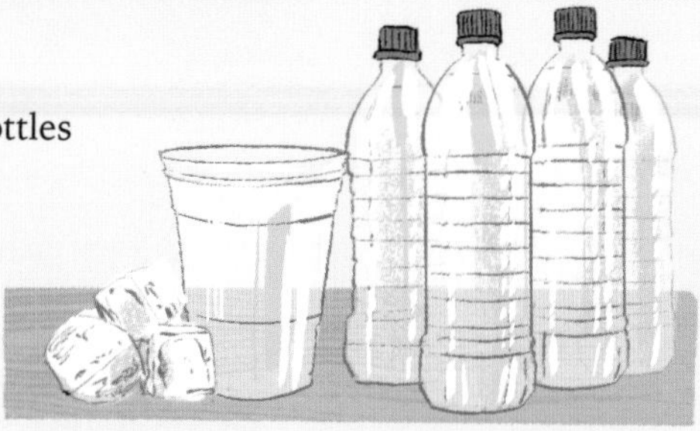

HOW TO MAKE INSTANT ICE

1. Leave the unopened water bottles at room temperature for about 4 hours. Then put them in the freezer for 2.5 to 2.75 hours. (You might have to experiment with the amount of time. This is not an exact science!)

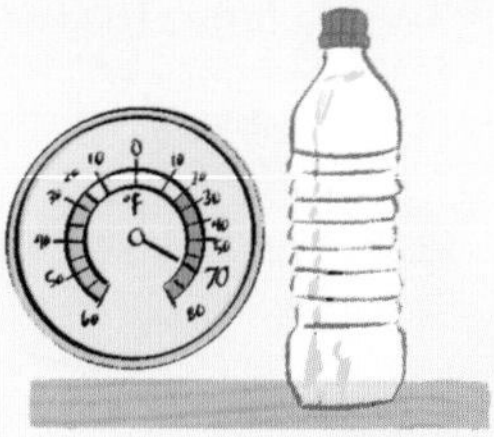

2. After taking the bottle from the freezer, test it to make sure it's cold enough. Hit the super-chilled water bottle onto a hard surface. If your water is supercooled, ice crystals inside the bottle will form and the water inside should turn opaque white as it flash freezes. Proceed to step 3. If not, put your bottle back in the freezer for another 10 to 15 minutes.

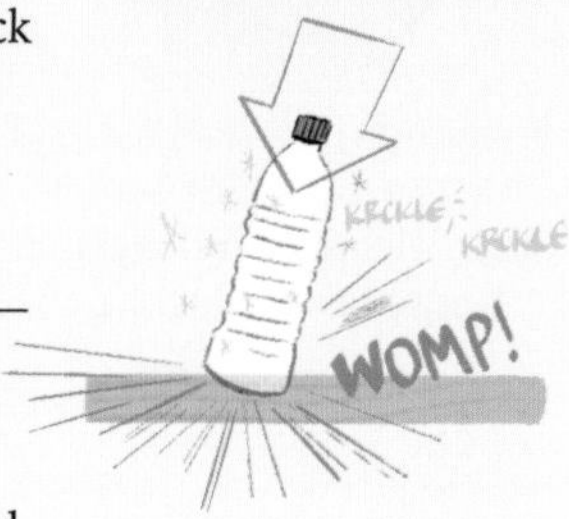
KRCKLE
KRCKLE
WOMP!

The next 2 steps should happen in quick succession:

3. Take a supercooled bottle from the freezer and open slowly—be careful not to jostle it!

4. Next, put an ice chip into the plastic cup. That ice chip is going to be your nucleation point, the point at which the liquid water starts to form crystals—and become ice.

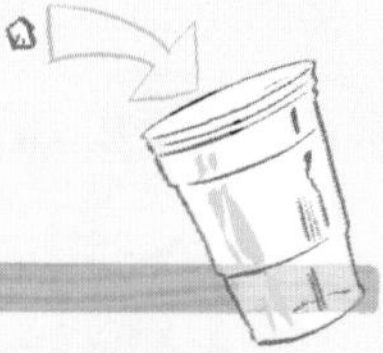

5. Gently open the bottled water and pour the water very slowly into the cup. Ice should begin to form around the ice chip. Cool! Instant ice!

6. Recycle or reuse those plastic bottles and cups.

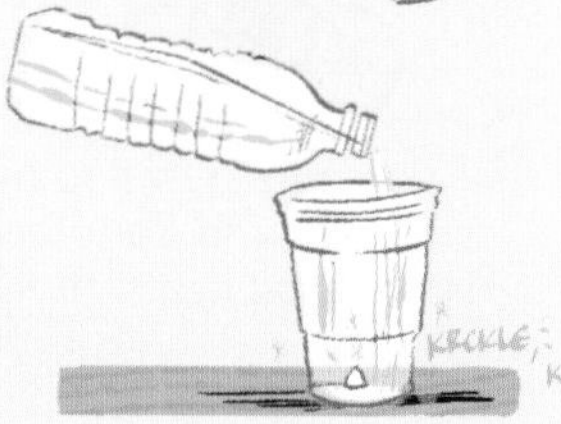
KRCKLE
KRCKLE

HEY, QUITO, WHY DOES IT DO THIS?

WHEN WATER FREEZES, INTERCONNECTED CRYSTALS FORM LIKE SNOWFLAKES ON TINY LITTLE IMPURITIES IN THE WATER. SINCE YOU'VE USED FAIRLY PURE SPRING WATER AND SLOWLY SUPERCOOLED IT INTO A METASTABLE STATE, IT'S HARDER FOR ICE CRYSTALS TO FORM. WHEN YOU INTRODUCED THE ICE CHIP, YOU DESTABILIZED THE WATER AND TRIGGERED THE FORMATION OF THE CRYSTALS. ICE CRYSTALS THEN BUILD ON THEMSELVES UNTIL YOU SEE THE MINI ICE AGE IN YOUR CUP.

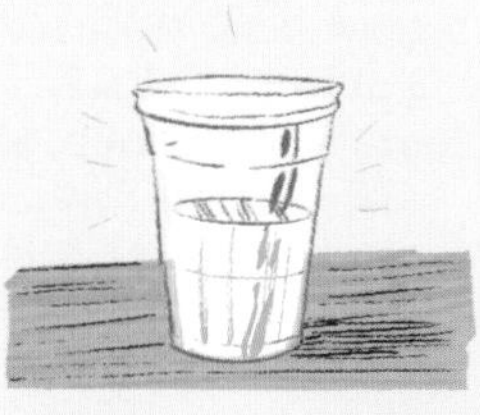

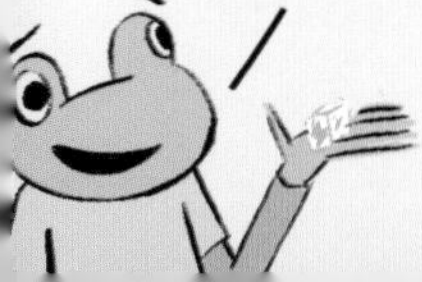

FURTHER READING

BOOKS FOR YOUNG READERS

Herman, Gail, John Hinderliter, and Kevin McVeigh. *What Is Climate Change?* New York, NY: Penguin Workshop, 2018.

Hoare, Ben, and Tom Jackson. *Endangered Animals.* New York, NY: DK Children, 2010.

Sabuda, Robert, and Matthew Reinhart. *Enclycopedia Prehistorica: Mega-Beasts.* Somerville, MA: Candlewick Press, 2007.

Sewell, Matt. *Forgotten Beasts: Amazing Creatures That Once Roamed the Earth.* London, UK: Pavilion, 2019.

Torday, Piers. *The Last Wild.* New York, NY: Puffin Books, 2015.

Zoehfeld, Kathleen Weidner, and Franco Tempesta. *Prehistoric Mammals.* Washington, DC: National Geographic Kids, 2015.

BOOKS FOR OLDER READERS

Carson, Rachel, Linda Lear, and Edward O. Wilson. *Silent Spring.* Boston, MA: Houghton Mifflin, 2002.

Greenberg, Joel. *A Feathered River Across the Sky: The Passenger Pigeon's Flight to Extinction.* New York, NY: Bloomsbury USA, 2014.

Kalmus, Peter. *Being the Change: Live Well and Spark a Climate Revolution.* Gabriola Island, BC: New Society Publishers, 2017.

Kolbert, Elizabeth. *The Sixth Extinction: An Unnatural History.* New York, NY: Picador USA, 2015.

O'Connor, M. R. *Resurrection Science: Conservation, De-Extinction and the Precarious Future of Wild Things.* New York, NY: St. Martin's Press, 2015.

WEBSITES

kids.nationalgeographic.com
passengerpigeon.org
reviverestore.org
worldwildlife.org

BIBLIOGRAPHY

Wray, Britt, and George Church. *Rise of the Necrofauna: The Science, Ethics, and Risks of De-Extinction.* Vancouver, BC: Greystone Books, 2019.

Macfarquhar, Neil, and Emile Ducke. "Russian Land of Permafrost and Mammoths Is Thawing," August 4, 2019. See: www.nytimes.com/2019/08/04/world/europe/russia-siberia-yakutia-permafrost-global-warming.html.

Expedition Unknown, Season 4, Episode 5, "Cloning the Woolly Mammoth." Written by Thomas Quinn. Aired on December 28, 2016, on Travel Channel.

Expedition Unknown, Season 4, Episode 6, "Journey to The Ice Age." Written by Thomas Quinn. Aired on January 4, 2017, on Travel Channel.

ACKNOWLEDGMENTS

The book you hold in your hands is my attempt to raise awareness of climate change and species extinction. Mercifully, I had a team as great as the Extincts to help me with it.

This book would not exist without my brilliant and beautiful wife, Christy, and my brave boys, Owen and Daniel. In addition to their endless patience with me, they read early drafts and shared their thoughts. I hope this book is worthy of all that time we were apart. I thank my parents for instilling in me a deep appreciation for nature and for their support as I worked on this book. Thank you, I love all of you.

To my agent, Paul Rodeen—your early and ongoing enthusiasm for this project was a key part of its genesis. To my editor, Russ Busse, who gave me wide-open creative fields in which to roam, mammoth-like, I am grateful. To Andrew Smith for remembering me and the old days in Cambridge, and for giving me this opportunity. To the whole team at Amulet Books for bringing the Extincts to life. Heartiest thanks to all of you.

To my brother, Zach, and my friends Jon D., Sean T., Dave L., Geoff L., and Chris S. for sitting through countless descriptions of what this book was going to be. Just think, we can do it again with Book 2.

To Matt Tavares for his *Hoops* graphic novel camaraderie, "and Ryan Higgins also, I guess." You guys are the best.

To Patrick McGee, for giving my comic strip *Duct Tape Man* a chance all those years ago at the Northeastern News. One thing lead to another and here we are.

To Jerry Jamowski, for not taking it from anyone. WFUZ's music kept me drawing late into Thursday nights. Thanks, man!

To the teams at my local public library and town forest. Liz Whitelam and her team at Whitelam Books—and indie booksellers everywhere.

To George Lucas and Larry Hama, for the inspiring imaginary adventures, and to Josh Gates, for the real ones. To Isabella Stewart Gardner, for getting me out the door. Or maybe it was in the door.

And a special thanks to YOU for reading my words and looking at my pictures. I hope you'll be back for Extincts Book 2.

AUTHOR/ILLUSTRATOR *Scott Magoon*

HABITAT: New England
TEMPORAL RANGE: Late Holocene
DISTRIBUTION: Worldwide
SIZE: 6'1", approx. 190 lbs
AGE: Late 40s
FUN FACT: Collects vintage Star Wars and GI Joe action figures and vehicles.

WRITING AND DRAWING FOR AGES

Scott was born back in the 1900s. He earned a BA in English Literature from Northeastern University sometime before the dawn of the 21st century. More recently, he was a children's book art director at major American publishers. Now he writes and illustrates books full-time. He's a lefty and, like his ancestors, enjoys running long distances, good food, and good music. He and his family travel to new places together from their Boston-area home.

He's illustrated thirty picture books and written five. This is his first graphic novel.

Visit scottmagoon.com to learn more about him and his books, and to get in touch. While you're there, sign up for his newsletter, *The Magoon Tribune*, for quarterly updates on all the latest and greatest.

You can also visit goextincts.com to find out more about extinct and endangered creatures and to access behind-the-scenes stuff from the Extincts, free downloads, teacher's guides, and special Extincts merchandise—the profits of which benefit environmental causes.

It is not the strongest
of the species that survives,
nor the most intelligent
that survives.

It is the one that is most
adaptable to change.

—Charles Darwin

For the Earth and her endangered species
—S.M.

PUBLISHER'S NOTE: This is a work of fiction.
Names, characters, places, and incidents are either the product of
the author's imagination or used fictitiously, and any resemblance to actual persons,
living or dead, business establishments, events, or locales is entirely coincidental.

Library of Congress Control Number for the hardcover: 2021932219

Hardcover ISBN 978-1-4197-5251-3
Paperback ISBN 978-1-4197-5250-6

Book design by Heather Kelly

The interiors of this book were printed with soy inks on FSC certified paper.
Approximately 3% of the power used at the facility where this prints comes from solar energy.

Printed and bound in China
10 9 8 7 6 5 4 3 2 1

Amulet Books are available at special discounts when purchased
in quantity for premiums and promotions as well as fundraising or educational use.
Special editions can also be created to specification. For details,
contact specialsales@abramsbooks.com or the address below.

ABRAMS The Art of Books
195 Broadway, New York, NY 10007
abramsbooks.com